MW01148446

Insights

Battling Demons, Volume 5

Kris Morris

Published by Kris Morris, 2016.

This is a work of fiction. Similarities to real people, places, or events are entirely coincidental.

INSIGHTS

First edition. November 15, 2016.

Written by Kris Morris.

This is an unauthorised work of fiction. All royalties paid to the author will be donated to TheHorseCourse, a children's charity in Dorset, England. Thank you for supporting the work they do with abused and neglected children!

Thank you to my dear husband for believing in me, my sons for inspiration, and my friends Carole, Abby, Janet, and Anneke for ceaseless encouragement and for tolerating my insecurities.

Special thanks to my dear friend Abby Bukofzer and my son Karl for assisting with editing. And to my talented husband, Tim, for designing my book covers.

Chapter 1

Louisa was awakened by a whispered pelting of heavy mist being driven against the cottage by the wind that had come up overnight. She rolled on to her side and watched for several minutes as her husband slept, hesitating before reaching across him to turn off the alarm clock, pre-empting his otherwise inevitable wake-up call.

Sleep doesn't come easily to someone being treated with external fixators, and Martin, despite his attempts to convince his wife otherwise, was no exception. He packed pillows in around his legs and elevated his arm either on pillows or, at times, on his wife's hip when he happened to be spooned up against her.

But much needed rest usually eluded him as he tossed and turned throughout the night, positioning and repositioning himself in any manner necessary to take some of the pressure off his fractured limbs.

He appeared to be sleeping soundly, a rare occurrence for her energetic husband, so Louisa decided to reverse their usual morning routine and be the first one out of bed. A shiver went through her as her feet hit the cold, hardwood floor, and she reflexively pulled her arms around her sides to preserve her body heat.

Stopping at the table by the bed, she examined one of the perfectly shaped, creamy white flowers on the gardenia Martin had given her the night before, leaning over and breathing in its scent.

He had told her once that he found her difficult to understand in the best of times. Is that what he meant when he described her as mysterious? She made her way quietly out of the room and up the stairs to prepare for another workday.

Martin began to stir a short while later, pushing himself up and grabbing for the alarm clock. "Ohhh, *jolly good!* This bodes well," he muttered, mentally kicking himself for having forgotten to set his alarm.

A gust of wind blew harshly against the cottage, causing the old timber framing to creak and complain. He glanced up, scowling at the rivulets of water cascading down the outside of the window. Trying to stay dry on a day such as this was always a challenge, but given his current limitations, which would prevent him from either using an umbrella or hurrying from the car to the school building, he knew that he would be spending much of the day wet and cold.

The mere thought of the morning he had ahead of him made his bones ache, and he loitered in the shower, only swinging his legs back over the edge of the tub when he heard a tapping on the door. He balanced on his own two feet long enough to give himself a partial drying before taking three crutch assisted steps over to flip the lock and turn the knob.

"Of all your suits, that one has to be my favourite," Louisa said as she reached to pull the towel from around his shoulders before rubbing at his wet head.

He gave her a puzzled glance before looking abashedly at the floor. "Sorry. I didn't want to keep you waiting, so I just..." He made an awkward gesture towards the door. "Mm."

Martin could be painfully shy, and he embarrassed easily, so Louisa tried to remain nonchalant in situations such as this, but she could feel the corners of her mouth resisting her efforts.

This did not go unnoticed by her husband, and he tugged the towel from her hands, trying in vain to wrap it around himself.

"Damn!" he hissed under his breath. The rectangle of terry cloth now lay at his feet. But it could have been sitting on a shelf at Marks & Spencer for all the good it would do him as he stood with his crutches wedged under his arms.

Louisa leaned over quickly, picking it up from the floor. And in one easy movement, she wrapped it around him from behind and tucked the corner in at his waist. "There. Is that the look you were going for?" she asked, as she took a step back and gave him a once-over.

"Yes, thank you," he replied, tugging at his ear and clearing his throat.

She slipped her arms under his and folded her fingers together behind him.

"Good morning," he said before leaning over to kiss her.

Reaching up, Louisa smoothed down his hair, pushing it to the side a bit in a more relaxed variation on his usual proper coif. "*That* is a nice look on you."

"Hmph. I need a haircut." He wriggled himself from her grasp and went to the sink to carry out his ablutions.

"You nervous about today ... the assembly?" she asked, cocking her head as she watched him run a brush through his hair, effectively erasing the hairdo she had left him with moments before.

"Not really. I *had* hoped you could come up with a slightly more dignified way for me to deal with Evan, though. I'm sure to be fodder for playground gossip, you know. *Which*, by the way, will travel straight home with those children to their eager parents' ears!" he said, pointing emphatically with the hairbrush.

Louisa sidled up behind him and massaged his shoulders. "Martin, you've been fodder for gossip and eager ears since you arrived in Portwenn. I think the villagers find you rather ... exotic."

"*Exotic!*" He scowled at her reflection in the mirror. "Nonsense."

"Well, think about it, Martin. For many people around here, a trip to Truro is a major excursion. Some of the villagers have never ventured farther east than Exeter. So yes, you are exotic. Big city doctor ... London surgeon and all that."

He laid the brush down next to the sink and pushed past her. "I need to get dressed," he said brusquely.

She followed after him, perching herself on the edge of the bed. "This is a good thing you're doing ... for Evan."

Glancing over, he gave her a grunt before pulling open his top drawer, yanking out a pair of boxers and a pair of socks. He dropped into a chair and began to work the boxers over his fixators.

Louisa worried her lip as she watched him pull roughly at the garment, causing it to catch on the protruding pins.

She knelt down in front of him. "Martin ... let me," she said softly, backing them off his legs to begin the process anew. "This will be such a confidence builder for Evan. He's so excited about being in charge of answering all the questions."

Martin sat unresponsive, staring distractedly out the window.

Gesturing for him to stand, she finished manoeuvring the fabric over the hardware penetrating his thigh.

"This could very well have the opposite effect on him, you know." He hoisted the waistband over his hips and sat back down. "He could be seen as an apple polisher for the tosser doctor ... suffer repercussions because of ... it."

"Ah, but you forget that the tosser doctor is married to the headmistress." Louisa gave him a wary smile as she pulled a sock over his still-swollen foot. "And I don't think the villagers see you as the tosser they used to think you to be. They may still find you to be gruff and rude, but I do think you've earned their respect."

"Can you hand me my trousers ... please," he said wagging his finger at the clothing laid out on the bed. "If they respect me, they certainly have a strange way of showing it."

She returned to his side and knelt down again. "Well, yes ... they do." She grimaced as she glanced up at him. "I'm sorry about that. I grew up in Portwenn, and I'm used to the somewhat ... *unusual* personalities that can be found here. And they may complain a bit, but—"

"A bit! Louisa, they're never happy unless they're ... where they aren't!" he sputtered. "Maybe if I set out cafe tables in the reception room and dressed Morwenna up in a black dress and a frilly white pinafore ... served tea and scones rather than dispensing medical advice. Yes, *then* maybe they'd be happy.

"Until that time, I can look forward to a steady stream of whingers, somatisers and ungrateful patients who refuse to take my advice and then come—*mithering*—to me because they've seen no improvement in their conditions!" He yanked his vest over his head, catching the sleeve on the metal pins in his arm.

"Martin, calm—down." Louisa looked up at him from her perch on the floor, her brow furrowed. "Is this about next week? About seeing patients again?"

He stared out at the harbour and took in a deep breath before letting it rush back out. "It's been almost three months since I saw my last patient. And I—"

He pressed his palm to his forehead. "I've noticed that I'm not as quick as I was before, Louisa. I don't know if it's just the effects of the morphine and it'll pass, or if it's a result of the accident."

She tipped her head to the side and studied his eyes. "Well ... I'm sure that would be normal after what you've been through," she said, trying to project an air of confidence she didn't feel. "I haven't noticed any change. Are you sure this isn't just a ... I don't know ... a—"

"Figment of my imagination? Louisa, you know me better than that."

He slipped his right arm through the sleeve of his shirt, then his left, before rolling the right sleeve back to his elbow. "Sometimes I have to grasp for words ... medical terms. I get them; I just feel sluggish." He glanced at her taut expression. "It—it's probably nothing though. I don't want you to worry about it."

"What does Ed say?"

"I haven't told him yet," he mumbled. "I thought I'd discuss it with him tomorrow. But like I said, it's probably nothing." He peered down at his chest as he struggled with a button. "Maybe you should check on James. He should be awake by now."

The subject of her husband's concerns now closed, Louisa got to her feet and left the room.

Jeremy dropped Martin at the school shortly before nine o'clock. An early morning assembly, Louisa had reasoned, would be less disruptive to classroom activities and would shorten the period of time Martin had to dread the affair—or to come up with an excuse to back out of it.

Evan was peering around the door of Louisa's outer office, watching for him, and he bounced down the hall, meeting him midway in the corridor. "Hi, Dr. Ellig-am! Are you all ready?" he said as he latched on to his wrist.

"About as ready as I can be, Evan. How are you this morning?" he asked, taking note of the child's dirty fingernails and untied shoes.

"Fine." The boy pulled up his feet and jumped as they passed over a crack in the flooring. "I know just what I'm gonna say. Mrs. Ellig-am practiced with me this morning."

"You better get those laces in hand before you trip and break your arm again, don't you think?" Martin stopped and poked a finger at the boy's feet.

The smile that had been fixed on the child's face faded, and he stared down at the floor. "I think they're okay. I'll be careful." The smile returned as he looked up at Martin. "I like them this way. It's more comfortable."

"Don't be ridiculous, Evan. It can't be comfortable to have your shoes flapping around like that. Tie 'em up so we can get down to Mrs. Ellingham's office."

The boy glanced up before bending over and stuffing the laces between his shoes and his feet. "There! Now I won't trip *and* they're comfortable!"

"Evan, just tie them up properly ... now!"

He looked up at Martin, his eyes filling with tears. "But I don't know how, Dr. Ellig-am."

"Mm, yes. I see." Martin brushed his hand across his head. "Let's be on our way, then."

Pippa Woodley was sitting behind her desk in the outer office when Martin arrived with Evan in tow.

"Mornin', Doc. You here to entertain the children?"

"Of course not!" he snapped. "I'm here to see my wife."

Pippa glared back at him. "Well, you'll hafta take a seat. She's with a student right now," the woman said as she got to her feet. "You just sit there on the sofa, Evan. I need to run down the hall for a few minutes."

She turned back to the doctor. "If I leave you alone with him, can I trust that you won't scare the poor child half to death?"

"That's silly!" Evan giggled. "Dr. Ellig-am isn't scary, Miss. He's my friend. Aren't you, Dr. Ellig-am?"

"Erm, yes. Something like that, I suppose," Martin said, ducking his head.

The boy scrambled on to the sofa and pushed himself back, his legs straight in front of him. "You wanna sit by me, Dr. Ellig-am?"

Martin cleared his throat and dropped down next to him.

"Well, I never!" Miss Woodley mumbled under her breath before leaving the room.

The doctor listened to the fading sound of the woman's heels clicking sharply against the linoleum and then turned to the boy. "Give me your foot, Evan."

He swung his leg up and Martin took hold of it, resting his heel above the injury to his thigh before tightening the lace and tying a bow. "The other one now," he said, wiggling his fingers.

The laces secured, Evan turned himself around and straightened his legs, admiring the neat bows that now adorned his shoes. "You're good at lots of stuff, aren't you, Dr. Elligam," he said, reaching over and putting his hand on Martin's arm.

"I wouldn't know about that," he mumbled back.

Louisa's door opened, and she followed a lanky blonde girl into the outer office. "And remember, Becky, you may *not* print that until I've authorised it first. Understood?"

"Yes, Mrs. Ellingham." The girl glanced in Martin's direction, giving him a roll of her eyes.

Louisa's tight-lipped expression softened as she turned her attention to her husband and his young charge. "Well, this is a big day, isn't it! Are you two ready?"

Evan pulled his feet under him and got up on his knees. "I'm all ready, and I remember just what I'm s'posed ta say."

"Good for you, Evan. Shall we head down to the gymnasium, then?" Louisa reached out and took the boy's hand.

After breathing out a resigned sigh, Martin struggled to his feet. "Gawd," he muttered.

When they arrived, the gym was filled with Portwenn primary students. Two chairs had been placed in the front of the room. Louisa directed Martin and Evan to take a seat before moving to a microphone that was situated on a stand nearby.

"Quiet everyone ... please!" She clapped her hands, and a hush fell over the room.

"Thank you. As you all know, the Portwenn surgery will be reopening next week. This will be wonderful for all of the people in the village, because it means fewer trips to Wadebridge to receive medical care. *And* it means you lot now get to see my husband if you're ill or hurt. And I happen to think Dr. Ellingham is the best doctor in Cornwall, so this is something to celebrate!"

Applause broke out in the room, and Martin looked uncomfortably from his wife to the floor. Evan kicked his feet vigorously back and forth, barely able to contain the excitement that was building in him.

As the applause faded, Louisa began again. "Now, as you are all aware, Dr. Ellingham was involved in a car accident several months ago, and he broke a number of bones."

The teacher walked over and took Evan's hand, leading him to the microphone. "As some of you know, this is Evan Hanley. He broke a bone recently, so he knows a lot about how our bodies repair fractures and about the things that doctors can do to help our bodies make those repairs. He's very kindly agreed to talk to you today about that. I want you all to give him your full attention."

She pulled the microphone from the stand and walked back to the two chairs where Evan reclaimed his seat.

Crouching down beside them, Louisa glanced up at her husband, giving him a smile.

"Evan, please tell the students a little about your broken bone. What did you break and how did they fix it?" she said, holding the microphone out to the boy.

He tentatively wrapped his fingers around the base, taking it from Louisa and pushing the business end of the device against his lips. Heavy breathing could be heard through the speakers as the child froze, suddenly aware of the eyes focused on him.

Martin leaned over, whispering into his ear, and a smile spread across his face.

He put a small hand over his mouth to stifle a giggle and then pulled his feet under him. "I broke my arm. But a pastor from Paris made me a cast, and the doctor put it on there. And now it's all better ... see!" he said pulling up his sleeve and waving his arm in the air.

"But Dr. Ellig-am couldn't have casts 'cause he might get a 'fection, so he gots these things on his bones," the child explained, jumping down from his chair and taking hold of Martin's hand.

He pulled his arm up and pointed at the hardware. "This is called a *fiss-a-tor*," the boy said. It fixes his broken bones with these metal things that stick into him." He tapped a finger against a pin. "And see, he gots one on each side." Evan lowered Martin's arm down to prove his point.

The child had the rapt attention of the other students as he continued with his demonstration. He squatted down on his haunches and pulled the Velcro fastener on the bottom half of the doctor's trouser leg open. Martin leaned forward to see what he was doing and wagged his finger back and forth at him. "Evan, that's not necessary!" he whispered.

"But I'm just showing them how you put your clothes on, Dr. Ellig-am," the boy said as he pulled the fabric away, revealing the deep wounds in his shin and calf. A murmured reaction rippled through the audience.

"*Louisa!*" Martin hissed.

The headmistress reached down quickly and fastened her husband's trousers shut again. "Sorry!" she whispered back.

She stood up and took the microphone from the boy. "If any of you have questions, I'm quite sure that Evan would be happy to answer them."

A smattering of hands shot up around the room, and the teacher turned the microphone back over to the small host of the gathering.

"Just one question per student, though!" she added.

"Ella?" she said, standing on her toes and pointing to the back row. "What's your question for Evan?"

"Do those fissators hurt?"

Evan hesitated and then took Martin's head in his hands, talking into his ear. After considerable discussion back and forth, the deepening furrow in Martin's brow revealed his growing impatience.

"Oh, for goodness' sake, Evan. Just tell them what I told you!"

"But, Dr. Ellig-am, you didn't an—" The boy paused mid-sentence when he saw the glower on the doctor's face.

He turned to his peers. "I don't know if they hurt, 'cause he won't tell me."

"I *did* tell you!" Martin squeaked.

Evan's shoulders drooped as twitters of laughter spread through the room. "You *told* me that it hurt when you broke your bones, but you *didn't* tell me if it hurts to have the fissators on there. You're *s'posed* to answer the question."

Martin looked down at the abashed little boy and sighed, realising he was the source of the child's embarrassment. He gestured with his finger, beckoning him. Then he hoisted him on to his lap, trying to hide a grimace.

Taking hold of his hand, which still gripped the mic, he positioned it properly. "Can you hold that there for me?" he asked, forcing a small smile.

Evan nodded, his face brightening as he settled in, content in his new role as microphone holder.

"Breaking a bone is painful, as Evan can tell you. And the external fixation devices ... or fixators ... *are* painful at times, other times just uncomfortable," Martin explained. "But they're necessary for my bones to heal properly."

Louisa gave her husband an approving smile before turning back to the audience. "Any other questions?" She scanned the heads of the younger children in the front row. "Gracie, what's your question for Dr. Ellingham?"

"How do they get those to stay on? Do they use glue?" the youngest of the Bollard girls asked.

"Huh! That's what I thought, too!" Evan said, pulling the mic to his mouth. "But they don't gots glue. These metal pokey things go into Dr. Ellig-am's bones, then these things keep them from getting all wobbly," he said, rubbing his palm along the bar on the side of Martin's arm and shoving the amplifying device towards his face. "Isn't that right, Dr. Ellig-am?"

Martin cleared his throat. "That's right. The surgeons made incisions, or cuts, through the skin and the subdermal layers ... erm, muscle tissue. They then drilled holes into the bones before screwing the long metal pins ... *pokey things* ... into them."

A collective *"Ewww!"* went up throughout the room. The presenters' heads whirled around as they turned puzzled faces towards the head teacher.

"Maybe just a bit more than they needed to know, Martin," she whispered.

He pulled in his chin and continued his explanation. "Once the pins are properly positioned, this bar is attached to hold everything in place. Quite an effective treatment method for this type of fracture, actually. Mm."

"Thank you, Gracie. That was a very good question. Anyone else?" Louisa's attention was attracted by a vigorously waving hand. "Adam?"

"How many of those fissators do you have?" the boy asked as he scratched vigorously at the side of his head.

Perhaps I should check that one for lice, Martin thought to himself.

Evan pushed the mic back in the doctor's direction.

"Adam—the floor-licker, right?" Martin said, pointing a finger at him.

"Martin!" Louisa hissed, shooting her husband a warning look. He cocked his head and raised an eyebrow at her.

Evan pulled the mic back and spoke into it. "He gots seven of 'em." Jumping down, he began to point at each one as he counted out, "One, two, three, four, five ..." He took hold of Martin's arm and lifted it up. "... six, seven. See! But those ones down there are bigger than those ones on his arm 'cause those bones are bigger."

Climbing back up on his chair, he positioned himself on his knees and flung an arm around the doctor's shoulders. "That's what you told me, isn't it, Dr. Ellig-am?"

"Mm, yes. That's right." Martin shifted in his chair and reached for his crutches. "Good. That's everything sorted. We done here, then?" he said, looking up at his wife.

Louisa glanced at her watch and gave him a nod. "This has been very helpful and informative, and I think everyone will feel more comfortable when they come to see you at the surgery, Dr. Ellingham. Let's all show our appreciation by giving Evan and our special guest a round of applause, shall we!"

The room erupted a final time. Once the noise had died down, Louisa returned the microphone to its stand.

"All right, all right! I want you *all*..." She tipped her head down and peered up at the children until she had regained the attention of the room. "I want you all to walk quietly back to your classrooms."

The large flock began to move towards the exit doors and Louisa yelled out a last directive over the growing din. "And keep your hands to yourselves, please!"

Martin pulled himself upright and retreated towards the corridor with Evan trotting along beside him.

"Very well done, you two! Evan, you may return to your classroom as well. Thank you very much for your help today," Louisa said as she tousled the boy's hair.

He gave Martin a smile. "See ya, Dr. Ellig-am. Let me know if you wanna do this again," he said before skipping down the hall.

Louisa glanced around them. Then deeming the corridor free of onlookers, she wrapped her arms around her husband's waist. "Nicely done, Dr. Ellig-am."

"Mm, yes." He looked around furtively and then bent his head down to place a kiss on her lips. "Will you be home for lunch?"

"I will. Hopefully, Poppy will have a pot of hot soup for us today."

"Erm, I should check on one of your students—the floor-licking boy. I saw him scratching earlier."

"Martin, the *floor-licking boy* has a name. He's Adam Trevathan. His family has the farm store this side of St. Endellion ... where we get our strawberries?" She tipped her head as she watched for any sign of recognition from him.

"Yes. Could be head lice. Best not wait too long or everyone in the village will be scratching. Jeremy and I'll be at the surgery this afternoon. The boy's parents should bring him by."

Louisa gave her head a shake. "Yes, *Mar-tin*. I'll take care of it straight away." She stormed off with her ponytail swinging petulantly as her husband watched her retreating form.

A sinking feeling came over him as he realised he had done something to upset her. "Louisa?"

He breathed out a sigh as she disappeared around the corner.

Chapter 2

Louisa dropped into the chair behind her desk, her jaw clenched tightly. *Oh, that man! Why does he have to talk about people in such an insensitive manner? He couldn't care less what that child's name is. He latches on to a symptom and that's all he can see!*

And he drives me halfway to Bodmin when he tells me how to do my job! Do I tell him how to do his job? No! 'Best not wait too long or everyone in the school will be scratching.' Errr! I know that, Martin Ellingham! Ohhh, that man! Why does he always have to tell me how to do my job? Why does he always think he knows better? I don't tell him how to do his job ...... do I?

Resting her elbows on her desk, she dropped her chin into her hand. *Well, I may have made suggestions on occasion, but I was just trying to be helpful ... mostly ... wasn't I? I mean, I have pointed out that his patients would benefit from a warmer bedside manner. And there has been the odd time or two when I may have mentioned an article I read ... a study done that may have contradicted his medical opinion.*

A pile of papers sitting on the desktop was shoved abruptly into a folder before she let out a heavy sigh. *Maybe it's his superior tone. My suggestions are well intentioned, his are ... well, I guess they're probably well intentioned, too, in a Martin kind of way.*

But it's not his job to decide how I should deal with my students! He's not their teacher! He should keep his nose out of what goes on here at the school and stick to caring for his patients.

Louisa rubbed her hand over her forehead. *Although, I s'pose they are his patients ... technically.*

But still, this isn't his surgery! This is Portwenn Primary and I am the Portwenn Primary headmistress. These children are under my care when they're here at the school, not his.

She sat, drumming her fingers on the desktop as she bit at her lip.

Be realistic though, Louisa. This is Martin we're talking about. His patients are his responsibility wherever they are.

And I s'pose if he just ignored Adam's scratching when he suspected a problem ... and he's usually right when he does suspect a problem ... and there was an outbreak of headlice, he'd feel he hadn't done his job.

Oh, Martin! It is sooo frustrating when you're right!

She slapped her hand down on the desk before glancing at her watch. It was a good time to take a break and walk down to the teacher's lounge.

Pippa Woodley was dividing her hours between her usual classroom teacher duties and temporary, part-time secretarial duties this term while the school's secretary was spending time with her ailing mother.

"I'm going for a cuppa. You want anything?" Louisa asked as she walked into the outer office.

The temp looked up from her paperwork. "Nope, I'm fine. Did the good doctor manage to get through the assembly without making any children cry?" she asked. Her eyes were focused on a sheet of paper lying on the desktop, but the smirk on her face was quite evident.

"Something amusing in the school lunch menu, Pipper?" Louisa glared, tight-lipped as she reached out and snatched it from under her nose.

She had considered Pippa to be one of her closest friends, but the woman had made her feelings about Martin known, and the frequent negative remarks had begun to chip away at their relationship.

"Actually, Martin handled things beautifully. And little Evan Hanley adores him," she said making a concerted effort to keep her tone positive.

"I know he does. Can't for the life of me understand why. I, erm ... heard you arguin' down at the end of the hall earlier. Honestly, Louisa, I don't know how you put up with that man."

"It takes *two* to argue, Pippa."

"You mean tango, don't you?" she quipped.

"I'm just *saying*, we weren't arguing. Martin said nothing. It was just ... me. *Not* that it's any of your business. And Martin and I tango quite nicely, if you must know."

She moved towards the hall before taking several steps back, slapping the sheet of paper down on the temp's desk. "This isn't mine."

"I was just making a little joke is all," Pippa said, furrowing her brow at her. "You okay today?"

Louisa crossed her arms in front of her. "I'm perfectly fine. But, Pippa, I'm warning you ... if you *ever*...make another derogatory comment about my husband, the words that come out of my mouth will make one of Martin's famous tongue lashings seem gentle by comparison!" she said, flicking her ponytail for emphasis.

She took a short breath and huffed it out. "I've changed my mind. I'm going to take an early lunch. I'll be back around half twelve. And I *will* keep this after all." She reached out and grabbed for the lunch menu one last time before dashing down the hall.

Louisa didn't realise she had left her coat in her office until she reached the exterior doors. Not wanting to have to face Pippa, she buttoned her jumper, wrapped her arms around her and plunged into the cold, wet wind.

The shock of the icy mist hitting her skin as she pushed her way down Fore Street felt refreshing as it cooled the anger on her face. But by the time she rounded the turn on to Middle Street she had begun to tremble from the damp chill that had penetrated her clothing.

As she turned to ascend the hill leading to Ruth's cottage, a gust of wind blew through between the houses, pelting her with rain. She reached a hand up to wipe the drips of moisture from her face before climbing the steps to the porch.

"Mrs. Ellingham, you must be freezing!" Poppy said as Louisa pushed the front door closed behind her.

"I am!" She stood, shivering as her teeth chattered. "Where's Martin?"

"He came home wet, too. I think he went to take a shower and change into dry clothes. Want me to make you a cup of tea? Warm you up?" the childminder asked as she looked worriedly at her.

"That would be lovely, Poppy. I'll be right out. I just want to say hello to Martin first." She looked about the room. "Is James napping?"

"Mm-hmm. Should be up anytime, though."

Poppy helped her out of her wet jumper and took it to the laundry room, and Louisa went in search of her husband.

"Martin?" she said softly as she peeked into the bedroom. The sound of running water could be heard coming from the shower. Not getting a response as she tapped lightly on the door, she stuck her head into the bathroom. "Martin ... it's just me. Can I come in?"

He pulled the shower curtain back. "Louisa! What are you doing home already? What time is it?"

She closed the door behind her. "Almost eleven thirty. I decided to take an early lunch break. Hope you don't mind."

"Nooo! Not at all! I'll be out in a minute," he said, pulling the shower curtain shut again.

"Erm, mind if I join you. I got kinda cold walking home in the rain," she said sheepishly.

He hesitated. "Ah, no ... no. That'd be fine ... good."

Peeling off her soggy clothing, she got into the shower, wrapping her arms around his warm body.

"Geesh, Louisa! You're freezing!" he said, sucking in a breath as he pulled back.

"Sorry."

He stood for several seconds, waiting for his breathing to slow and then released his grip on the assist bar and embraced her. "How the bloody heck did you get so cold ... and *wet*?" He ran his fist over her soggy ponytail.

"I walked home without my coat. Got a bit soaked."

"Obviously. How could you forget your coat on a day like today?" he asked, peering down at her incredulously.

"I didn't *forget* my coat, Martin. It just sort of got—left. Now, be quiet and warm me up. Please."

He brushed the rogue wisps of hair away from her face before tipping her head back to kiss her. "I, erm ... I'm sorry for what I did to make you angry, Louisa."

"And what exactly is it that you think you may have done?"

He gazed back at her, his face softening as his head tipped to the side. He blinked his eyes. "I, erm—I—" he faltered. "I *do* remember now where we get our strawberries."

She pulled him in closer and laid her head against his chest. Steam rose from his body along with the fresh, slightly-spicy smell that was so quintessentially her husband. "It wasn't *about* where we get our strawberries, Martin. I was annoyed because you referred to *Adam* as the floor-licker."

"But he *is* the floor-licker. Perhaps you don't remember last summer term when your janitor had been inhaling fumes from the paraffin heater he'd been using to heat the shed behind the school. He'd—"

Louisa put her hand over his mouth. "Mr. Coley isn't *my* janitor. And I understand the origin of Adam's unfortunate nickname. But that's not the reason I was angry. I thought you were telling me how to do my job ... telling me how to deal with my students."

Martin picked up the bottle of bath soap and squirted a puddle into his hand. "I'm not sure what you're getting at. All I have to go by is the example set by my parents and the headmaster and housemasters at boarding school. I hardly think *I'm* the kind of person who should be allowed to deal with child—"

He breathed out a heavy sigh. "I'm just saying that *you* are much better qualified to deal with children and make decisions regarding your job than I could ever be, and that it has never been my intent to try to do otherwise," he said, a scowl now fixed on his face.

"Hmm. Maybe I need to remind you that you *did* criticise me once for taking too relaxed an approach to discipline at my school."

The ever-present furrow in his brow deepened. "I may have been wrong in my assessment of the situation. I have a slightly different perspective now on what's appropriate in regard to discipline."

Louisa glanced at his still soap-filled palm. "I could use some of that if you're not going to do anything with it."

He looked down. "Mm, of course," he said, holding it out awkwardly.

She took hold of his hand and pressed it to her chest, working the soap into a lather. A small smile peeked out from one corner of his mouth as he allowed his palm to glide slowly over her breasts.

"Mmm, that's nice." She closed her eyes and let the firmness ... the gentleness of his touch ease her tensions.

"We, erm ... could skip lunch if you like," he suggested as his hands slid down her sides. He pulled her to him.

She took in a slow breath before releasing it. "We could. But then we'd have to rush things. And I don't want to have—to—

rush," she said, punctuating her words with kisses placed down his front. "And *your* stomach is growling, and your bones need to be fed. So, we'll just have to anticipate, won't we?"

She gave a little sigh and an apologetic smile. "Don't let go of me until you have your hand on the assist bar, hmm?"

His shoulders dropped. "Mm, yes,"

Poppy had made a pot of crab soup for lunch. Which Martin, much to Poppy's delight, said rivalled the soup made by Marilyn, the cook at the small cafe and seafood shop up the hill from the school.

Louisa rewarded her husband with a smile and a pat on his knee. She knew he wasn't particularly fond of Marilyn's soup. He found the sodium content to be disturbingly high, so he always avoided it.

With dry clothes and warm bellies, both Martin and Louisa felt ready to face going back out into the inclement weather. Martin and Jeremy dropped Louisa at the school before heading back towards Roscarrock Hill and the surgery. This would be their last opportunity to prepare for the reopening on Monday, and Martin had a number of files he wanted to go over with his assistant. Not the least of which was Malcolm Raynor's colourful medical history.

Chapter 3

Martin was feeling more than a little apprehension about ceding some of the control of the practice to his assistant. Communication failures could cause his patients the inconvenience of having to travel to Wadebridge unnecessarily. But more worrisome was the possibility that Jeremy could overlook a serious health issue in his efforts to protect Martin's well-being.

"So, this patient you were telling me about on the way over here ... what dreaded lurgy is he likely to present with?" Jeremy said from his perch on the desk in the reception room.

"Gawd," Martin muttered, limping towards the file cabinet. "The man's a hypochondriac in every sense of the word.

"If there's any mention in the news of some sort of outbreak occurring, you can bet Mr. Raynor will be making an appearance in the surgery the following day, having thoroughly researched the symptoms, the expected duration, likely modes of transmission, and possible complications.

"And for future reference, he will have squirrelled away any information he's been able to suss out on the incidence of recurrence," Martin said as he pulled a file and tossed it to his assistant.

"Look through that carefully. Mr. Raynor's thespic skills are really quite impressive. And he's not as stupid as he looks.

"Keep in mind, too, that he does present occasionally with *genuine* medical symptoms. I have concerns about some pulmonary scarring resulting from his hypersensitivity pneumonitis. It bears watching. It would probably be best to consult with me before sending him to Wadebridge."

Jeremy dropped into the receptionist's chair and pulled the records from the folder. "It sounds like this village harbours more than its share of eccentric characters. Or are you just exaggerating to make your life appear more exciting than it is?"

"Let's have this discussion again in a few weeks. See what you think once you've had a thorough indoctrination."

Setting a stack of files on the desk, he said, "You can start in on these after you've finished with that one."

The aide's head snapped up. "All these for one guy? You've got to be kidding!"

Martin stared back at him for a moment, deadpan. "I don't kid." Turning, he headed towards his consulting room. "I have some work to do. Knock if you need me for anything."

He had an appointment with Dr. Newell the following day. The therapist had asked him to consider what emotions a child might be expected to feel when being subjected to the sort of punishments that Margaret and Christopher Ellingham had inflicted on their son. And up to this point, he had nothing to show for his efforts.

He leaned back in his chair and closed his eyes, trying to recall his dream from two nights before, paying particularly close attention to the body language and facial expressions of the boy as the oneiric sequence played out in his head.

The child flinched at the first harsh words uttered by his father and then began to back away, even though the man hadn't made any physically threatening moves as of yet. Did that mean the boy was anticipating that he would? If that was the case, he'd likely be feeling fear ... dread.

The child's eyes were wide and fixed, only leaving his father's face occasionally, to dart towards the woman on the desk. The younger of the Ellingham's two maids, hardly more than a teenager, Martin now remembered. *Clarice? French maybe? Probably one of Dad's souvenirs,* he thought, his lip curling involuntarily.

Apart from being a gifted surgeon, Martin could think of no other redeeming qualities in his father. Out of the long list of unflattering adjectives that could be used to describe the man, the most felicitous had to be smarmy. His father was the very definition of the word, and it caused a visceral reaction in him to witness the old man *in action*, particularly with the fairer sex.

Louisa told him once that he was being smarmy, when in actuality he was making a concerted effort to be nice, a characteristic for which she seemed to find him lacking. *Best not attempt nice.*

Focus on the boy! He took in a deep breath and tried to relax into the chair ... to let his mind drift back to the dream.

The boy glanced over again at the maid's face. Her red, moisture-filled eyes seeming to trigger a similar response in the child himself.

His heightened emotional state further enraged his father, and the man did not mince words in expressing his disgust with the boy. This seemed to exacerbate the child's distress, and he pulled his arm up over his face to hide it. *Shame?* Martin could see the boy continuing to spasm involuntarily as he took in deep sobbing breaths. But was he distraught because of the maid's anguished state or the fear of his father?

Could be he's embarrassed by his own childish behaviour, Martin thought, suddenly finding the boy's blubbering infuriating. "For God's sake, stop it!" Martin snarled inadvertently before taking in a gasp of air as his eyes popped open. He rubbed a palm over his head and cleared his throat before settling back into his chair.

The boy was sobbing uncontrollably, and his father was angry with him, grabbing on to his neck and shaking him, causing his head to flop front-to-back.

His eyes were open wide, and his hands pulled desperately at his father's fingers. But his small body couldn't match the size and strength of the man's, and he gave up, allowing his hands to drop limply to his sides. *Submission ... hopelessness?*

Watching as his father demanded an apology from the boy, Martin felt an anger building in him as the child struggled to force the words through his constricted airway. *God, you should have just told the bloody bastard to go to hell!* He tried to block out his growing sensation of nausea, keeping his thoughts fixed on what he could remember of his dream and the memory it triggered.

His father dropped the child to the floor, much as he would a bag of rubbish into the bin, before pulling his belt from the loops around his waist. The boy reflexively pulled his arms up across his face and head. He rolled to his side, pulling himself into the foetal position.

Martin's legs jerked suddenly, and he was jolted back to reality as the fixator in his thigh hit sharply against the underside of his desk. A sharp wail slipped from his mouth as a deep, searing pain reverberated through his femur, and he fought to contain the contents of his stomach.

He had rolled his chair back and was bent over, retching into the bin when his aide hurried into the room. "Martin, are you okay?" He went to the sink and pulled several paper towels from the dispenser, running them under the tap before handing them to his patient.

Martin leaned back in his chair. "I'm fine now," he said as he wiped the towels over his sweaty face.

Jeremy pulled the rolling exam stool over next to him and took a seat. Taking hold of his wrist, he felt for a pulse point.

"I'm *fine*, Jeremy!" Martin snapped as he yanked his arm away, the movement causing his head to spin. His face blanched and he listed in his chair.

The aide stood up and pushed him forward on to the desktop. "Stay there and be quiet." Grabbing the blood pressure cuff from its place next to the exam couch, he resumed his gathering of vital signs in silence. This time, Martin didn't resist.

"Okay, what happened?" Jeremy stared fixedly at him, waiting for an answer. "Martin?"

"Ohhh, just leave it, Jeremy. I'm fine now."

"Aside from your racing heart and elevated blood pressure you mean?" Jeremy pulled out the bin liner and held it up. "And the fact that your lunch is now going to end up on the back terrace with the rest of the day's rubbish."

Martin rested his forehead on the desktop and folded his hands behind his head. "I was—I was trying to—" He swallowed back the uncomfortable lump in his throat. "It was an assignment ... for my therapy session tomorrow."

"Must'a been pretty intense." The aide reached over and began rechecking his patient's vitals.

Martin sat up and took in a deep breath. "I've alluded to my less than idyllic childhood."

"Yeah." The young man pulled the blood pressure cuff from his arm.

"It resulted in physical injuries."

"What do you mean by injuries?"

Martin glowered at him. "Why do you need to know all the sordid details?"

The aide gave the top of the bin liner a twist before tying it shut. "Sorry, Martin, I'm not trying to pry. I *am* interested if you want to talk about this stuff. But just tell me to bugger off if I'm getting too nosy."

He stepped out of the room with the bag of rubbish, returning shortly and taking a seat again on the stool. "And you and your mum were never close?"

"God, no! I thought it was me. Up until a few years ago, I think I held out some hope that as I got older she might find some redeeming quality in me. I told you about my difficulty understanding emotions, and I thought maybe I'd misunderstood her feelings. But a few years ago, she made it clear, in no uncertain terms."

The aide reached for his patient's wrist again, checking his pulse rate one last time. Martin huffed but allowed him to do his job.

"So today ... what was that all about?"

Martin tapped his fingers on the armrest of his chair, peering up at the young man guardedly. "I've had some ... difficult memories to try to come to terms with in recent months. I haven't handled it very well," he explained. "It contributed to the depression, no doubt. I suppose I was dragging Louisa down with me. She'd had her fill and left with James several months ago. She said she was going to go to Spain to see her mother, but ... I don't think she would have come back.

"Fate intervened and gave me another chance to get things sorted. So, here I am. This is what you've gotten yourself into, I'm afraid."

"Well, you're damned lucky I thrive on a healthy challenge, then, aren't you mate."

The front door to the surgery opened, and a gust of cold wind pushed into the building. "I'll go check on that. You just sit tight," the aide said.

Martin watched the young man as he left the room, and then he laid his head back down on his desk.

He was roused moments later by Jeremy's rap on the doorjamb. "What is it?"

"Karen Trevathan's here with her son, Adam. She says you wanted to see him this afternoon. Should I check him over and send him in?"

Martin pressed the heels of his hands to his eyes, and shook his head. "Erm ... yes. Get a temp on him, check the lymph nodes, and go through our list of questions. If nothing jumps out at you, have them come through."

"Okay." The aide handed him a sleeve of patient notes and then turned to leave the room.

"Jeremy!" Martin called out. "Could you check the refrigerator in the kitchen ... see if Ruth has some orange juice or something?"

"Yeah, I'll do that first thing."

Martin was scanning the boy's records when the door to the consulting room opened and the Trevathans stepped in, followed by Jeremy. "Would you mind if I sit in on this one, Dr. Ellingham?" the aide asked.

Martin looked over at Mrs. Trevathan. "Are you comfortable with that?"

"I don't care if the whole village sits in. Just get rid of them godawful head lice!" The woman reflexively scratched at her arm.

Martin picked up his crutches and pulled himself up from his chair. "Have a seat on the exam couch," he told the boy.

Jeremy saw his patient's face blanch before he leaned back against the desk to steady himself. He cleared his throat and then pulled himself to his full height.

"You doin' okay, Doc? You look a bit peaky, if you don't mind my sayin'. Sure yer up ta this?" Mrs. Trevathan said.

"I'm fine." Martin pulled on a pair of exam gloves and began to examine the child's scalp for the tell-tale nits. "How long has he been scratching?"

"Must be goin' on a couple of months now. 'Ere I thought it was just a nervous habit. Lord, if I'd knowed it was creepy-crawlys I'd have had 'im in 'ere long ago!"

"I don't know that it *is*—creepy-crawlys. That's just a possibility. Lie back on the couch for me please, and undo your trousers," Martin said, gesturing.

The boy looked at him, wide-eyed. "Why? Do you think I got 'em down there?"

"Oh, for goodness' sake!" the doctor said, rolling his eyes. "I don't have a clue at this point as to what's causing you to dig at your head like you do. But the only way we're going to find out is if you unzip your trousers and let me examine you."

Martin and Jeremy made brief eye contact, Martin taking note of the young man's incredulous expression.

The boy laid back and did as he was told. Martin tugged at his shirt and began to palpate his abdomen. Adam grimaced as his eyes filled with tears. "That hurts!"

"Have you been experiencing diarrhoea—gas—bloating? Any vomiting?" Martin asked as he pushed the boy's sleeves back, examining his arms.

"He's got a touchy tummy, Doc. Always *has* had a touchy tummy. Even when he was a baby," the mother explained. "Some things seem to give 'im the runs, but most seem ta send 'im the other way. Bind 'im up something awful."

"And when did this rash develop?" Martin asked, lifting the child's arm to examine the underside.

"Rash? What rash?" Mrs. Trevathan peered over the doctor's shoulder. "*Adam Jacob!* Why didn't you tell me 'bout that all over yer arms?"

Martin grimaced as the woman's voice sent a sharp pain through his head.

He took a step to the side and pushed the woman back with his elbow. "What about his sleep habits? On weekends ... how late does he sleep?"

"Oh, he'd sleep till we bring the cows in, if we let 'im. But don't all boys that age?" the woman said, roughly tousling her son's head.

"No. That's not typical of a prepubescent child. I'm going to refer you to a paediatric gastroenterologist in Truro. They'll run the appropriate tests over there, but I suspect Allen may— erm—"

Martin's eyes drifted closed briefly. "Celiac disease. I think your son may have Celiac disease. Has anyone else in the family been diagnosed with it?" he asked as he peered into the child's ears with his otoscope.

"Never 'eard of it. That's not serious, is it?"

"It's a treatable condition. It's an autoimmune disorder.

"Gluten, a protein found in many foods, triggers an abnormal immune response that leads to damage of the villi that line the small intestine. The body can no longer absorb nutrients effectively so, in children, we see a failure to thrive. That's why Allen is small for his age."

The woman looked from her son to the doctor. "He's not *small!*"

"Haven't you noticed how he compares to his classmates?" Martin hissed a breath through his nose and gave her a scowl. "It's very effectively treated with proper dietary modifications, and any damage that *has* occurred will correct itself once the appropriate dietary changes have been made."

He walked back to his desk and sat down, scribbling notes in the boy's file. "You can close up your trousers now, Owen. We're finished."

"My *name* is Adam." The boy said as he zipped his trousers. "So, I don't got lice then?" he asked anxiously.

The doctor looked up from his patient file. "No, you don't *have* lice. Your scalp looks clean. Try not to scratch though. The itching is a symptom of the Celiac disease. I'll see what I can do about expediting the process over in Truro. If the boy tests positive for the disease, you'll want to ask the consultant about testing the other family members as well. There's a strong hereditary link."

Martin sent the Trevathans out the door with strict instructions to not make any immediate dietary changes that could affect the results of the tests that would be run in Truro.

"You have a very ... *unique* style with your patients," Jeremy said as he returned the last of the folders to the file cabinet.

Martin pulled up his lower lip and shrugged a shoulder. "They're unique patients. A unique style seems appropriate."

Jeremy opened his mouth to say more, but thought better of it. "Can you use an extra pair of hands on Saturday ... getting moved back into the surgery?" he asked as he held the door for him.

"I'd appreciate that, Jeremy. I had my doubts about that contractor Louisa lined up, but he seems to have done an adequate job in the end," he said, wagging his finger in the direction of the stairs. "It'll be good to have things back to normal."

Martin moved on to the terrace, and Jeremy pulled the surgery door shut behind them.

"Well, you ready for tomorrow ... the pin removal?"

"Yes. A few qualms, but I'm looking forward to having it over with. I haven't discussed it much with Louisa. I suppose I should prepare her for what to expect," he sighed.

Jeremy pulled the door of the Lexus open. "Yep. Louisa doesn't strike me as the ignorance-is-bliss type."

Martin hesitated, considering the aide's words for a moment, and then lowered himself into the seat.

They rode in silence, neither of them speaking until Jeremy parked the car at the bottom of the short walk to Ruth's cottage.

"That was a really nice catch today ... with the Celiac disease," the aide said.

"It was a relatively simple diagnosis. *If,* that is, the test results come back as I expect them to."

"They will."

Martin's right crutch caught on a cobblestone, throwing him off balance, and Jeremy grabbed on to his shirt to steady him.

"Thank you," he said, glancing up at the young man.

"You're welcome. I'll stop by tomorrow evening to see if you need anything for the pain ... change dressings and such."

"Yep. Have a good night, Jeremy," Martin said as he stepped into the house and pushed the door shut behind him.

It had been a long and emotionally tiring day, and Louisa found him already in bed when she came downstairs after tucking James Henry in for the night. She slipped under the blankets and nestled into his warmth.

"Martin ... are you still awake?" she whispered.

"Yes."

"What was it that you whispered to Evan at the assembly today ... that made him laugh?"

He slid the straps of his wife's nightdress from her shoulders and ran his fingertips lightly along her collarbone. "He was nervous. I told him to imagine all the students were frogs, and they weren't staring at him, they were staring at the fly that had landed on his head."

Louisa smiled and reached up, placing a kiss on his cheek. "That was very sweet."

Martin traced a finger across her eyebrow and down her jaw. "I'm not sure it was wise advice. What if it turned out the boy's ranidaphobic?"

Louisa cocked her head at him. "Ranidaphobic?"

"Mm, yes. A fear of frogs. It's fairly common, actually. In some cultures, frogs are considered to be a bad omen. And in our own culture they, along with toads, are often illogically assigned blame for causing warts and other maladies. Although today, the fear usually stems from concern over whether or not a particular frog species is poisonous."

"Are you trying to seduce me, Martin Ellingham?" Louisa said, pushing him on to his back.

INSIGHTS

"Of course not! You seemed somewhat perplexed by my use of the word ranidaphobic, and I was merely trying to clear up the confusion."

"Shame. It was working." She pressed her lips to his in a suggestive kiss. "You were very caring earlier today. Warming me up and all," she said, nuzzling her nose into his neck.

"Yes, well." He cleared his throat. "Getting a chill in and of itself won't cause illness. However, if you're harbouring any viruses in your body, it could theoretically stress your immune system enough to allow the virus to get a toehold."

Her eyes fixed on his as he continued. "Also, a recent study done by a group of scientists at Yale University suggested that the lowering of the temperature in the respiratory tract compromises the cells lining our noses and airways, limiting their ability to defend against viruses," he explained.

Pulling up his vest, Louisa leaned over and began to place gentle kisses on his belly. "You're tempting me, Martin ... your beguiling ways and all. And if I remember correctly, we got a start on something in the shower earlier. I don't think we should leave it unfinished ... do you?"

"Ah, I see." He wrapped his arm around her and pulled her close, finally picking up on the earthy game that she was playing. "Where did we leave off?"

Chapter 4

Martin took hold of his wife's wrist, preventing her from leaving the bed Friday morning. "Louisa, wait."

She giggled and rolled back to face him. "Martin, we just did that last night."

"Mm, sorry. That's not—I mean I wouldn't mind if—if you wanted—that. But I need to talk to you actually."

"Oh? What do you want to talk about?"

"I want you to know what to expect with the procedure today."

"What do you mean? I thought you said it would be a quick in-and-out kind of thing. Martin, you're scaring me now," she said as her chest tightened. "Is there more to it than that?"

"No, no, no, no, no! It *is* a simple and quick procedure. But I just want to make sure that you're aware that there *could* be some pain as well as some bleeding afterwards, especially with the heparin I've been getting.

"I don't want you to think that I'm slipping back into old habits. And you do tend to want to know more than I would expect. So, I'm just trying to not ... bollocks this up. I don't want you to think I'm hiding anything." He reached over and caressed her cheek. "Any questions?"

She furrowed her brow and worried her lip. "I guess I should have known there'd be pain, but I hadn't thought about it. Maybe I didn't *want* to think about it."

"And that's good. I think that's good ... to not dwell on these things. I don't think it would be of any benefit. And I don't want you to worry. I can deal with all of this." He massaged his thumb across her forehead, trying to ease the visible tension in her face.

"But, Martin, I want to be prepared for whatever they're going to be doing to you. It's *not* going to be good if you let me go into these upcoming procedures ... surgeries ... clueless. You *will* prepare me, won't you? Tell me everything ... not keep me in the dark."

He breathed out a heavy sigh. "Louisa, it has never been my intention to keep you in the dark. I hope you know that."

"Hmm, well I don't think this is the time to get into a discussion about why *either* of us behaved as stupidly as we did in the past. I *am* still in the dark as to what was going through your head during our ... difficult time. But like I said"—she pushed him on to his back and kissed him— "now is not the time for deep discussions. We need to get up and get going or you're going to be late."

Louisa noticed signs of her husband's growing apprehension as they drove to Truro later that morning. He continually shifted in his seat, wiped the perspiration from his palms on to his trousers, and cast frequent glances in her direction.

"I hope you don't mind, Martin, but I'd like to come back with you this morning ... be with you until they take you to do the pin removal," she said, reaching over to caress his thigh.

"No, that's fine. If ... that's what you'd like. I mean, if it would make you feel better. That would be fine. That would be good. Mm," he said, his punctuational grunt emphasising the fact that he was merely concerned for her emotional welfare.

She turned her head towards the side window to hide the smile that had slipped across her face.

The smile faded as she remembered the look of fear and desperation on his face the night of the accident. If she should ever again doubt her importance in his life, she would remember that night.

Traffic was heavy as they passed the park-and-ride and navigated their way through the final roundabouts before the turn towards the hospital.

A driver behind them honked his horn, communicating his unhappiness with what he perceived to be her slow rate of speed. "Tosser," she grumbled. "I certainly won't miss these trips between the hospital and the village."

Martin turned away, but she noticed the tilt of his head and knew that a grimace likely accompanied it. The look that adorned his face whenever he felt he had annoyed or angered her in some way.

She manoeuvred the Lexus under the canopy at the patient drop off. "I'll go and park the car. Wait for me in the reception area, okay?"

"Yes." He gripped his crutches and raised himself from the seat.

Martin had checked himself into outpatient services and was sitting in a chair in a dimly lit corner of the waiting room when Louisa entered the building. She flashed him a smile as she approached, and he returned it with a tip back of his head.

"Any trouble finding a parking spot?" he asked as she dropped into the seat next to him.

"Nope. There are a few parking places behind the bus stop that people don't seem to notice. Seems to always be an open space available. Being a veteran has its upsides, too, you know," she said as she reached up and gave him a peck on the cheek.

He glanced around them furtively, clearing his throat. "I should have had Jeremy come over with me today. I'm sorry about this."

Louisa linked her arm in his. "No, Martin! I *want* to be here!"

He gave her a dubious look, his brow furrowed. "Erm, we should get going," he said as he pulled himself to his feet and headed for the doors leading into outpatient services.

Their first stop was at the laboratory where Martin had blood drawn for the tests ordered by Mr. Christianson. Louisa got up as he re-entered the reception area and she joined him at the desk.

"All right, Dr. Ellingham," the phlebotomist said, perusing a sheet of paper in her hand. "It looks like Mr. Christianson wants some pictures before he gets started with your procedure. Do you think you can find your way to radiology? I can get someone to help you if you like."

"I managed to find my way *here*, didn't I?" he replied tersely. "I don't need a chaperone."

Louisa looked over at the woman. "Sorry, I think we're both a little nervous."

Martin cast a fiery glance at her before heading off towards the doors. Louisa hurried to catch up to him.

He whirled his head around as soon as she approached. "Why did you do that?"

"Why did I do what?"

"Apologise for me!" he sputtered, colour rising in his neck and face. "It's like my mother!"

Louisa trailed after him as he stormed down the hall the best he could, turning at the next corridor to make his way towards radiology. She took hold of his arm and steered him towards a bench.

"Martin, sit down," she insisted.

He huffed and lowered himself on to the seat. "I need to get these CTs done, Louisa," he growled.

"Well, then you better listen up so we can get this ... disagreement straightened out quickly. But I *will* not let them take you off to theatre with angry feelings between us! Got it?"

He took in a deep breath and closed his eyes for several moments. "Fine. What is it you want to talk about?"

"Martin? You're angry with me. That's what I want to talk about. Tell me why my apologising for your rude behaviour has you so upset."

He worked his jaw as he stared at the wall ahead of him. "I wasn't rude."

"Yes, Martin, you were. That poor woman was trying to be helpful. You could certainly have found a politer way of turning down her offer of assistance!"

Footsteps could be heard coming down the corridor, and Martin waited for two doctors to pass them by before responding.

"What was rude about what I said? It was the truth, wasn't it?"

"Well yes, it *was* the truth. It just came out sounding very harsh. Like you were annoyed with her."

"I *was* annoyed with her!" he squeaked. "She called me *Dr. Ellingham!* She must know I'm not a complete imbecile!"

"Martin, even doctors can get turned around, or need directions on occasion. Maybe you should have given her the benefit of the doubt ... not assumed she thought you were an imbecile."

He rolled his eyes and gave an exasperated snort. "Maybe the less I say, the better. Should I have just said, I don't need any help, and left it at that? Is that what you're saying?"

She gave him a timid smile. "That would have been a *bit* better, I suppose."

He blinked his eyes at her and shook his head. "Can we go now?"

"In a minute." She took his chin in her hand and turned his head towards hers before placing a kiss on his lips. "*Now* we can go."

The CT scans completed, they sat in the radiology department a short time later, waiting to receive further instructions.

Ed Christianson entered the room. "Good morning, Martin ... Louisa. You ready to go?"

"Erm, yeah. Everything looks good, then?" Martin asked as he picked up his crutches and got to his feet.

"For the most part. Let's get you back to a room, and we can go over a couple of things. Then we'll get you on down to theatre."

Martin and Louisa followed the surgeon through the automatic doors and into an outpatient cubicle.

A nurse stepped in and handed him a hospital gown and a pair of socks. "I'll give you a minute to change, then we'll get a line going for you, Dr. Ellingham. Mrs. Ellingham, you're welcome to stay if you like, or you can wait in the reception area if you'd prefer."

"No, here's good," Louisa said, giving her a smile.

"I need to chat with Dr. Ellingham for a few minutes, so give us a little extra time, please," Ed said to the nurse.

"Yes, Mr. Christianson."

He waited for her to leave the room and then pulled up another chair, gesturing for Martin and Louisa to take a seat.

"Is there a problem?" Martin asked apprehensively.

"Just an area of concern. The CT scans showed some possible infection developing around one of those pins that took a hit in your recent fall. Could be related ... could be coincidental. Have you noticed any more pain than usual? Or has your temperature been elevated?"

"I've had more pain in the arm, but I attributed it to being more active. I don't know about fever. I haven't checked it in several days. What about my white blood cell count? Any leucocytosis?" Martin asked, shifting quickly into medical mode.

"Yep, it's elevated. But you *are* under a lot of stress, and I don't need to tell you, your body's sustained a heck of a lot of damage.

"I think we've caught this early, Martin. My plan is to remove that pin, get some bone and soft tissue samples, debride with saline, then backfill the cavity with vancomycin and tobramycin pellets. I'll close with an absorbable running deep fascial stitch and a nylon dermal stitch.

"We'll give you IV antibiotics here, and I'll instruct Jeremy Portman on what to do with you when you get home." Ed slapped his hands down on his knees. "Any questions?"

Martin breathed out a heavy sigh and rubbed his hand over his eyes. "I can go home today?"

The surgeon leaned forward, resting his elbows on his knees. "Yeah. We'll get you into theatre within the next half hour. Have you out again by half ten, or so. You'll need to stay until we get the antibiotics into you, but if all goes well we should be able to cut you loose early this afternoon."

"What about the other pins; will you still pull those today?"

"Nope. I want to hold off. I don't want to give the bacteria in your system any more opportunities to get a toehold. We'll get the other pins in another week or so." Ed stood up and picked up the hospital gown, tossing it to his patient. "I'll see you in theatre, mate."

"Ed ... before you go," Martin said. "I've noticed some mental sluggishness. It's probably the morphine, but it's been a concern."

Mr. Christianson turned and leaned against the door jamb. "Any headaches, nausea, vision changes?"

"Headaches, yes. No vision changes, but some sensitivity to sound and some light-headedness. And I've been grasping for words at times. I get them; it's just slow ... different. Some nausea, but I'm thinking now it may all be related to a brewing infection."

"Could be. I'll set something up with one of the chaps up in neuro though, just to rule out any delayed symptoms from the concussion. It may be you've been experiencing concussive symptoms but have been blaming it on the pain meds. Or the pain meds could have been masking symptoms that are showing up now that you've cut back on the morphine. It's best to check things out. I'll let you know when they can get you in."

Martin gave a nod of his head and Ed stepped out the door.

Louisa pulled the curtain shut and gestured for her husband to get to his feet before wrapping her arms around him. "It *will* be fine, Martin. Just a bit of a bump in the road is all, hmm?"

"Mm, yes," he said as he began to undo the buttons of his shirt. Louisa took hold of his wrists and tugged his trembling hands down. "Let me do it. You take some deep breaths and try to relax."

She pulled his arm from the left shirt sleeve and then worked the right sleeve over the fixators. Undoing his waistband, she slid his trousers down and he stepped out of them.

"One day, this will all be over. Until then, I'll be with you every step of the way," she said, wrapping the surgical gown around his back and tying it shut.

She went to place a kiss on his cheek but was brought up short by the pained expression on his face.

"I'm sorry that you have to be, Louisa," he said as he sat down on a chair and tried to work one of the hospital socks over his foot.

She knelt down and took the sock from his hands. "Sorry that I have to be? I don't understand."

"This isn't what I want for you," he said, shaking his head.

"*You* are what *I* want for me, Martin. And just so you know, I may not like making this drive over here for appointments and such, but like you put up with living in Portwenn so that you can be with me, I will put up with the traffic and pushy drivers so that I can be with you." She leaned forward and pressed her cheek to his. "You're worth every horn honk and rude gesture."

"Everyone decent in there?" the nurse called out before sliding the curtain aside.

"We're ready," Louisa replied, giving her husband an encouraging nod.

"All righty, then. Let's get your IV going," the woman said as she examined the back of her patient's hand in search of a prime puncture site.

Martin closed his eyes as the woman inserted the catheter, breathing a sigh of relief that she was competent and one jab was all that was necessary to get the needle in the vein.

As they wheeled him out of the room, he looked up at his wife. "I, erm ... love you," he said softly.

"You have a good rest, and I'll be here when you wake up," Louisa said, kissing his forehead as she brushed her hand across his head. "And I love you, too," she whispered in his ear.

Chapter 5

Martin was groggy but awake when two nurses wheeled him back into the outpatient cubicle a little more than an hour later. Louisa could see from the tautness of his face that he was in pain, but his level of discomfort did not seem to compare to what he felt following his previous surgeries.

His eyes searched for her as they adjusted his freshly assaulted arm, elevating it and encasing it in the familiar blue cold packs.

She moved to his side. "Hello," she said softly, touching her forehead to his. He returned her greeting with a soft grunt.

"Does it hurt, Martin?"

"Yesss ... but, not too bad. They gave ... me some ... thing. Milazodam ... I think."

A smile came to Louisa's face at her husband's rare mispronunciation. "I think it was midazolam. And I think they must have given you a generous amount."

"Mm, yes. Thas how much ... how much Ed *said* he was going to give me." His eyelids drifted shut momentarily as his wife stroked her fingertips against his cheek. When he opened them again, he fixed his gaze on her. "I think ... I'm fery lucky."

"Yes, you are *fery* lucky. Ed's a very skilled surgeon."

Martin squinted at her, reaching up to pull down her lower eyelid. He tipped his head back, examining her critically. "You're ssluring your ... your words. You ... said fery, not *fery*. Per ... perhaps I shh ... should have Ed look at you."

"I'll let him know you mentioned it, how 'bout that." She ran her palm over the top of his head before letting it come to rest against his cheek.

"Mm ... yes." He stared at her, glassy-eyed, before knitting his brow. "I meant ... I'm fery lucky because I'm awkward. An' strange ... my mother says."

Louisa bit her cheek, trying to focus her thoughts away from the tears that were stinging her eyes.

An' you ... everybody likes you. An' you're ... beauqiful."

She drew in a breath. "Thank you, Martin."

He pulled his head back to focus on her face. "On our wedding day ... I couldn't believe you married me. Then when you leff for Spain..." He squeezed his eyes shut. "My mother said she wasn't surprised you ... my mother wasn't surprised you walked out ... on me. I should ged used to being on my own."

Louisa took his hand in hers and brought it to her lips. "No, Martin. You shouldn't get used to being on your own, because I'm not going anywhere."

He gave her a tired smile. "My father thought ... I'd have to drug you to keep you. But you're still here. So, you see ... I'm fery, fery ... lucky."

Louisa tried to smile back at him in response to his words. The medication not only slowed her husband's speech and thought processes, it released him from his usual inhibitions. His sentiments were bittersweet. His flattering words about her were so nice to hear, but it made her heart ache that he still saw himself through his parents' eyes.

"I guess we're both lucky then because you are a *handsome* and *extraordinary* man, and I get to be your wife," she said as she pressed her lips to his forehead.

His eyes drifted closed again, and he fell back to sleep. He woke about an hour later, a low groan alerting Louisa. She got up from the chair she had been dozing in and moved to his side. The sedative had cleared his system enough that he was much more coherent, but he was now feeling more pain and he grimaced, reaching for his arm.

A nurse entered the room and hurried over, pushing his hand back, far more aggressively than Louisa thought necessary. "Don't touch, Dr. Ellingham!" she ordered as she checked the drip rate on his IV.

The woman gave him a cold stare, and he averted his eyes. "Your surgeon will be in to see you in a while. Let him know if you need something to make you more comfortable."

As she pulled the ice packs from Martin's arm, Louisa's small gasp drew her husband's attention to the surgical site. He pushed himself up on his elbow, now anxious about the source of his wife's concern. Blood had soaked through the bandage and had formed a sizable pool along his arm. Martin stared with glazed eyes at the dark red puddle, the colour draining from his face. He swallowed several times, attempting to stave off the threatening emesis as Louisa reached for the basin next to the bed. He glanced apprehensively at the nurse before searching out his wife. He looked at her with fear in his eyes as his breaths quickened.

"Martin, are you all right?" Louisa asked, her concern growing.

"I need your help!" he whispered before collapsing on to the bed."

The nurse immediately began searching his wrist for a pulse, furrowing her brow when she felt it, weak and rapid. She pressed the call button on the cord around her neck and another nurse hurried in. "Get Mr. Christianson down here," she ordered.

"What's going on?" Louisa asked, the nurse's tone adding to her own anxiety.

Footsteps could be heard approaching in the hallway before Ed hurried through the door. He pulled the stethoscope from around his neck and placed it against Martin's chest. "What's his BP?" he asked.

"One fifty-five over eighty a few minutes ago."

He snapped his fingers at the blood pressure cuff in the woman's hands.

"He *was* fine, Mr. Christianson. Suddenly, he seemed to be having trouble catching his breath, and he lost consciousness."

"Ed, I think it was the blood. I think he had a panic attack," Louisa said.

"Oh, are you a trained medical professional, Mrs. Ellingham?"

"No, but—"

"I think you should let Mr. Christianson make that determination then," the nurse said patting her arm.

"Shut up," the surgeon said abruptly, glaring angrily at the woman.

Ed looked up at Louisa and nodded his head, his shoulders relaxing visibly. "His BP's fine now. I think you're probably right, Louisa." He smiled at her reassuringly before turning to the nurse. "Get me a cold wet towel. And get this blood cleaned up."

The nurse looked at her patient's wife askance, then left the room, returning shortly with the requested towel.

Ed passed it to Louisa. "I suspect he'd rather wake up to you caressing his face than me," he joked. The humorous moment broke the tension in the air, and Louisa heaved a heavy sigh.

Martin's eyelids began to flutter as his wife wiped the sweat from his face and consciousness returned. He glanced around him, confused momentarily by his whereabouts, looking up at her, wide-eyed.

"I can see to things here, Ms. Turner," Ed said to the nurse. "Why don't you go tend to other patients."

The woman left the room, and Ed pulled the curtain shut before moving a chair up next to the bed. "Martin, you experienced a syncopal episode. I'm quite sure it was just a panic attack. How are you feeling? Is the blood back in that thick head of yours?"

He blinked his eyes and licked his dry lips. "Yeah. May I have a drink?"

"Sure, let's see what we can do about the pain as well," Ed said as he adjusted the IV. "I want to bring you up to speed on what I did to you this morning. Are you up to it, or should I come back later?" he asked, raising the head of the bed and handing his patient a glass of water.

"I'm … I'm fine, go ahead." Martin pushed himself back so that he was sitting upright and gave his head a shake.

"Well, there *was* a bit of infection in there, but it seemed to be confined to the soft tissue. I collected some samples, then debrided and irrigated the wound. We'll see what the cultures grow, but I'm really pleased with how things looked before I closed up. I did also pack the cavity with vancomycin and tobramycin pellets. You'll be hurting for a few days, but I don't think this'll set you back too much."

Ed glanced over at his patient's wife as her eyes flitted between the surgeon and her husband. "All these trips over to see me payed off today, Louisa. We caught this in its initial stages and should have no trouble managing it. Make sure he's not overdoing things, getting enough rest, eating well. You know the drill."

"So, it's not serious then?"

"No. It could have been serious, but as in most things in medicine, the earlier we catch it the easier it is to treat. And the better the outcome will be."

The surgeon turned his attention back to his patient. "I'm going to have Portman give you a two-week course of parenteral antibiotics, just to make sure we have our arses—" He glanced at Louisa. "Erm, just to be sure we've covered our bums. Then we'll switch you to a course of oral antibiotics.

"I want to keep you here until later this afternoon … just to monitor your blood pressure and the bleeding from the wound. You can probably go home around four or five o'clock."

"I have an appointment with Barrett Newell at four. Do you think I can be out of here in time to make it there?"

Ed hesitated. "I think that'll be okay, but I want you to go directly home afterwards. Think you can get around with one crutch for a few days? I don't want you to put weight on that arm. It could get the bleeding started again."

"I can manage. I've been doing a bit of that already."

"Good. I'll have a chair sent down to get you from here to Barrett's office. And we'll send you home with a sling. Use it when you're up and about. Keep it elevated otherwise."

Martin pulled his hand away from Louisa's and held it out to the surgeon. "Thank you, Ed. Very much."

"You're quite welcome. You made my day actually." The man stood up and moved towards the door. "I'll want to see you back here in a week. We'll take some more pictures and think about removing those other pins."

Martin watched as Ed left the room and pulled the curtain closed behind him. Then he turned to Louisa and gave her a smile. The first genuine smile she'd seen from him in many months.

"*You* look happy," she said as he reclaimed his hand.

"Yes." He grimaced as a pain shot through his arm, and he reflexively squeezed on to her until it eased. "Sorry," he said, loosening his grip and stroking his thumb across the back of her hand. "Did I hurt you?"

"Maybe just a teeny bit. It's fine. Are *you* better now?"

He swallowed and nodded his head. "Louisa ... I want to apologise for earlier ... for embarrassing you. I really *wasn't* trying to be rude."

"Maybe it's an area we can work on with Dr. Newell. And I know that it's not right for me to be making apologies for you. I guess I may have to resort to wearing a rubber band on my wrist after all."

Martin's brows pulled down. "I'm sorry?"

"Dr. Newell suggested that I either pinch myself or wear one of those band thingies like Mrs. Tishell has. Give it a snap when I find myself treating you like a child."

Martin curled his lip at the thought of his wife wearing anything suggestive of the barmy chemist. "I think I'd rather have you treat me like a child."

She leaned over to kiss him but was interrupted by a rustling in the hall. Chris Parsons stepped into the room. "Hi, Mart ... Louisa," he said picking up the chart on the table by the bed. "I ran into Ed upstairs. He told me he had you in theatre this morning. Is the arm hurting?"

Martin shrugged his shoulders. "It's not bad ... I've experienced worse."

Chris gave him a wry grin and then looked down, scanning the patient notes. "Has Ed said when you can get out of here?"

"Later this afternoon. I have a four o'clock appointment next door that I'll be out in time for. What time is it now?" he asked, looking around for a clock.

"Twelve fifteen. Why, you getting tired of our accommodations already?"

"No, I'm getting bloody hungry." He scowled at his friend. "Would you mind going to the canteen for me?"

Chris set the chart back down on the table. "I'd be happy to. What do you want? And don't say monkfish."

"I wasn't going to. Just get me a cheese sandwich and some carrot and celery sticks. Maybe some yoghurt ... a couple would be good. And a carton of milk."

Chris took a couple of steps towards the door before he added, "And I could use a couple of high protein shakes as well."

"Anything else...*Martin?*" Chris tipped his head down, narrowing his eyes at him.

"Mm, no. I think that should be adequate for now."

"Right." Chris made it just past the doorway before he heard Martin call out, "Chris!"

Louisa worried her lip when she could see her husband was beginning to annoy his friend.

"What?" Chris asked testily.

"If they *should* happen to have monkfish could you—"

"Yes!" Chris stomped off down the hall.

Louisa adjusted the blanket covering her husband's legs. "You *are* hungry!"

"Not really. I was just playing with him," Martin said, dipping his head contritely.

Louisa peered down at him with her sternest teacher's expression.

"What?" he asked, raising an eyebrow.

She shook her head. "Nothing."

Having polished off the requested lunch items that Chris had picked up for him, minus the monkfish, Martin fell asleep. He was awakened later in the afternoon by the nurse, Ms. Turner, as she rustled through patient records and hospital papers.

"Mr. Christianson has given you permission to be discharged. Would you like some help getting dressed?" she asked.

Martin rubbed his tired eyes and looked around the room. "Where's my wife?"

"She went to the loo. The woman crossed her arms in front of her and stared down at him imperiously. "I asked you a question. Would you like some help or not? I do have other patients to see to."

Martin screwed up his face at her. "Not. Just get me my clothes."

He had woken with a headache, and he rubbed a palm over his forehead trying to ease it.

Ms. Turner removed the IV from his hand and then sat down to add notes to the patient chart.

Air hissed from Martin's nose as he glanced at the clock. "I do have somewhere I need to be *Ms*. Turner. Can't you get your work done out at the nurse's station?"

Not getting a response, he added, "I thought you had other patients to see," he growled.

"Don't get impertinent with me," she said, finally looking up from her lap. "You may have gotten away with that up in London, but I won't tolerate it."

"Oh, for goodness' sake," he mumbled, kicking his legs free of the blankets. He sat himself up on the edge of the bed. "I don't think it's unreasonable to expect a little privacy. I have an appointment to get to. So, hand me my things and leave me be. I'll get dressed myself and be on my way."

The woman stared back at him for a moment. "I don't take orders from patients, Dr. Ellingham. I don't care who they are. I'll be done here in a minute. And then, if you can keep a civil tongue about you, I'll help you with your clothes."

Martin slid to the floor, balancing himself against the wall as he made his way towards the small wardrobe.

He staggered back towards the bed with his clothes in his left hand and his right hand held over his head to ease the throbbing. He cast a fiery gaze at the nurse. "If you want to potter about in here, be my guest. Just don't complain about being at the receiving end of my—*bare arse!*"

The nurses head shot up. "Well, I never!" she said as she got to her feet.

Louisa had arrived just in time to hear the choice words uttered by her husband, and she pulled the curtain aside quickly. *"Martin!"*

Ms. Turner pushed by her, grumbling, "He's all yours, love."

Martin threw his head back. "Gawd! *She* doesn't reflect well on the quality of care in this hospital."

"That was terribly rude, Martin."

He opened his mouth to respond but instead huffed out a breath. "Of course. It's always my fault," he muttered as he pulled on the ties at the back of his neck.

"Here, lean forward," Louisa said reaching around him.

"I'll *do* it!" he barked, brushing her hand aside. The pounding in his head, the throbbing in his arm, the difficult nurse, and his wife's immediate assumption of his guilt, had thrown Martin into a very foul mood.

She stood back and watched him struggle until she began to fear for the safety of his new wound.

"Martin, please ... let me help you."

He glowered back at her as he sat on the edge of the bed, shaking his left arm, trying to free it from the constraints of the hospital gown while simultaneously attempting to keep his right arm elevated.

"Errrgh! Dammit!"

Louisa moved forward and wrapped her arms around his chest. She could feel his heart pounding as his breaths rushed past her ear. When she felt him begin to relax, she held him out at arm's length. "Doing better?"

He gave her a lethargic nod. "I just want to get out of here."

They worked together in silence to get him dressed and ready to leave. Louisa knelt down and assisted him with his socks and shoes. "There you go," she said, patting his foot, signalling the end to their struggle with his clothes.

"Mm, thank you." A stream of air hissed from his nose. "Louisa, it's not always my fault. That woman was—was—"

She stood up and embraced him again, nuzzling her face into his neck. "I'm sorry. That wasn't fair. Maybe we can talk about it later. I'll try to do better in future, but I might need you to remind me, hmm?" She pulled back and put her hands on his cheeks, peering into his face.

He hesitated, and then gave her a strained smile. "Or ... maybe you could just snap your rubber band."

"Mar-tin."

Chapter 6

"Martin, if Dr. Newell has the time, I'd like to be included in part of the session today. But only if there's time," Louisa said as she flipped through a magazine in the waiting room of the therapist's office.

"Why?"

She narrowed her eyes at him. "You could just say yes or no."

"Well, yes, of course you can. But what is it you want to talk about?"

Louisa twisted her purse strap in her hands and peered up at him. "I'm worried about the effect this whole thing with Evan could have on you. I'd just like some reassurance from Dr. Newell that it won't be harmful to you if it's not a happy outcome."

"Mm." Martin's eyes shifted to the window as he stared absently.

A door could be heard opening down the hall, and Dr. Newell's deep, husky voice resonated into the waiting area.

A tall young man walked past them, followed by the therapist. "Martin, come on back," he said, giving a wave to Louisa.

"How are you, Dr. Newell?" she asked as she slipped her coat from her shoulders and hung it over the chair next to her.

"I'm doing well, thank you. Would you like a hand there?" the man asked, looking down as Martin struggled with a crutch.

"Nope, I've got it," he replied, gripping on to it with his left hand and pulling himself to his feet. He closed his eyes for a few seconds, waiting for the room to stop swaying.

"Are you all right?" the doctor asked, putting a hand on his shoulder to steady him.

"I'm fine. I had a bit of work done this morning. The anaesthesia's just...I'm fine now," he said, making his way towards the man's inner-sanctum.

"So how are you progressing ... physically?" The psychiatrist swung the door shut behind them and helped Martin into a chair.

"It's slow, but things are coming along. They found a bit of infection in the arm so Ed Christianson went in and cleaned that up this morning. A bit of a setback, but it certainly could have been worse."

The man dropped into his chair and pulled a folder from a stack on his desktop. "And mentally ... how have you been holding up with all the issues you're trying to deal with?"

"There's been a lot going on lately ... a lot to try to get my head around. And the surgery will open again on Monday. Just two hours a day to start with. I have some trepidation about it."

"Trepidation about?"

"Do I need to remind you of my physical condition?" Martin gave the man a scowl. "The villagers are going to be coming into my surgery just to gawp ... like I'm an item in a curiosity shop. And I'm having to relinquish much of the control over which patients I see to Jeremy Portman."

The psychiatrist pushed himself back in his chair. "He seems like a very competent and professional young man. What are your concerns?"

"He *is* competent and professional. But that doesn't provide me with any guarantees that he won't send someone with an emergent health issue to Wadebridge in an effort to protect me."

He grabbed for his crutch as it began to slide from its resting place perched against his chair. "I've been trying to familiarise him with the patients registered at my practice, but mistakes could be made."

"It will take some time for a trust to develop between the two of you, I'm sure. But from everything that Ed Christianson and Chris Parsons have told me, you couldn't have chosen a better assistant."

Martin brushed at his trouser leg with the backs of his fingers, keeping his eyes glued to the floor. "Jeremy says he thinks of me as a friend, and it bothers him that I don't ... that I don't trust him." He shifted in his chair as his arm began to throb.

"Well, as I said, that'll come with time." Dr. Newell pulled his chair forward and jotted notes into the file.

"No. He doesn't think I trust him with my *fee*—" his body tensed as a sharp pain shot through his freshly assaulted appendage. "I'm sorry, do you mind if I elevate my arm?"

The psychiatrist jumped up and hurried around to assist him, turning his chair so that he could rest his arm on the desk.

"Better now?" the man asked.

"Yes, thank you," Martin said, tucking his chin. "I'm sorry."

"No need to apologise. So, you were saying that Jeremy thinks of you as a friend and?"

Martin glowered at him. "You know what I was getting at. Do I really have to spell it out for you?"

The psychiatrist perched on the corner of the desk and leaned back on his hands. "I'm not trying to torture you, Martin. I just want to be sure I'm understanding you. Jeremy thinks of you as a friend and? Please finish what you were going to say."

Martin wrinkled up his face. "He thinks that I don't trust him with my—my feelings."

"Ah, I see. What do *you* think? Or better yet, tell me who you *do* trust."

"What do you mean by trust?"

"I'm referring, in this instance, to a faith ... a belief that you can confide in someone without having that person abuse that confidence in some way. That you can share your emotional pains ... ecstasies without any fear that it'll be used in a way that could cause you harm, particularly emotional harm. And that what you tell them will be kept between the two of you."

Martin's eyes drifted shut and he breathed out a heavy sigh. "I suppose I have the most trust in Chris Parsons ... and his wife, Carole. I *have* confided in Jeremy on occasion, but time will tell as to whether or not he's trustworthy. Chris and Carole have never given me any reason to distrust them in the twenty or so years we've been friends. Yes, I'd say I trust the Parsons."

"What about your wife?"

"I want to ... to trust Louisa. But she's found my—*feelings*—Gawd, I hate that word. Let's just say my...*feelings* have been a source of amusement for her at times. I'm taking a risk every time I admit something to her. There are things that I can't bring myself to confide in her about. It just seems too risky."

"Care to elaborate?"

"Things that have happened that still bother me."

The psychiatrist slipped from the desk and returned to his chair. "You know, what's discussed inside the four walls of this room goes no further, Martin. This might be the time to get this off your chest."

Martin's fingers tapped on the armrest of his chair. "It was back in medical school ... a classmate. She was struggling in a particular class. It was an area that came easily to me—cardiovascular pathophysiology—and she asked me for assistance."

Taking time out from his anxious drumming, he wiped his sweaty palm on his trousers. "I didn't find her especially attractive, but when she began to show more than a collegial interest in me, I let myself get emotionally involved. We spent a lot of time together.

"Bloody hell, this could hardly be more humiliating!" he spluttered, rubbing his fingers roughly through his hair. "I don't know what purpose this is going to serve."

He looked up into the therapist's unflinching gaze and breathed out a sigh of resignation. "I think my judgement was clouded by the fact that someone of the opposite sex seemed attracted to me. It was my first relationship and I thought she..."

He cleared his throat before continuing. "We were sitting in my living room one night. It was cold and I had a fire going in the fireplace. I wanted her to try a single malt that I liked, and we were both feeling relaxed ... romantic. She *said* she loved me. And I admitted to loving her. One thing led to another and..." he waved his hand in the air, gesturing vaguely.

"She seemed to want to spend every spare moment with me after that. I don't know why I didn't notice that our time together always worked to her professional advantage in some way. Helping her with papers, swotting for exams, accompanying her to parties where she'd introduce me as her partner. Never failing to mention honours I'd been awarded and my familial relationship to Christopher Ellingham. It got her noticed, and it eventually got her a position with an American hospital."

"And she left you behind here in England?"

"Not before I made a complete arse of myself." He groaned. "God! I was twenty-five years old before a woman ever looked at me, let alone allowed me into her bed! It felt at the time like I'd never have another opportunity if I let her slip away, so I decided to ask her to marry me."

Taking note of his patient's sweaty brow, Dr Newell got to his feet and came around the desk. "Let's take a little break. I'll let your wife know that we might be a little while. Then I'll fetch a couple glasses of water before I come back." He put his hand on Martin's shoulder. "You try to relax a bit while I'm gone."

"Mm, yes," Martin answered, watching as the door swung shut behind him.

Louisa glanced up when she heard a rustling in the hall. "Finished already?" she asked as she began to get up from her seat.

"No, no. Stay put a bit longer. We could be a while yet. Are you doing okay out here? Need a cup of tea or a glass of water?"

"Nope, I'm good. I brought my own," she said lifting her water bottle into the air.

"I do have a question, though, when you have time."

He glanced around, taking note of the empty reception room, and sat down next to her. "Shoot, I'm all ears,"

Louisa hesitated, suddenly feeling it a bit of a betrayal to be discussing the subject without her husband present.

"Martin's been helping a student at my school. His father drinks and has abused him in the past ... broke the boy's arm. The child adores Martin, and Martin's ... well, I think he's rather emotionally invested in the boy. It's a huge stress on him. Will he be able to deal with it if things go badly?"

"What about state services? Maybe they should be handling this."

"Children's Services doesn't want to get involved until there's more evidence of what they consider to be imminent danger. I think Martin's going partially on his instinct, but he fears for the boy's safety. Enough so that he's provided him with a mobile to use if he needs help. He's taking a chance doing this. There could be action taken against him if the parents find out and file a complaint against him."

Louisa worried her lip as she watched the man. "Is Martin's involvement posing a risk to his own well-being? His emotional well-being."

Dr. Newell sat quietly for a minute. "I think the benefits outweigh the risks. Martin could learn a great deal about himself through this child. And it sounds like the kid bloody well needs an advocate. Try to be supportive. I'll keep this in mind when I see him in our sessions. If you have any further concerns don't hesitate to call me."

The psychiatrist rose from his chair and began to move away when Louisa spoke again. "Why doesn't Martin seem angry?"

"I'm sorry? Angry about what?"

"All of this. The abuse by his parents, the abuse of this little boy ... his accident. I mean, he hasn't said a single word against the driver of that lorry that hit him. I'm just wondering where he has it all stashed away."

"It's in there. And it may come out bit-by-bit as he works through these things with me, or it may come out more violently at some point. Just try not to overreact if you *do* see some outbursts that seem to be out of character. And you know how to reach me if you should need my assistance ... anytime, day or night."

"Thank you, Dr. Newell."

The doctor returned to his office, setting a water glass down in front of his patient before taking a seat behind his desk. "All right, you were telling me that you'd decided to propose. Can you take it from there for me, Martin?"

Martin picked up the glass, taking a long, procrastinating drink. He had hoped the man might give him a reprieve ... perhaps a continuation at a later session. But he sat watching him intently.

"I made a complete fool of myself with the proposal. I wrote her a poem, and I..."

Turning his head towards the window, he focused on the gulls passing by on their way to the river. "I played the piano at the time, and I had worked up a piece of music that she was particularly fond of ... added some embellishments of my own."

He looked across at his therapist. "Is it really necessary to go any further?"

"If you'd like to move on from this, then yes, I think it is. Take your time and remember that what you have to say stays in this room."

Hissing a breath of air through his nose, Martin continued. "I sank a ridiculous sum of money into a special evening. Rented out an upscale restaurant for two hours, hired a florist to decorate the place, had them prepare her favourite dishes ... all expensive, of course.

"She seemed quite pleased with the restaurant ... didn't notice the flowers."

"And the two things you probably put your heart and soul into ... the music and the poem. How did she react?"

"I couldn't bring myself to look at her when I played the piano piece. When I returned to the table she was chatting it up with the waiter. I stood there while the imbecile finished his conversation with her. When I *could* finally get back to my seat I believe her response was, *well done, Ellingham. You're improving.*"

Martin rested his elbow on the armrest of his chair and tipped his head into his hand. "I gave her the poem. She read it, and then she started to hand it back to me before changing her mind. She put it in her handbag.

"She didn't say *anything*. And I— Well, as you know, I have some difficulty making sense of facial expressions. I was clueless as to how she felt about it. She'd been raised in a home that was as equally devoid of sentiment as the Ellingham home. I excused her reaction to the poem as awkwardness. I trusted her."

He rubbed his palm across his face before slapping it down on his thigh. "I should have trusted my instincts, but I went ahead with my plan for the proposal. The only thing I did right that night was not getting down on bended knee when I asked her to marry me!"

He closed his eyes and shook his head. "I still feel humiliated by my idiotic behaviour. I was nervous. I felt like this was the only chance I'd have to—"

Dr. Newell folded his hands on his desk and spoke softly. "Your only chance for ... what, Martin?"

"To have someone to ... to—to—to have a family!"

"And what do you mean when you said you should have trusted your instincts?"

"I wouldn't be very good at it. Any of it."

"What do you mean by, any of it?"

"Proposing ... marriage. But ... I was tired of being alone. I told her how I felt about her ... that I ... that I loved her. That I didn't want her to leave to take the position abroad. I asked her to marry me."

"And did she accept?" the therapist asked, knowing the answer he would hear.

"She didn't turn me down straight away. She said she'd give it some thought and get back to me. She patted my hand and asked if I was ready to go. That was the end of the evening.

"There was a gathering of department chiefs from King's at my parents' home the next night ... a dinner party. Edith got wind of it and wanted to attend. My parents liked her, especially my mother. The feeling was mutual. I had hoped that she'd realise the opportunities being an Ellingham would afford her and that it might influence her decision," Martin said as he tried to shift his weight to his other hip.

"I found it to be a miserable evening, but Edith seemed to be having a good time, so I sat in the corner and watched her as she worked the room. She finally settled in next to my mother.

They were talking and laughing. Now and then, she'd look in my direction and smile. I felt sure that she'd made the decision to accept my proposal.

"When everyone moved to the dinner table, Edith sat down next to my mother ... across from me. She'd never been a drinker, but she'd been sipping at wine all evening and had several more glasses with the meal. It was obvious that she was becoming inebriated.

"We were just finishing the main course when she stood up and asked for everyone's attention. She announced that she'd been offered a position in the United States, but that I had complicated things the night before by proposing marriage. That she'd had a difficult decision to make, and I'd made it even more difficult by writing her the poem.

"She pulled it out of her purse and started reading it aloud. What was I supposed to do ... jump up and grab it out of her hands! I sat there while she shared my innermost feelings with that table full of my parents' self-important, stiff-necked friends!" he sputtered.

He took in a ragged breath. "Although, I suppose in all fairness to them, they didn't appear to be enjoying my discomfort any more than I was."

He cleared his throat and looked over at his therapist. "Could I get another glass of water?" he asked.

"Certainly. Close your eyes and try to relax while I'm gone, Martin."

Dr. Newell took his time, giving his patient an opportunity to compose himself. Martin looked tired and drawn when he re-entered the room.

"Think you're okay to continue, or should we take this up again next week?" he asked as he handed him the glass of water.

"I just want to get this over with." Martin drank half the glass and set it down on the desktop with a thud.

The psychiatrist went back around and lowered himself into his chair. "Whenever you're ready," he said.

Martin lifted his arm and repositioned it, searching for a more antalgic position. "So, she'd thoroughly humiliated me, but I blamed it on her alcohol consumption. Once the hilarity that followed her telling of my pianistic farce had abated, she looked down at me and said that I was all mouth and trousers on the home front, so to speak, and that love was a *difficult* word. That she didn't think I completely understood the concept. Then she thanked me for getting her through medical school, lifted her glass to me, and sat back down to resume her conversation with my mother.

"My mother had a smirk on her face. My father looked like he was completely disgusted by the turn the evening had taken. I tried to act like I was unfazed by it all, but I—"

The therapist sat patiently, swivelling back and forth in his chair.

Martin shook his head. "I couldn't keep the tears from my eyes. That embarrassed my father ... to have his son show that kind of emotion in front of his professional colleagues. He yelled at me to stop being such a bloody big girl's blouse and grow a pair.

"I had to get out of that house, so I handed Edith the keys to my car, and I walked home ... seven miles in a cold rain with no coat. I didn't even feel it."

Dr. Newell sat quietly for several moments before clearing his throat. "Martin ... first of all, let me say that I can certainly see how such an experience would have a lasting impact. If that had happened to me, I think it would have been devastatingly painful. I'm very sorry you had to go through all that."

"Mm." He pulled in his chin before his gaze shifted to his lap.

"Have you shared this story with anyone before now?"

"My aunt Joan was aware of certain details. Enough for her to have very strong feelings about Edith after that. But I suppose you could say I was economical with the truth."

"How are you feeling about having been more generous with the truth today?"

Staring off absently for a moment, Martin shook his head. "I'm not sure."

"That uncertainty is completely understandable. You took a giant leap of faith in revealing a very painful memory to me. I'm honoured that you feel you can trust me with that information, and I can assure you it will go no further than the four walls of this room."

He leaned forward on his desk and folded his hands in front of him. "You said a little while ago that the experience still affects you. In what way?"

Martin fidgeted in his chair. "I used to write poetry. Up until that night it seemed to be a safe way for me to ... unwind. Piano ... I just can't do it without having that whole horrid scenario resurrected. Neither pursuit brings me relief or enjoyment anymore."

Reaching for his glass, he took another sip of water. "Louisa found out recently that I played. I know she was hurt that I hadn't told her, and she wanted to know why I quit. It made me angry when she persisted. She let the issue go for the time being, but she expects an explanation at some point ... soon."

Dr. Newell leaned back in his chair and steepled his fingers. "Would it help if you could talk it through with her here, in a session?"

Martin furrowed his brow. "It'll be an awkward conversation that I think would be best conducted between the two of us, privately. Louisa has her own issues with Edith. It's complicated."

"Louisa knows Edith, then?" Dr. Newell asked.

"Mm. She resurfaced during Louisa's pregnancy. She was her obstetrician. Edith made the emotional aspect of the pregnancy much more difficult for Louisa, by design. And Louisa misconstrued the professional relationship that I had with Edith to be more than it was.

"If I'd known what she was thinking I could have explained. It makes no difference now, of course, but it makes any discussion about the piano issue quite ... problematic."

"I assume then, that you and Louisa have discussed what went on during that period ... that Louisa understands your relationship with Edith during that time was a purely professional one?" Dr. Newell's chair creaked as he pushed back and stretched out his legs.

Martin cocked his head and tugged on his ear. "Well ... yes. That's the way she understands it."

"I see. Are you saying there may have been more to it?"

"I'm *saying*, nothing beyond a professional interaction occurred, generally speaking."

The psychologist reached for his biro before adding notes to the file. "Maybe we can take this up a bit more at a future session. For now, let's focus on the more delicate issue of your impending discussion over your previously hidden talent.

"Bear in mind, Martin, that you and Louisa have sorted many things out and that a trust has developed between you.

"Be open when you tell her about that horrible experience all those years ago. If you try to downplay the effect that Edith's behaviour had on you, it may play into Louisa's insecurities about the woman."

Martin stared at the man. "You do realise that I don't need her sympathy, don't you?"

"There would be nothing wrong with benefiting from your wife's sympathy, Martin. And Louisa may find reassurance in knowing there's a need she can fill that Edith couldn't. That she can face those awful memories with you. These are the sort of shared experiences that can help to build a bond in a marriage."

"Mm. I see." He rubbed his sweaty palm on his trousers. "I, erm ... you asked me last week to think about the emotions I might have felt as a child ... during punishments. I was having difficulty with that, but I had a dream the other night about an incident when I was a boy. It seemed to help me to see things from a different perspective."

"Was this another memory triggered by a dream?"

Martin stretched out his legs and rubbed a hand up and down his thigh. "No, I had always had full recollection of everything before the dream. I just hadn't really thought about the details. I guess to use your psychological vernacular, I'd been remembering the incident through my child eyes, and the dream allowed me to think back on it through my adult eyes."

"Well now you've piqued my interest. Can you explain what you mean?" Dr. Newell worked the rubber ball in his fist.

"I was watching the incident play out in my dream ... watching myself as a child. I'd walked into my father's office unannounced. He was quite angry with me for having forgotten to knock first. He had me—the child—by the throat, shaking me. Then he dropped me to the floor and pulled off his belt. He lashed out at me—the boy on the floor, I mean. But I—as an adult watching—I grabbed on to the belt before it could hit the child.

"I'd wondered at the time why my father's trousers were unzipped. And our maid was sitting on his desk with her dress pulled up around her waist. She'd—she'd been crying."

"And you had some recollection of this before your dream?"

"Mm. I just hadn't given it any thought. I didn't know anything about sexual intercourse at that age, obviously, so it wasn't until I thought about the details after I had the dream that I was able to put everything into the proper context. I'd—I—I interrupted while he was—"

"This wasn't consensual?"

Martin shook his head. "I don't believe so. I tried to remember the dream ... to name the emotions. I was helpless, and I knew it. I tried to pull his hands from around my neck, but I wasn't strong enough. I suppose maybe at one point I felt fear, I just don't remember it.

"I couldn't breathe. I think I felt a sense of panic when I couldn't get any air in. When my father pulled off his belt, the maid looked at me—" he shook his head "—like she felt sorry for me. I don't know if I was more afraid or humiliated. I can remember being uncomfortable around her after the incident. I would say it was probably embarrassment."

Martin looked over at the therapist, waiting for some sign that he'd completed the assignment to the man's satisfaction. "Is that what you were wanting from me?"

Dr. Newell picked up a rubber band from the desktop and toyed with it. "You know, there is no right or wrong with these assignments I give you."

Martin furrowed his brow and cocked his head at him. "What's the point in doing them, then?"

"Much of the value is *in* the doing ... becoming more comfortable with thinking about these things."

The doctor scratched at his ear as creases etched his forehead. "Martin, imagine yourself trapped in a hedge maze, and there are a limitless number of paths out and a limitless number of paths that lead to dead ends.

"My job is to keep you moving towards the paths that will get you out of the maze ... to keep you from veering off on to a path that will lead you to a dead end, destined to go over and over the same wrong route time and time again.

"These assignments are intended to keep you moving forward on a path that will lead you out of the maze. It doesn't matter which path you take ... how you do these assignments ...

as long as you stay on a path that will lead you to an exit. Eventually you'll find it."

Martin gave the doctor a scowl. "Eventually, that's not very specific, is it? Am I getting close ... to the way out?"

Dr. Newell let the rubber band fall to the desk. "Clos-*er*... you're getting clos-*er*. Neither of us knows how long it'll take you to find your way out of the maze your parents left you in. But the hedges are getting less dense the closer you get to the end, and your view is getting clearer ... less obstructed. This *will* become easier in time."

Martin fidgeted nervously, picking at the Velcro seam around the fixator in his thigh. "I wanted to ... to ask you about something that happened after I woke up from the dream."

He glanced uncomfortably up at the therapist before his eyes darted back to the floor. "Louisa and I made love ... or had sex, rather. I know it was wrong, but at the time, right or wrong was the farthest thing from my mind. And...well, the way I went about it was inexcusable. I felt no better than my father."

Dr. Newell tipped his head back. "I see. You felt like the act was one-sided. That Louisa wasn't a part of it."

Martin released a sigh of relief and nodded his head. "I've never experienced anything like that before."

The psychiatrist came around and perched on his usual corner of the desk. "Martin, I know I don't need to tell *you* this. I'm sure you learned it *way* back in The Birds and The Bees 101. But I'll just remind you ... when we have sex, a cocktail of hormones is released, resulting in a sense of well-being.

"You've been dealing with a tremendous amount of emotional and physical stress. I would imagine the midnight realisation of what a truly horrible man your father was tipped you over the edge a bit. How did Louisa react to what transpired?"

"She was far more understanding of me than I deserved. She was very ... she dealt with it very well."

"Then I would say it may have been an experience that helped to strengthen the bond between the two of you ... in a couple of ways. *You* were reassured that she's there for you, and *she* was provided with an opportunity to be of help to you. To feel useful at a time when she probably feels quite useless.

He got down from his desk and moved towards the door. "It was also a trust building experience. She showed you that she's there to catch you when you fall, and you showed her that you trust her to be there."

Martin had been holding his breath, uncertain about how the doctor would judge his behaviour. He released a heavy sigh. "Mm, I see. Thank you, Dr. Newell."

"You're very welcome, Martin. I think we better wrap this up. You're looking rather tired, my friend."

The psychiatrist got down from his desk and moved towards the door. "You know, Martin, I think it's quite significant that in your dream, you came to the aid of your child self. You stepped in now and put a stop to something you had no control over as a boy. I hope you'll think about that. Perhaps that hedge is getting a little less dense."

Martin stared down at the floor for a moment before giving the man a grunt, getting to his feet, and following him down the hall.

"Ready to go?" Louisa asked, her face brightening when she saw her husband come through the small corridor.

"*I'm* finished, but you had a question, didn't you?"

Dr. Newell gave his patient's wife a wink. "I think we got that question talked out while you were taking a bit of a break earlier. Let me know if anything else comes to mind though, both of you."

"Thank you, Dr. Newell," Louisa said as she slipped her coat on before helping Martin into his.

"How was your session?" Louisa asked as they exited the building and walked towards the Lexus.

"It was ... fine. *Good,* really," he said before tipping his head down to place a lingering kiss on her lips.

Chapter 7

Saturday was moving day at the Ellingham home, and Louisa woke early, anxious to get a start on settling back into their own house. Martin was spooned against her back with his right arm resting on her hip. A soft smile spread across her face as she closed her eyes and allowed herself to take in all the sensations being created by his close proximity.

His body was warm and solid against hers, a luxury on a chilly November morning. The gentle wafts created by his slow, somnial breathing tickled the back of her neck, causing a wisp of her hair to flutter across her cheek and to stir the air just enough to carry a redolence of the soap and shampoo he had used the previous night.

She wondered, as his arm lay heavy on her, his fingers twitching occasionally in his sleep, what dreams might be passing through his head.

The leisurely start to her day was interrupted by happy toddler chatter emanating from the second-floor bedroom. Sighing, she reached for her husband's wrist, lifting his arm and wriggling out from under him.

The cold room was in stark contrast to the warmth and security she had left behind, and she reached quickly for her thick, terry robe, wrapping it tightly around her before hurrying off to see to the baby.

She was frying the protein rich sausages that Martin had learned to tolerate when he appeared in the kitchen doorway. James squealed an excited, "Da-ee!" when he looked up from his high chair to see his father.

"Good morning, James," Martin said softly as he walked over and stroked the backs of his fingers over the boy's head.

Louisa turned to see him bend his tall frame, placing a kiss on the child's head before nuzzling his nose into his neck. James released a string of giggles and chortles, grabbing at his father's ears.

Martin straightened himself, and noticing his wife's gaze fixed on him, he ducked his head self-consciously. "Mm. I think I'll make myself a cup of coffee now," he said as he moved towards the counter.

Louisa came up from behind and wrapped her arms around his chest. "That was lovely to see, Martin ... you and James. It makes me happy for both of you."

"Ah." His eyes scanned the counter top. "Have you seen the filter basket?" he asked as he lifted a pot in the draining rack next to the sink to search underneath it.

"The what?" Louisa's asked, her attention now back on the sausages sizzling on the hob.

"The *filter basket* ... for the coffee machine. Shiny ... makes a nice noise when you bang it on the table," he said sharply, a nod to his wife's reason, on a previous occasion, for allowing the appliance's component to be used to entertain their son. He quickly surveyed the pile of toys in the middle of the floor.

She shifted the last sausage from the frying pan to a platter and then glanced over her shoulder. "I'm not sure *where* it is, Martin. Check the high chair tray."

"Well *that's* not where it belongs, is it?" He hissed out a breath of air as his eyes sifted through the scattering of baby toys, plastic utensils, and bits of banana and half-chewed pieces of toast laid out in front of his son.

"It's not there!" he grumbled. "How am I supposed to make coffee without a filter basket?"

Louisa came over and rested her hand on his shoulder as she set the platter of sausages on the table. "It'll turn up; don't worry."

She moved a pile of freshly folded baby clothes from the table top to a chair and picked up the dish towel. "Oops, here it is. See, I told you it'd turn up. Now relax and make your coffee," she said, handing him the misplaced piece of equipment and giving his bum a pat.

"Ohhh, good gawd! *Look* at this!" he moaned. He shoved the basket in front of his wife's face. "It's full of—*something*!"

He peered closely at the item and furrowed his brow. "What the bloody hell *is* that?" he said before lifting the basket to his nose and giving it a sniff.

"Martin, watch your language," Louisa admonished. She peered over his shoulder. "Oh, I think James was pushing peas through it last night. Can't you just wash it out?" she said, giving him a wary smile.

He gave a communicative huff and flipped the handle on the faucet. "I shouldn't *have* to wash it out. We buy James toys for a reason, you know."

He shook the basket around under the running water and then picked up the dish brush and began to scrub at it roughly in frustration. He grimaced as the nerves in his arm sent pain messages to his brain, and he threw the basket into the sink before storming off down the hall.

Louisa watched as his broad back disappeared around the corner, and then she turned her attention back to her son. "I think your mummy may be in the proverbial dog house, James Henry," she said as she wiped the child's face and hands.

The boy batted playfully at her mouth. "Mum ... mum ... mum," he syllabized.

"Okay, my sweet boy! Let's go find your daddy." She pulled the bib over her son's head then hoisted him from the high chair.

She found Martin on the sofa in the living room, a medical journal in his lap as he sat with his feet up and his eyes closed.

"Tired today?" she asked as she squeezed on to the cushion next to him.

"A bit." He pressed two fingers to his son's forehead, making a quick check of his body temperature and refusing to make eye contact with her.

"Are you angry with me?" she asked.

Creases formed in his forehead as he tried to make sense of the emotions bubbling in him.

"Martin, did you hear me?" She gently bounced her son on her knee in an attempt to mollify him.

"Yes! I heard you!" he snapped as his fiery eyes locked on to hers. His face softened when he saw her anxious expression. "I'm sorry. I don't know whether I'm angry or not."

Reaching over, she brushed her fingers back through his hair. "Is it your arm? Is it hurting you today?"

The fire was rekindled in his eyes again as he pushed her hand away. "Don't blame this on my injuries, Louisa!"

James began to struggle to get down and away from his father's angry voice. Louisa gathered some toys together and placed them in the middle of the floor before settling the baby in front of them.

"Talk to me, Martin," she said as she took a seat on the coffee table next to the sofa.

He breathed out a heavy sigh. "What do you want me to say, Louisa? That I'm this upset because James made a mess of the basket from my espresso machine? I know it sounds childish, but that *is* why I'm upset!"

She tipped her head down and peered up at him. "But James doesn't know any better, Martin. He's just a baby."

Exactly, he *is* a baby, but *you're* not! Why do you give my things to him?"

"I'm just trying to provide him with a stimulating environment. You want that, too ... don't you?"

"Yes, of course I do!" he sputtered. But does it have to be at the expense of something I enjoy? I just want a damn cup of coffee in the morning! Am I asking that much?"

Louisa sat silent for a few moments before her brow furrowed, and she reached out to wrap her arms around him. "No, you're not asking that much, and I'm sorry. It was disrespectful and inconsiderate of me to be so thoughtless about your personal things."

She placed a kiss on his cheek and then picked James up from the floor, heading back towards the kitchen. "You can relax a bit more. I'll call you when breakfast is ready."

Blinking his eyes slowly, Martin watched her move away. Perhaps they were learning to work through their differences more effectively.

He was awakened a short time later by James's juicy kisses on his neck. "Mm, sorry. I guess I must have dozed off," he said to Louisa as she laid the boy carefully on his chest.

"That okay? He's not too heavy, is he?"

"No ... no, it's fine. It's nice." He peered down at his small son, his eyes drawn again to the miniature replicas of his own hands. He loved this little boy dearly, and James was so obviously his child, a part of him. For a few startling moments, he experienced a novel sensation. It felt *good* to be Martin Ellingham.

Noticing tears welling in his eyes, Louisa quickly reached for the child, assuming them to be tears of pain. "Are you all right?"

He grasped on to his son, shaking his head. "Don't touch us!" he whispered, trying desperately to hold on to the good feeling. But he could feel it quickly slipping away.

James Henry seemed to sense a need in his father, and he laid his head down on his shoulder. Slowly, Martin felt himself adjusting to the emotions that had washed over him. He looked up at his anxious wife's face, giving her a shy smile. "I didn't mean to worry you. It was just a moment of—of—it was a very nice moment."

"I'm sorry I interrupted it." She tipped her head down. "Are you sure you're all right?"

"I'm fine, but I *am* getting hungry."

She picked up the baby and then handed her husband his crutch.

When Jeremy and Poppy arrived, Louisa extended an invitation to them to stay for breakfast. Martin eyed the platters of food. Jeremy had an appetite typical of a young man, and he wasn't sure he liked the idea of having to compete with him for food.

"How's the arm this morning, Martin?" the aide asked as he poured himself a glass of orange juice. "Any pain in the night?"

"Some. I did all right, though," he said as he spooned a generous portion of scrambled eggs on to his plate.

James squawked and reached his hand towards Poppy's plate, wiggling his fingers back and forth in a display of preverbal communication.

The childminder took his bowl and added a small serving of eggs to it, along with a few bits of sausage. "What did they have to do yesterday, Dr. Ellingham?" she asked.

Martin gave a dismissive shake of his head. "Just remove a pin and clean up a bit of infection that had developed around it."

"Oh, here's Ruth!" Louisa said as she saw the elderly woman pass by the kitchen window. Several seconds of silence elapsed before the anticipated rap on the door was heard.

"Come on in, Ruth!" Louisa called out from her place at the table.

"Good morning, family," Ruth said in her unique, flatly cheerful manner.

"Morning," Martin muttered, mentally subtracting yet another sausage and scoop of eggs from their respective containers.

"Have a seat, Ruth. Let me put another plate on the table," Louisa said as she got to her feet and went to the cupboard.

"Well, Martin, how did it go yesterday?" she asked as she pulled a chair up next to him.

"It could have gone better," he grumbled.

Louisa shot her husband a warning look and air hissed from his nose.

"There was some infection around a pin in my arm that they had to take care of, so they'll remove the other pins later," he said impatiently, the words pattering from his mouth.

"I see. Well, lets hope it doesn't develop into anything more serious. Osteomyelitis is nothing to sneeze at, so don't be trying to hide any further problems."

Martin screwed up his face and shot her a black look before stabbing his fork into another piece of sausage on the platter.

"Well, Ruth, are you ready to be back in your own home?" Louisa asked in a tone that Martin found to be overly ingratiating. He gave her a slight scowl.

"I'll be ready to bid those long walks up Roscarrock Hill goodbye," she said as her nephew watched her out of the corner of his eye.

"And there'll be no love lost between that ancient boiler and me! Martin, you *really* should do something about that. Do you want your wife and child to freeze this winter?"

He dropped his fork on to his plate. "Yes, Ruth, that's *just* what I want."

He was spared any more chastising when a loud pounding was heard coming from the front of the house.

"Good lord! What is *that* all about?" Ruth said, craning her neck to see down the hall.

The door flew open and slammed into the living room wall, followed by a metallic clatter and a grunt. "Ouch!"

"This is PC Joseph Penhale! Surrender yourself immediately! Or if there's two of you, surrender *yourselves* immediately! I have you cornered!" The adenoidal voice of the village constable reverberated through the house.

James burst into tears, startled by the sudden clamour, and Louisa grabbed him from his high chair, trying to quiet his fearful sobs. Martin struggled to his feet and headed for the living room, his lips taut and his face reddening.

"Penhale, shut—up!" he whispered stridently. "What do you think you're *doing*? You can't just barge into someone's home like this!" he sputtered, glancing towards the kitchen where James Henry was still wailing uncontrollably.

Ruth walked into the room and stood behind her nephew. "Why don't you tell us what this all about, constable," she said in a voice that could calm the most bolshie of criminal offenders.

Having quieted her son, Louisa now joined the others and stood watching from behind her husband.

"Don't get your knickers in a twist, Doc. That's probably not good for someone in your condition. I had a perfectly legitimate reason for making my somewhat *unconventional* entrance into your domicile. Well, actually—technically speaking it's Dr. Ellingham's domicile. The other Dr. Ellingham, that is."

Martin breathed out a heavy sigh. "All right, let's hear it."

Joe brushed dust from his standard police issue sweater and hoisted up his tool belt. "Well, as I was making my approach to the premises, I detected a suspicious looking substance on the steps. Upon further investigation, I was able to determine that said substance appeared to be blood—probably. Well, possibly. If I had to guess—which I did.

"I found further, more incriminating evidence of a crime in a puddle on your porch—er, your aunt's porch. Unfortunately, I have yet to ascertain the location of the injured party. Or worse, but I'd rather not go there just ye-*t*."

"Just *show* me, Penhale," Martin growled.

The constable led his small entourage outside, past the broken door frame. "You ladies may want to avert your eyes." Joe looked up at Martin and grimaced. "You too, Doc."

"Don't be ridiculous!" he snapped. He looked down as Joe pointed to a small red puddle by his feet.

A wave of nausea swept over Martin, threatening to bring up his breakfast, and he whipped his head to the side.

Aunt Ruth stepped forward and examined the substance, following several red drips to the far end of the porch. "I believe *this* may be your victim here, Penhale. Here, under the bench."

Joe walked over to investigate. "What would the perp want with a poor innocent rabbit?" he said as he rose from a crouching position. He turned, his eyes narrowing as he set his jaw. "This is worse than I'd hoped. We may have a homicidal maniac on our hands."

"Oh, for goodness' sake! There *was* no perp!" Ruth said with a sigh. "And we most certainly do *not* have a homicidal maniac on our hands.

"After Mr. Moysey's mishap a while back, I convinced him he might not be so lonely for his wife if he had a pet. He got a tabby cat not long after. The creature has a *very* unpleasant habit of leaving its prey, half-eaten, on my front porch."

"So, *this* is your justification for breaking into our home?" Martin said, rolling his eyes.

Penhale tilted his head at him. "In a situation such as this, where innocent citizens may have become victims of grievous bodily harm, an officer of the law can't wait for test results to come back from forensics, Do-*c*." he explained slowly.

"But you broke our door down!" Martin squawked.

The constable gave him an oafish grin. "*Really,* Doc, you wouldn't expect me to ring the bell and wait for the perp to invite me in, would you? I'm not *that* stupid."

"Of course I wouldn't; the—*perp*—is a cat!"

"Hmm, you may have a point there." Joe wrinkled his brow and then gave his fingers a snap. "Maybe I should cancel the call I put in to the tactical firearms unit." He flashed the GP a sheepish grin. "I'll be right back."

Martin sighed and moved towards the kitchen to join the others. "Great, now my breakfast is cold," he grumbled.

"I'll warm it up for you," Poppy said, pulling the plate out from under him.

"Is that what you mean by unique?" Jeremy asked, pointing his fork towards the living room.

Martin curled his lip. "Penhale's more than a bit peculiar. Let's leave it at that."

"Oh, Joe's okay," Louisa said as she set her cup of tea on the table. "He means well, anyway." Pulling out a chair, she took a seat beside her husband. "And I should remind you, he *was* very helpful the night of your accident, Martin."

"Mm, yes."

"All taken care of," the policeman announced when he emerged in the kitchen doorway.

"Maybe you should tell us what you came to see us about in the first place, Joe ... before you got side-tracked," Louisa said.

"No, you shouldn't," Martin said dryly. His wife turned a rankled expression on him.

"Oh, Doc. Always the kidder, aren't ya," Joe said, giving him a punch in the shoulder and pulling up a chair. "That looks good," he said, eyeing the food on the table.

"Oh, would you like something to eat, Joe?" Louisa asked. "I can warm it up if you're hungry."

"A bit of breakfast would go down a treat. I just had time for a cup of coffee before duty called this morning."

Poppy set Martin's plate back down in front of him, and he stabbed angrily at a sausage.

After rewarming the remainder of the eggs and meat in the microwave, Louisa returned the platters to the table. "There you go, Joe."

"Gee, thanks, Louiser!" The policeman licked his lips and rubbed his hands together before jabbing his fork into two of the three remaining sausages. He then heaped scrambled eggs on to his plate.

"So, Joe, what was it you wanted to see us about?" Louisa asked, handing her son a piece of Melba toast.

"I wanted to assure you that I'll be staying on top of the traffic situation today ... during the big move. One less thing for you to have to worry about, Doc."

"We're moving a few boxes, not the entire structure, Penhale," he grumbled.

"That's very thoughtful, Joe. But I think Martin's right. We should be able to deal with the traffic. Thank you all the same, though."

"Suit yourselves. You know how to reach me if you should change your minds."

Martin slipped his last bite of sausage into his mouth and glanced over at the solitary patty that remained on the platter in the middle of the table. He gave the policeman a sideways glance and then reached for it with his fork.

Joe snapped his hand out, meeting the doctor's in mid-air, their forks clinking together, signalling the commencement of the duel for the patty.

The two men stared each other down for several seconds, the sunlight coming in the kitchen window glinting off their weaponry.

Martin narrowed his eyes threateningly at his adversary. Joe flinched, and then flashing him a vacuous smile, he drove his fork down in a race for the platter. The GP responded with lightning speed, spearing the hapless sausage and yanking it out from under the constable's fork.

His reflexes were bang on. However, the dexterity in his left hand was lacking, and he lost control of the fork, allowing it to fly over Aunt Ruth's head and clatter to the floor as the patty sailed smoothly in the opposite direction, landing on James Henry's high chair tray.

The boy burst into a fit of giggles as he picked it up in his fist and brought it to his mouth.

Martin's head whipped to the side, and he stared wide-eyed at his wife.

"Well, that settles that then, doesn't it," she said as she stood and whisked her husband's now-empty plate out from under him.

Chapter 8

Al Large arrived at Ruth's cottage shortly after the Ellinghams and their guests had finished with breakfast. He and Jeremy hauled in an assortment of boxes containing Ruth's appurtenances, mostly clothing and food items. They then began the more arduous task of getting Martin and Louisa's belongings, as well as all the accoutrements that accompany the raising of a baby, moved back to the surgery.

It was after four o'clock that afternoon before Louisa had unpacked the last box and dropped down on to the sofa to relax next to her husband. "Well, Dr. Ellingham, how does it feel to be back under your own roof?" she asked as she nestled in under his arm.

He gazed down at her. "*This* feels very nice."

She closed her eyes and took in a slow, deep breath. "It doesn't quite smell right, though."

"No, it smells like Bengay in here," Martin said, wrinkling up his nose.

"Mar-tin, Ruth was very kind to let us use her cottage for a while. Don't look a gift horse in the mouth, hmm?"

"Mm, yes." He tightened his grip on her, pulling her closer. "Next sunny day we get we'll need to give things a proper airing"

She caressed her palm back and forth across his stomach and peered up at him. "I actually meant I'm missing that familiar, homey aroma of antiseptic and broiled fish."

"Ah, I see."

James, who had been playing in the middle of the floor with his stacking blocks, crawled over and pulled himself up next to the coffee table. He slapped his fire engine down, setting off the high-pitched wail of the siren. Martin grimaced and yanked his arm from behind his wife, pulling his hand to the side of his head.

"Martin, what's the matter?" Louisa asked.

"Why do they have to make those bloody toys so loud, for God's sake?" he snapped, grabbing the still-screeching vehicle and shoving it into the drawer of the end table. The now muffled whine continued.

"Oh, it's not that loud. Quit your fussing." She went to the pile of toys on the floor and retrieved James's frog puppet and his plastic giraffe. "Here you go, James," she said, squeezing the giraffe several times to make it squeak."

Martin closed his eyes and set his jaw, inhaling deeply before picking up his crutch and walking off. Louisa could hear his uneven footsteps on the stairs.

After shutting the bedroom door behind him he sat on the edge of the bed, a knot of anxiety beginning to tighten in his stomach.

This sensation was disturbingly familiar. Was being back in the surgery making him tense ... or possibly his apprehensions about opening the practice on Monday? He swung his legs up and lay back, rubbing at the piercing pain that had now spread across his forehead.

When he was awakened by his wife's kisses some time later, it was dark in the room. "Mm, sorry. I guess I fell asleep. What time is it?"

"Almost half six; you must've been tired." She leaned over and laid her head on his chest, listening to the steady beat of his heart. "Are you doing okay?"

"Yes. I'm ... fine."

"Hmm."

"Did you come to tell me supper's ready?" he asked in an attempt to distract her from her scrutinising gaze.

"I did. And we better get downstairs before that son of ours gets tired of being left alone in his playpen."

"Mm, yes."

Martin had been opposed to the use of that particular piece of baby furniture and had only agreed to its purchase with his wife's assurances that it would only be used for safety reasons and for brief periods of time. He quickly pulled himself from the bed and headed for the stairs to free his son from his confinement.

He eased his way down the steps and, bracing himself against the side of the playpen for stability, he hoisted up his son with his left arm before setting him down on the floor to roam freely. "What are we having? It smells good," he said.

"James and I went to the market for a fish while you were having your lie-down. It's baked cod with roasted potatoes and broccoli. And it's ready, so come and have a seat at the table," she said as she reached into the cooker for their dinner.

Martin had just lowered himself into his chair when there was a loud metallic bang as his wife straightened suddenly and slammed the door of the appliance shut.

"Crikey, that hurts!" she squeaked, hurriedly setting the dish in the middle of the table before twisting her arm to look at it.

"What's happened?"

"I burned myself. Got my arm against the—the—" she wagged her finger vaguely towards the business end of the kitchen— "the whatsit!"

"Well, get some water on it. Put it under the faucet. Get some cool water on it. I'll come and take a look," he said as he pushed himself up from the table and struggled to his feet.

He limped to the sink and took her arm in his hands, inspecting the fiery red welt that had been raised on her skin. "Mm, not serious, but I'm sure it hurts. Keep it under the tap;

I'll get something for that," he said as he began to walk off towards the hallway.

Louisa glanced behind her, taking in a gasp at the sight of both of her Ellingham men standing in front of her on their own two feet. Martin, unassisted by a single crutch, and her son, in the middle of the living room floor with his frog puppet in one hand.

James gave his father a self-satisfied grin and took two tentative steps towards him before toppling over with a giggle.

"Did you see that?" he asked as he turned towards his wife.

"I did! James Henry, you took your first steps!" She grabbed the tea towel and patted her arm dry before hurrying to scoop up her son. She stepped back up on to the slate kitchen floor and picked up her husband's crutch. "You better use this, Martin. *You* have a lot farther to fall than James does, and there's a whole lot more of you to hit the floor."

"Mm, yes." He took it from her and wedged it under his arm. "I'll go and get something for that burn."

Reaching out, he brushed his fingers across the baby's cheek. "Well done, James."

As he turned towards the hall, Louisa caught a glimpse of the tears that had welled in his eyes. "Your daddy's very proud of you, James Henry," she whispered to the boy as she watched her husband move away.

The Ellingham family was sitting around the dinner table a short time later when there was a knock on the back door.

"I'll get it," Louisa said, as her chair screeched across the floor.

Martin cringed and pressed the heel of his hand to his eye as he tried to alleviate the intense pain shooting through it.

The headache eased quickly, leaving behind a warm, anaesthetised sensation.

"Hey, Martin," Jeremy said as he stepped through the door. "I just dropped Poppy at her place. Thought I'd come by and check up on you before heading back home. Is all good?"

Martin glanced uncomfortably at his wife. "I'm fine. What did you and Poppy do tonight?" he asked, again attempting to divert the conversation away from his own health.

The young man pulled out a chair and took a seat across from him. "I took her over to Truro for dinner. It was kind of a special day." He picked up the pepper mill and toyed with it, rolling it back and forth between his palms.

Louisa leaned over, caressing her husband's shoulder. "Maybe I'll go get James ready for bed ... leave you two to it, hmm," she said softly in his ear.

"Yes." He looked up and gave her a half-smile.

Jeremy watched as mother and child disappeared under the stairs before rocking back in his chair. "It's our one month anniversary today, so I took Poppy out for a nice dinner."

"I didn't realise you two had made it official."

"Made what official?"

"We didn't get an invitation to the wedding." Martin said, pulling a bone from his fish before lifting a forkful to his mouth.

The aide crossed his arms in front of him. "Are you trying to wind me up again?"

He peered up at him sheepishly. "No."

"So, anyway, Poppy was happy." Jeremy tipped forward, resting his elbows on the table. "She didn't think I'd remember it was a special occasion."

Martin furrowed his brow. "Can you tell me again why this was a special occasion?"

"It's one month since our first date! Geesh, mate! Are you paying any attention?"

"Yes I am. But technically, it's not an anniversary. It's one month. But I do understand that when it comes to anniversaries, semantics seem to be irrelevant to women."

The aide gave him a grin. "I'm beginning to think I could get myself into trouble taking relationship advice from you."

"I think that's a safe assumption." Martin set his silverware on his plate and wiped his mouth with his napkin.

"Here, I'll take that," Jeremy said as he picked up the dirty dishes and got to his feet.

As he turned from the table, the knife slid from the plate and clanged loudly against the slate floor, triggering another stabbing pain behind Martin's left eye.

"Hey, you okay?" the aide asked as his patient put his head down on the table, covering it with his arm.

Martin held up a hand to silence him as he waited for the piercing headache to pass.

He straightened back up slowly, blinking back the tears that the brief but intense cephalalgic event had triggered. "It's better now."

"Did you talk to Mr. Christianson about this?" the young man asked as he put the dishes in the dishwasher.

"He knows about it. He wants me to see a neurologist next week ... just a precaution. It's most likely post-concussive symptoms."

"Do the headaches seem to be noise induced? Was it the knife falling on the floor that set it off?"

Martin rubbed his palm across his now numbing forehead. "Yeah. It was James's fire engine earlier this evening. I'm sure it'll pass in a few weeks."

"You should keep a diary of when the attacks occur ... their severity, time of day, what seems to trigger them. And I'll stop in at City Music tomorrow and pick up some musician's earplugs for you."

"Mm, thank you, Jeremy."

Louisa came in from the hallway, carrying a pyjama-clad James Henry. "What are you getting musician's earplugs for?"

Martin breathed out a heavy sigh. "I'm having some trouble with noise induced headaches. Ear plugs will reduce the decibel level of noises and, hopefully, reduce the headaches."

"Oh." She eyed him briefly. "James would like to say goodnight, Martin."

He turned in his chair and reached a hand out before his wife set the boy on his lap. "I could put him to bed tonight ... if you can carry him upstairs for me." He glanced over at his aide. "If you'll excuse me, Jeremy."

"Yeah, sure. I just came by to see how you were doing ... see if you needed anything before I head back to Truro. Did you get your antibiotic infusion taken care of yet today? Want any help with it?"

"I'll do it after James is down for the night. And Louisa can help me if I need it." His scrutinising doctor's gaze settled on the young man. "Erm, you've had a lot of driving today. If you're tired you could spend the night here. There's a bed in James's room."

"Thanks just the same, but I'll be okay. I've actually been looking for a place to rent, either here in the village or in Wadebridge. Cut down on the amount of time on the road."

"Sounds sensible," Martin said, giving him a small smile before shifting his attention to his son who had latched on to one of the fixators on his arm. "You need to leave that, James. It's not a toy."

Jeremy smiled at his over-sized friend's attempts to wrest the tiny fingers from his hardware. "Well, I'll see you bright and early on Monday."

"Goodnight, Jeremy. Thanks for checking in," Louisa said before flipping the lock on the door behind him and turning to her son and husband. "Well, Master Ellingham, shall we get you off to bed?"

James still had a hand wrapped firmly around his father's fixator, but had settled in and was quickly growing sleepy. Louisa pried his fingers loose and lifted him from her husband's lap.

"Maybe you could give me a head-start?" Martin suggested as he got up from his chair. He had found himself to be quite self-conscious about his gait, and especially about how he might appear to his wife as he took on the stairs. The distraction of knowing that she was watching only added to the difficulty of the task.

"Erm, sure. James and I'll check that the doors are all locked, and we'll join you in a minute," she said as she stretched up to place a kiss on his lips.

"Mm, yes." His eyes fixed on hers before he averted them and cleared his throat. He moved off down the hall, leaving his wife watching him with a smile on her face.

James had dropped off to sleep quickly as his father read to him from an unillustrated book of Thornton Burgess animal stories. The glossy, colourful pictures of the board books that were shared with him by his mother seemed unnecessary to the boy when Martin read to him.

He was captivated only by the sound of his father's voice and, Louisa suspected, by the vibrations he could feel as his voice resonated through his upper body. She had often seen the boy with his ear pressed to his father's chest and a hand resting against his neck.

Martin lay in bed a short while later, scanning the latest issue of the *BMJ* while his wife made her night-time preparations. His eyes shifted, discreetly and frequently, as she removed her jeans and folded them over a hanger. He noted the pale blue knickers with the white lace trim that she was wearing, a particular favourite of his for the way they fell across her hips, accentuating her curves.

She glanced over, catching him in his moment of voyeuristic pleasure.

He dipped his head and his eyes dashed back to the page in front of him. Finding himself no longer capable of focusing on the words, he allowed his gaze to drift once again.

Louisa moved to the dresser and removed a nightdress from the drawer, laying it out in front of her. She could feel his eyes watching her from behind, and she slowed her pace, pulling her blouse languidly over her head and letting it drop to the floor.

Martin watched, mesmerised, as she reached behind and unhooked her bra before sliding the straps from her shoulders. His attention was drawn slowly from the chestnut hair flowing down her back to the image in the mirror as the undergarment was allowed to fall away from her.

She smiled knowingly as she heard a soft sigh behind her. Reaching for her nightdress, she paused when she heard his throaty voice.

"Louisa ... you, erm ... you could wait with that. For just a bit."

She turned to look at him, the expression on his face igniting her own desire.

He pulled the blankets back, and she pushed the last remnant of clothing over her hips before slipping in next to him.

As they lay together later that night, Martin thought back to the day, so many weeks ago, when he had stopped at the school to assure his wife that he loved her. She had made him a promise before he left on that unpropitious trip that afternoon.

"Louisa?"

"Hmm?" she sighed as she lay watching him, tracing circles around his ear with her fingertip.

"Do you remember the day of the meeting at the Royal Cornwall ... about the air ambulance?"

"Martin ... I could hardly forget that day. Try as I might."
She ran her palm down his arm and picked up his hand,
bringing it to her lips. "That was a horrible, *horrible* day."

"Not entirely. I remember a nice moment at the school.
And I believe you said something about a proper kiss when I
got home that night. I was very much looking forward to that."

"Yes, I *do* remember something about a proper kiss ... I
think."

"Well, I *am* home now, and I think I still have it coming."

"You already collected on that ... several times."

"No. I didn't."

"Yes, you did. Before one of your surgeries. You probably
don't remember because you were pretty fuzzy."

"Well *that* doesn't count, then, does it?" he said, frustration
beginning to register in his voice.

"Hmm, maybe not," she said as she leaned over and placed a
proper kiss on his lips. "Goodnight, Martin. And welcome
home."

Sunday had brought a welcome respite from the usual
intense daily routine that had come to define life in the
Ellingham home. James had allowed his parents the luxury of a
lie-in, no visitors had knocked on their door, and Martin was
headache and relatively pain-free all day.

He had spent his time working on Ruth's grandfather clock
in the solitude of his consulting room while Louisa and James
baked cookies, replacing the odour that they had found
reminiscent of a menthol body rub with the much more
pleasing aroma of toasted oats and nuts.

Martin woke Monday morning feeling more rested than he
had since before his accident. The anxiety that had troubled
him on Saturday had lifted as well, and he felt much more
confident about facing the questions and stares that he knew
he would have to deal with that morning.

The surgery would be open from ten o'clock until noon to begin with. More hours would be added to the schedule as his health improved and his stamina increased.

He was standing at the hob cooking his breakfast when Jeremy knocked on the door. "Come!" he called out. The sizzling intensified as he flipped the sausages over, and several spatters of molten fat erupted from the pan.

"Morning, mate," the aide said. He walked over and leaned against the counter. "That smells really good."

Martin gave him a sideways glance. "Are you hungry?" he asked as he squirted a bit of washing up liquid on to the counter and wiped away the rogue grease.

"I kinda overslept this morning. Just had time for a cup of coffee before I left my flat. So yeah, I *am* hungry."

"I assumed you would be. I made extra. Have a seat at the table."

"Where are Poppy and James?" Jeremy asked as he pulled out a chair.

"I'm not sure. Poppy said something about porridge and hair. Then they were gone."

He turned and reached his hand out, snapping his fingers. "Hand me a plate."

"Let me do it, Martin. You sit down," the aide said as he got to his feet.

"I can do it! Just hand me a bloody plate!" Martin snapped. He turned his head away momentarily and took in a deep breath. "I'm sorry, that was uncalled for. But please, just give it to me."

Jeremy handed him the dish and sat back down. "How have the headaches been? Any better or worse?"

"It's been fine. I haven't had any trouble at all since the episode Saturday evening." He slipped several sausages on to his aide's plate and gave it back to him before tossing a hot pad on the table.

"I suspect it's just post trauma headaches and they'll pass. You want some eggs?" Martin asked, setting a bowl down next to the bottle of orange juice.

"Yeah, that'd be great."

Keys could be heard rattling in the front door, followed by a loud shout from Morwenna Newcross. "Mornin', Doc!"

Martin gave an annoyed glance down the hall before looking over at the clock and emitting a short grunt. He held out his hand again. "Other plate, Jeremy." He snapped his fingers once more. "If she's not late, she's early," he grumbled. He turned and reached out, dropping his breakfast on to the table in front of his chair.

"Not a bad aim there, Martin."

The doctor watched, his lip curling slightly as the young man slathered a liberal layer of marmalade on his toast, but he kept his opinions to himself.

The jangling of the receptionist's bracelets and necklaces grew louder as she approached from under the stairs. "Hi ya, Doc!"

"Morwenna," he replied, giving her a slight nod of his head before taking a seat.

She deposited the brown bag containing her lunch into the refrigerator and then squeezed in behind him to make herself a cup of coffee.

"Gettin' a square meal in before the hordes descend on you this mornin', I see. Good idea, that."

Martin looked up at her with alarm. "How many appointments did you schedule?"

"Calm down," she said, resting her hand on his arm. "I'll keep 'em under control."

He pulled away and picked up the pepper mill, eyeing her uncertainly. "Mm, yes. Jeremy, don't forget to call Chippy Miller today," he said.

The aide took a small notebook from his shirt pocket and flipped it open. "Yep. Got it on my list." He dug deeper into his pocket and pulled out a small packet. "And I, er ... got you something."

"Oh?" Martin looked expectantly as the young man reached across the table with the item and dropped it into his hand. "I see. The earplugs. Thank you, Jeremy." He laid the packet next to his coffee cup and pulled out his wallet. "Will fifteen pounds cover it?"

"Ten's plenty. You know, with any luck, you won't even need to use those," he said, piling another spoonful of eggs on to his plate.

The receptionist cocked her head. "What would *you* be needin' earplugs for, Doc?"

"That's none of your business, Morwenna," he replied sharply, fixing his eyes on his newspaper.

"All right. No need to get all narky. I'm just curious is all," she said as she walked out of the kitchen and down the hall.

Jeremy waited until the cacophony of rattling jewellery had dissipated and then peered up at him. "You know, it might be a good idea if Morwenna was kept up to speed on your health concerns."

"Why?"

"Well, for one thing, she'll better understand your limitations. And she'll feel more like a member of the team."

Martin's head shot up. "The *team*?"

Jeremy scowled back at him. "Are you going to get all dainty with me about my semantics?"

He eyed him for a moment before shifting his attention back to the news of the day.

"Martin, hear me out ... please."

Folding up the paper, Martin tossed it aside. "All right, I'm listening."

Jeremy cleared his throat and straightened himself in his chair, making an unconscious attempt to even the vertical score with the doctor. "You have a long way to go yet before you can put this all behind you. And in some ways, the tough part of this ordeal is just beginning.

"It's going to be a hell of a lot easier if you let yourself trust a few people ... let them know what your vulnerabilities are so they know when you might need a hand ... or when you just need a little extra time and a bit of space to do things yourself."

Martin stared past him for several seconds before re-establishing eye contact. "Morwenna? No. I haven't known her that long."

"But she told me she's worked here for more than a year," Jeremy said, a deep vertical line forming between his brows.

"Just *barely* a year!" Martin's expression was one of frustration teetering on the edge of anger. "And not only that, I need to maintain some semblance of professionalism between us. Keep a proper professional distance, obviously."

He got up and turned to put his dishes in the sink but lost his tenuous right-handed grip on his plate. The dissonance created when the ceramic plate and metal utensils crashed on to the slate below triggered a pain in his head so intense that it caused his legs to buckle beneath him, sending him to the floor.

Jeremy yelled for Morwenna as he jumped from his chair and ran to the doctor's side. He lay with his arm pressed against his head and his eyes tightly shut.

"What's goin' on?" the receptionist asked, her eyes widening when she noticed the state Martin was in. "Oh, gawd! Should I call an ambulance?"

"No, stay with him," the aide said, his voice measured. He ran to the consulting room for a stethoscope and a blood pressure cuff before hurrying back to the kitchen.

"Doc, you *need* ta lie still!" Morwenna said as Jeremy wrapped the cuff around his patient's arm.

He relented and allowed his body to relax against the cold tiles. The pain eased quickly, and he blinked to clear the moisture from his eyes.

"Another headache?" the aide asked as he watched the seconds tick off his watch.

"Yeah." Martin brought a trembling hand up to wipe the sweat from his brow, revealing several small cuts on his left forearm and a bruise developing on his elbow.

"Well, your BP's slightly elevated, but it's not significant. Think you can sit up?"

He nodded and pushed himself off the floor with his good arm.

"Morwenna, can you go upstairs and get a wet flannel from the bathroom?"

The receptionist took off without answering and returned quickly. She began to wipe at Martin's face.

"What on earth are you *doing*?" he hissed as he batted her hand away.

"Doc, just hush up."

He sat in silence, his embarrassment growing at the receptionist's solicitude.

"Morwenna, that's not necessary. I can—"

"Doc, just be quiet and let me help. I was so worried about you after yer accident, and there wasn't anything I could do. Now there is, so please just—just let me—help."

Jeremy quickly cleared away the ceramic shards and had Morwenna hold kitchen towelling over the cuts on Martin's arm while he wiped the drops of blood from the floor.

"Okay, mate. Let's take you in and get you cleaned up."

With his aide's help, Martin was able to get to his feet and limp into the consulting room.

Jeremy treated the cuts. "Here, keep the ice on that elbow," he said, pressing a cold pack into his hand. I need to go consult with Dr. Parsons and Mr. Christianson about the wisdom of allowing you to see patients today," he said as he began to walk off.

"Ohhh, that's not necessary! I'm fine as long as there are no sirens going off or dishes falling on the floor."

"Sorry, Martin. This one's my call." He headed towards the kitchen to retrieve his mobile.

"Doc?" Morwenna said apprehensively as she stuck her head in the door.

"What!" he snapped, rolling his sleeve back down over the fresh bandages.

The receptionist took a hesitant step into the room. "I just wanted to say ... I'm sorry for yellin' at you. And I want you to know it wasn't angry-yellin', it was scared-yellin' ... if you know what I mean."

Martin stared back at her and his stony face softened. "Mm, I *do* know what you mean. Erm, why don't you pull up the stool over there and have a seat. I need to talk to you, and this is as good a time as any, I suppose."

"Crikey, just tell me, Doc. You're scarin' me now!" Morwenna worried the beads hanging around her neck and stared back at him.

"I've developed some noise sensitivity in the last week. Then the headaches started. They seem to be triggered by certain sounds. But it can be hard to determine the exact cause of these things. I'll be seeing a neurologist sometime this week, and they'll probably do a CT scan to rule out the slight possibility that a clot could have developed. Any questions?"

A smile slid across her face and settled in. "Can I give you a hug?"

"Oh, don't be ridicu—" Martin's screwed up face surrendered to the girl's smile, relaxing into a less oppositional expression of resignation.

She stepped forward and wrapped her arms around him before brushing a kiss across his cheek.

"Mm." He cleared his throat and dipped his head when he felt the tell-tale warmth of a flush spreading up his neck.

"I'll just go ... get back to work then," Morwenna said as she hurried towards the door. "Let me know if you need anything."

"Mm, yes."

"Oops, excuse me, Jeremy!" she said as she do-si-doed past him.

The aide leaned back against his boss's desk and folded his arms across his chest. "Okay, Mr. Christianson wants you over in Truro at two o'clock today. They'll do the CT, then you'll meet with one of their neuro guys. He also wants to see you in his office before you head back home. I can take you over if you like."

Martin furrowed his brow and gave him a shake of his head. "But what about patients this morning?"

Jeremy turned his arm over and looked down at his watch. "It's only half nine. Let's check your vitals in fifteen minutes, see how you're feeling, and then decide."

Martin went to the kitchen to tidy up and then looked in on Poppy and James before returning to his consulting room.

Jeremy was reviewing the files for the patients that they would be seeing that morning when he walked in. "Oh, good. I had a question about the Dingley woman who's on the schedule for today. I see in her records she had the pre-exposure rabies series. What's up there? She a veterinarian?"

"God, no! She runs a sanctuary for every flea ridden, worm infested feline in the Portwenn area. She comes around begging for money on a regular basis."

He took the file from the younger man's hand and scanned it over. "We should draw a blood sample today ... check her serum antibodies. She probably won't let you near her with a needle until after she sees me, though."

"A bit wary of new faces, is she?"

"No, just odd. I think the woman spends far too much time in the company of cats.

"My former receptionist did the draws for a while. She was convinced that Pauline was harvesting blood from patients and selling it to the blood bank in Wadebridge. She's likely to suspect the same thing of you."

"Good to know." Jeremy glanced at his watch. "Let's get your vitals," he said, pulling the stethoscope from around his neck.

The instrument hissed rhythmically as the aide squeezed the bulb. "Well, your blood pressure is back down to your usual one hundred over sixty-five, and your heart rate's fine. Any headache?"

"No, I'm okay. They're severe when they hit, but they're brief."

The aide rubbed at his jaw. "All right. We'll go ahead as planned."

Martin moved towards the door.

"But you have to promise me that you'll let me know *immediately* if you begin to feel off at all," Jeremy said.

"Yes, I know!" he snapped back as he ducked through the doorway into the reception room.

"That was a rubbish excuse for a promise!" the aide called out, following after him.

Martin stopped and turned. "What? Are you going to get all dainty with me about my semantics?"

"Yes, I am. I don't want to get any, technically-I-never-actually-promised, excuses later!"

"Fine. I promise to let you know if I feel *off* at all! Now, if you don't mind—I need to get my tie!"

"Hey!" Jeremy held up his arm and tugged at his sleeve. "You might wanna change your shirt. You've got a bit of blood there, mate."

Martin glanced down before whipping his head to the side. "Gawd."

Morwenna sat at her desk, watching as he disappeared up the stairs, then turned to the aide. "Wow, Jeremy! You really know how to handle the doc!" she said in an undertone.

"Mm," he grunted before walking out to the terrace to get some air.

Chapter 9

"How's he doin'—the doc?" Lorna Gillett asked as Jeremy inserted a thermometer into her ear.

"I think that's a question for Dr. Ellingham, don't you?" He pulled an antiseptic towelette from the round plastic dispenser on the desk and gave the instrument a thorough rub down.

"Well, the doc isn't exactly one to go on about himself, is he?"

"Open wide and say ahh, please, Mrs. Gillett," Jeremy said before sticking a tongue depressor in the woman's mouth.

"Ahh." She cocked her head at him and gave him an apologetic smile. "I don't mean to be stickin' my nose in where it doesn't belong. It's just ... well, the poor man seems so sad all the time. Now with all that's happened ... it's hard not ta worry, ya know?"

Jeremy took in a deep breath and stared at her. "Again, Mrs. Gillett, if you have a question for Dr. Ellingham, you need to *ask* Dr. Ellingham."

He took a seat at the desk and pulled her patient notes from the sleeve. "I do have a few questions to ask *you* though, then I'll send you back out to the reception room."

Picking up the binder containing the written guidelines that Martin had typed up for him, he read directly from it. "Have you experienced any of the following symptoms in the past forty-eight hours—sore throat, body aches, stomach pain, diarrhoea, vomiting, or cough?"

Lorna shook her head slowly. "No, none of them. 'Cept for the body aches, of course. The doc says it's not arthritis, but my joints are stiff as a gate post, some days."

"Hmm." The assistant scanned through the woman's records before returning to the binder. "Have you been around anyone in the last forty-eight hours who's been ill?"

"No."

He tipped his head to the side and pulled Lorna's lower eyelid down. "The joint pain is a complaint you discussed with the doctor on a previous visit, then?"

"Yeah. But it doesn't seem to be gettin' any better. I thought once the chromo-tomo-whatever-it-is was all set straight, the pain'd go away."

Jeremy palpated the lymph nodes under her jaw and at the base of her neck, scribbling a few more notes in her patient file. "All right, Mrs. Gillett, you can have a seat in the reception room. Morwenna will send you in when the doctor's ready for you."

"Oh, it's not missus. It's just plain ol' Lorna, love," she said as she got up from her chair and turned towards the entryway.

The door to the consulting room opened, and a tall man, with hair a shade of yellow that could only come from a bad dye job, strode out. "Seems I'm s'posed to make another appointment fer next month, darlin'," he said giving Morwenna a leering grin.

The receptionist shifted uncomfortably under the man's gaze. She kept one eye on him as her fingers clacked away on her computer keyboard.

"How does December sixteenth at half ten work for you, Mr. Britton?" she asked, giving him what she hoped would be perceived as a neutral smile.

"If *you're* gonna be 'ere my lover, then it ought'a work out right fine."

He glanced towards the consulting room. "You got a right crackin' pair'a Thrupney bits there," he said surreptitiously as his eyes shifted to her chest. "I hope yer not wastin' 'em on some young git who don't appreciate 'em, proper-like."

Morwenna's face reddened at the man's crude remark. "Mr. Britton, that was inappropriate," she said, attempting to project a false air of confidence.

She heard the familiar squeak of Martin's chair as he reclined to peer into the reception room, and she glanced over at him.

The man took a seat on the edge of the desk. "'Ere's what ya wanna do. Git yerself a bloke with some *experience.*"

Martin got up and moved over, watching from the doorway, unnoticed. He couldn't hear what was being said, but Mr. Britton's manner set him on edge. He stepped into the hallway, straining to pick up his patient's end of the conversation, the words he was able to make out triggering a feeling of protectiveness for his employee. He craned his neck trying to make eye contact with her, but she had her gaze fixed on the appointment card she was filling out.

"Get off my desk, *right—now*, Mr. Britton," Morwenna said through clenched teeth.

"Oh, don't go gettin' all hoity-toity on me, girl." He leaned forward, laying a palm over the appointment card. "I'm tryin' ta do you a favour. *I* got experience, and I could teach you a few things you'd *never* ferget," the man said lubriciously.

Martin's jaw clenched, and reflex rapidly replaced reason when Morwenna poised her fountain pen over the man's hand, glaring at him.

"I'm warning you—get off my desk or you'll be screamin' for the doc to come out and surgically remove my biro from that disgusting, grimy meat hook of yours."

Lorna Gillett, absorbed in the magazine she was thumbing through, was incognisant of the minor drama playing out. She glanced up at Martin as he moved out into the reception room. "You ready for me, Doc?" she asked as he limped past her, crutchless and without so much as a grunt of recognition.

He crossed the room and grabbed on to the back of Mr. Britton's coat with his left hand, pulling him off the desk. "You plug-ugly, hyper-concupiscent, maggot! Get out of my surgery!" he yelled, giving the man a shove.

The patient turned, pulling his fist back, ready to throw the first punch, when Jeremy hurried into the room and grabbed his arm. "Okay! Okay! That's enough!"

He looked over at Martin, seeing the fury on his face. "Apparently, this office visit is over. It would be best if you left now, Mr. Britton. Dr. Ellingham will be in touch with you if he'd like to see you again."

Britton turned and gave Martin a dark look before storming out of the building.

Morwenna got up from her chair and hurried off under the stairs, and Jeremy turned to his boss. "Well, as I've said before, you *do* have a unique style with your patients."

Martin pushed past him. "I need some air," he grumbled.

The aide glanced over at a confused Lorna Gillett. "My apologies for the wait, Mrs. ... er, Lorna. We'll be with you in a few minutes."

The crisp, late autumn air and a few moments of silence had helped to cool Martin's anger, but he now felt an uneasy smouldering of regret for his behaviour. He walked slowly around to the back of the house, working his left hand along the stone structure for stability. When he entered through the kitchen door, Morwenna was sitting at the table, seemingly focused on the cup of tea sitting in front of her. He took a seat in a chair on the opposite side.

"I'm sorry, Morwenna."

The girl shook her head, and then looked up at him. "It's not *yer* fault, Doc! I'm sorry I let him get to me like that. I would'a just let 'im have it except Lorna Gillet was sittin' right there. I didn't want to come off looking unprofessional."

"The man's a moron, Morwenna." Noticing a discomfort, Martin glanced down. His left hand had been curled into a tight ball, and he flexed his fingers in an attempt to get the blood flowing again. "Well, I'm sorry you were subjected to that, especially here in my surgery."

The receptionist gave him a shy smile, "It was bound to happen at some point, I guess. I should'a just sloshed him a good one, eh?"

Martin pressed his fingers to his eyes. "It never occurred to me that you could be unsafe here, Morwenna ... if I'm in my consulting room with the door shut. But especially if I get called out ... if I'm not here."

The receptionist peered up at him with a small smile. "Well, one thing's for sure ... I know I'm safe from any plug-ugly maggots when you *are* here."

Martin cringed. "Oh, gawwd," he moaned as he pushed himself up from the chair. "Come on, we have patients, Morwenna."

"Yeah, okay. But you wait right there," she said before hurrying down the hall and returning with his crutch.

"Yer scarin' me, runnin' around without that, Doc," she said as she handed it to him. "And it might be a good idea if you didn't go pickin' any more fights for a while. Leastwise, not until you've got all the hardware off ... you know?"

"Mm, yes."

Martin returned to his consulting room and settled in behind his desk to review Lorna Gillett's patient notes. He took in a deep breath and closed his eyes for a few moments before calling out, "Next patient!"

"Hello, Doc," Lorna said as she closed the door behind her.

"Mrs. Gillett, have a seat please," the doctor said, pointing a finger towards the chair on the opposite side of his desk. "What seems to be the trouble?"

"It's my joints, Doc; they *still* hurt. I thought you said takin' the blood would fix that."

"Yes. You should, at the very least, have seen noticeable improvement by now."

He shuffled through the woman's patient notes again, his brow furrowing. "I don't see any serum ferritin test results. Do you recall what your level was when the doctor in Wadebridge last checked it?"

Lorna gave her shoulders a shrug. "I don't know. I s'pose the doc over there does, though."

Martin picked up his phone and flicked a button. "Morwenna, Lorna Gillett's test results aren't in the records the clinic in Wadebridge sent over. Call over there and have them email them to me." He hissed out a breath and rubbed at his throbbing head. "No, now. The serum ferritin results. *All* of them."

He replaced the receiver and got to his feet. "All right, Mrs. Gillett. Have a seat on the exam couch, please."

Lorna did as she was told, watching as he limped towards her. "How are *you* doin', Doc?"

Martin hesitated, his eyes taking a rapid inventory of the visual signs from his recently acquired lexicon of nonverbal communication.

She leaned back in a nonthreatening manner as she propped herself up with straightened arms, and she tipped her head slightly at him, suggestive of a genuine curiosity. But her eyes were soft, not as intense as the eyes of someone who was merely gathering information.

Her face was relaxed, and her mouth curled up at a gentle angle in the corners, as opposed to the sharper angle one might expect to see in someone lacking sincerity. His eyes darted about the room as he quickly thought through his answer.

"I'm better. Thank you for asking," he managed as he pulled his stethoscope from around his neck and plugged the ends into his ears. "Can you undo your blouse for me, please?"

Lorna slipped the top three buttons through the buttonholes.

Martin's eyes locked on to a beige plaster on her chest. He pulled the stethoscope from his ears, quickly depositing it into the hand of his injured arm. "What in the world is that? Is that a *nicotine* patch?"

Lorna glanced down at her chest. "Oh, please don't be angry, Doc. I been meanin' ta quit, but I just can't do it on my own. Usin' the patch is better than not tryin' at all, isn't it?"

"Well yes, but not for someone with haemochromatosis! Nicotine increases the iron levels in your blood!"

Air hissed through his nose as he scowled and jammed the stethoscope back into his ears. "I don't suppose you thought to inform the doctor in Wadebridge that you were using the patch," he grumbled.

"*He's* the one that tol' me to try it, Doc. Said it'd make it easier for me ta quit."

Martin breathed out a heavy sigh. "Well, your heart *sounds* strong, but I'm sending you to get a CT scan of both your heart and your liver. I'll write an order for that before you leave today. I also want my assistant to check your blood glucose levels," he said as he moved towards the door.

"Is there somethin' yer not tellin' me, Doc? Yer scarin' me just a bit."

Martin shook his head. "Haemochromatosis *can* lead to a build-up of iron in the heart, liver, and pancreas, which can result in complications. I just want to make sure I haven't missed something."

He pulled the consulting room door open and called out to his receptionist. "Morwenna, did you get those test results I asked for?"

"'Fraid not, Doc. Seems they never did 'em over there. They said Lorna was feelin' better after seeing you so he wasn't takin' blood every month anymore. 'Cause of that he didn't do the tests either."

"What!" Martin screwed up his face. "How in the bloody hell are they going to know if the patient requires a phlebotomy if they don't check her ferritin levels?"

Morwenna gave him a shrug of her shoulders. "Don't ask me!"

He turned and re-entered the consulting room. *"Idiots!"* he muttered.

Taking in a calming breath, he looked at his patient. "All right, Mrs. Gillett. I'll have Mr. Portman check your blood glucose and draw for a serum ferritin test. We'll see what that shows and take it from there. For the time being, I'll write you a prescription for a stronger analgesic that should help with the joint pain. Any questions?"

Lorna gave him a smile. "Yeah. Do you think you can trust me with just a little more than, *I'm better*?"

Martin furrowed his brow and cocked his head at her. "What do you want to know?"

"Could you let me see yer arm?" she asked as she tried to peer into the sling that covered the wounds and the fixators.

"Mrs. Gillett! That's none of your—"

"Doc, I'm not askin' because I'm a nosy parker or I wanna go 'round gossiping about it. You've been good to me, and I *care* about you. That's all."

"Oh, gawd," he groaned.

She gave him an apologetic smile. "Call me overly maternal, I guess."

Martin remembered his aide's advice to him early that morning, and he closed his eyes momentarily, steeling himself against the nausea that was beginning to churn in his stomach.

He lifted his arm from the sling and held it out briefly.

"Oh, Doc. I'm real sorry."

"Mm." He cleared his throat, and then, avoiding any eye contact with her, he returned to the protection of his desk, where he slipped the wounded appendage back under the cover of the sling.

"This should get you through until we can get your ferritin levels down, but don't hesitate to call if it doesn't control the discomfort," he said, scratching his notes on to his prescription pad before ripping the sheet away and handing it to the woman.

He pulled himself from his chair and walked to the door, pulling it open. "I'll call you as soon as I get any information back on your CTs and your bloodwork."

Crossing the reception room, he ducked under the front doorway. "Mr. Portman, could you get a blood sugar reading on Mrs. Gillett and do a draw for a serum ferritin test?" he asked.

"Sure, have a seat, Lorna." Jeremy gave the woman a smile then answered Martin's quizzical look with a shrug. "She said she prefers I use her Christian name," he whispered in his ear.

"I see."

"You take care now, Doc. And let me know if there's any way I can be helpful to you." She leaned over and gave him a hug before his battered body would allow him to jump out of the way.

"Mm," he grunted.

Moving back towards his consulting room, he gave a nod to the elderly woman sitting next to the door. "I'll be with you in a minute, Miss Prynns," he said before pulling his mobile from his breast pocket and dialling his wife's number.

Chapter 10

Louisa removed her watch and laid it on the desk in front of her before returning her attention to the letter she was typing.

The holidays were fast approaching, and preparations were underway for the annual Christmas Festival. Trisha Soames and Katherine Griswold, the year two's teachers, had proposed the idea of adding a German Weihnachtsmarkt, or Christmas Market, to the traditional evening of music, punch, and biscuits.

The students would donate items, either handmade, hand baked, or preowned, that could be sold for a penny to a pound each.

It was hoped that the market would provide all of the children, even those from families of more modest means, with an opportunity to purchase gifts for their family members. Proceeds from the sales would be used for the purchase of a gift to the village of Portwenn. What the gift would be had not yet been determined, but it would be handled by the Board of Governors.

Louisa was now faced with the mildly inglorious task of appealing to the more well-heeled members of the community for cash donations, which would be used for the purchase of decorations and other needed supplies, as well as advertising for the event.

She bit at her lip as she mulled over how to word her letter of supplication. In other words, how to grovel graciously.

Her fingers drummed against the wood desktop, the sound resonating through the drawer below with a rich fullness reminiscent of her husband's voice. She sighed and, picking up her watch, strapped it back on her wrist.

She had just gotten up from her chair to go to the teacher's lounge for a cup of tea, when her mobile rang. She felt a familiar swelling of her chest when she heard Martin's voice on the other end.

"Hello. I've been thinking about you all morning."

She juggled her purse, teacup, and a file that she was going to pass to Pippa on her way through the outer office.

"Oh, that was quick. I didn't think he'd be able to get you in to see someone until later in the week." Her face registered an instant unease with the apparent haste of the scheduling of her husband's appointment with a neurologist.

"No, no! I want to be there with you. I'd rather get the information first-hand," she insisted.

"Martin, I don't want to get into one of our mini-rows over this. I *am* going with you!" She huffed out a breath and pressed her fingertips to her temple.

"Tell Jeremy, thank you just the same. I'll see you for lunch."

She listened intently, a soft smile slipping across her face. "I miss you too, Martin. Love you."

Dropping the device back into her purse she stared out her window. It seemed odd that Ed Christianson would have an appointment with a neurologist lined up so quickly. But he and Chris had bent over backwards since the night of the accident to make sure that Martin had the best of care, so maybe today's expeditious visit wasn't cause for concern. Perhaps this neurologist had a timely cancellation and an appointment slot had opened up.

Okay then, get the cuppa and get back to the gracious grovelling! she told herself.

Martin was in his consulting room when Louisa arrived home for lunch. Poppy had James in his high chair, already tucking into a bowl of tuna casserole, when she walked in the back door.

"Hello, James! Did you have a good morning?" she said in her lilting mother's voice as she leaned over to kiss the top of her young son's head.

"He did a lot of walkin'. Maybe he's makin' up for lost time since he started late," the childminder said as she laid the silverware out on the table.

Louisa slipped her coat from her shoulders and hung it on the rack by the door. "I think all the upheaval with Martin's accident threw him off his stride a bit. He seems to be back on track now, though, doesn't he?"

"I think so." Poppy moved the casserole dish from the hob to the table and filled the glasses with water. "But I'm not sure it's so much the accident that slowed him down as it was James always havin' his nose in a book or investigating things around the house. Maybe walking wasn't that interesting to him."

The baby gave her a broad smile before bursting into giggles as he tossed a piece of macaroni on the floor.

"You are going to get your lunch taken away from you if you keep that up young man!" Louisa said in mock admonishment.

"I think I'll just run in and say hello to Martin," she told Poppy before heading under the stairs.

A quiet tapping on the doorframe got his attention, and he shifted his eyes from his bookkeeping.

"Hello," she greeted him softly.

He got to his feet as she moved towards him.

"Hello," he said, pulling her in close and tipping his head down to nuzzle his face into her neck.

He took in a deep breath, her scent having a relaxing effect on him. "You know ... you wasted your money on that lavender oil."

"Is that right, Dr. Ellingham? Explain it to me." She tightened her grip around his middle and pressed her ear to his chest.

"This. *This* … is what I needed," he said as he exhaled the accumulated stresses of the morning.

Louisa's smile faded, and she squeezed her eyes shut. "I'm … sorry, Martin."

He put his hands on her shoulders and pushed her back, peering into her face.

"Louisa, did I say something wrong?" he asked, brushing the tears from her cheeks.

"All those sleepless nights, Martin. *All* … those sleepless nights and what you needed was *affection*?"

He blinked down at her and swallowed hard. "I don't know what I needed, Louisa."

His manner changed abruptly, and she could see the confusion on his face. "Martin, it's okay," she said softly.

He cleared his throat and backed away from her. "Erm … we should go eat. We should leave for Truro soon."

She watched as he turned the corner and headed down the hall. This was one of those verbal exchanges where her husband left her at sixes and sevens.

Martin didn't utter more than the occasional no thank you during lunch. Louisa maintained a steady banter with Poppy and James but kept one eye on him. Something about their brief conversation in the consulting room had rattled him.

"How did the first morning back at the surgery go?" Louisa asked as they rolled over the narrow twisted lanes between Portwenn and Wadebridge.

"Pretty mundane." Martin pleaded silently with her to leave him be, but she persisted.

She turned, giving him a small smile. "I guess I was thinking more in terms of how *you* did. Was it tiring? Did you do okay with pain? That sort of thing."

He rolled his eyes and heaved out a breath. "Yes, I'm tired. But it's nothing I can't deal with. And I don't know what you want me to say about pain, Louisa. We've been over and over that with Ed and Chris. It's there, and there's only so much I can do about it. So, let's not bring it up, all right?"

She worked her hands around the steering wheel and focused her eyes on the road.

Martin's head was whirling with emotions he couldn't distinguish at the moment. He was sure that he had hurt his wife's feelings with his words, but trying to discuss things now would be as futile as planning a course of treatment before a medical history had been taken.

Her comment earlier had knocked him off balance. *What you needed was affection?* Needed? No, he had outgrown his neediness long ago. If there was anything good that had come from his relationship with Edith Montgomery, it would be that she had forced him to grow up.

Her impromptu recitation of his poem a year and a half ago had been a harsh reminder of that—of the previous time he had heard her quote those words. *On my own no more. The beat of my heart echoes in time with another. And now, sore with longing, it runs like a child to its mother.* How callow those words had sounded to his ears when *she* spoke them. *I hope you're not expecting **me** to mother you, Ellingham!* Her words reverberated in his head.

But *had* he outgrown his neediness? Less than three years ago, when he'd picked his parents up at Bodmin Parkway, he had reached to hug his mother, partly out of a sense of filial duty, but also, if he was honest with himself, with the hope that his expression of love for her would finally be reciprocated.

He couldn't deny the fact that he had felt a terrible emptiness, a need still left painfully unsatisfied when his affections were met with the usual acrimonious tolerance, if not unmitigated disgust. Maybe he *was* still needy, and maybe he was expecting his wife to appease that need.

"Oh, gawd," he moaned under his breath.

"Did you say something?" Louisa asked, glancing over at him.

"Mm, no. Just thinking aloud." He cleared his throat and turned towards her. "How was your morning?"

"It was good. Kinda *mundane* as well." She looked over at him. "Are you just trying to make polite conversation, or do you really want the details?"

"No. No, go ahead."

She brushed the hair off her face. "I worked on a letter that's supposed to be mailed out to all the business owners and ... hmm, let's just say the people with the deepest pockets. I feel like a bit of a cadge. I know it's part of my job and everything, but ... I mean, asking for money?"

"Well, *you're* not really the one asking for money. You're just a mouthpiece for the children, Louisa."

His wife's black look was not missed, and he quickly added, "I *mean* that it's the children asking for donations. You're just communicating the request. For that matter, is it even necessary for you to put your name on the letter?"

"You mean just sign it, from the students of Portwenn Primary?"

"Problem?" he asked, raising an eyebrow at her.

She gave her head a shake. "No, Mar-tin. No problem."

She hated when her husband pointed out something so obvious. Something she should have thought of herself. It made him seem intellectually superior.

She watched him from the corner of her eye and saw his head drop to the side as he screwed up his face and huffed softly.

He sat quietly for several minutes. "I said something wrong ... didn't I?"

Louisa reached over and caressed his thigh. "No, Martin. I'm just displaying my own insecurities."

"Oh ... good."

Louisa's mouth quirked at her husband's gift for the ambiguous response.

"I'll drop you at the entrance and then go park the car, hmm?" she said as they turned into the hospital car park.

Martin pulled his arm up and glanced at his watch. "We're early. I have a bit of time yet before I need to be at radiology, so I could walk with you."

"I'll probably have to park fairly far from the entrance. Down by the bus stop. You sure you can make it?"

"I could do with a bit of fresh air. And it's flat ground. It's a good place to get some practise."

Louisa pulled the car into a parking space and got out, walking around to take her husband's hand.

"This is nice. It feels a bit like the walks we'd take on the Coastal Path ... before your accident," she said as she moved closer and shifted her arm up and around his waist.

"I think I could manage walks up to the top of the hill now that we're back in the surgery." He stopped, and after glancing around him, he leaned over and kissed her.

Louisa smiled up at him. "If it weren't for the fact that we're on our way to see a neurologist, I would feel quite ... *normal* right now."

"Well, that makes a change I suppose," he said, giving her a shy smile. "I'm sorry about earlier ... in the car. Perhaps we could talk after we go to bed tonight?"

"Gives me something to look forward to." Louisa caressed his arm and rested her head on his shoulder.

If her husband was going to discuss an uncomfortable topic, he preferred to do it under a blanket of darkness. She felt a small wave of trepidation, but opted to brush it aside and enjoy a beautifully banal moment with him.

The hospital staff were ready and waiting when they arrived at radiology. She gave him an encouraging smile from her seat in the waiting area, watching as he disappeared through the doors.

Picking up the newspaper lying on the table next to her, she began to visually sift through the columns of celebrity gossip and attention-grabbing crimes against her fellow man to find something that resembled actual news.

"Louisa, hello," a familiar voice said.

She looked up into Barrett Newell's warm, craggy face. "Oh, hello! What are you doing here?"

"A patient ... getting an MRI done across the hall. How about you? Everything okay with Martin?" he asked as he dropped into the chair next to her.

"Yeah, yeah!" Her smile faded as her brow creased. "Well, I guess that's what we're here to find out. He's been having some headaches, and they want to check things over ... just a precaution."

Dr. Newell scrutinised her face. "What kind of headaches?"

She shook her head at him. "Headache—headaches, I guess. He says they seem to be triggered by noise. He's not really complained about it to me, so I don't think it's been a real issue."

She hesitated then gave the man a sideways glance. "You don't think it sounds like anything to worry about, do you?"

Dr. Newell held his hands up in front of him. "I have no way of making that sort of determination, and it's not my place to say even if I did. You'll have to wait until the verdict comes down from Mr. Christianson, I'm afraid."

"Mm, the neurologist. He has an appointment with a neurologist after this."

"Ah, I see." The therapist brushed a piece of lint from the leg of his trousers then glanced around the empty room. "How are you doing? You've had a lot of turmoil to deal with lately."

Louisa sat thoughtfully for a moment. "Well, I guess pretty well, all-in-all. Of course, I worry a lot about Martin. He's doing so much better ... physically *and* emotionally. But he has days when it's like there's something just under the surface. I don't know if he's just trying to not let this all get to him ... to not let his frustration show. But there are days when I feel like I'm living in the shadow of Mt. Vesuvius." She looked over and gave Dr. Newell an uneasy smile.

The door squeaked open and Martin walked through, his eyebrows raised as he focused in on his therapist seated next to his wife.

"A patient across the hall," the man explained. "How's it going, Martin? Louisa tells me you've been having some headaches."

He shook his head dismissively. "Just noise induced post-trauma headaches most likely."

He glanced down at his wife and then gave a nod towards the doors. "We should go. I have an appointment with the neurologist in ten minutes."

Louisa hurriedly refolded the newspaper and laid it back down on the table. "Yeah, of course. It was nice to see you, Dr. Newell."

"Yes, you too, Louisa. Martin," he said, extending his hand. "I'll see you on Friday."

"Mm, yes."

Minutes later, Martin and Louisa were sitting in the neurologist's office, the consultant looking intently at Martin's CT scan images on his computer monitor. He swivelled the apparatus around so that his patient could see the screen.

"As you can see, Martin, your scan looks perfectly clear," Dr. Shekar said with the alveolar trill typical of Indian dialects. "Tell me about these headaches. What brings them on? Describe the quality ... the duration."

He gave his wife a furtive glance and pulled at his trousers, attempting to straighten the opening around the fixator in his femur. "They're noise induced. Loud, sharp, high pitched noises seem to trigger them. Chairs scraping on floors, things being dropped on the slate ... that sort of thing."

He removed a sheet of paper from his shirt pocket and slid it across the desk. "I've kept a record of the episodes as they've occurred."

The consultant scanned over his patient's makeshift journal and then leaned back in his chair, steepling his fingers.

"According to your records, you've experienced them at least five times in the last five days, three of them occurring on Saturday. Was Saturday a typical day for you?"

Louisa listened attentively, realising she was unaware of much of what her husband had been dealing with.

"We had a busy day ... a stressful day I would say."

Dr. Shekar leaned forward and jotted some notes into his patient's file, then pushed back into his chair again.

"Describe the headaches for me. Are they consistent or do they vary? Dull—sharp—do they come on suddenly or gradually build in intensity?"

"They've been the same every time, aside from the first one. That was not as severe and very brief. The mother of a patient was leaning over my shoulder as I examined her son, talking in my ear." Martin scowled at the thought of Mrs. Trevathan's warm moist breath and strident voice.

"And that day ... was it stressful as well?"

"Most of Martin's days are stressful," Louisa interjected before giving her husband an apologetic smile.

He cleared his throat and refocused his attention on the consultant.

"Yes, it *had* been a stressful afternoon," he said, recalling his distressing reaction to the exercise he was trying to complete before his Friday therapy session.

"Describe the pain for me."

"Very sharp ... intense. But the episodes are brief, seconds to a minute or two in duration."

"What do you mean when you say intense?"

Martin huffed out a breath and gave the man a stern look. "Shall I define the word for you?"

Louisa reached over and placed her hand on his thigh, giving him a warning glance.

Dr. Shekar swivelled his chair side to side and stared his patient down. "That won't be necessary, Dr. Ellingham. Despite what my accent may suggest, I've been speaking English for almost as many years as you have."

He cleared his throat before referring back to Martin's sheet of notes.

"Try to be as specific with your description of the headaches as you can."

Martin looked over at Louisa then back at Dr. Shekar. "They're momentarily incapacitating. The episode this morning took my legs out from under me. Not that it takes much at the moment."

Feeling his wife's eyes on him, he squirmed in his chair.

"Did you lose consciousness or lose your sense of balance?"

"No! Don't you think I would have specified if I had? I'm a doctor for God's sake!"

Martin glared at the man, forcing him to avert his gaze and pick up his biro.

Louisa watched her husband warily as he closed his eyes and inhaled deeply.

"I apologise, Dr. Shekar."

"Apology accepted. I'm sure this must have been weighing very heavily on you, especially given your recent medical history."

"I tried not to dwell on it ... to keep busy."

"Well, as you know, Dr. Ellingham, the exact aetiology of these sorts of symptoms can be difficult to pinpoint. I can, however, say with confidence that there's no indication of a blood clot or a bleed."

The man got up and came around to the front of his desk. "I suspect that what you've been experiencing are ice pick headaches, brought on by a combination of stress and certain noises. We also need to consider that residual trauma from shear force stresses on the cervical vertebrae could be contributing to the problem as well.

"I would suggest that you try working with a physiotherapist. Many of my patients have gotten significant relief from massage therapy. It's certainly worth a try. Get yourself some musician's earplugs as well."

Louisa took hold of Martin's hands as soon as Dr. Shekar's door closed behind them, pulling him to her.

"Louisa, I'm sorry if this came as a surprise to you. I didn't really—"

She pressed a finger to his lips. "Shhh. I don't even want to discuss why you didn't tell me about all of this. For the moment, I just—want—to breath a sigh of relief together that there's nothing seriously wrong."

Chapter 11

Martin reached out and pressed the button. Waiting for the lift doors to open, he looked anxiously at his wife. "Louisa, I did tell you about the headaches. Saturday night ... when you asked about the earplugs."

She released his hand from hers and crossed her arms in front of her. "Well, you weren't very forthcoming about how severe they were."

"You didn't ask me any more about it, and you didn't seem that interested in hearing any more about it. The subject was changed quickly and—and well, I don't know what you think I should have done differently!"

Louisa turned as rapid footsteps could be heard approaching from down the hall.

"Mart ... Louisa! Hold up!" Chris Parsons called out.

"We'll continue this later, Martin," she clipped before flashing a smile at their friend. "Hi, Chris. This is a surprise."

"Yeah, I wasn't sure I'd catch you before you headed up to Ed's office." He inhaled deeply, trying to catch his breath. "How did it go with Shekar?" he asked, giving a nod down the hall. "Get any answers?"

The arrow overhead turned green, and the lift doors opened as the electronic ping signalled its arrival.

"I'll ride up with you, if you don't mind," Chris said, reaching his hand out to keep the doors from closing again before Martin could get across the threshold.

They rumbled softly as they slid shut. "So ... was Shekar helpful at all?" he asked, peering up at his much larger friend.

"Somewhat. He was able to rule out a serious problem. He thinks the headaches might be being triggered by a combination of stress and noise. Could possibly be a whiplash type problem involved as well."

"Sounds plausible," Chris said, pulling his hands behind his back.

The lift pinged again and the doors parted.

"Shekar thinks that some physio work on my neck could be helpful," Martin said, glancing at his watch. "We should—" He gestured towards Ed's office with his thumb.

"Yeah, yeah, of course," Chris said as he absentmindedly toyed with the coins in his pocket. "I should let you go, but I do have orders from Carole to convey a message. She's wondering if you two want to have supper with us before you head back to Portwenn."

Louisa looked up at her husband, expectantly. "Martin, can we? I haven't seen Carole in ages."

Martin drew his brows together. "Well, if you want to, that'd be fine."

"Good, give me a call when you finish up with Ed," Chris said. He gave them a wave of his hand and moved down the hall a few steps before turning back around. "Mart, you should talk to Portman. He's had therapeutic massage training. It could be helpful if it's a cervical issue."

"Mm, yes."

The door to Ed Christianson's office was open when they arrived, and hearing the soft clicking of his patient's crutch, the surgeon looked up from his desk.

"Come on in," he said as he typed a few final words on to his computer keyboard before closing the window. Martin dropped heavily into a chair, and Ed stood up to stretch his back.

He pulled a chair over from the wall. "Louisa, it's nice to see you. Have a seat, please."

He leaned back against his desk with his arms folded in front of him. "Well, I received Dr. Shekar's report a few minutes ago. It's good news, albeit not terribly helpful in deciding how to proceed from here. What's your thinking on it, Martin?"

Martin's lower lip twitched as he tipped his head to the side. "It was a relief to get the clear scans. Not a surprise, but a relief just the same. I'll try using the earplugs and do what I can about eliminating stress, but—"

"Life *is* inherently stressful at the moment," the surgeon said, completing his patient's sentence."

"Mm."

"What about his recommendation for physiotherapy? Are you open to that?"

"Jeremy Portman can help me with that. So yes, I'm open to it."

Pulling the bandage from Martin's arm, he inspected his most recent work. "This looks good. How's it feeling?"

"Better. Still pretty tender, and I don't think I want to be putting weight on it yet."

"How are you managing with one crutch?"

"There haven't been any issues." Martin hesitated, glancing quickly at his wife. "I'm ... wanting to start driving again. I realise I won't be able to do that until the headaches are under control, but as far as my legs and arm ... is there any reason I can't be back behind the wheel?"

"No. You certainly have the strength back and the flexibility needed. But you're right, as long as you're having the ice pick-type headaches you absolutely should not be driving."

Louisa leaned forward in her chair. "Could you explain these ice pick headaches for me, Ed?"

"Well, if you're wanting a description of what it's like to experience them, your husband would be better able to answer that. But they're sudden, intense, although brief, headaches.

Like an ice pick being jammed into your head, hence the name. I've had patients describe it as feeling more like a hot poker than an ice pick. The point being, they can literally bring a person to their knees, so it would, obviously, be unwise for your husband to be driving if he's experiencing them."

Louisa laid her hand on Martin's and gave it a gentle squeeze. "Do you think these headaches are stress related?"

The surgeon slipped around to the back of his desk and took a seat.

"If you remember, your husband sustained some mild bruising on his brain, just above his right ear. We can get a rough idea about what's going on in a person's head using CT or MRI scans, but there's always damage to small blood vessels and nerves that won't show up on the scans.

"It's quite likely that some of Martin's issues are related to the healing process going on in his head. Headaches are extremely common after a concussion. They're usually transient, rarely continuing for an extended period of time."

Martin stared at the floor, working his jaw back and forth. "How long, then? How long do I need to be headache free?"

"Well, let's see how you do this week, then we'll talk about it again."

He got up from his chair and moved towards the door. "I'd like you to stop down at the lab before you go, Martin. Check your leucocytes. The arm looks good though. We'll talk the end of the week about pulling some of those lower limb pins."

"Thank you, Ed," Louisa said as he pulled the door open for them.

"How are you feeling about today's appointments?" Louisa asked as they once again waited in front of the lift doors.

"Well, the clear scan was good news, but—" Martin rubbed his palm across his face. "Maybe we could not discuss this right now. Just get done at the lab and go have dinner."

"Sure, I'll give Carole a call; see where they want to meet."

Martin and Louisa arrived at the restaurant ahead of the Parsons and had ordered several starters before their friends walked through the door. Martin had missed his usual mid-afternoon meal and was tucking into garlic-grilled prawns when Carole leaned over him from behind and wrapped her arms around him.

"Hello, Martin. How are you doing?"

He pulled his head back and peered at her incredulously. "Carole! For God's sake!" He reached up to uncoil her from his body.

"Sorry." She patted her hand on his cheek before throwing her arms around Louisa. "And, how are you? It seems like ages!"

"It does. This was a wonderful idea." Louisa embraced her friend as her husband squirmed in his chair, glancing over his shoulder.

"Did Chris fall out along the road somewhere?" he asked as he pulled a prawn from a skewer.

Carole dropped into a chair on the opposite side of the table and gave him a shake of her head. "No, wise guy. He ran into someone he knows. He said he'd be right in."

"Mm."

Louisa pulled her purse from the back of her chair and stood up. "Can you keep my husband out of trouble for a few minutes?" She leaned down and whispered, "I need the loo."

"I think we'll manage."

"I'll be right back," Louisa said, brushing her hand lightly across Martin's cheek as she walked by."

Carole reached for the water pitcher and filled her glass. "Chris tells me you've been having some problems with headaches."

"It's nothing. Probably just stress." he said, jabbing at a prawn with his fork.

Her fingertips drummed lightly on the table before she looked at him, hesitantly. "You know, *music* can be a great stress reliever."

Martin froze as his eyes snapped up at her. He sat motionless for a moment before poking his knife in the direction of the skewer-filled platter. "Would you like some shrimp?"

"No, thank you. I want to save my appetite for dinner."

She breathed out a sigh and tilted her head at him. "Martin, you used to enjoy music. In fact, Chris said once, back when you two were in medical school, that he could tell when you'd had an especially bad day because you'd go right to that piano you had in the flat. That you wouldn't even stop to take your coat off some—"

"I don't play anymore, Carole. You know that. Why are you bringing it up?"

She reached across the table and put her hand on his. "I'm bringing it up because it makes me heartsick that you had a gift taken away from you years ago. That you've given up something that you love because of someone like Edith Montgom—"

"Is *this* why you wanted to meet for dinner tonight? So you could get me to tell you what happened between Edith and me?" Martin's eyes flashed with anger and defensiveness as he tossed his fork down on to the table.

"Martin, hear me out, and then I won't ever bring the subject up again ... okay?"

He stared across at her, unflinching. "Say what you have to say, and say it quickly before Louisa comes back," he said tersely.

Carole pulled her napkin from the table and laid it across her lap. "I don't need to know the details, Martin. Chris and I figured out years ago ... when you suddenly refused to join in with our impromptu ensembles, had that piano of yours hauled off by the bin man *and* didn't even try to get any money for—"

"Is there a point to this?"

"Well, we figured it had something to do with Edith's sudden absence.

"Chris and I knew when you started dating Edith that you were going to get hurt. It was horrible to watch the effect she had on you. I'm sorry that I didn't do more to help you back then. But I'll be damned if I don't try now!"

Martin focused his attention on the food in front of him. "You sure you don't want any of this shrimp?" He asked as he reached out to pick up a skewer.

Carole yanked the platter out from under his hand. "Forget about the bloody shrimp, Martin! I am *trying* to talk to you!"

She gave an exasperated huff. "It would be uncomfortable at first, I'm sure. But it would be so good for you emotionally *and* physically to get those keys under your fingers.

"You can use the piano at our house if you like. I'll find something Louisa and I can do and you can have the house to yourself. You could start with something strictly technical— those godawful Hanon exercises—or scales. Think of it as therapy for that arm and hand. Now's the time to be working on that you know."

Martin shifted his gaze from his plate and looked at her. "I'll think about it."

His eyes flitted to the platter, now out of reach. "May I have my shrimp back now?"

Carole gave the plate of prawns a shove. "Let me know, Martin. Whatever I can do to help, okay?"

"Yes," he said, dipping his head as he grabbed for a skewer.

"Here come our better halves," she said softly.

Chris pulled out the empty chair left between his friend and his wife and took a seat. "Looks like the appetite's holding up fine," he said with a grin as he took a visual account of the empty skewers on Martin's plate.

Louisa smiled as her husband's ears reddened slightly, and he tucked his chin.

"So ... how, erm ... did the first day back in the surgery go?" Chris asked.

His tone put Martin on alert. "Why?"

He glanced over at the two women, already involved in a conversation about their children. "I ran into Harry Cannon out in the parking lot."

"Oh, gaawd," Martin groaned.

Harry Cannon was a member of the NHS's Commissioning Board and was in charge of fielding complaints against the group's practitioners.

"Judging by your reaction, I don't have to tell you what he and I were discussing out in the carpark."

Martin gave a grunt. "Britton didn't waste any time."

"Well, to hear your patient's version of the story, he has a legitimate gripe."

"The man's an idiot."

Chris picked up a skewer of prawns and slid them on to his plate. "According to Mr. Britton, you called him a plug-ugly moron."

Martin waved his fork back and forth. "No, no, no, no, no. I called him a plug-ugly, *hyper concupiscent* moron."

"Oh, I see. I'm sure Harry'll let the incident slide then."

"The man was verbally harassing my receptionist, Chris!"

The raised voices of the two men had attracted the attention of their wives. "When did this happen, Martin?" Louisa asked.

He hissed out a breath. "This morning. I haven't had a chance to tell you.

"The man was vulgar. I heard some of what he was saying, and I guess—I guess I lost my temper."

Chris leaned back in his chair, flinging his arm up on to the top rail. "Britton says you took a swing at him."

"I did no such thing! I grabbed the back of his coat and showed him the door. Told him to get out of my surgery."

"So, no punches were thrown, then?"

"Of course not!" Martin looked at his friend in disbelief, then glanced down at his broken limbs. "Chris—really?"

"All right, point taken."

The matter was dropped and the rest of the evening was spent with the men discussing medical studies and treatment options, and the women discussing everything from the latest village news to the upcoming open house at Ruth's farm.

"I hope you and Chris can make it over on Saturday," Louisa said as she folded her napkin and got up from her chair.

Carole gave her a nod of her head. "We'll definitely be there. We haven't been there since Chris and Martin were in medical school. I have very fond memories of that weekend," she said, giving her husband a knowing smile.

He cleared his throat as his gaze darted from his wife's face to his friend, who was struggling to get himself pushed out from under the table.

Pushing the table back, Chris grabbed on to Martin's arm, giving him a boost to his feet. "Don't worry about this thing with Britton, Mart. I told Cannon I'd handle it and, well, I understand why you reacted the way you did. Consider the issue dealt with, mate."

"Mm, thank you." Despite his friend's reassuring words, Martin had an unsettled feeling in his stomach.

Chapter 12

Louisa said nothing about the incident that had occurred at the surgery that morning, deciding to give her husband a chance to bring the subject up first. But he was quiet as they drove back from Truro that evening, giving the bare minimum of information whenever she asked a question.

"You doing okay?" she finally asked, reaching for his hand.

He hesitated. "I'm ... fine."

Louisa released an inaudible sigh and tightened her grip on the steering wheel.

Several minutes passed before Martin's voice broke the silence. "I want to have locks put on the doors between the family area of the house and the surgery area. And better locks on the exterior doors."

"Oh?" He pulled his hand away from hers, and she glanced over at him. The slight furrowing of his brow and the downward tip of his head betrayed his unease.

"Martin, I'm sure you don't have to worry about this man who was harassing Morwenna. He sounds like a very repulsive person, but he's probably harmless. The crime rate around Portwenn is ... well, outside of the occasional melon from someone's veg patch going missing, little else happens. I *really* don't think you have to worry."

"How can you say that, Louisa? How long has it been since you were in tears in my arms because that idiot ... Maynard threatened you at the school?"

"Bollard."

"What?"

"Bollard, not Maynard, Martin. The man's name is Bollard." She patted his hand and gave him a tepid smile.

"Mm, yes."

They crossed the River Camel as they came into Wadebridge. Louisa watched her husband out of the corner of her eye. The flashes of light as they passed under the street lamps illuminated the vulnerability in his face.

"Whatever you think is best, Martin." She forced a reassuring smile and patted his arm before returning her hand to the wheel while she navigated the roundabouts through town.

It was almost seven o'clock when Louisa pulled the Lexus into the parking place next to the surgery. James whirled his head around and released a loud and enthusiastic squeal when he saw them walk through the door.

Martin grimaced and stopped in his tracks, waiting for the pain in his head to abate.

Louisa moved to her son's side, unaware of her husband's discomfort as he trailed behind her.

"Hello, you two!" she said, leaning over to nuzzle her nose into her son's neck. "Thank you so much for staying late, Poppy."

"Did everything go okay?" the childminder asked as she wiped the floor under James's high chair.

"Yes, I would say it went fine, wouldn't you, Martin?"

He raised a hand to rub the residual tension in his forehead and gave his trademark, taciturn, "Yes."

His eyes shifted to the pasta sauce and spaghetti still littering the unwashed area of the floor. "I see James has had his supper."

"Yeah ... made a bit of a mess tonight," Poppy said with a shrug of her shoulders and an apologetic grin.

Martin went to the high chair and reached down to unfasten the strap around his small son before leaning over and hooking his left arm around him, pulling the boy to his chest. "We need to work on your table manners, James," he said softly as he pulled him in a bit closer.

Louisa eyed him nervously. "Here, Martin. You'd better let me take him," she said, pulling the boy from her husband's reluctant arm.

"I was fine, Louisa!" he replied. His features tightened as he watched James move out of reach. Lowering his arms, he tried to shake his coat from his body.

"Poppy, I can finish that up. You get on home. It's been a long day for you." Louisa made a mental note to include a generous bonus in the girl's next pay cheque.

"Thank you *so* much for staying late. You have no idea how much we appreciate all the extra time you've put in for us in the last several months."

"It's no big deal, Mrs. Ellingham. I like spendin' time with James."

"Well, we do appreciate it, don't we, Martin?" She gave her husband the exaggerated nod that meant he should reinforce her statement.

"Yes." He eyed her indignantly as beads of perspiration broke out on his upper lip and forehead, a result of the continued struggle with his coat.

"And we realise this isn't what you signed on for. We've asked an awful lot of you, and I'm sure it's been an inconvenience," Louisa continued as she guided Poppy towards the hall.

Martin stood alone in the middle of the floor, the women's voices growing softer as they moved away from the kitchen. He gave up on his coat and shrugged it back up over his shoulders before heading out the back door.

There was a damp chill in the air and a stiff wind blowing, but it felt refreshing to him. He was hot, tired, his bones ached and his nerves were frayed.

Walking to the side of the cottage, he dropped on to the bench that was perched on the slate walkway. Louisa's voice could be heard as she chatted briefly with Poppy, a chortle or two from James punctuating the conversation.

It was eerily quiet. The gulls had found sanctuary for the night, and the cottages, for the most part, were vacant. Only the hardiest of souls had any desire to visit Portwenn during the winter months. Most of the year-round residents lived in the homes up on the hill, where it was safe from the flooding storms.

He listened to the goodnights being exchanged and watched, unseen, as Poppy descended the slate steps and headed off down Roscarrock Hill. The childminder *had* done a more than adequate job, and the demands placed on her as a result of his accident *had* been great. Martin liked Poppy—she loved his son.

The waves sloshed against the cliff rocks. Ruth found the sound obtrusive, but Martin found it soothing. It was continual reassurance that this shoreline had existed for countless millennia and would no doubt exist for many more. It may change course slightly over time as weather and geological forces ate away at the cliffs, but the sea's waves would continue to rush in to kiss the granite rocks until the day that some cataclysmic event obliterated the Earth.

He sighed and pulled himself to his feet to leave the quiet and solitude and return to the pressures he felt inside the house.

"Where have you been? I thought you were in your consulting room!" Louisa said as he pushed the door shut against the wind.

"Getting some air ... cooling off. I was hot," he grumbled.

"You didn't try to walk up the hill on your own, did you?"

Martin gave her a challenging glare. "Are you going to tell me that I'm not capable of taking a walk without someone holding my hand?"

Louisa put the last of the dishes in the dishwasher before pulling the tea towel from the door of the cooker. "I'm not *saying* that. Well, not exactly. It *is* a steep hill, though, and it's dark. If you fell there'd be no one around to help you, Martin."

"Right, I'll add it to the list!" he yelled back as he ducked under the stairs.

There was a loud bang as the consulting room door was slammed shut. Louisa gathered James from where he was playing on the kitchen floor and took him upstairs for his bath.

Her husband was still sequestered in his office when she came back downstairs. She tapped softly on the door. Not getting an answer, she opened it and peeked in. "*Oh, Martin,*" she whispered as she walked to her husband's desk and leaned over to kiss him as he lay, slumped over, sound asleep.

"Martin," she said softly, tickling the back of his neck with her fingertips.

He took in a deep breath and sat up abruptly, rubbing his eyes and trying to get his bearings. "Mm, sorry."

"James is asleep and you're tired. Maybe we should call it a night too, hmm?"

Yawning, he leaned back in his chair, momentarily closing his eyes.

"Come on, sleepy head; I'll give you a hand," she said as she reached out to pull him up.

"Nope, I've got it," he mumbled. "We'll both end up on the floor if you try that. Why don't you go on? I'll close things up and be there in a few minutes."

He waited until she had disappeared around the stair rail, and then he got to his feet and went to the kitchen to make sure the lock was set. Passing the front entry, he flipped the deadbolt. He gave the door a tug to assure himself that it was secure before turning to ascend the stairs.

Louisa was in the lavatory brushing her teeth when he came into the bedroom. Dropping down on to the edge of the bed, he sat watching her. The suggestive language that Mr. Britton had used with Morwenna that morning played in his head. It was infuriating to hear those things being said to his receptionist, but he couldn't bring himself to think about them being said to the woman he cherished more than anything in the world.

Morwenna seemed to have the impression that he had been valiant by coming out and giving the degenerate a tongue lashing before throwing him out of the surgery. But truth be told, Martin had found himself intimidated by the man when he was shut behind the consulting room door with him.

Britton was a bully, and bullies prey on people with weaknesses. It didn't take a very keen nose to smell weakness in Martin right now. No, it wasn't valiance, it was a primal response, a knee-jerk reaction.

A moronic knee-jerk reaction, Ellingham. You could've easily been at the receiving end of that punch if Jeremy hadn't stepped in. You could have ended up with a zygomatic fracture ... or a fractured jaw. That's all you need. What an idiot!

As Louisa leaned over the sink to spit the toothpaste out of her mouth, Martin's eyes were drawn to her upturned bum. He pulled in a ragged breath as the sight had nature's intended effect on him.

Louisa turned and, catching her husband in his libidinous gaze, stretched her arms up and yawned.

"Oh, my. I am shattered! And judging by your catnap on your desk, you are as well. So, I better clear out of here so you can get ready for bed, hmm?"

"Mm, yes," he said, a tinge of disappointment in his voice.

He stood in the bathroom doorway a few minutes later, toothbrush in hand, watching her as she rubbed lotion on to her arms and hands before settling in under the covers.

"We don't have to, erm ... go to sleep right away."

Louisa rolled over and looked up at him. "Oh, yeah, I forgot. You said you wanted to talk, didn't you?"

He cocked his head as he tried to read her intentions.

"Yes. Yes, I did," he said, the tinge more palpable.

He returned to the bathroom, and Louisa lay listening to the buzz of his toothbrush, a small satisfied smile on her face. She was delighted with this new eager husband she seemed to have acquired, but Martin had said he wanted to talk, and she wasn't going to let the precious opportunity slip by.

When he emerged from the bathroom, he leaned his crutch against the table by the bed and sat down, fiddling with his watch.

She pulled the covers back and patted the mattress. "Come on, crawl in here with me before you get a chill, you silly man."

He pulled the watch off and laid it on the table before flipping the switch on the lamp and sliding in next to her.

"Not such a great first day, then?" Louisa asked as she twirled her finger around a curl of hair behind his ear.

He pulled his shoulders up and grimaced. "It was all right. Aside from one patient in particular. That and the discovery that the GP over in Wadebridge is so incompetent as to be dangerous."

"Well, I've said it before. No one's gonna fill *your* shoes, Dr. Ellingham." Louisa moved closer and laid her head on his shoulder.

"No. I mean, this idiot bollocksed things up so badly that his failures could result in organ damage for one of my patients!" Martin scratched roughly at his head.

"Oh, dear. That does sound serious. Will you have to report him?"

"Of course, I will! A proper doctor would have been aware of the need to run the necessary tests before discontinuing treatments!"

"I'm sorry. I know you don't like having to grass people up." Louisa pushed herself up and pressed her lips to his forehead. "Then you had the plug-ugly moron to contend with as well, hmm?"

"Hmph. Hopefully, it's the last we've seen of him."

"Who did you say the man was?"

"I didn't say. And I can't. Sorry."

"Well, he must have said something pretty rubbish to upset you like he did."

Martin rolled on to his side and wrapped his arm tightly around her, burying his face in her hair. "I don't want you to *ever* be subjected to a man like that, Louisa."

"Is that why you want the locks on the doors? Are you afraid he could come in sometime when James and I are at home?" she asked softly.

He rolled to his back and flung an arm over his face. "He's not a nice man. And he's not the only one in the world with ill intentions, either. I'm sorry that I'd never given the matter any thought before today. I've left you and James vulnerable. All the people in and out of our home."

Louisa reached over and turned out her light before curling up to face him. "I hadn't thought about it either, Martin. I think in a tiny village like this where we know everyone, it's easy to become complacent ... to forget that there are bad people anywhere you live. No place is immune."

"Louisa, I can't protect you right now. When Brit— When the imbecile was in my consulting room I—"

He took in a deep breath and tried to free the lump in his throat. "The man knew I couldn't defend myself, Louisa. I don't think he would've bothered Morwenna if I wasn't in the state I'm in. I haven't felt so outmatched since I was a teenager. What am I going to do if you need me?"

Louisa lay quietly. Martin had expressed the same concerns while he was still in hospital, but she had reassured him, and he seemed to have moved past those fears. "You defended Morwenna. You threw the man out of your surgery. I'm sure you'd be even more motivated if it were James or me that seemed to be in danger."

He pushed himself up to a sitting position. "No! I *didn't* defend Morwenna. I wasn't thinking when I went storming into the reception area. The way I handled things this morning could have made things worse. If Jeremy hadn't been there I probably would have found myself laid out on the floor, and God only knows what could have happened to Morwenna."

"Well, granted, I didn't have the misfortune of meeting this man, but I suspect he's all mouth and trousers. They usually are."

All mouth and trousers ... Edith's words. There was a painful silence before Martin spoke. "I'm going downstairs for a glass of water," he said abruptly, his words obscured as he swallowed back emotions.

"Martin?" Louisa got up from the bed to follow after him, but something told her to give him some space.

She had drifted off to sleep before he finally returned. Waking as he sat down on the edge of the bed, his back to her, she rubbed her eyes and shook the grogginess from her head.

"Everything okay?" she said, stifling a yawn.

"Yes. I'm sorry for going off like that. I think I'm ready to talk ... if you're still ready to listen."

"I *would* like to listen," she said as she pushed her pillow back against the headboard.

Martin cleared his throat nervously and leaned forward, his forearms resting on his thighs. "Do you still want me to tell you why I quit playing the piano?"

Louisa held her breath for a moment, taking a mental step back before answering. "If you're ready to tell me, yes, I *would* like to know."

"It was something that happened with Edith Montgomery. If you remember, she was your obstetrician when you were pregnant with James."

"Oh, for goodness' sake, Martin. I haven't forgotten who my obstetrician was ... try as I might."

"If this is going to upset you, Louisa, I'll stop right there!" he snapped.

She crawled to the side of the bed and sat back on her feet behind him, wrapping her arms around his chest. "I'm sorry. I can handle this gracefully ... I think. Please, go ahead."

"I made a fool of myself with her. I thought I loved her when we were in medical school together. I think it felt like love then because I had nothing to compare it to. Aside from Joan that is, and that had been many years before.

"I planned a special night out so that I could ask her to marry me. I wrote her a poem and worked up a piece of music that she was particularly fond of. I played it for her on the piano at the restaurant that I'd rented out for the evening.

"Her reaction was ... indifferent. She told me I was *improving*," he said with a sneer. "When I asked her to marry me, she said she'd think about it. Like I was trying to sell her a bloody kitchen appliance. Then she asked me if I was ready to go. That was it ... the end of the evening.

"The next night, we went to a dinner party at my parents' house. She made a fool out of me in front of them, as well as all the department heads at King's hospital. She read the poem that I had written for her and told them about my serenading her the night before. Everyone had a hearty laugh before she turned down my proposal in front of all of them.

"She said that love was a *difficult* word. That I didn't understand the concept. Which I suppose, in retrospect, was true. Then she said something that hit below the belt, so to speak. It was the most humiliating experience of my life, Louisa. Vomiting and passing out in front of my surgical team when the blood sensitivity hit ... that paled by comparison."

Louisa pressed her cheek against his back and tightened her grip around his chest.

"I gave her the keys to my car, and I left. I walked the seven miles home, locked the bedroom door and laid awake all night.

"I heard her come home ... heard her knock, wanting to come in and go to bed, but I couldn't bear to face her. I didn't want her near me. She slept on the sofa that night, and I slipped out the next morning before she woke up."

Louisa raised up on her knees and kissed his cheek. Then draping her arms over his shoulders, she pressed her hands to his chest and her lips to his head.

"I drove to Portwenn. I'd brought Edith to the farm a few months before so that Joan could meet her. I don't think she approved. She didn't come right out and say it, but I could tell she didn't like Edith."

He took in a deep breath and rubbed his eyes. "Joan saved me that day, Louisa. Like Ruth saved me the day you left for Spain."

Louisa had tried to stay composed—strong for him. But the pain she felt for her husband now overwhelmed her and the tears began to flow freely.

"I am so, so, sorry, Martin. I'm sorry you've had the awful experiences that you've had in your life, and I'm sorry you had no one there for you when you really needed someone. But you have someone now."

He reached his left arm back and wrapped it around her waist before pulling her into his lap. His gaze was penetrating as he studied her eyes in the moonlight filtering through the bedroom curtains.

Her fingers touched his chest as she said hesitantly, "You used the same words when I told you I loved you, you know. The day after I got you drunk."

"I'm sorry?"

"That love is a difficult word. After we'd been drinking and you woke up on the kitch—"

"*Yes.* You don't need to remind me."

"I'm just saying ... I did know, Martin. I did know then that I loved you."

"Mm, yes. Maybe I was the one who was confused. But I do understand the concept now."

Raising his hand, he brushed the tears from her cheeks with his thumb.

"You are so very beautiful, Louisa."

She took his face in her hands. "I'm very happy that you could share such a very painful and intimate experience with me. To know you trust me—need me. Well, it makes me feel safe."

He blinked back at her. "I don't understand. Why would my *needing* you make you feel safe?"

Her fingers toyed with his ears. "It makes me feel secure. Makes me feel like an important ... or necessary person in your life. I know you won't leave me because you need me in your life."

"I won't leave you because I love you and would never do that to you. Not because I *need* you, Louisa."

"You don't *need* me?"

He threw his head to the side. "Neediness is not a very attractive quality. Strictly speaking, a person shouldn't *need* someone else. Obviously, James needs us at this point in his life. But for me to say that I need *you* would be—would be—be— well, rather thoughtless, opportunistic, and potentially egomaniacal."

"Really? So, you're saying you don't need me, then?"

Martin tried to ignore her hands which had begun to wander. "I'm *saying* ... that I appreciate that you listened to me tonight, but I don't need you to placate me. Don't you think that would be a bit narcissistic?"

Louisa reached under his vest and caressed his chest, allowing her thumbs to trace leisurely circles around his nipples. "No, I don't think that would be the least bit narcissistic." She leaned forward and nibbled gently on his earlobe. "I think I would enjoy very much, placating you."

He pulled his head back and screwed up his face. "I'm *trying* to say that I don't want you to feel I'm needy." A stream of air hissed from his nose. "I'm sorry. Perhaps I'm not expressing myself well."

"I think you're ... *expressing* yourself quite well, actually," Louisa said, giving him a coy smile as her eyes drifted south. "Hmm, quite well." Her fingers stroked lightly across his belly.

"Stop—that!" he said, batting her hand away.

"Martin ... there is absolutely nothing wrong with needing love and affection from another human being. Nor with needing to *give* love and affection—to give it and have it accepted. And when it comes to you, Martin, I can be rather insatiable on both the giving *and* the receiving end, so don't worry that head of yours about being needy."

She got up from his lap and crawled back into the bed. Now, if you don't mind, your expressing yourself has left me feeling quite—needy."

"Mm, yes."

Chapter 13

Jeremy stood at the counter the following morning, watching a pair of gulls squabble over a bit of rubbish that hadn't made it into the neighbour's bin.

The clear aggressor, the smaller of the two birds, lunged at the other, grabbing at its throat with its hooked bill. The larger gull was driven back against the concrete partition demarcating the property. It ducked its head and conceded defeat before flying off over the cottage roofs.

The aide pulled his now-full coffee cup out from under the wand of the machine. "So, what was that all about yesterday … with that patient you threw out of the surgery?"

Martin pulled an earplug from his ear, screwing up his face. "What did you say?"

"I *said* … what was that all about yesterday … with Mr. Britton!"

"For God's sake, Jeremy!" Martin said, grimacing. "You don't have to shout; just don't mumble! And turn around when you're talking to me!"

The young man returned to the table and pulled out a chair, taking a seat. "Sorry. Put that back in," he ordered, wagging a finger at the ear protection. "I'll speak a little louder. What was that all abou—"

"Well, I've heard the question now! You don't have to keep repeating yourself!"

Jeremy raised his eyebrows at him as he filled his glass with orange juice.

Martin pulled out the other earplug and scratched at his ear. "The arse was on the pull. I heard him saying some things to

Morwenna—which I won't repeat, so don't even ask—and I lost my temper. I guess. I'm not sure."

Jeremy cocked his head at him. "You're not *sure* if you lost your temper? I always feel pretty clear about it when I've thrown a wobbler."

He looked on as the distrait doctor stirred orange marmalade into his coffee.

"You mean you went into defensive mode?" he asked.

Martin took the pitcher of milk from his aide's hand and drizzled a bit on his toast. "Nooo! That's what's bothering me. I was standing in my consulting room one minute and the next thing I knew—" He waved his hand vaguely through the air and took a sip from his cup. "Next thing I knew, Britton was about to belt me in the face." He pulled his chin back and wrinkled up his nose at the cup before setting it back down on the table. "If you hadn't intervened, the idiot probably would have laid me out on the floor. So ... thank you."

"No problem, mate."

Taking a bite from his toast, the doctor wrinkled his nose and tossed it back on to his plate.

"Soggy, is it?" Jeremy asked.

Martin looked up at him, his brow furrowed. "Mm."

"You might find your coffee a bit lumpy as well." He picked up his boss's plate and cup and took them to the sink, then put two more slices of bread in the toaster before returning to the table with clean dishes.

"So you heard what the guy was saying and you went primal? You saw red?"

"I don't know. If that's the claptrap terminology for it, then yes, I guess I ... went primal."

There was a metallic pop as the toast sprang out of the toaster, and Jeremy got up from his chair to retrieve it. "There was a study done that suggested people who were first presented with threatening scenarios were more likely to see the colour red as being predominant when shown a picture that was actually equally red and blue.

He laid the toast on the doctor's plate and handed him the marmalade before refilling his coffee cup. "The same study showed that people who preferred the colour red were more likely to indicate they would harm another person."

"Sounds like an American study."

"Yeah, North Dakota State University if I remember correctly."

"Thought so."

"You should talk to Dr. Newell about it on Friday. He could probably explain the phenomenon in physiological terms. But don't let this get to you too much. It's happened to all of us at one time or another."

"Really? You, too?"

Jeremy gave him a crooked grin. "More times than I care to admit. I'm afraid we all have moments when our baser instincts get the better of reason. My dad seems to know how to push my buttons, and sometimes I can't think straight he makes me so furious. I lose control and say things I regret."

"So, it doesn't bother you to not be in control?" Martin asked, wagging his toast in the air.

"Yeah, it *bothers* me. You gonna eat that last sausage?" the aide asked, his fork hovering over it.

"Yes." Spearing the chunk of meat, the doctor flopped it on to his plate.

Jeremy sank back into his chair and crossed his arms in front of him. "Yeah, it *does* bother me. I've lost sleep over it a time or two. But there's nothing I can do about what's already happened, so I try not to worry about it. I just try to handle things differently the next time."

"I see." Martin pulled up his lower lip and nodded his head.

"You look tired. Did you sleep okay last night?" the young man asked, cocking his head at him.

"I was up late."

"Take a while in Truro, did it?"

Martin peered up at him self-consciously before taking another sip of his coffee. "No."

His aide gave him a knowing smile. "Ah, I see."

"What do you mean ... *I see?*" Martin snarled, narrowing his eyes at him.

"Nothing. Nothing." Picking up the pile of patient notes he'd been reviewing, he tapped them on the kitchen table, hesitating before saying, "Although, as the person charged with looking after your health care needs, it behoves me to remind you that getting an adequate amount of rest must be a priority. You might want to schedule your—*activities*—for a bit earlier in the evening."

"Mm." Martin grunted, staring back at him. "Perhaps it behoves *me* to remind you that sometimes our baser instincts get the better of reason."

Jeremy's eyes darted away from the doctor's penetrating gaze before he diverted the conversation away from the man's personal *activities*. "So, the patient list today ... anything I should know about?"

"No, it looks to be a rather prosaic lot. I do want to drive out to check up on Beth Sawle right after lunch, though."

"Martin, it's your second day back. You're not trying to sneak extra hours in already, are you?" Jeremy asked as he got up to put his dirty dishes in the dishwasher.

Martin tipped his head back to get the last drops from his cup before pushing himself up from the table. "If I was trying to *sneak* hours in, I wouldn't be announcing it first."

The aide leaned back against the counter and crossed one ankle over the other. "Well, just remember, I have the final say about how much is too much."

Lowering his head, the doctor gave the young man a sideways glance. "Rrright." He limped over with his plate and cup, passing them to his assistant before reclaiming his seat at the table.

Louisa breezed into the room with the baby perched on her hip. "Good morning, Jeremy!"

She brushed her hand against her husband's cheek as she walked up behind him. "Martin, remember, school dismisses at noon today—staff training. So, I won't be home for lunch. And ... erm, do you think you could handle James until Poppy gets here? I need to be at work early to meet with a mum before the kids start arriving."

He cleared his throat and reached for his son.

"You won't try to stand up with him, will you?" she asked, eyeing him uncertainly as she lowered the child on to his thigh.

"If you don't trust me with him, Louisa, then perhaps you shouldn't leave me alone with him!" He hissed out a breath and scowled.

Leaning down, she kissed him on the top of his head before pulling the high chair over and setting it next to him. "I trust *you* completely, but I'm a bit twitchy about those legs of yours."

Jeremy pushed himself away from the counter and moved towards the doorway. "I'll be in the consulting room if you need me, Martin. You have a good day, Louisa," he said as he left the kitchen.

"You, too, Jeremy."

Martin's gaze was fixed on her as she hurried over to grab her coat. She was wearing a pair of form-fitting black jeans that he found particularly attractive.

She turned around and, catching him in his perusal, she gave him a smile. "You know, I'm very much enjoying seeing that expression on your face again. I can't believe there was a time when I thought it was creepy."

"I believe we covered this already and determined that I *wasn't* being creepy. I was merely doing my job."

Louisa sighed. "All those opportunities missed—shame. Well, I guess I'll just have to make up for lost time, hmm?" She placed a gentle kiss on his lips before hurrying out the door, leaving him blinking his eyes at the empty space she left behind.

He looked down at his small son. "James, if you ever figure your mother out, perhaps you could enlighten me."

The boy let out a stream of giggles and squealed loudly. "*Daaa*-ee!"

His startled father braced himself for the ice pick onslaught, but aside from the adrenaline induced whoosh of blood surging through his ears, he was pain free.

"Maybe you *should* go in your high chair James, just to be on the safe side, hmm?"

After Poppy arrived to take over with the care of the baby, Martin went upstairs and had a short lie-down. When his alarm went off an hour later he went to the bathroom and splashed cold water on his face before taking on his nemesis— the stairs.

"Mornin,' Doc!" Morwenna greeted him cheerfully as she slipped into her chair and tossed her bag on to the floor. Her eyes flitted up and zeroed in on his ears. Craning her neck to get a better look she asked, "What'd ya got there, hearin' aids?"

"Don't be ridiculous, Morwenna. They're earplugs ... to reduce noise. Hopefully, it'll prevent any more headaches."

"Gawd, I hope so," she said, gathering together the morning's patient notes. "You nearly scared me to death yesterday, you know."

"I'm sorry about that." Martin toyed briefly with a kitschy figurine on her desk before adding, "Erm, Morwenna, I'm going to have someone come in to do some work on the surgery ... make it more secure. I'd like to have a proper reception desk put in for one thing. Wall off an area ... have a door with a lock. And a window you can close and lock as well."

He grunted and pulled a patient file from the stack in the girl's hands before limping off. "Send Mr. Moysey in when he arrives."

Morwenna watched, slack-jawed, as the consulting room door closed behind him. *Oh, crikey. You've gone and got the poor man all worked up about you now.*

Martin dropped into his chair, pulling his patient's file from its sleeve.

A dietician from Social Services had been working with the man for the last five months, and meals on wheels had been providing him with a nutritious dinner several times a week.

He had been coming in twice a month, prior to Martin's accident, and the doctor had been seeing steady improvement in both his overall physical condition as well as his mental affect. However, in the few times that Martin had occasion to speak to or be spoken to by him recently, his mood had seemed dark.

There was a rattling of the latch on the door, and the man entered the room.

"Hello, Mr. Moysey," the doctor said as he jotted the day's date down in his records.

"I was beginning to think I'd be dead and gone before you finally got back to seeing patients," the old man curmudgeoned. "It's been very inconvenient, you know. Driving all the way over there to Wadebridge every two weeks! And that quack over there doesn't even know how to conduct a proper examination!"

Martin halted the old man's downward movement into the chair abruptly. "Not there. If you're wanting a *proper* examination, then you need to get up on the couch." He waved his biro towards the other side of the room before shoving it into his breast pocket.

Mr. Moysey walked stiffly across the floor and climbed on to the table.

Pulling out his earplugs, the doctor stuffed them into his pocket. "Unbutton your shirt, please," he said, reaching for the blood pressure cuff.

He removed the stethoscope from around his neck and inserted the ends into his ears. "Are you getting plenty of fresh fruits and vegetables?"

Whispers of air whooshed from the bulb as the doctor inflated the cuff.

"I try. Your aunt drops a bag by now and then, and Social Services comes with my meals on wheels."

The elderly man gazed around the room. "You still diddle around with those kinds of things?" he asked as he poked a finger at the antique barometer sitting on the mantle.

"That was a one off. It's usually clocks that I *diddle* with."

"Don't you have anything better to do with your ti—"

"Stop talking," Martin said brusquely as he listened carefully to the old man's pulse sounds.

Ripping the cuff from the man's arm, he moved the bell end of his stethoscope to his chest. "Take a deep breath for me."

Mr. Moysey inhaled deeply, the action triggering a coughing spell.

Martin grimaced as the sound sent a stabbing pain through his left eye. He turned his head away from his patient and grabbed hold of the edge of the table to steady himself.

"Are you all right?" the elderly man asked in a tone two-thirds of the way between concern and annoyance.

"I'm fine. Let's try this again, Mr. Moysey," he said, returning the instrument to its previous position.

The creases deepened in Martin's brow as he listened to the wheeze in the man's airway. "How often do you use your inhaler?"

"I don't know. Couple times a day, I suppose."

"You shouldn't be needing it that frequently. And you shouldn't be labouring to breathe like this. That *cat* of yours—does it sleep with you?"

The old man's eyes snapped up at him. "What if it does?"

"That's a yes, I take it, then?"

Mr. Moysey's expression eased into one of chagrin. "The animal gets cold at night."

Martin wrapped his stethoscope around his hand and then laid the instrument on the table next to the couch. "I'm going to send you over to Truro to see an allergist and a pulmonologist. They'll—"

"No, you're not! I'm not driving all the way over there just because you can't be bothered!" The old man pulled his shirt closed and began to slip the buttons through the buttonholes. "It was hard enough to get to Wadebridge. How do you expect me to get all the way over to Truro?"

Martin hesitated, taking note of his averted gaze and rapid blinking. "Mr. Moysey, is there a problem you'd like to discuss with me? Do you have difficulty driving? Is your vision an issue?"

"Read your notes; I'm getting old!" His eyes darted up, making brief contact with the doctor's. "I find it ... intimidating. To be out on the highway, you know. It makes me nervous," he grumbled.

"If I could make arrangements with Social Services to have someone help you with transportation, would you be agreeable?"

Mr. Moysey raised his head slowly. "Do you really feel it's necessary?"

"I do. I suspect we may not have accurately identified the cause, or causes, of your breathing difficulties. I think we might be able to improve your quality of life if we can get you started on the proper treatment."

"Ohh, all right," he growled.

Martin returned to his desk and began to scratch notes into his patient's file.

Mr. Moysey slid off the exam couch and took a seat in the chair by the desk. "So, you still repair clocks then?" he asked.

"I do. I'm working on my aunt's grandfather clock at the moment."

"So, you probably wouldn't ... have time to take on another one then?"

The chair squeaked as Martin leaned back. "You have a grandfather clock that needs repairing?"

"No. It's a mantle clock. It quit working a couple of years back."

The doctor hesitated. "Would you like me to stop and take a look at it. Could be it's a simple fix."

Mr. Moysey gave him a small smile. "If you don't mind; I'd appreciate it."

Pushing himself up from his desk, Martin moved towards the door. "I'll have Social Services contact you about transportation over to the Royal Cornwall. And I could stop by this evening to take a look at your clock—if you don't already have plans."

The elderly man's head shot up, and he looked at him incredulously. "Plans? No, I don't have any plans."

"Good." He held the door for the man and walked with him into the reception room.

"Morwenna, could you please get Social Services on the phone for me."

"Yeah, course, Doc," she said, pulling a lollipop from her mouth and quickly wrapping it back up before shoving it into her desk drawer.

"Mr. Portman, could you draw a sample on Mr. Moysey and get it sent over to Truro—check his serum ascorbic acid level?" Martin asked.

"Yep, come on over and have a seat, Mr. Moysey," the assistant said as he pulled a syringe from a box on the desk. "Mr. Moysey, did you remember to fast after eating last night?"

Martin gave his patient a final glance before returning to his consulting room.

Chapter 14

It was half twelve by the time Martin and Jeremy had seen to the last of the morning's patients, and Martin's fatigue was obvious, even to Morwenna.

"Doc, yer draggin'. You oughta go have a lie-down before you *fall* down, don't you think?" she said as she followed him across the reception room.

"Be quiet, Morwenna. Get your bag and go home now," he said, snapping his fingers towards the door. "Jeremy, I'm going to grab something to eat before we head out to Beth Sawle's. I'll make something for you as well."

The aide gave his boss a scrutinising stare. "Morwenna's right. We'll get some lunch, and then I'll get your IV going. You can rest while it's infusing."

"Mm, we'll have to do it later. I told Miss Sawle we'd be out there between one and two o'clock," he said as he ducked under the stairs.

Jeremy pursed his lips and turned to the receptionist. "Morwenna, please call Beth Sawle and tell her it'll be closer to half three before Dr. Ellingham will be to her place."

Martin turned and limped back through the hallway. "Are you rescheduling my appointments?" he asked incredulously.

"I can *cancel* the home visit if you'd prefer. But *you're* not going anywhere until you've had some rest," the young man said, folding his arms across his chest.

The doctor glared back at him for several seconds then opened his mouth before snapping it shut. He hissed out a breath and abruptly left the room.

Morwenna watched the exchange, wide-eyed. "Wow, Jeremy! You're like The Doc Whisperer!" she giggled.

The aide shot her a black look. "Don't say that. Do you think I *like* talking to him that way?"

The grin on Morwenna's face fell away quickly. "Sorry, I didn't mean anythin' by it—honest."

Jeremy took in a deep breath. "It's okay," he said, raising a palm in front of him. "I do want to make it clear, though, that I have the utmost respect for that man."

He turned on his heel and went to join Martin in the kitchen.

Poppy had made egg and cress sandwiches, sliced tomatoes, and a fruit salad, sparing the two men from having to fend for themselves for lunch. It was a kind and unnecessary gesture that had not gone unnoticed by her employer.

"This is quite good, Poppy. And very nutritious as well," Martin said, avoiding eye contact with the girl.

Jeremy gave his girlfriend a nudge with his elbow. When she glanced up at him, he added a wink and an approving nod of his head, causing a pink blush to spread across her cheeks.

"Jeremy, Ed Christianson mentioned that you've had some training in therapeutic massage." Martin kept his eyes on his plate as he chopped up pieces of melon and banana before depositing them into his son's bowl.

"Yeah. It was in conjunction with the workshop on lymphatic massage. Why, does he think it's something that might prove helpful to you?"

"Da-ee. Uh—uh—uh—*uh*—*UH!*" James grunted and kicked his feet as he reached for the dish of carefully prepared fruit that his father held in his hand.

Martin looked up at him, following the boy's gaze. "Mm, yes," he said, setting the demanded bowl of food down on the high chair tray. James gave him a satisfied smile before plucking a bit of fruit from the bowl.

"He and Dr. Shekar, the neurologist, seem to think the headaches could be indicative of some cervical trauma. And yes, they both feel therapeutic intervention could be beneficial."

"I'd be happy to help you out. We could get your antibiotics taken care of while I look at your neck."

"Mmmm ... yes," Martin said, trying to stifle a yawn. "Rationalising time. Good idea."

"You go up and have a lie-down. I'll help Poppy with the clean up and be up in a bit," the aide said as he got to his feet and began to clear the table.

Martin gave a single nod of his head before pushing himself up and disappearing under the stairs.

"Is he okay?" Poppy asked, wagging a finger towards the hall. "He looks really, really tired."

"He *is* really, really tired." Jeremy gathered together the carton of milk and what was left of the bowl of fruit. He carried them to the refrigerator, shoving them on to a shelf before closing the door a bit more forcefully than necessary. "He doesn't have his strength back yet; he's, no doubt, not sleeping well; and despite the pain meds, he's gotta be hurting. Pain's exhausting. And between you, me, and the gatepost, he went back to seeing patients *way* too early."

Poppy slipped the plates into the rack in the dishwasher and then pulled a clean flannel out of the drawer. She ran it under the tap and began to wipe James Henry's face, followed by the high chair tray.

"I thought his doctors were friends of his. Why'd they tell 'im he could go back to work if it wasn't gonna be good for 'im? Seems kinda stupid." She lifted the baby from his seat and placed him on the floor in front of his toys.

Jeremy picked up the dishrag and swiped it back and forth across the table. "The convalescence period is very difficult for someone like Martin. He's used to being busy and needs to feel useful." The aide glanced up at his girlfriend. "And helping you with the dinner clean-up won't cut it," he said with an apologetic grin. "I think he feels…"

Clearing his throat, he took a seat, reaching for the newspaper lying on the chair next to him. "I've probably said more than I should have already, Poppy. Let's just say that in Martin's case, letting him go back to what he loves doing *is* good for him. It's just really nerve-wracking when you're the guy who's supposed to be watching out for him."

The childminder came up from behind and wrapped her arms around him. "Thanks for talkin' to me about it, Jeremy. I feel better now."

He leaned forward, double checking that the coast was clear, and then pulled Poppy into his lap. "I think it's very sweet that you're worried about him," he said tapping a finger on her nose. "And I'm glad you can see he's not just a grumpy old tosser."

The childminder's eyes grew round as she pushed back from him. "Oh, no! I mean … yeah, I used ta think he was scary. But then I figured if Mrs. Ellingham loves him enough to marry him, he must be okay. I think everyone in the village thinks that."

She tipped her head down and furrowed her brow. "I think there are still people who blame him for the Sports Day thing, though."

"The Sports Day thing?"

The girl opened her mouth to answer, but decided quickly to keep the words to herself. "I think *I've* said too much now. You probably should talk to Dr. Ellingham about it. I just heard it from someone who heard it from someone. You know."

"I see." Jeremy took a final glance down the hall before taking the girl's face in his hands and pressing his lips to hers. He took in a deep, ragged breath and shook his head. "I, erm … should go up and check on Martin."

"Yeah, I better get James off for his nap," she said as she slipped from his lap.

Martin was still sleeping when Jeremy looked in on him a short time later, so he pulled a chair in from the baby's room and sat, reading the day's news.

The sun, now very low in the sky throughout the short daylight hours, had dropped past the top window casing and shone through the curtains on to Martin's face. He squinted as he began to stir, and he pulled a hand up to shade his eyes. Propping himself up on his elbow, he rubbed his palm roughly over his face.

"Hope my paper rustling didn't wake you up," the aide said as he got to his feet. "You feeling any better?"

"I feel more rested, yes."

Jeremy went to the bathroom and returned with a tray of supplies. "Let's get this going, then I'll take a look at your neck," he said as he wiped the catheter port in his patient's wrist with an alcohol swab, flushed it with saline, and then snapped the tubing that snaked from the bottle hanging above the bed into the catheter. "Okay, let me take a look at you. Lie back down."

Martin began to roll to his stomach but Jeremy stopped him. "Nope, I need you on your back," he said, pulling the pillow out of the way and pressing his patient back on to the mattress.

"Try to relax." He leaned over and cupped his hands under Martin's neck, palpating along the muscles, starting at the base of his neck and working his way up. "Yeah, you're really tight back here. Feels like you have metal cables holding you together in there, not soft tissue. Blimey, Martin, this has to have been bothering you! Why didn't you say anything?"

Martin winced occasionally as the young man hit a particularly tender area. "It *wasn't* bothering me before you started poking around there," he grumbled. "And I do have a few more prominently painful bits to distract me."

"Yeah, I get that. These muscles are really ropey ... and crunchy," the aide explained as he massaged the area.

"Ropey and crunchy? That's your medical diagnosis, is it? Ropey and crunchy muscles?"

Jeremy rolled his eyes at him. "A considerable amount of fibrosis has developed where you've had tears in the muscle tissue. It creates a crunching sensation when I palpate the area. I'll work on that to get it broken down.

"And the muscles have tightened and shortened. The fibres have hardened. That's what I mean by ropey. I'll work on that as well. But first things first.

"Tell me if anything feels particularly sensitive back here," the aide said as he worked his fingertips up his patient's neck.

"Mmrrg! Martin groaned loudly and raised up when the young man's palpations reached the base of his skull. He squeezed his eyes shut as the pressure that Jeremy was applying to the back of his neck elicited a severe stabbing pain behind his left eye.

The aide held him down with his forearms, continuing his compression of the muscles as Martin pushed back, attempting to roll away from him.

The struggle between the two men continued as the aide mentally counted off ten seconds before releasing his grip.

"Well, that certainly activated your jump reflex," Jeremy said.

Martin lay, blinking his eyes to clear the tears and then pushed himself on to his elbow. His jaw tightened as his brow furrowed and his nostrils flared. "What—the *bloody hell* was that!"

"I think we found the source of your problem," Jeremy said, the right side of his mouth pulling up slightly into a nervous smile. "It's your left sub occipital muscle," he said, wagging a finger. "Where it's attached to the base of your skull. I'll apply several more ischemic compressions to the area today, and then we'll work on you a bit more over the course of the next few weeks."

"Oh, no we *won't!*" Martin said as he fired visual daggers at his aide. "You could've warned me that was going to hurt, you presumptuous little prat!"

Jeremy dropped down, taking a seat on the edge of the bed. "Look, Martin, I didn't warn you because I didn't want you tensing up. I wanted an honest reaction."

The doctor's face softened as he glanced over at him. "Was that honest enough for you?"

"I think you made yourself clear. I know it hurts, but I feel almost certain the damage to that muscle is causing the headaches. How does it feel now?"

Martin reached back and rubbed his hand across the nape of his neck. "Warm ... and a bit numb."

"Good, that's what we want." Jeremy glanced down at his watch and then gestured with a nod of his head. "Lie back down."

Peering warily at the aide, Martin huffed out a breath and lowered himself back on to the mattress.

Chapter 15

"I'm sorry ... about calling you a presumptuous little prat earlier," Martin mumbled as they wound their way out of the village.

Jeremy gave his shoulders a shrug. "I'll get over it."

"No. Presumptuous prat was uncalled for, and I'd like to apologise."

The younger man hesitated and furrowed his brow. "I think I can forgive you for the presumptuous prat part. It's the *little* part I'm going to have trouble getting past."

Martin snapped his head to the right and stared at him uncertainly. "Well, I wasn't intending for you to—to—I mean, it wasn't meant to be—to be—emasculating."

"Oh, really? You weren't trying to make me feel inferior, then? Yes, you are a lot bigger than most blokes, but there's no need to rub it in."

"Now wait a minute!" Martin spluttered. "I never suggested that you were in any way inferior because of your—your—vertical challenges. I just meant that—"

"Martin, calm down. You are so easy to wind up, mate." Jeremy shot him a broad grin and gave him a punch on the arm, causing him to flinch.

Martin's head whipped back to the left, and he fixed his gaze out his side window.

"Did I hurt your shoulder just now?" Jeremy asked. "Sorry if I did. I was trying to be careful."

Martin waved off the young man's concern. "That's not—I mean it didn't hurt. I just don't—it—" He regarded the young man with a contemplative eye. "Never mind."

Jeremy fidgeted as a period of awkward silence followed. "How did you think things went this morning?"

"Erm, fine. Better than yesterday ... most definitely."

"So, this Mr. Moysey ... is he always so morose?" the aide asked as he folded a stick of gum into his mouth. "You want some?" he offered, holding the pack out.

Martin's eyes darted up at him then back to his hand. "No. I don't like gum. But ... thank you."

"You're welcome. So, Mr. Moysey?"

"Yes, he *is* always that morose. *And* the man's about as recalcitrant as Churchill ... though not nearly as charismatic."

"That's kinda the impression I got." Jeremy reached over and turned down the heat. "That okay? You're not cold, are you?"

"No, a bit warm actually."

"So, what's Moysey's backstory?"

Martin yawned, running his palm over his face. "I don't know a whole lot about the man. His wife died a couple of years ago, and I think it threw him into a depression. He began hoarding. Filled his cottage to the rafters with stacks of newspapers, magazines, all manner of rubbish. He couldn't throw anything away.

"About five months ago, he began to have nose bleeds, joint pain, fatigue, and shortness of breath. I found a therapist to treat the depression and got him started on regular doses of ascorbic acid to treat the scurvy he had developed from his diet of tinned food. Meals on wheels delivers to him several times a week, and Ruth brings fruit and vegetables by periodically."

Jeremy turned the Lexus into the long driveway leading to the Sawle home.

"This shouldn't take long, Jeremy. I just want to listen to the woman's chest, make sure her lungs sound clear," Martin said pulling her patient notes from his shirt pocket.

The aide pulled the vehicle up next to the house and shifted it into park. "I'll go check things out then come back for you," he said, pushing the car door open.

The sound of a rooster's crowing was carried from a nearby farm by the gentle breeze that was blowing, reminding the doctor of the upcoming open house on Saturday. The door closed behind the aide with a solid thunk, and he leaned his head back and closed his eyes.

Louisa was excited about what she kept referring to as *the big day*, but he was dreading it. It wasn't just the questions about his health he knew he would be peppered with. He felt an emptiness at the farm now since all the changes had been made.

He used to feel a bit of a connection to Auntie Joan when he was at the farm. Ruth had tidied the place up, but there had still been reminders of his deceased aunt everywhere.

Books he could remember perusing as a child. Those about nature and the books of maps being favourites.

The bowl of *the keepers*, as Joan used to say—seashells they would find on their walks on the Northwest Cornwall beaches.

The old three-legged milking stool with the funny handle sticking out from the side of the seat, relegated to the back corner in the kitchen until it was called upon for higher duty.

Those early mornings with Auntie Joan had been magical for a small boy from the city. The morning dew would be glistening on the grass, and a chorus of reed buntings would fill his ears with their bubbly song as they walked to the barn.

Joan, the milking stool swinging from her hand, would shake her head and give him a wry smile as he pretended to hold a cigar between his fingers. First bringing his hand to his lips, he would then pull it away again as he blew out a breath, imagining the moisture that condensed in the chilly, damp, Cornish air to be a puff of smoke.

But now, most of the mementos had been carried off by the bin man so the house could be made *presentable* to future paying guests.

Seeing his aide approaching, Martin took in a deep breath to relieve the tightness that had developed in his chest. Then he pushed his door open and pulled himself to his feet.

"All okay?" he asked.

"Yep. She appears to be healthy. Let me give you a hand, the ground's pretty uneven," Jeremy said as he came around the car. "She's a sweet old thing, eh?"

Martin gave him a quick glance before refocusing his attention on the path ahead of him. "Yes, she's quite ... nice."

Beth Sawle sat by the living room window in a dingy-green wingback chair.

"Oh, Dr. Ellingham, you shouldn't have troubled yourself to come all the way out here just to check up on me!" the old woman said as she smiled at him, self-consciously smoothing out the front of her blouse.

"Nonsense, Miss Sawle. You're my patient, and it's my duty to follow up on your recent illness. How have you been feeling? Any residual cough?"

"I'm fine, Doctor. Those antibiotics work wonders, don't they?"

"Yes, they do. Jeremy, could you, erm ... give me a hand?" he asked, pointing a finger towards the dining room.

Jeremy pulled a chair away from the table and set it next to Beth before the doctor took a seat.

"Could you ... erm ..." Martin gesticulated again, this time towards his medical bag, just out of reach on the end of the coffee table.

The aide set the bag down beside him and pulled out the stethoscope. "There you go."

"Mm, thank you," Martin said as he plugged the ends into his ears.

"Could you undo the top three buttons of your blouse for me, please, Miss Sawle."

Jeremy looked on as his boss scrutinised his patient.

"Take a deep breath in. And out. And in again."

He shifted the instrument up slightly and listened to the woman's heart before pulling the stethoscope from his ears and flipping it behind his neck.

"How's your appetite?"

The old woman straightened in her chair. "Oh, much better now that I'm over the pneumonia, Doctor. Like I said, those antibiotics work wonders. I eat like a teen now!"

"It's a bit chilly in here. Are you warm enough with it this cool?" He wrapped a blood pressure cuff around the woman's arm before reinserting the stethoscope into his ears.

"Oh, I'm fine. I think my thermostat's gotten a bit unreliable in my old age. I used to always be too *cold*." she said with a brittle laugh.

Martin took hold of her fingers and examined them. "I noticed your hands were trembling when you were unbuttoning your blouse. Does that cause you difficulty when you're trying to hold a cup of tea, or eat soup ... that sort of thing?"

"Well, yes. But you just wait. It'll happen to you, too, in another thirty years or so. You can't stop Father Time ... or Mother Nature for that matter."

She shifted uncomfortably under the doctor's penetrating gaze.

"What about your toilet habits? Have you noticed any changes there?" Martin asked.

Beth's eyes darted from one man to the other as her face flushed. "Well, I do have to run to the loo more than usual. If that's what you mean."

"Bowel or waterworks?"

Miss Sawle folded her hands in her lap and gave him a sideways glance. "The first one."

"I see." Martin coiled his stethoscope around his hand and pushed it back into his bag. Then, leaning forward, he began to palpate the woman's neck.

He reclined in his chair and took in a deep breath. "Miss Sawle, I'm going to have Mr. Portman draw some blood. I'd like to check your thyroid levels. Make sure that your— *thermostat*—is working properly. I should get the results from the lab in a couple of days. I'll plan to stop by again on Thursday afternoon between one and two."

"Better make that three to three-thirty, Dr. Ellingham," Jeremy interjected. "I think you have some commitments earlier in the afternoon."

Martin glanced over at him. "Thursday, between three and three-thirty, then."

The sun had dropped behind the trees by the time Martin and Jeremy pulled away from the Sawle home, and Martin was once again beginning to feel weary. He laid his head back and closed his eyes, dozing off quickly.

He was awakened a short time later by a firm tap on his arm. "Martin, wake up. Isn't that your little mate there?" the aide said, slowing the Lexus to a crawl.

He rubbed a hand over his face and shook his head. "Yeah, stop the car." Pushing his door open, he pulled himself from the vehicle.

A bicycle lay in the verge, and Evan Hanley's small form was hunched over as he sat in the middle of the gravel roadway.

"What on earth is going on, Evan? Get out of the way of the traffic for goodness' sake!" Martin said.

The little boy tipped his head back to look up at him, tears streaking his dusty face. "I skinned my knee, Dr. Ellig-am, and it hurts!"

"Can you move your leg? Wiggle it around for me," Martin said, his eyes darting from the child to the roadway as he watched for oncoming vehicles.

Evan straightened his leg out and wiggled his foot back and forth. "It works, but it hurts!" he sobbed.

"Okay, okay. Get on up, and I'll take a look at you. But you can't sit there in the middle of the road." Martin reached down with his left hand and pulled the boy to his feet.

"Jeremy, would you set him on the boot for me please? Then get my bag."

The aide hoisted the boy up on to the Lexus, and Martin limped over to examine his second patient of the afternoon.

He pulled his handkerchief from his back pocket and wiped the child's face before tucking it into his hand. "All right. It's okay now. Let's see what you've done to yourself."

He peered into the rip in the child's jeans, then back up at him. "Well, Evan, I can either pull your trousers off to treat you, or I can cut that tear open further."

The boy laid back and stuck his feet up in the air. "You better pull 'em off. My mum will want to patch 'em. I don't gots that many."

"Mm, yes. Jeremy, could you lend a hand here? Evan, you know my assistant, Mr. Portman, don't you? Can he help you with your trousers?"

The seven-year-old looked from Jeremy back to Martin. And, after a slight hesitation, he nodded his head.

He kept his gaze fixed on the doctor as the aide set the medical bag down on the boot lid. Jeremy then removed the child's shoes before pulling his jeans down over his legs.

"Well, you've done a jolly good job on this knee, but I think you'll live," Martin said, giving the boy a small smile.

"Jeremy, do you have an unopened bottle of water in your backpack?"

"Er, yeah ... hang on."

"What were you doing out here on your bike, Evan? It's not a safe place to be riding, you know. Drivers can't see around the curves. You could have been hit," Martin said as he inspected the child for any other injuries.

"I was looking for Potato," he said, turning glum. "He ran off, but I couldn't find 'im. He's not very 'sponsible, and he might get *lost* on his own."

Gravel skittered behind them suddenly as a large red dog bounded up, sliding to a stop next to the car.

"Oh, gawd! What's that?" Martin groaned.

"*That's* Potato!" Evan said, a broad grin spreading across his face. "He's my dog! He's an Iris shredder! Miss Babcock says that's his brand."

"Potato?" the doctor said, screwing up his face. "That's a ridiculous name for a dog!"

"Nuh-uh! It's not! You should see 'im dig up the potatoes in Miss Babcock's garden. He's really, *really* good at it.

"Miss Babcock doesn't like it, though. She yells at him. And she yells *really* loud at him when he digs up her flowers.

"She says he drives her clear to Bodmin when he does that. But I told her he can't help it, 'cause that's what he was made for. It's her own fault; she should'a gotten a different brand. I don't think it's very fair to tell Potato he can't act like he was made to act, do you, Dr. Ellig-am?"

"Mm, perhaps not. Let's get this knee cleaned up, shall we?"

Martin washed the blood and grit away from the boy's wound, swallowing back the saliva that kept filling his mouth and turning his head to conceal the occasional gag.

"Want me to do it?" the aide asked.

"*No!*" Evan said. "I want Dr. Ellig-am to do it!"

The doctor wiped the perspiration from his brow with a swipe of his sleeve and shook his head. "I'm okay, Jeremy. Can you hand me some gauze pads and the lidocaine spray? And I'll need the disinfectant."

Martin patted the boy's knee dry with the gauze then applied the lidocaine to numb it.

The corners of Evan's mouth spread out across his face. "Wow, that feels lots better!"

"Good. I'm going to put some disinfectant on the wound now, and that might sting a bit. Okay?"

"Errrr, do you gots to? Maybe you could just put the bandage on it. *That'll* keep the germs out."

"Yep, I have to," Martin said, flooding the area with the bacteria killing liquid before the little boy could protest any further. "There, all done."

Evan sat himself up, inspecting his wound. "Hey, it looks like I've been in the wars, doesn't it, Dr. Ellig-am? Maybe it'll even leave a scar."

"Yes, Evan. That should leave you with a really good scar. And yes, it *does* look like you've been in the wars."

Martin jumped as Potato suddenly stood up, stretching his front legs out in front of him on the lid of the boot.

The animal's manoeuvre earned him a look of derision from the doctor. "Disgusting," he sneered.

As if on cue, the setter swung his head over, getting a quick shot in at Martin's face with his tongue. A long string of viscous drool dripped from the dog's mouth, accumulating in a puddle on his sleeve before spilling over on to the boot lid.

"Oh, gawd. Look what it's done now!"

He gave his arm a shake, trying to rid it of the worst of the remaining slaver. "Gawd!"

"I can help you with that, Dr. Ellig-am," Evan said as he took the handkerchief and smeared the slippery deposit around on the doctor's sleeve.

Martin screwed up his face as he watched the mess being extended further up his arm.

The boy reached up and gave him a pat on his shoulder. "All shipshape and Bristol fashion now, Dr. Ellig-am."

"Mm, right. Let's finish up here, shall we."

Pulling a Telfa pad from the drawer in his bag, Martin placed it over the boy's knee before taping it on securely.

He turned to put his supplies away, and the Irish setter seized the opportunity, reaching his large head over and taking a swipe with his tongue at the boy's freshly bandaged knee.

"Noo! You'll contaminate the wound!" Martin yelled pushing the dog away.

The animal fell back on its side, yelping repeatedly in apparent agony.

"Oh, come on! It's not that bad!" Martin said defensively as his assistant hurried to Potato's aid.

"I think you broke his leg, Martin," Jeremy said, running a hand along the wounded appendage.

"I didn't! I barely touched him!"

Potato let out a blood-curdling wail and struggled to his feet. He staggered in concentric circles, one hind leg held in the air.

Martin looked on, horrified, as the dog finally dropped to the ground at his feet.

It stared blindly, its eyes fixed and unblinking for several seconds, before giving a few last feeble yelps of pain.

The animal's eyes rolled back in its head. Then the lids slid shut before its mouth gaped slightly, opening and closing as it struggled for air in its death throes.

Watching the drama play out, Martin's eyes grew round. *Oh, bloody hell! I've killed the boy's dog!* he thought, his heart sinking.

He took in a deep trembling breath then glanced over at his aide. "Jeremy, help me get down there, then bring me my bag!"

The young man hurried over and supported Martin as he lowered himself to the ground. Groaning, he put his weight on his left knee while trying to move his less flexible right leg out of the way. Then he dropped on to his backside.

"Here you go, Martin," Jeremy said as he set the medical bag down before joining him in the dirt.

Martin took a moment to gather his thoughts, then taking hold with a gauze pad, he lifted the dog's upper lip, checking the colour of the mucous membranes.

Pulling the lower lid down, he looked at the conjunctival lining of the animal's eye. It appeared pale to Martin, but then again, dogs weren't his speciality.

The eyelid remained open as he moved his hand away. The closed, milky-coloured nictitating membrane, or inner eyelid, gave the dog an appearance that he found reminiscent of his medical school cadaver.

He then ran a large palm gingerly along the dog's ribcage and down the injured leg. Potato responded with a barely perceptible whine.

A panic grew in Martin as the fuzzy, red chest rose one last time before the dog breathed out heavily then quieted completely.

He grabbed frantically for his stethoscope, plugging the ends into his ears and slapping the bell to Potato's chest. *Lub-dub, lub-dub, lub-dub.*

His brow furrowed as he cocked his head at the dog. "It has a heartbeat. Sounds perfectly normal. And normal respirations, too ... if I remember correctly," Martin said, thinking back to his times spent with the mongrel dog of his childhood.

"Evan, is there any chance Potato could have gotten hold of something toxic?"

The boy sat on the lid of the boot, looking down at the scene on the ground. He furrowed his brow and scratched at his head. "Are jelly babies toxic?"

"Strictly speaking, yes. But I was thinking more in terms of a poison of some sort. Rat poison, perhaps?"

Evan shook his head vigorously. "I'd *never* feed Potato rat poison, Dr. Ellig-am! It wouldn't be good for him!"

Martin closed his eyes and sighed heavily. "Yes, I realise that, Evan. I *am* a doctor. I'm merely trying to work out the cause of your dog's aberrant behaviour."

He looked from the dog to the boy and his shoulders sagged. "Evan—if I hurt your dog—" He tried to swallow back the constriction in his throat. "I'm very, very sorry."

He began to struggle to his feet and Jeremy hurried over to assist him. "Let's see if we can get him into the back seat of my car, Jeremy ... get him over to Wadebridge. There must be a veterinarian there."

"Is a veterinarian like a librarian?" Evan asked. He sat cross-legged with his chin in his hand, seemingly unfazed by the sorry state of his pet.

"No, it's a doctor who treats animals. Potato obviously needs medical assistance, and I don't know anything about treating dogs."

"Oh, you don't gots ta take 'im to the doctor. He's just pretendin'."

"Pretending?"

"Yeah, he gots a *really* good imagination."

Martin's head swung down, and he leaned closer, peering inquisitively at the setter.

The dog's eyebrow twitched slightly and his eye opened. He leapt suddenly to his feet, his tongue lolling happily.

Martin blinked back his astonishment. "*That* creature was somatising!"

Evan slipped off the car and dropped to the ground. "He's not s'tising, Dr. Ellig-am, he's zagerating."

"Somatising, Evan. And that animal *was* somatising!" he said, wagging a finger.

"What's s'tising, Dr. Ellig-am?"

"*So—ma—ti—sing*! It means that dog of yours is presenting physical symptoms with no apparent physical cause. I've never seen anything like this!"

The seven-year-old gave him a quizzical look and Martin huffed. "He's pretending, Evan."

"Dr. Ellig-am, Potato's not *really* my dog. He's Miss Babcock's dog. I'm just *so—ma—ti—sing*."

Chapter 16

"Well, now what?" Jeremy asked as he looked from Evan, who stood with his arm slung over Potato's neck, back up to his boss.

Martin hissed out a heavy breath and shook his head slowly. "I guess we'll run Evan on home," he said. Pulling his arm up, he glanced at his watch. "I better call Louisa or she'll be thinking the worst. Could you get Evan's bicycle into the boot?"

"Yeah. Can you help me out, Evan?"

"Sure, I'm good at helping!"

"Here, Evan. How 'bout you be in charge of the keys," Martin said as he took them from his assistant's hand and held them up in front of the boy.

The child looked up at him, wide-eyed. "Can I really?"

"If you promise not to lose them ... then, yes."

"Oh, I won't lose 'em! Thanks, Dr. Ellig-am!" he said before gambolling up to the young assistant.

Martin walked wearily to the passenger's side of the car and pulled the door open before letting himself fall into the seat. The sun had just dropped drop below the horizon, and in late autumn the blue hour was short-lived. It would be dark by the time they reached the Hanley home.

He pulled his phone from his breast pocket and rang his wife.

The left corner of his mouth pulled up, ever so slightly, when he heard Louisa's voice on the other end of the line.

"Hello," he answered her softly. "I just wanted to let you know that Jeremy and I are running late. Don't wait dinner on me. I'll reheat a plate when I get—

"Louisa, I realise that. But this was unavoid—

"Can we talk about it when—" Martin began to squirm at his wife's increasingly frosty tone.

"Louisa—

"Louisa! Yes, I *am* aware of the promise that I made, but this was unavoidable. I can explain it all la—

"Yes, I *am* tired, but I'll get home as soon as I can."

He closed his eyes, his arm feeling noticeably heavy as it supported the phone.

"Louisa, I need to go. I'll see you when I get home," he said, his fatigue threatening to get the better of him.

He rang off, returned his mobile to his pocket, and then let his head drop back against the headrest.

He was awakened a short time later by a sharp tug on his sleeve.

"Dr. Ellig-am!" a small voice whispered. "Potato wants to say goodbye to you!"

"Mmmm ... what?" Martin slurred huskily from that murky place somewhere between sleep and wakefulness.

"Do you wanna say goodbye to Potato before he has ta go back home?"

"I don't care what you do with the potatoes."

The little boy giggled, then flopped forward suddenly, laying his upper body across the doctor's legs. "I don't gots *that* kind of potatoes!" he said, no longer bothering to use his *small voice* as Jeremy had requested.

Martin shook his head and straightened himself in the seat before clearing his throat.

He glanced down at the small, warm body stretched out across his lap, and his place in time and space began to come into focus.

The child kicked his feet up behind him, smacking his heels against his bum, and Martin tried briefly to worm his way out from under him as the boy's pestle-like elbows ground into the tender wound in his thigh.

"Evan, you're hurting me!" he yelped hoarsely.

The boy pushed himself back before rubbing his hand lightly across the doctor's leg. "You okay now, Dr. Ellig-am?" He squatted down slightly and cocked his head, peering up at him.

"I'm fine, Evan," Martin said, gritting his teeth against the sting that still remained.

"We're at Miss Babcock's house, so Potato gots ta say goodbye to you."

"Mm, yes. Jeremy, could you—"

"I'm already on it, mate," the aide said as he gave a tug on the dog's collar. "Come on, Evan. Let's get your buddy home."

Martin watched the boy bounce along next to Jeremy. The child seemed to have an almost irrepressibly positive temperament. That had worked in his favour thus far, but as Martin knew all too well, abuse could chip away at the sunniest disposition. Though he had never heard the word *sunny* used to describe his own congenital constitution.

He might still be the shy, introverted, gruff, rude and monosyllabic tosser that he was if he had spent his entire childhood in the loving care of Joan and Phil. In the words of his philosophical young friend—*sunny* is just not what he was made for. It was not his brand.

He was jarred from his self-reflection by the solid metallic click of the latch on the rear car door, and the air was filled suddenly with childish chatter.

"...should cook 'em up and let 'im eat 'em for dinner. *Then* they wouldn't just be endin' up in the bin!"

"How do you suppose Potato prefers his—potatoes?" Jeremy asked the boy, giving him a gentle poke in the stomach as he flopped back into his seat.

Evan looked back at him, screwing up his face and furrowing his brow. "Probably in bangers and mash. He likes sausage a lot! Miss Babcock could boil up all those potatoes he digs up, squish 'em up with some bangers and give 'im that for his dinner. Then she wouldn't have ta buy dog food. She's always complaining about him eating her out of house and home. She could save herself a lot of money doin' that, I bet!"

"Yeah, she could do that I suppose. But it'd be quite a bit of work for Miss Babcock. Having to cook meals for her dog as well as something for herself. She's not getting any younger you know," Jeremy said as he snapped the boy's seat belt into place.

Evan scowled at the aide. "You can't get *younger*, just *older*."

Jeremy opened his mouth to explain himself, but was brought up short by his boss. "Jeremy, leave it! Let's get the boy home. *I'm* not getting any younger waiting for you two to discuss the dietary habits of that animal."

"Watch your fingers!" the assistant said, shoving the child's door shut before getting into the driver's seat.

"Have you met Miss Babcock?" the aide asked as he turned the key in the ignition.

"The name's not familiar. Could be she's been into the surgery, though, and I don't remember it." Martin squeezed his palm against the back of his neck and pressed his chin to his chest, releasing a soft, inadvertent groan in the process.

"Well, she seems awfully frail to be living all the way out here by herself."

"Aw, she's not so frail; she's just really old," Evan piped up from the back seat. "I think maybe like ... mmm, *fifty* or something."

"Wow, fifty! And she still manages to drag herself out of bed and get the paper in off the front steps every morning!" Jeremy said, giving his boss a smirk.

Martin narrowed his eyes at him.

"Yeah, she's old. But she gots a few good years left in her," Evan said, pushing his feet against the back of Martin's seat.

The doctor peered behind him. "Get those filthy shoes off of there, Evan! Now I'm going to have to clean that up!" he groused.

"Oh, that's okay. You'll have to clean all the dirt and dog slobber that came outta Potato anyway. You can just do the other at the same time. Piece of piss!"

Martin looked incredulously at his assistant then back at the small mouth which had just uttered the vulgar words.

"I beg your pardon?"

"What's a pardon?" the boy asked guilelessly.

"Evan, piece of piss isn't a proper thing to say."

"But the *other* means something different, Dr. Ellig-am."

"*What* other?"

"The other *word!*"

Martin shook his head as he tried to tamp down his growing annoyance. He twisted in his seat to look back at the boy, sending pain shooting through his ribs and abdomen.

"Bloody hell!" he squeaked as he held his arm against his front, waiting for his agony to ease.

"Bad move there, mate. You okay?" Jeremy asked as he scrutinised him.

"I'm—fine!"

Evan attempted to justify his choice of words. "See, if you say piece of piss, it means something's really, really easy. But if you say piece of—" The boy clamped his mouth shut when he glanced up at the doctor's glare.

He stared glumly at the floor. "I wasn't going to say the actual *word*. I was just *tryin'* to s'plain to you." the boy said, his voice cracking as he smacked his fist twice on the seat next to him.

All three sat in silence as the Lexus traversed the gravel drive leading to the Hanley farm. Jeremy shifted the car into park, and Martin heard Evan's seat belt click.

The boy jumped out and slammed the door demonstratively before stomping off towards the barn behind the house.

The doctor's head dropped to his chest as he closed his eyes and let air rush from his nose. "I'll be back in a few minutes."

Jim Hanley answered the door and stepped out on to the porch, preventing Martin from entering the house. "What are *you* doin' 'ere?"

"I brought your son home. He had an accident with his bike on the road near St. Kew's. He skinned up his knee pretty good, but I cleaned it up and dressed the wound. I'll take a look at it again tomorrow. But in the meantime, I'll leave this Calpol with you. He'll be uncomfortable once the anaesthetic that I used wears off," he said, handing the bottle to the man.

"Boy's always wanderin' off. Gettin' 'imself into trouble. I'll give 'im a right good rollickin' so's he doesn't bother you again, Doc."

"That's not necessary, Mr. Hanley. It wasn't a bother at all. My assistant and I happened to be passing when we saw him.

"I do have a bit of a mess left in my car, however. I was thinking that having Evan come over after school to help me clean it up might be a more appropriate disciplinary action than a rollicking would be."

"Well, long as you bring 'im home when yer done with 'im. I don't wanna hafta be drivin' all the way into the village to collect 'im."

"Understandable. It's a jolly good mess, so we may need a bit of time. I might have to bring him back after dinner, but I can bring him back with a full stomach."

Martin took a step away from the house before hesitating. "How are you doing? Is the issue with the alcohol sorted?"

"Yeah, yeah, yeah. Sure, Doc. Everything's good there. No need fer ya ta give it another thought," the man said, forcing a smile.

"Good." Martin stared pointedly at him and added, "He's a fine boy, Mr. Hanley. You should be proud of him. He's going to have a very sore knee for a while so maybe you should give him a pass this time—skip the rollicking."

Jim gave Martin a sharp grunt and then turned to go back inside.

The doctor limped around to the barn and found Evan huddled up against the same rock ledge where he had found him months before.

"May I join you?"

The boy shot a quick glance up before tipping his head back down, but not before the yard light illuminated the tears on his cheeks.

Martin sank back on to the wall and patted the rocks next to him.

Evan reluctantly climbed up and took a seat.

"I'm sorry that I was impatient with you, Evan. I'll try to do better in future."

The boy's shoulders shuddered as he spoke between ragged breaths. "Please don't think I'm bad 'c-cause I didn't say it— properly. I *know* I'm not supposed to say the *s* word. We g-get 'tention at school for sayin' *that*. But we *don't* get 'tention f-for sayin' piece of—of—of—" he pulled in a wet breath through his nose. "Of the—the other thing. What *you* said wasn't proper."

"Ah, I see." Martin now understood Evan's frustration and confusion caused by the inconsistencies in rules.

"Well, I'll try to be more understanding in future. But I do want you to try to understand what *I* was saying.

"There are certain words and phrases that many people find offensive. Words that give them a bad feeling when they hear them. We say those words are *vulgar,* and it's best to try to remember not to use them."

"Kay." The little boy scuffed the heel of his shoe against the wall and looked up at the doctor. "Do you still like me, then?"

Martin swallowed back the lump in his throat. "Yes, Evan. I still like you. You're a very fine young man."

Evan pulled his feet under him and rose up on his intact knee, wrapping his arms around the doctor's neck. Martin tensed at the unaccustomed bodily contact. His arms rose stiffly, and he gave the boy an awkward hug in return.

He cleared his throat as the boy jumped down from the rocks. "Evan, I'd like for you to come to the surgery after school tomorrow and help me clean up the mess in the back of my car. I'm not punishing you, but you're the one responsible for the mess being made, so you should be the one responsible for cleaning it up."

Evan's eyes shifted to the house. "I don't know if my dad will allow me to be 'sponsible."

"I already spoke with your father, and he gave his approval."

The little boy's pursed lips spread into a broad grin. "That'll be fun! You can be my assistant!"

"Mm, yes. Well, just don't forget to show up."

"Nope, I *won't!*" Evan ran several yards towards the house before reversing course. "Dr. Ellig-am, I just thought I should tell you. You shouldn't say 'bloody hell'. It's not proper, and some people might find it 'fensive."

"Yes. Thank you, Evan. Goodnight."

Martin walked to the car feeling a perplexing stew of emotions.

"Those dainty semantics get you into trouble?" Jeremy asked as Martin got into the Lexus and pulled the door shut behind him.

"Something like that. Now be quiet and drive."

Chapter 17

It was almost half six by the time Martin and Jeremy returned to the surgery. Louisa glanced up as she saw them pass by the kitchen window and she took in a deep breath. "Don't lose your temper with him," she mumbled to herself.

Martin hesitated for a few seconds before taking hold of the knob and pushing through the door.

James and Louisa had just finished eating, and Louisa was putting the last of the dishes into the dishwasher. She looked up at him briefly, her lips taut as she dropped a handful of silverware into the rack. It clattered sharply as it fell against the other utensils.

Martin went to the high chair and stroked the backs of his fingers across his son's warm, silky head.

"Just set my bag in the consulting room please, Jeremy, then head on home. I appreciate you staying so late today."

"No problem. Try to get to bed earlier tonight. You're worn out," the young man said as he headed under the stairs.

Martin scowled his annoyance at him. The innocent comment would not serve to strengthen his position in the row he sensed coming.

He let his hand slide down so that his palm rested against James's cheek, watching his wife's abrupt movements as she worked with her back to him.

He waited for some time, his hand in constant contact with his son, the sensation easing the stress he was beginning to feel. His wife had barely acknowledged his presence, so he released a silent sigh and moved towards the hall.

"Oh, no you don't, Martin Ellingham! Don't you dare go off before we discuss this!"

Martin stopped in the doorway and turned slowly. "Louisa, I didn't in—"

"Don't make excuses, Martin," she said as she yanked the tea towel from her shoulder and wiped the drips of water from her hands. "You promised, when I agreed to let you go back to work this soon, that you would start out working *two* hours a day. And what time is it now?"

Martin opened his mouth to speak, but his words were clipped short before they reached the air.

"And don't you *dare* remind me you only worked two hours *yesterday*! I don't want to hear any excuses for your eight-hour day today, either!"

Martin shrugged his shoulders and shook his head at the futility of continuing the conversation any further.

"Martin! Where are you going?"

"Shower!" he snapped back.

Louisa watched as he disappeared around the corner, a righteous indignation smouldering in her. She pursed her lips and squeezed her eyes shut, slapping the tea towel against her thigh.

Martin made his way up the stairs, too tired even to bend over and pick up James Henry's purple dinosaur, which was lying on the top step.

He pulled his tie from around his neck and tossed it on to the dresser as he came into the bedroom. His shirt landed on the chair next to it before cascading off the seat and on to the floor.

When he stepped into the shower a short time later, he turned the nozzle to the side, leaned his forehead against the wall and allowed the warm water to soothe his aching body.

He watched as a brown thread from one of the bath towels floated aimlessly at his feet before being caught up in the vortex of water that was being sucked down the drain. He had about as much control over his life at the moment as that hapless piece of thread.

Louisa hesitated on the opposite side of the door. She wanted to knock, to go into the bathroom and wrap her arms around him, telling him how much she loved him. But she was also angry, and her anger sent her in the opposite direction. She decided to leave him be to go bathe James and get him ready for bed.

Feeling somewhat better after his shower, Martin returned to the bedroom and began to gather up the clothes he had left strewn haphazardly around the room.

As he leaned over to pick his shirt up from the floor he spotted James Henry's soft cat which had long ago gone missing. It lay, hidden, under the foot end of the bed.

He dropped on to the mattress and reached down, retrieving the wayward animal. The cat led to the discovery of a number of other items, mostly articles of his wife's clothing. He also found one unused nappy, several elastic hair bands, an item that Louisa referred to as a scrunchie, and the purple sleeping mask that she had taken to using for a period of time.

He gathered up the cache of stray objects, piling them on the table next to her side of the bed. *For a woman who won't leave the house without being perfectly arrayed, she certainly doesn't have an issue with leaving the house in disarray!*

The mantel clock over the fireplace ticked steadily, and Martin stroked his fingers over its curved top.

He groaned, remembering the commitment he had made to Mr. Moysey. Sighing, he pulled a clean set of clothes from his drawer.

Louisa lifted her son from the bathwater, his arms and legs flailing in protest. "Oh, stop that young man; look at these pruney fingers! You've been in there long enough," Louisa said as she dried his solid little body.

"You're getting to be such a big boy, aren't you!" James babbled back at his mother, his nonsensical baby chatter interspersed with the occasional "Mum, Mum, Mum" as he reached for her ponytail.

"Let's go find your Daddy ... say goodnight." Louisa made her way downstairs with the boy balanced on her hip. She expected to find Martin in the lounge reading one of his medical journals, but all was quiet.

Carrying the baby to the kitchen, she set him in the high chair to eat his bedtime snack of cereal and milk. A bright pink sticky note in the middle of the kitchen table caught her attention. She peeled it away and read her husband's familiar scrawling script. *I told Mr. Moysey that I'd stop tonight and take a look at his clock. I'll be back shortly—Martin.*

She fought back an immediate sense of panic, taking in a deep breath before ringing Ruth.

About the time Ruth answered her phone, Martin was knocking on Mr. Moysey's door. He was breathing heavily and his limbs ached. But he had made it on his own. And venturing out in the dark meant that he didn't have to endure the stares and comments that were sure to come from the villagers during the daylight hours.

"Well, it took you long enough!" the old man groused as he stepped to the side to let the doctor into the house. "I was beginning to think you'd taken a wrong turning and gone over the cliff."

"I didn't come here to listen to your monotonous cavilling, Mr. Moysey. Where's the clock?" Martin asked, his head snapping side to side as he conducted a quick visual search.

"It's a *mantel* clock. That should be your first clue," the old man grumbled.

Martin's patience was rapidly growing thin with the man's disobliging attitude. "Well, if you can point me in the general direction, then perhaps I can unearth it from the dregs of your pitiful existence."

"It's over there." The elderly man said, softening his surly tone when he noticed the doctor's pained face as he moved across the room.

Working his feet in between the slate hearth and the cardboard boxes full of used, washed and stored Styrofoam plates and cups, Martin wagged his finger. "I hope you don't ever build a fire in this with all the kindling you have sitting here."

Mr. Moysey gave a small growl. "It hasn't been lit since my wife died."

Martin hesitated, taking in a deep breath and trying to hold his fractious mood at bay. "Mm, is this the clock here?"

The old man leaned his arm on a stack of newspapers and nodded his head. "It won't run."

"It's a nice clock," Martin said. "Boxwood case—basic spring-driven movement, but a quality maker."

He slid the latch and opened the back. "It's in good condition overall, but it could do with a jolly good cleaning and lubrication."

"I'm afraid I over-wound it. Can you fix that?" the old man asked.

Martin pulled out his pocket torch and shined it into the clockworks. "You really can't overwind a clock. You'd have to tighten it to the point that the mainspring actually breaks. Once the coils are in firm contact with one another, the spring can't be wound any tighter."

He turned towards the man. "This is a 1920s-vintage clock. It's pretty dirty—probably never been cleaned. That's likely to be the problem."

"How much would you charge to get it working again?"

Martin eyed him for a moment. "This is a job you could do yourself. I could loan you a few tools—give you some clock oil."

"Mrrg, I don't know anything about clocks," Mr. Moysey grumbled. I don't want to damage it. My wife gave it to me as a wedding gift. It never gave me a bit of trouble until the day Eleanor died."

The doctor's brow lowered.

Mr. Moysey looked down to adjust his tie before glancing back up. "I don't mean to suggest that one thing has to do with the other. It's just a coincidence," he said. "I feel like if the clock was working, I could move on as well, though. Can you do the job?"

Martin gave a small sigh. "I'm at a loose end with only being back to work part-time right now. Why don't you come up to the surgery tomorrow with the clock, and we'll work on it together?"

Mr. Moysey stared silently at the timepiece. "Fine. What time do you want me there?"

"I'll plan on seeing you at three-thirty," Martin said as he moved towards the door.

He said his goodbyes to the old man and manoeuvred his way down the the front steps before hesitating to survey the steep, dimly lit cobblestone slope leading towards Dolphin Street. Then continued on.

Ruth had been somewhat taken aback by her nephew's wife when she called that evening. Louisa was an emotionally reactive individual; that had been obvious since her arrival in Portwenn just under a year and a half ago. But tonight, that reactivity seemed especially pronounced.

If she was understanding the younger woman correctly, Martin had left a note informing her that he had walked down to see Mr. Moysey. She seemed convinced that some horrible fate was about to befall her husband.

Ruth attempted to point out the realities of the, admittedly, very real risk that Martin was taking by walking down

Roscarrock Hill by himself. Yes, he could fall, but he had left a note saying where he would be. And aside from the slight possibility of an additional fracture being sustained, the greatest risk would be to his ego should a fall occur.

But Louisa was frantic, ready to bundle the baby up in a blanket and set off into the cold, dark night to rescue her husband.

"Louisa, you need to calm yourself down. Martin is almost certainly fine. He's a very cautious individual. He'll take it slow, I'm sure, and watch his step. I *really* don't think you need to be fretting so much over this," Ruth said, rather ineffectually.

The elderly woman's words had done nothing to appease Louisa's distress.

"I'll tell you what, dear. I'll go knock on Mr. Moysey's door and let Martin know that you're concerned. He can tell me when he's going to head home, and I can watch him until he gets to the bottom of the hill. You can watch for him from the terrace. If he takes a tumble, one of us is likely to see it, and we can make sure that he gets help."

It wasn't a satisfactory solution in Louisa's eyes, but it seemed to relieve her worries to some extent.

Ruth rang off and stepped out her front door, her foot poised to step down off the porch when she noticed her nephew making his way down the cobblestones in front of her house.

"Martin!" she called out. She saw him turn his head before his form disappeared into the shadows on the ground with the sound of metal scraping harshly against the pavement.

Chapter 18

"Martin, are you all right?" Ruth asked as she leaned across the porch rail to peer down the hill. Her nephew's unmoving form was obscured by the tall perennials which lined the path, with only his lower legs visible. "Martin!" she called again, her breath catching in her throat.

"I'll be right there, Martin!" the elderly woman said as she hurried into the house, returning quickly with her coat around her shoulders and a torch in hand. The cobblestones under her feet were precarious for an eighty-one-year-old woman, and she inched along, side-stepping her way down the hill.

She feared the worst as she approached the motionless form on the ground. She knelt down beside him, shining the torch on his face.

He was trying to get a breath in, emitting small grunts as he gasped for short puffs of air.

"Should I call for an ambulance?"

He shook his head vigorously and held up a palm.

"I'll ring Louisa, then," she said as her hand searched her coat pocket for her mobile.

"Don't—call L—Lou—isa!" he whispered between breaths. "Give me—a min—ute."

Ruth ran the beam of light up and down his body, checking him over the best she could under the given circumstances. The knuckles and back of his left hand were abraded and bleeding, but it was hard to see with the night-time shadows and the glare of the harsh artificial light.

The spasms in Martin's diaphragm began to ease, allowing his doctor's mind to shift to an assessment of possible injuries.

He moved his limbs and quickly determined that no additional damage seemed to have been done to his fractured bones. There was a persistent pain in his left hip, which felt like nothing more serious than a deep bruise. His left hand and forearm were stinging, and his elbow and cheek pulsed hotly as blood rushed into the contused areas.

"Can you sit yourself up?" Ruth asked, taking hold of his upper arm.

He shook himself from her. "I've got it!" he snarled.

The hard rocks bit at Ruth's knees, and she let herself drop to her backside.

"Go inside, Ruth. You're going to get cold," Martin snapped. "I'm fine."

"I'm not going anywhere, Martin! Not until I've ascertained that you've not suffered an injury requiring immediate medical assistance!"

"I just winded myself. Just—go back inside and leave me be. Please!"

"Hush up and lean back against the post there," Ruth said, snapping her fingers. Her voice was now soft, but commanding. "How did you land?"

"On my left side, I think," Martin mumbled, staring at his lap. "Please, just go back inside, Ruth."

Perhaps she just knew her nephew well enough to know what he was likely to be feeling at that moment, but even in the poor visibility, Ruth was sure she could see the humiliation written on his face.

"All right. I'll be in the house then. But I must insist that you let me check you over before you head back home."

"Aunt Ruth, I'm—"

"Mar-*tin!*"

He blew out a breath of air through pursed lips. "Pfft—*fine!*"

"Good, I'll leave the door ajar. Call if you need me," the old woman said as she pushed off her nephew's shoulder to struggle to her feet.

Martin watched as she traversed the cobblestones to return to her cottage before turning his attention to his immediate predicament.

He shifted himself further down the hill to more level ground. Then, leaning against a nearby lamp post, he used his crutch to pull himself to a standing position. He took a moment to catch his breath and wipe the sweat from his brow before making his way back up the path to the porch.

"I'm in the kitchen!" Ruth called out when she heard the metallic clicking of his crutch.

"Sit down at the table, Martin, and let me take a look," she said as she filled a glass with water and set it down in front of him.

"I'd be home by now if you hadn't distracted me, you know," he grumbled, dropping into a chair.

"I'm sorry. Louisa called and was quite concerned. I told her I'd check up on you."

Martin tipped his head back and shook it side to side. "I don't *need* looking after! The accident didn't damage my intellect!"

He winced as his aunt grasped his head and turned it so she could examine the abrasion on his face and the lump that had been raised on his cheekbone. "Why does everyone think they know better than I do what's good for me?"

Ruth went to the refrigerator and returned with a bag of frozen peas. "Well, I can certainly understand your frustration," she said, pressing the vegetables to the side of his face and pulling his hand up. "Hold that there."

The elderly woman slid a chair over next to him and took a seat. "It must be galling to have gone from being head of vascular at a prestigious medical facility to sitting helplessly on the ground in a little fishing village in Cornwall."

Martin blinked his eyes as his mouth dropped open. "This has absolutely *nothing* to do with my former position!"

Ruth rolled his bloodied left shirt sleeve back and raised her eyebrows at him. "Well, this is a mess. Come to the sink and I'll clean you up."

He yanked his arm away. "I'll take care of it when I get home," he grumbled as he got to his feet.

"Oh, Martin, stop it! I'm not going to argue about this. You'll make yourself sick trying to treat this on your own, and that's the last thing you need right now," she said as she put a hand on his back and nudged him towards the sink. "I'd like to hear what this *is* about if it's not about how far you've fallen since your glory days in London."

Ruth turned on the tap and pulled his arm under the water.

"I didn't realise I'd fallen," he said quietly, his eyes downcast.

"Well, Doctor, how do you think we should proceed?" the elderly woman asked, pulling her nephew's arm up so that he could evaluate the damage.

Martin turned his head away and closed his eyes as his blood pressure plummeted. He waited for the effects of his blood sensitivity to ease and then cleared his throat. "Just leave it, I'll tend to it back at the surgery."

Ruth stared at him for a few moments before patting his arm. "I'll get a clean tea towel to wrap around it, just to get you home. Sit back down," she ordered. "And where's your coat? It's cold out there tonight!"

Dropping into his chair, he scowled at the woman out of the corner of his eye. "I *am* capable of dressing myself, you know." He watched as she wrapped his arm and fastened the towel in place with several safety pins. "I get hot. I have to exert when I'm moving around and I ... get hot."

"I see. Your wife said you hadn't eaten any supper so I've made you a sandwich," she said, setting a plate and a glass of milk in front of him.

"Mm, thank you."

Ruth sat quietly, thumbing through a magazine as her nephew finished eating. She glanced over at him, and as he drank down the last sip of milk from the glass she flipped the pages shut and tossed the magazine aside.

"You and Louisa have been through a lot in the last months, Martin. She's very fearful about losing you and tends to overreact. Try to keep the lines of communication open," the old woman said.

He stared back at her. "Well, thank you for that bit of unsolicited advice, but if I remember correctly, communication's a *two*-way process. Now if you don't mind, I'll be on my way."

After saying a final goodnight, Martin headed back down the hill once again.

Alone with his thoughts as he worked his way home, he mulled over his aunt's allusion to his fall from grace. He bristled at her implication that his job as a GP in this remote fishing village was somehow less consequential than his position as head of vascular at a renowned hospital. It smacked of the same ignorance displayed by his father when he last visited. Certainly, she of all people must appreciate the unique challenges that accompanied his job here.

He rounded the corner on to Roscarrock Hill, stopping to gaze out at the harbour. Several small fishing vessels, illuminated by their interior lights, bobbed in the water, tugging against their moorings.

They glowed warmly in contrast to the crisp air around him, and he tried to picture the men on board. Playing a card game, reading in their bunks, or, perhaps, talking about their families.

To think about family made his heart ache. He had longed for a family when he was a boy. To be like the other boys who would be welcomed home from school on holidays by loving parents. He was an eccentricity, spending all holidays, but for the too-few summers with Joan and Phil, at school.

He'd filled that void left by his parents with work. His free moments outside the classroom spent in the library or in his room studying.

His jaw clenched as he recalled his parents, having stopped at St. Benedict's one July, just long enough to collect him to be shipped off to Portwenn, accepting accolades for having reared such a gifted and accomplished child.

Tears had stung his eyes as his efforts were overlooked, and the credit was given to the two people who loathed him. He realised then that no one was aware of how bereft he was of parental love.

He had excelled, despite his abysmal upbringing, and yet it wasn't enough that Christopher and Margaret Ellingham had denied him the love that a child needs and deserves, they managed to deny him even the distinction of being a self-made man. For many years, his successes had been routinely discounted, attributed to his father's reputation as a gifted surgeon or his mother's social standing.

His fingers drummed against his crutch, an agitation and anger building in him suddenly. He forced those thoughts aside and continued on up the hill.

There was no sign of his wife when he entered the back door of the surgery. He hoped that, perhaps, she had gone to bed, and any discussion of the evening's events would wait until morning.

He moved through the hallway and under the stairs before turning into his consulting room, closing the door behind him.

After pulling together the supplies needed to care for his wounds, he dropped heavily into his chair and leaned back, closing his eyes and letting his mind wander back to those little fishing boats in the harbour.

He was awakened some time later by his wife's warm lips on his neck.

"Mmm, sorry. I must have dozed off," he said as he straightened himself in his chair, grimacing as his weight shifted to his bruised hip.

Louisa didn't say a word but pulled up a chair next to him before wrapping her dressing gown around her and sitting down. She removed the tea towel that was around his arm. "Oh, Martin," she sighed as she inspected the deep abrasions covering the back of his hand, forearm and elbow.

"What do I do here?" she asked, digging through the supplies on his desk.

"I can do it, Louisa," he said as he picked up a white bottle of antiseptic.

She took the bottle from his hand and applied the medication to his wounds. He clenched his jaw and sucked air in through his teeth as it triggered nerve endings to send pain signals to his brain.

"Sorry," she said, giving him a sympathetic smile.

He handed her a small stack of non-stick gauze pads, a roll of elastic bandage material, and tape before she set to work silently dressing his wounds.

"There, all done. Let's go to bed." She leaned over and kissed the darkening bruise on his cheekbone and moved out the door.

Martin blinked back his surprise as she walked away. Then he pulled himself to his feet, went to the kitchen for a glass of water, and locked the doors.

Louisa was already in bed and appeared to be asleep when he entered the bedroom, so he readied himself for the night before quietly slipping in next to her.

"I'm sorry," she said as she rolled to her side and wrapped her arm around him. "I didn't really give you a chance to explain yourself earlier."

"Mm. I am, too. I mean ... for worrying you." He hesitated, knitting his brow. "It's been an odd day."

"Anything you want to talk about?" She asked, propping herself up on an elbow.

"I'm not sure." He pulled a bandaged hand up and rubbed his palm across his forehead. "Maybe we should talk about it tomorrow ... when things are clearer."

She kissed him gently, letting her lips linger on his, and then rolled on to her back. "Goodnight then."

"Mm, goodnight." Martin flipped the switch on the table lamp next to the bed and lay in the dark, his thoughts flitting from Mr. Moysey, to his spill on the path in front of Ruth's, and then to young Evan Hanley. He knew how the boy must feel, living in a home where he's seen as an inconvenience at best.

The child's words came back to him. *He can't help it, 'cause that's what he was made for.* Martin knew that he had upset his wife tonight. Perhaps that's how it would always be. Him, time and time again, saying or doing something to upset her because that's what he was made for.

"Do you ever wish you'd gotten a different brand?" he said, absentmindedly.

"Brand of what?" Louisa asked as she pulled her elbow underneath her again.

He turned his head away from her puzzled face. "Mm, nothing."

"Martin, don't ask me a question and then leave me hanging. What do you mean, a different *brand?* Brand of what?"

He hesitated, glad for the darkened room to conceal the flush he felt spreading up his neck. "I didn't mean to say that. I was just thinking about something Evan Hanley said today. Just ... thinking aloud, I guess."

"And ... you were thinking about what Evan said about brands of what?"

"Dogs."

"Dogs? You mean *breed* of dog, Martin."

He heaved out an exasperated breath. "I'm familiar with the word, Louisa. Let's just drop this and go to sleep. We can take it up tomorrow."

He lifted his head and kissed her before dropping back heavily on to the pillow. "Goodnight."

"Hmm, goodnight." Louisa traced her fingertip down the bridge of his nose before rolling on to her back and pulling the blanket under her chin.

She tossed and turned, mulling over how she had handled, or rather *mis*handled, her husband's earlier non-compliance.

His breaths were now slow and deep, characteristic of his typical sleep pattern. She sat herself up in the bed and watched him, his deep chest rising and falling regularly, and she brushed her fingers lightly over his hair.

What in the world did he mean by, do you ever wish you'd gotten a different brand? Different brand of what?"

She began to take a mental inventory of her most recent purchases. Outside of the new car, the only purchases she had made since Martin's accident were incidentals. She had picked up some groceries at Lidl's in Wadebridge late last week. *But that was just some potatoes, fruit and veg, nappies ... oh, and some mouthwa—"*

She slapped a hand to her forehead. *Oh, bugger! I got a different brand because they were out of what I usually get. Maybe that's what he was referring to?*

Cupping her hands over her mouth, she breathed out heavily. *Hmm. I don't notice anything. But he must have noticed my breath when I kissed him."*

She glanced down at her sleeping husband, tempted to wake him to verify her theory.

You're going barmy, Louisa. Leave the poor man be and go to sleep. Any further discussion would have to wait for morning.

Chapter 19

Martin lay staring at the ceiling the next morning, taking note of a new crack which had formed overhead. He knew he was going to need to have someone come in and make some much needed repairs around the cottage.

He had put the project on the back burner when he had hopes of returning to a surgical post in London, and when the baby was born things seemed so tense that he didn't want to add to the existing turmoil. And now, there were days when he was barely holding it together. He didn't think he could tolerate the inconvenience and frustration that accompanies any sort of home maintenance project.

He jumped and glanced over at his wife as her fingers lightly touched the bruise on his cheekbone.

"Sorry, did that hurt?" She brushed the hair away from her face.

"Mm, not much. You just startled me. How did you sleep?"

"Once I *got* to sleep—good. It just took a long time to get there."

Martin hesitated, watching her guardedly before asking, "Would you mind if Evan Hanley came home with you today? He and his—" he curled his lip at the thought of the animal "—*dog* friend made a mess in the back of the car, and I told him he should come over after school today to clean it up. I spoke with his father about it already. I also want to check the scrape on his knee ... make sure there's no infection developing. We'll run him home after dinner ... *if* you don't mind."

She gave him a small smile. "I don't mind at all. I'll collect him after the last bell, and he can wait in my office for me until I'm ready to leave."

She pulled her knees under her and drew the covers away from his legs.

"Louisa, what are you doing? It's cold!" he squawked, grabbing for the blanket.

"You may have it back once I've gotten a look at you. Now shush ... and lie still," she admonished, pushed him back on to the bed.

She began at his feet, visually inspecting every inch of him as she ran her palm along his leg. "I'm sure you would have called Ed or Chris right away if you thought there was any chance you could have done yourself any real harm." Her eyes darted up to meet his. "Wouldn't you?"

He looked back at his wife's narrowed eyes and taut lips. "Yes, of course I would!"

Her hand brushed over a raw area on his knee and up his left thigh where her eyes spied the bruise on his hip spreading down his leg and peeking out from under his boxer shorts. She grabbed his waistband and pulled at the fabric, releasing a small gasp as the deep purple swelling was revealed.

"Oh, Martin! What in the world got into you last night? Going off like that. Taking chances."

"I'd told Mr. Moysey that I'd stop and look at his clock. When I came downstairs after my shower, you weren't there."

"Of course not. I was upstairs getting James ready for bed! You should have come up and talked to me before making the decision to go over there!"

He swung his legs over the side of the bed. "Louisa, I'm perfectly capable of walking down to Mr. Moy—"

"Obviously *not,* Mar-tin!" she said, waving a hand vaguely in her husband's direction. "Look at you!"

"Yes, I fell. That's bound to hap—"

"Don't you dare take a chance like that again, Martin!" she said, blinking back tears. "I didn't say anything about this after you came home last night because we needed to tend to your injuries and get you off to bed."

She tipped her head down and peered up at him, softening her tone. "That and ... well, Ruth called me while you were walking home. She suggested I postpone any discussions until this morning."

"Did she!" Martin was still stinging from his aunt's unceremonious remark the night before.

"She thought you might be feeling a bit—" Louisa winced "—a bit red-faced about what hap—"

"She needs to mind her own bloody business!"

"Martin!" She stared at him, taken aback. "I really don't think she meant to interfere. I think she's trying to be helpful ... in the only way she knows how. We're all trying to be helpful. We just want what's best for—"

"Well, that's just it! Everyone's well-intentioned to the point of intrusion! May *I* please have a say in what's best for me?"

He got up from the bed and limped off into the bathroom, slamming the door shut behind him.

Louisa slumped back on her heels as she listened to the water begin to flow in the shower. *Well, you handled that brilliantly, Louisa.*

Martin was sullen and withdrawn when she joined him for breakfast later, barely making eye contact with either her or James.

The latch rattled as Jeremy hurried into the house, pushing the door shut against the cold, blustering wind.

"Gonna be a right good soaker today, I think. You can feel it in the air," he said as he pulled his mac from his shoulders and hung it on the coat rack behind him.

"Morning, Jeremy. How are you?" Louisa asked.

"Need a cup of your coffee this morning, Martin. Didn't get much sleep last night."

Martin peered up at him from behind the newspaper and grunted an acknowledgement of sorts, giving a jerk of his head in the direction of his espresso machine.

Jeremy glanced over questioningly at Louisa who answered with a furtive shake of her head.

The aide slipped a cup under the appliance as it hummed ambitiously before spewing out the black brew. Then he took a seat at the table.

"I was up late last night. I found a place to rent up on the hill, so I got a bunch of unpacking done before I headed back to Truro. Should be able to get the furniture moved on Friday. It'll be bloody brilliant to not have to make that drive every day."

"And you'll be closer to Poppy," Louisa said as she stood up with her dishes, pausing to tap the aide on the arm before giving a subtle nod towards her husband.

Jeremy glanced over at his boss, finally noticing his bandaged hand and bruised face.

"Crikey, Martin! What happened to you?" he asked, shoving his chair out behind him and getting to his feet.

The screech of the chair legs against the slate floor triggered another stabbing pain behind Martin's eye, and he grunted as his hand went to his head.

"Where are your earplugs?" the aide asked as he stood watching him, his hands on his hips.

Martin shook his head as the pain began to abate, leaving him with a woozy feeling. "I think—I think I forgot them." He squeezed his eyes shut to clear the tears as the pain eased into a warm ache.

"Getting better?" the young man asked.

"Yeah. Sit down and finish your coffee."

Jeremy hesitated and then returned to his seat before picking up the sports section of the paper.

Louisa looked incredulously at the two men, then pulled her son from his high chair and left the room, her ponytail whipping side to side as she disappeared down the hallway.

Jeremy finished reading the latest football match results and then lowered the paper, staring pointedly at Martin. "Okay, let's hear it. What happened?"

Martin glared back at him for a few moments before pushing himself up from his chair.

"I walked to Mr. Moysey's—got distracted—took a tumble—scrapes and bruises—end of story. Now if you'll excuse me, I have some work to do in my consulting room," he snapped.

The aide listened to Martin and Louisa exchange goodbyes as they passed each other under the stairs and glanced up at Louisa as she entered the kitchen.

She set James down on the floor with a plastic container and his wooden blocks before straightening up. Propping a hand on her hip, she stared pointedly at her husband's aide.

"Well, you were a lot of help!" she quipped sarcastically.

Jeremy jumped to his feet. "Oh, did you need a hand with something?"

"No, Jeremy. With Martin! Couldn't you have told him how silly it was for him to go to see Mr. Moysey last night?"

Jeremy swallowed hard. He didn't know what to say. The only thing worse than making his boss angry would be to make his boss's wife angry.

He tipped his head to the side and stammered out, "Well, he—I'm sure—what I mean is, he most likely—I mean, he *did* tell Mr. Moysey he'd stop by. And since he can't drive, he'd *have* to walk, so technically it wasn't—silly."

"Jeremy! You saw his face! Have you looked at his arm?" Louisa blustered.

"I was just going to head down to the consulting room, Louisa. I'll check him over, but—" He hesitated, knowing that what he had to say would not be what she was wanting to hear.

"Martin's going to have some mishaps. It's inevitable whenever a patient is on crutches. He has a long recovery period ahead, and he knows the more he can use those legs the better they'll heal—the faster they'll heal."

Louisa began to gather together the papers she'd worked on earlier and shoved them into her satchel. "But he went off without so much as discussing it with me first last night!"

"Well, I *will* talk to him about that. He does need to let someone know where he's going to be. I'm surprised he didn't leave you a note or something."

Louisa picked the newspaper up from the table, deposited it in the bin and turned to the aide. "He did actually leave me a note," she said sheepishly. "But *still*, I don't like the idea of him walking up and down these hills. I mean, look at what happened!"

The young man pulled the chair out next to him and gestured for Louisa to take a seat.

"James is learning to walk," he said. "He's going to have some mishaps. Skinned knees, bumps on his head, lots of bruises ... right?"

"Yeah, but James is a *baby*. They're kind of made for falling. Not too high off the floor—their bones don't break as easily."

"That's true. But try to think about it the same way when you find yourself getting nervous about Martin.

"It *would* be a whole lot easier on the two of us, though, if we could put them both in a padded room for a while, wouldn't it?" the aide said as a grin spread across his face.

Louisa returned a tepid smile. "But James doesn't already have two broken legs and a broken arm, does he, Jeremy. And ... he didn't nearly die three months ago."

The aide rubbed a palm over his face. "Look, I know it's going to be really nerve wracking. But the exercise is good for Martin physically. And the independence, sunshine, and fresh air is good for him mentally. Just try to be encouraging."

"I'm impressed that he was able to make it all the way down there and back, especially after taking the fall. That's not just humiliating for patients, it's bloody scary."

"Martin took the spill out in front of Ruth's cottage. She called me while he was walking home. She told me she was to blame for the fall—that she'd distracted him by calling out to him as he went by. She said he was embarrassed and wanted her to leave him be, but she insisted he come in so she could check out his injuries."

"Well, it's good that he can go out on his own but have the assistance if he needs it."

Louisa got up and picked up the dish rag from the sink before wiping the crumbs from the table. "I helped him with his scrapes last night, but I took Ruth's advice. I didn't bring up the fall until this morning, hence the foul mood."

Jeremy pushed his chair away from the table and leaned over to build a small tower of alphabet blocks which James Henry immediately knocked over, prompting a gale of laughter from the child.

"Don't make a big issue out of his accomplishments, Louisa. I don't have to tell you, Martin's not real eager for that kind of attention. But encourage him, and let him know you support him. Be there to help him with the bumps and scrapes when they do happen. And I'm sorry about this, but I can guarantee there'll be more."

Jeremy stood up and moved towards the hall. "I better go and take a look at your husband. You have a good morning," the young man said, taking a step back to tousle the baby's hair before continuing towards the consulting room.

"Mm. You too, Jeremy," Louisa said as she worried her bottom lip. "Let me know if you see anything that worries you," she called after him.

Martin glanced up from the patient files in front of him when he heard the click of the latch on the door. His aide strode into the room and went to the supply cabinet, jerking his head in the direction of the exam couch.

Martin glowered back at him but pushed himself up from his chair.

"You gave your wife a pretty good scare last night, you know," Jeremy said as he took the crutch from him and leaned it against the chair next to the couch. "And you should be using two crutches again now that the arm's better."

The aide ignored his patient's eye roll and guttural mumblings, unbuttoning his cuff and rolling his shirt sleeve back. He peeled the gauze pads away from his arm. "Jeez, you did this up good, mate. Come over to the sink, I want to wash off that exudate, so I can get a better look," the young man said as he handed the doctor his crutch.

"So, you left Louisa a note and walked down to Mr. Moysey's. Some reason you didn't talk to her about it first?" the aide said as he held his patient's arm under the running water.

"What do you think Louisa would have said if I'd told her first?" Martin said, braving a peek at his wounds. "Any third-degree areas?"

"Possibly a spot on your elbow. I'll take a better look at it when we're done here. So, you left her a note and snuck out?"

"I didn't *sneak* anywhere! You make me sound like a ten-year-old. Ouch! For God's sake, be careful there!" Martin spat as he pulled at his arm.

The aide gave him a quick glance before patting the wounds dry with several gauze pads. "All right, go sit back down," he said as began to wipe up the water on the counter.

"So, you left her a note and went off down the hill. Don't you think it would have been better to discuss it with her? I mean, women are hardwired to be suspicious—think the worst if we're not open with 'em."

Jeremy pulled the magnifying lamp over and began to examine his patient's arm.

"When did you become so conversant with the inner-workings of the female brain?"

The aide glanced up. "Hmm. It looks like one small avulsed area here on your elbow. I'll call Mr. Christianson, let him know what you've done to yourself. But I think this'll heal up without any problems."

Martin yanked his arm away from his aide. "Answer my question! Why does everyone think it necessary to give me relationship advice? What works for you, and for most people for that matter, doesn't seem to work for me."

Jeremy picked up the bottle of antiseptic spray and doused his patient's arm liberally. "I'm not sure I know what you mean. But what I'm saying is that if you'd talked this through with Louisa first, she wouldn't be so upset about it."

Martin sat silently for several moments, scrutinising his aide's technique as he applied fresh bandage material. "People don't listen to me. What point is there in discussing something if my side isn't going to be heard anyway?"

"There, how'd I do?" Jeremy asked as he began to clear away the supplies.

"You slapped some gauze and tape on my arm. You didn't repair a severed radial artery," Martin snipped.

He glanced up, noticing the aggrieved expression on his aide's face as he turned to walk away. "Jeremy," he said as the young man pulled the consulting room door open. "Thank you. Well done."

He turned and leaned around the door. "You're welcome, Martin. And, erm ... you might try talking to Louisa again. Maybe she'll be more receptive."

Chapter 20

Morwenna pushed the door to the surgery open and stooped over to pick up the morning's mail. She flung her bag over her desk and on to the floor below before sorting through the stack of envelopes in her hand. Three of the pieces of mail she tossed on to her desk. Two, announcing that the *resident* may have just won a million pounds, went into the bin. The remainder she carried into the consulting room.

"Mornin', Doc! Got some mail for you," she said as she dropped the envelopes on to the ledger book in front of him.

"Do you mind? I'm working here!" he said, glaring up at her.

"What happened ta *you?*" She hurried around to the back side of the desk, looking him over, her mouth agape. "Looks like ya got into it with someone down at the pub! That what happened?"

"Don't be ridiculous!" Martin squirmed uncomfortably before shifting his gaze to his lap. "I fell. Now get back to work."

"Okay, okay!" She hesitated and then moved off towards the door. "Just don't tell me not ta worry, 'cause I'm gonna anyways," she said as she began to pull the door shut behind her.

"Morwenna!"

"Yeah, Doc?"

"Could you, er ... bring me a couple of cold packs from the freezer?"

"I'll be back before you can say knife!" she said, rushing off down the hall.

The morning began uneventfully, with the most pedestrian of ailments and rechecks filling the waiting room. Picking up a stack of patient notes that were ready to be returned to the file drawer, Martin bundled them together with an elastic band.

"Morwenna!" he barked.

The rapid flip-flapping of the young woman's seasonally inappropriate footwear grew louder, and he rolled his eyes, breathing out a soft sigh.

"What'd' ya need, Doc?" she asked as she burst through the door, wide-eyed. "Somethin' wrong?"

"Here ... take these and file them," he said, thrusting the stack of cardboard sleeves at her.

She leaned over and peered into his face.

"What in the world are you doing?" He rolled back in his chair as she looked him up and down.

"Just checkin' ta be sure yer all right."

"Well, of course I'm all right! Why wouldn't I be?" His vexation intensified as he fidgeted under her scrutinising gaze.

"There are all kinds of reasons *you* might not be all right. You could've contracted some sort of really fast developing disease, or you could've fallen then couldn't get yourself up off the floor on your own. Or maybe you could've had one of those pin prick headaches you've been gettin'. There are a lot more things that could've happened, too. You want me to go on?"

"Of course not! And it's *ice—pick* headaches. *Which* I didn't have! Now go put these back, and bring me the next patient's file."

"That'd be Sally Watson. Should I tell her to come on back?"

"Give me five minutes, then send her in."

Martin waited for the door to close behind the girl before resting his head on his desk, closing his eyes momentarily.

He was awakened a few minutes later by a soft voice and a hand on his shoulder. "You need to go have a lie-down, Doc.

Yer workin' too hard, ya know," Sally said as she patted his back.

Martin straightened himself in his chair, blinked his eyes, and took in a deep breath, trying to clear the fog from his head.

"Mm. Please ... have a seat, Mrs.—" he glanced down at the woman's patient notes— "Watson. Rubbing his palm across his face, he winced as his fingers bumped his forgotten injury from the night before.

He pulled himself forward in his chair and cleared his throat. "What seems to be the problem?"

"You been in the wars, Doc? You look somethin' awful!"

"No!" He hissed out a breath and stared the woman down. "Do you have a medical problem that I can help you with, or did you just come in here to glean bits of twaddle fodder for the village rumour mill?"

"Don't git yourself all worked up now," Sally said with a narcotic tone. She dug around in her handbag, finally pulling out the small cardboard box she'd been searching for. "It's these patches you told me to use for my hot flashes. I don't like 'em. I was wonderin' ... could you give me somethin' else, maybe?"

"What do you mean, you don't *like* them? Be specific."

"They're uncomfortable," the woman complained, rubbing at her abdomen.

"All right. Get up on the exam couch and I'll take a look." Martin pulled himself to his feet and trundled across the floor.

"Lay back please and pull up your blouse. Then undo your waistband."

Sally reached down and unsnapped the top of her jeans before reclining on the table.

"Irritation at the application site is a fairly common side effect of the oestrogen pa—"

His brows pulled together in a vee, and he leaned forward as the woman tugged at her top, revealing a solid row of white rectangles encircling her waist.

"What in the *world?*" He rolled the woman side to side. "You're only supposed to use one patch, not the entire box!"

"Oh, I didn't use the whole box in one crack, Doc. I followed your instructions exactly. I put a new one on every Sunday and Wednesday. It's just gettin' awful uncomfortable, and I'm runnin' outta places to stick 'em."

Martin screwed up his face and huffed out a breath. "You're supposed to take the old one off when you put the new one on! You don't just keep adding to the collection!"

"Well, I didn't know! You should'a told me that when you wrote the prescription."

"I told you to replace the patch with a new one every three to four days. *Replace!*"

He began to pull the rectangles from the woman's body as she wriggled on the table. "Oouch! Careful there, Doc!"

"I can't believe what you've done here!" he grumbled. "Have you been experiencing any nausea or bleeding?"

"A bit spotty off and on. I thought that was normal though. You know, when yer goin' through the menopause. But mostly, it's just been uncomfortable—itchy!"

"As I would imagine it would be!" He continued to work his way across the woman's abdomen, tossing the patches into a stainless-steel basin.

"Well, I don't think you've done yourself any harm. The amount of hormone delivered by the patch diminishes quite rapidly after four days. And you're obviously not exhibiting any signs of immediate distress.

"In future, I would recommend you listen to my instructions more carefully. And read the directions that come with the prescription."

"Sorry, Doc. I guess I didn't catch the replacin' part," the woman said sheepishly.

He wagged a finger at her. "Mm. You can put yourself back together now." Returning to his desk, he dropped heavily into his chair.

"I think you'll find yourself more comfortable now. I'm not going to discuss any alternate treatments with you until we see how you do without all the ... extra baggage." Clearing his throat, he shifted his attention to the woman's patient notes.

Sally sat watching him, winding her purse strap around her finger as his biro moved across the paper.

He looked up, raising his eyebrows at her. "Was there something else?"

"No, that's all." She gave him a hesitant smile as she got to her feet and left the room.

"Next patient!" Martin shouted out through the open door before slipping Mrs. Watson's notes back into the sleeve.

"Oh, gawd," he muttered when he glanced up to see Florence Dingley trudging in his direction.

"Doctor," the woman said as she doffed her feculent old hat and dropped it on to his desk.

"Mrs. Dingley, you do realise you're—" he glanced at his watch "—forty-nine and a half hours late for your appointment, don't you? I don't suppose you have an explanation for your untimely arrival?"

"I had an emergency to attend to. There was a crisis with my poor ca—"

"Yes, I thought not." He tossed his biro down on his desk. "Mrs. Dingley, I don't appreciate having my time wasted while you feather-bed those pestilence-ridden creatures of yours."

She pulled a glob of chewing gum from her mouth and wrapped it in a paper coaster from the stack on the doctor's desktop. "I had a flea infestation I had to get under control," she said in her whiny, wavering voice.

"I'm not surprised." Martin shook his head and wrinkled up his nose before making a note in the woman's file. "And, you're here today because?"

"I just thought you'd be wantin' to check my eyes ... that bloodshot thing you say I have. You want me to get on the table?"

"Birdshot chorioretinopathy. And no, take a seat here," he said, gesturing towards the chair as his eyes remained focused on the woman's notes.

Mrs. Dingley reached across the desk. "Here," she said flatly.

Martin extended his hand and the old woman deposited her wad of chewing gum into it.

"Eeww," he undertoned as he tossed the item into the bin before going to the sink to wash his hands.

He pulled a paper towel from the dispenser and turned to scowl at her. "I seem to remember making appointments for you with an ophthalmologist and a rheumatologist over in Truro."

The woman brushed at the front of her coat, sending a blizzard of cat hair into the air, before turning her gaze to the window.

"I went over there like you said, but never went back. A pair of idiots those two were," she said. "Wouldn't know a cow's head from its—"

"Mrs. Dingley, you have a serious disease that requires specialist care if you wish to preserve your eyesight!" Martin hissed out a breath before barking out to his receptionist. "Morwenna!"

The old woman donned the contrived, forlorn expression that she had perfected over years of wheedling for contributions for her feline sanctuary. "It's a long way over to Truro, you know," she said. "I s'pose *you're* runnin' over there all the time. Maybe I could just ride over there with—"

"Noo! If you require assistance with transportation, I'll make arrangements with social services."

"But they might want to take away my cats!" she screeched.

The woman's voice chafed at Martin's ears like a rusty gate hinge, and he made a mental note to thank his aide for the reminder to use his earplugs. "If they shut down that flea farm it'll be a step in the right direction," he mumbled.

"What'd ya need, Doc?" Morwenna asked as she stuck her head in the door.

"Call over to Truro and have them email Mrs. Dingley's patient notes ... A.S.A.P."

The receptionist flashed him a smile. "Can do, Doc! You doin' okay in here? Not gettin' yourself all worn out, are you?"

"Notes!" He pushed himself to his feet and waved his patient to the exam table.

Morwenna quickly retreated, and Mrs. Dingley shuffled to the doctor's couch.

"Take off your coat before you sit down."

"Why? It's my eyes you're lookin' at, isn't it?"

"Mrs. Dingley, if you want me to give you a proper examination you need to remove your coat. You can stand there and argue with me about it, or you can do as I asked and spare us both further aggravation."

She gave him a black look before pulling her jacket from her shoulders and dropping it into his hand. Martin screwed up his face and gave the grungy article of clothing a toss on to a chair before wiping his hand on his trousers. Then he pulled his stethoscope from around his neck.

"How long have you had these lesions on your arm?" he asked as he took hold of the woman's wrist.

"A few days. Just some scratches from my cats," she said as she shook him away from her. "And it's my *eyes* that I came to see you about, remember!"

"Shush! Lie back on the couch."

Martin snapped on a pair of exam gloves, unbuttoned the woman's blouse, and pulled her hand up over her head, palpating the lymph node under her arm.

"Ooow! What do you think you're doing?" she said, slapping at his hand.

"Have you been experiencing headaches or fatigue—loss of appetite?"

"Yes, of course I have. I'm worried about—"

"Your *cats*," the doctor sneered. "I'll need to draw blood and have it tested to confirm my diagnosis, but I suspect you've contracted cat scratch disease. As the name implies, you got it from those parasite-infested animals."

He gave another shout over his shoulder. "Morwenna!"

"I'll start you on a course of antibiotics, Mrs. Dingley, but you can't continue to care for those stray cats. Your health is already compromised with the chorioretinopathy. The last thing you need is to be dealing with an easily avoidable disease. You have to get rid of the cats."

The old woman's eyes welled with tears. "I can't! Where would they go?"

"I'll have PC Penhale contact the R.S.P.C.A."

The latch on the door rattled, and the receptionist stepped back into the room.

"Morwenna, could you please ask Mr. Portman to come in and draw a blood sample from Mrs. Dingley."

"Sure, Doc. But he usually does 'em out—"

"Morwenna, just do it," he said softly as he pulled a tissue from the box on his desk and handed it to his patient.

The receptionist's eyes darted between the doctor and the old woman. "Yeah, right. Here are the patient notes you asked for," she said slapping the papers down on the doctor's desk before hurrying out the door.

When Jeremy entered the consulting room a few minutes later he looked at his boss questioningly.

"I need you to draw for IFA testing on Mrs. Dingley," Martin said as he limped back and sank into his chair.

"Erm, sure." Jeremy went to the medical cart and gathered together his needed supplies.

The doctor finished poring over Mrs. Dingley's Truro notes and joined Jeremy as he stuck a plaster on the old woman's arm.

"Did you notice anything remarkable in the patient's presentation when you conducted your initial examination?" Martin asked, his head tipped back as he peered down at the young man.

Jeremy's brow lowered as he turned back to the old woman on the exam couch. "Did I miss something?"

"Examine her arms."

The aide took hold of Mrs. Dingley's wrists and turned her hands palm side down. "She said they're cat scratches."

"Yes, but how would you account for the lesions forming at the inoculation sites."

Jeremy wracked his brain, trying to retrieve any information he may have stored away from his nursing courses.

Martin handed him a clean pair of latex gloves. "Take a look at the axillary nodes."

Jeremy's eyes shifted uncomfortably from the doctor to the patient. "Mrs. Dingley, could you lie back for me, please?"

"I already did that for *him!*"

"Mrs. Dingley, I'd appreciate it if you'd let my assistant take a look at you," Martin said as he gave the old woman a reassuring nod. "Doctors learn from hands-on experience."

"He a doctor, then?" the old woman asked as she eyed Jeremy suspiciously.

"I'm just sizing him up right now."

The aide looked up at him apprehensively and then to the patient as she lowered herself back on to the couch.

"Hmm, some slight node suppuration," the young man said as he examined the old woman's underarm.

"Right. Anything ring a bell?"

Jeremy's gaze settled on his shoes for a moment before he looked up. "Bartonellosis?"

The left corner of Martin's mouth nudged up. "Mm-hmm."

"I'm sorry, Dr. Ellingham. I missed it. It's not contagious, though. Right?"

"No, it's only transmissible from cats to humans. And there's no need to apologise. The lymphadenopathy that occurs with this disease primarily affects the axillary nodes. You wouldn't have seen it."

Martin returned his attention to his patient. "I'll send your blood off for analysis, but I'm quite sure you have cat scratch disease. It's a bacterial infection that you've contracted from your cats. I'll get you started on a course of antibiotics immediately."

Jeremy held his hand out to the woman and helped her to a sitting position on the end of the table.

"You can button your blouse, Mrs. Dingley," the doctor said, giving her a nod. "I'll write you a prescription, and you can be on your way." He turned to his aide. "Thank you, Mr. Portman. I think that's all I need for now."

Jeremy hesitated and then left the room as Martin returned to his desk.

"Mrs. Tishell can fill this for you," he said, peering up at his patient. "I want you to get started on it right away." He tore the sheet from his prescription pad and slid it across the desktop.

"Are you *sure* I have to get rid of my cats?"

"Positive. I'll be contacting PC Penhale right away. And I'll call you when your test results come back. Social services will get in touch with you regarding a ride over to Truro for the appointments I'll arrange for you."

She pulled her hat from the doctor's desk and smashed it down on her head before leaving the room.

Martin laid his head back and closed his eyes.

Chapter 21

The kitchen had been filled with poorly disguised tension as Martin and Louisa shared lunch with Jeremy and Poppy. Both of them harboured a degree of resentment towards the other over the discord the night before.

They tried to mask their unresolved feelings by focusing their attention on unrelated topics. Louisa discussed the upcoming Christmas Festival with Poppy, and Martin discussed his frustration with their Bartonellosis case with his assistant.

"She needs to be taking steroids as well as immunosuppressants for the retinopathy. That should have been started weeks ago!" He stabbed at a hapless cherry tomato as it repeatedly scooted away from the descending tines of his fork. "Now we'll have to get the bacterial infection cleared up before we can treat the eye problem ... which could very well mean vision loss for the woman."

He gave the tomato one final robust jab, sending it bouncing off his plate where it slid across the table and on to the floor beneath James Henry.

"Uh-oh," the little boy said as he grabbed the side of the high chair tray to peer down at the now inert red orb. He looked up, round-eyed, at his father before bursting into a fit of laughter, bouncing in his seat. "Da-eee!" he squealed.

The tension in the room eased, and Louisa saw a sparkle alight in her husband's eyes. As his gaze met hers, a tacit temporary truce was reached between them before their son picked up his bowl and dumped out its contents, allowing the bits of vegetables which had been fished from the soup to join the tomato on the floor.

"I'll take care of it." Jeremy said. He got up from the table and pulled several sheets of towelling off the kitchen roll.

"Thank you, Jeremy." Louisa reached to grab for the now empty bowl before it, too, ended up on the floor.

James pointed a chunky finger down at the aide as he crouched next to the high chair. "Jeb—Jebby."

Poppy's head whipped up as her young charge startled her with his new word. "Jeremy, James knows your name!"

The young man stood up, his hands now full of vegetable laden paper towels, and looked incredulously at her. "*That* was Jeremy? You sure?"

"Of course, it was! He even pointed at you, didn't you James?" Louisa said, now on her feet extolling her son's most recent achievement with a congratulatory pinch of his cheeks and a kiss on the top of his head.

Martin exchanged befuddled glances with his aide, and Jeremy gave him a shrug of his shoulders.

"You need to go have a lie-down now, Martin," he said as he began pulling empty plates from the table before taking them to the sink.

"I need him for just a minute, Jeremy. Martin, could you see me out?" she said, jerking her head towards the door.

"Mm, yes." He pushed himself up from the table, and wedging his crutch under his arm, he warily followed her on to the back terrace.

She glanced at the kitchen window before reaching up, clasping her fingers behind his neck. "I just wanted to say that I *am* still angry with you for sneaking out last night, but—hmm, well maybe I'm not really *angry* anymore. I'm not sure. But I love you, and we'll sort this out tonight, okay?"

"Louisa, I—"

She slapped a hand over his mouth. "Shhh. I don't want to discuss it now. We always get ourselves into trouble when we try to talk things over where we're in danger of being interrupted." She shifted her hands to the sides of his head and tipped it down so that she could place a kiss on his lips.

"But, I wan—"

"Mar-tin," she warned softly.

He breathed out a resigned sigh. "Yes."

Louisa headed back to the school and Martin returned to the house to continue with what was to become his new afternoon routine—a nap while his antibiotics were administered through the catheter in his arm. When he woke around an hour later, his aide worked to loosen the knotted muscles at the base of his skull.

"Okay, roll over," Jeremy ordered as he dipped his fingers into a jar of cocoa butter, rubbing a liberal amount on to his hands.

Martin wrestled himself to his stomach, and the aide massaged his palms over the nape of his neck, attempting to soothe the tenderness left by the ischemic compressions that he had been using.

"How many of these sessions will it take before I see results?" Martin asked.

"You mean until the headaches are eliminated?"

"Mm. How long does it usually take to see improvement?"

"I'd guess a few more sessions should provide you with noticeable improvement. When you'll be headache free...? We're working on this every day rather than the twice a week schedule most patients are limited to, so a couple of weeks would be my best guess."

"I see." Martin closed his eyes and drifted back to sleep.

He was awakened some time later by several firm pats on his back. "Hey boss," Jeremy said, "You've got company ... Mr. Moysey. You want me to tell him to come back later?"

Martin pushed himself up on his elbows. "No. No. Just give me a minute," he said as he rubbed a hand over his face. The spicy aroma of fresh baked Cornish Fairings hit his nose, triggering a sudden hunger pang.

"Could you take him to the kitchen? Get him a cup of coffee or tea. I'll be down in just a bit."

"Sure. You need a hand?"

"No, I'm fine. Just see to Mr. Moysey ... please."

Jeremy hurried back downstairs, and Martin went to the bathroom to splash cold water on his face. He groaned as he straightened up and was confronted with his own reflection.

He took a moment to run his fingers gingerly over his swollen, abraded, and contused cheek, feeling a twinge of guilt for how his mishap had affected his wife.

But he couldn't cloister himself in the surgery for the rest of his life in hopes of saving her from any additional distress. The matter would have to be addressed, and they would need to come to some sort of understanding.

He pulled a towel from the rack and wiped his face before heading downstairs.

"Hello, Mr. Moysey. I'm sorry to keep you waiting," Martin said as he pulled one of his shakes from the refrigerator.

The old man stood in the middle of the room, clutching on to his clock as he eyed the doctor critically.

Opening up an old sheet, the doctor laid it out on the table. "Go ahead and set it down, and I'll show you how to take it apart. Then we can give her a thorough examination."

Mr. Moysey harrumphed and gave him a small smile. "You think it has female attributes, do you?"

Martin cleared his throat self-consciously. As a young boy, he had always pictured his *patients* as male or female, sometimes even assigning them names. It was a habit formed long ago that had carried over into adulthood.

He no longer endowed his mechanical patients with monikers, but he had continued to think of each clock and watch that he repaired as having gender specific characteristics.

"I'll leave the anthropomorphising to you." Martin glanced around quickly. "Did Mr. Portman ask if you'd like a cup of coffee or tea?"

"He did. I told him no, though. I, er ... well, you're a doctor! You know how it is when you get old!" The old man tugged at his beard and cleared his throat. "Don't want to have to keep interrupting our operation here."

"It *is* inconvenient, but allowing yourself to become dehydrated can have disastrous consequences. I can wait if you need to take breaks to run down the hall." He gave the old man an encouraging nod.

"Well, I suppose. It's getting cold out there; a cuppa sounds good."

Martin pulled two cups from the cupboard and handed them to his guest before filling the tea kettle and plugging it in.

The two men sat down on opposite sides of the table, and the doctor instructed the old man on how to dismantle the workings of his timepiece.

They had just gotten the internal organs laid out in a logical order in front of them when the back door flew open. The space in the room was immediately filled with the exuberant, slightly nasal chatter and energy of Evan Hanley.

"Hi, Dr. Ellig-am!" the boy said as he took several skipping steps before making a final two-footed leap, landing himself next to Martin. "Whatcha doin'?" he asked as he peered closely at the metal objects in front of him.

"Evan, this is Mr. Moysey. I'm showing him how to fix his clock."

"Hi, Mr. Moysey. Are you Dr. Ellig-am's friend, too?"

Mr. Moysey tugged at his tie and scowled at the child.

"Mr. Moysey is my aunt's neighbour. I'm just giving him a hand with his project," Martin explained.

The seven-year-old folded his arms on the table in front of him. "How come you gots ta fix it? Did you break it, Mr. Moysey?"

"No! It just quit working," the elderly man said sharply. He was clearly not yet taken by Evan's charms.

Resting his elbow on the table, the boy propped his chin in his hand. "Dr. Ellig-am's a good one for fixin' things," he said, his head bobbing as his jaw opened and closed. "He even made my mobile—"

He clamped a hand over his mouth and looked at Martin anxiously.

"I think we should wait and see how I do with Mr. Moysey's clock before you do anymore bragging about my abilities, don't you think?" the doctor said softly.

The child gave him a relieved smile as he kicked his leg back, resting the toe of his trainer on the slate floor and pivoting his foot back and forth.

"Let me get Mr. Moysey started on cleaning up these clock parts, Evan, then we'll go get to work on cleaning up my car."

Evan watched as Martin showed the old man how to remove the years of accumulated grime from the small metal bits using a brush and a rag saturated with rubbing alcohol.

The little boy's curious fingers crept ever closer to a small cog, lying in front of the doctor, until he could no longer resist. He pinched the little part between his thumb and forefinger to pick it up.

"Leave that be!" the old man yelled, grabbing for the child's hand.

Martin's arm shot out reflexively, grasping his wrist and pulling his arm back.

"Don't you dare!" he hissed.

Evan's eyes were locked on the old man's glowering face as he slid himself over, nestling in under the doctor's still raised arm.

Martin stared at Mr. Moysey for a few moments, and then he released his grip and took in a deep breath. His arm dropped down to encircle the small body next to him.

There was a rustling, and he looked up to see his wife standing inside the doorway watching them.

She set her satchel on the floor under the coat rack and slipped her jacket from her shoulders.

"Everything okay here?" she asked worriedly as she approached her husband.

Martin closed his eyes and took in a deep breath before letting it out forcefully. "Fine."

Louisa had just stepped into the house when the small dust-up began. She knew why her husband had reacted the way he did, and she reached down to discreetly caress his back.

Mr. Moysey cast an uncomfortable glance at the little Hanley boy and then at the doctor. "I'm sorry. I guess we were both protecting things that are important to us," he said gruffly.

Martin looked down at Evan and pulled his arm from around him, a flush working its way up his neck. He cleared his throat and picked up the small gear that had captivated his young charge.

"This is an escape wheel, Evan. See these little angled projections that stick out?"

"Uh-huh. They look like those pointy teeth Potato has." The boy pulled his lips back, tapping a fingernail against his upper canine.

"That's right. The teeth on the escapement wheel keep the hands on the clock going forward at a constant rate."

"See, Mr. Moysey, I told ya he's good at fixin' things."

Evan turned his back to Martin, reclining against him, when Louisa crouched down in front of him. "Evan, you shouldn't have run on ahead of me the way you did. Next time you come, you must walk *with* me."

He straightened up and gave her a smile. "So, I get ta come again?"

Martin raised an eyebrow at her.

"I guess I should have said, *if* you come again. It smells like Poppy made biscuits while James was napping. Would you like one? Maybe with a glass of milk?" she asked as she stood up and walked over to the jar on the counter.

"I think he should clean my car out first," Martin grumbled with feigned annoyance.

Louisa gave him a sideways glance. "Maybe you should have a biscuit and milk *before* you help Dr. Ellingham ... for the energy to do the job properly. Then you could have another biscuit after if Dr. Ellingham is happy with how his car looks." She laid a Cornish Fairing on a piece of paper towelling and set it down at the far end of the table, placing a glass next to it.

Martin rolled his eyes and threw his head back. "You'll spoil his appetite doing that, Louisa. I was hoping to get a solid nutritious meal into that stomach of his."

She peered down at the child. "I guess Dr. Ellingham has a point. We'll save the second biscuit for after dinner, hmm?"

The little boy pulled his shoulders back and rose up on his toes. "I get to stay for dinner?"

Martin pushed himself up from the table and scowled down, but the slight upturning of the right corner of his mouth betrayed his affectation. "If you don't hurry up and eat that biscuit you'll still be here for dinner tomorrow night as well," he grumbled before moving down the hall.

Chapter 22

"Good thing you gots Mr. Portman ta help you carry yer stuff, huh, Dr. Ellig-am?" Evan said as he watched him set the cleaning supplies down next to the Lexus.

Martin raised his eyebrows as the young man straightened himself up. "Mm. And he does a jolly good job of wiping up floors as well. I didn't realise you had all these hidden talents when I hired you, Jeremy."

The aide shook his head at him and reached a hand down to tousle the little boy's hair. "You should see the wonders I can work with this hoover here." He picked up the female end of the extension cable running from the surgery and plugged the appliance into it.

"Really?" Evan watched the young man, wide-eyed.

"Jeremy, you can work your wonders for Evan another time. He has a job to get done today."

"Okay, I'll leave you to it, then. Evan, come and get me if you need my help out here." He gave Martin a roguish grin. "Or if Dr. Ellingham goes rolling down the hill or something."

"Oh, very funny, Jeremy," Martin said as his aide climbed the steps to the terrace.

"I wanna try that!" Evan took a quick step towards the street before Martin grabbed hold of the hood on his coat, bringing him to an abrupt halt.

"Nooo, you don't. You'll get yourself run over doing something like that!"

The child peered up at him. "But I was *gonna* look both ways first."

"Evan, it was only yesterday that I found you sitting in the middle of the road over by St. Kew! I don't want to see you playing on any streets or roadways again! Understood?"

The child fixed his eyes on his shoes and scuffed his foot on the ground. "Yes, sir."

"And I need to check that knee," Martin added distractedly, wagging a finger at the boy's leg.

Evan unzipped his fly, unsnapped his trousers, and had them pulled down around his ankles before the doctor knew what was happening.

"Not here, Evan! For goodness' sake, what do you think you're doing?"

"I thought you wanted ta see my knee. I'm just tryin' ta be helpful." The boy stared dejectedly at his feet before tipping his head back to look up at Martin. "Are you cross with me?"

"No, of course not. It's just not the appropriate place to be doing that. Now pull them up. You have a job to do," Martin said, turning his head away and clearing his throat as he suddenly felt embarrassingly conspicuous standing at the top of Roscarrock Hill while his charge disrobed in front of the entire village.

"Kay, but remember, yer gonna be my assistant."

Evan yanked the bottoms of his school uniform back up around his waist and fumbled with the snap, his hands trembling as he worked his small fingers, trying to get the two sides to click together. "I can't get it," he breathed out heavily.

"All right, come here."

The little boy shuffled over and pulled his hands behind his back.

"We're going to be doing this in the dark at this rate," Martin grumbled, snapping the child's trousers shut.

"Naw, we'll have this done quick as a flash!" The boy scrambled over and picked up the wand of the hoover. "Are ya ready, Dr. Ellig-am?"

"Yes." Martin groaned, pressing his fingers to his eyes.

"Kay. When I say, you push the button. The one with the *O—N.*"

The seven-year-old climbed into the back of the Lexus and positioned himself for the task at hand. "I'm ready!"

Martin flipped the switch and then leaned back against the car and closed his eyes.

He listened to the whine of the machine, punctuated by the occasional exertional grunt from the little boy.

"Kay! You can shut it off now!" Evan called out a few minutes later.

The doctor shook the drowsiness from his head and stepped over, flipping the switch.

"She looks right as rain now. Huh, Dr. Ellig-am?"

He leaned over and peered into his car. Aside from a few small bits of gravel under the driver's seat, the child had done a surprisingly good job. "Well done, Evan. Now we just need to wash the effluvium off the seat."

"Is that the doctor's word for gunge?" the child asked through chattering teeth.

"I suppose you could say that." A cold wind had begun to blow in off the harbour, and Martin reached down, pulling the boy's hood over his head before snapping it shut. He pointed towards the bucket of hot water that his aide had carried out. "Get that sponge and we'll finish this up."

The child picked it up and carried it over, giving it a brisk shake and sending a shower of soap suds in the doctor's direction.

"*Care-ful!*" he squawked as he brushed the droplets from his face.

"Oops." Evan eyed him warily for a moment before holding the sponge up and squeezing it, watching as a puddle of white foam accumulated at his feet.

"Here, better let me ring that out. You get back in the car."
Martin took the sponge from the boy and did the best he could
to rid it of excess moisture, grimacing as his fractured arm
protested the twisting motion.

He handed it back to Evan who began to scrub furiously at
the dull smears on the leather seat. "There, don't see no more
'fluvlium." The boy sat back on his heels to admire the result of
his efforts.

"Good. Now you need to treat the leather. Spray this on the
seat, then wipe it with this dry cloth."

A wisp of a smile slipped across the doctor's face as his
young charge accompanied the spraying of the liquid with a
vocalised *pshew-pshew*, turning the bottle into a chimerical
weapon. It prompted in him memories of a time when he had
allowed himself to slip into such flights of fancy. A time before
his parents had made it understood that such childishness was
not what they expected to come from the large sums of money
they had expended for him to go to the most elite of public
boarding schools.

"There! Proper job!" the boy said as he hopped out of the
car. He brought a small hand up and wiped the back of it across
his forehead, then leaned against the vehicle and blew out a
breath. "Whew! *That* was hard work!"

Martin joined him against the car. "Well, sometimes a man
has to face up to his responsibilities, no matter how difficult
they seem."

The child grew quiet for a few moments. "Sometimes my
'sponsibilities are too difficult for upping my face to."

Before Martin could respond, the boy's solemn demeanour
shifted abruptly. "Can we go have dinner now?"

He reached out with his crutch and tipped the bucket over,
sending the soapy water down Roscarrock Hill.

"You gather together whatever will fit in that pail and carry it into the house," he said. "We'll take a look at that knee, *then* we'll have dinner."

By the time Martin had examined Evan's wound, and the boy had thoroughly washed his hands, Louisa had whole wheat spaghetti and meat sauce served up on plates along with a bowl of tossed salad and a basket of warm bread.

"You just missed Mr. Moysey. He said to tell you he got all of the little" —she waved her hand vaguely in the air and pointed to a tray sitting on top of the washing machine— "parts cleaned. You're supposed to let him know when he should come back."

"Mm, I see," Martin said, glancing into the laundry room.

"Evan, you may sit next to Dr. Ellingham. Can you help him if he needs it, Martin?" Louisa asked, giving him a nod.

"Yes."

She kept one eye on the boy as she cut pasta into pieces for James Henry.

Her husband placed an ample serving of salad in his bowl. The seven-year-old speared a chunk of green pepper and brought it to his nose before screwing up his face.

Martin seemed oblivious to the fact that his every move was being monitored by the child. Evan watched him as he poured vinaigrette on to his salad and then reached for the cruet and followed suit.

His eyes tracked the doctor's hand as he brought a forkful of salad to his mouth. Evan looked at his own bowl of greens and made a hesitant stab at it before taking a bite.

Louisa stifled a giggle as he wrinkled up his face and forced it down, finishing the act with a slight shudder of his shoulders.

The boy then picked up his glass and washed down the remnants of the greens with milk. Placing his elbow on the table, he rested his head in his hand.

"Dr. Ellig-am, how come you got so big?" he asked as he poked around in his salad. "Did you have to eat vegetables to grow that way?"

Pulling his napkin from his lap, Martin gave his mouth a quick wipe. "I've always liked vegetables. I don't know if eating a lot of them had any effect on my eventual height, but I do know that vegetables contain many vitamins and minerals that a child's body needs to grow properly. So, if you wish to reach your maximum growth potential you need to eat a balanced diet, get adequate exercise, and plenty of sleep."

The boy stared at him for several moments, his brow furrowing as he pushed out his lower lip. "Maybe I could just go to bed earlier," he said glumly, giving his greens a lethargic jab.

"How 'bout you just eat your spaghetti for tonight."

Louisa was taken aback as her husband gave the boy a playful poke in the ribs, provoking a giggle and an immediate improvement in the child's demeanour.

Feeling his wife's eyes on him, Martin glanced over at her, taking note of the perplexed expression on her face. He cleared his throat and straightened himself in his chair before returning his attention to the food on his plate.

Before they drove the seven-year-old home that night, Louisa wrapped several biscuits in cling film and slipped them into his coat pocket.

Neither the child nor her husband said two words beyond clipped yes or no answers to her questions as they wended their way from Portwenn to the Hanley farm. As she shifted the gearbox into park, Louisa heard her husband sigh softly before pulling himself from the car.

"Come on, Evan. I'll see you to the door."

Louisa glanced in the rear-view mirror in time to see the boy's hand brush at his cheek before he unbuckled his seatbelt and slid out, gravel crunching under his feet.

Martin's thoughts turned briefly to Auntie Joan as he approached the house with Evan's fingers clinging to his sleeve. Those inevitable trips back to Bodmin Station must have been almost as painful for her as they had been for him. He felt as if he was leading the child to the gallows or throwing him to the wolves, and his stomach began to churn.

When they reached the porch, Martin steadied himself, gripping the doorframe, then he leaned over to speak softly to the boy.

"Evan, do you still have the mobile in your closet?"

The child rubbed vigorously at his forehead and nodded. "Uh-huh. In the wall under my bed."

"Good. Call me if you need me. Or call one of the other two numbers ... okay?"

"Yeah," Evan said, his voice breaking.

The little boy turned and went into the house, pushing the door shut behind him.

Louisa watched from the Lexus as her husband descended the stairs and took a few steps towards the car before veering off around the side of the building. He re-emerged a short time later and made his way towards the vehicle.

"Where did you go?" she asked as his seat belt clicked into place.

"Ohhh, let's just go home ... please." Martin fixed his gaze out his side window.

They drove in silence for several miles before he mumbled softly, "I had to vomit. That's where I went."

Louisa said nothing, but moved her palm to his thigh and comforted him the best she could with a gentle caress.

When she joined him in bed later that evening she hesitated before raising the issue of their differences the night before.

"Martin ... we need to discuss your fall, or rather what led up to your fall."

"Oh, Louisa. Do we have to do that now?" he moaned as he rolled on to his back and flung his arm up over his face.

"That *was* the plan." She turned to him and nestled her head into his shoulder. "Maybe you could start by telling me why you sneaked off."

"I did *not* sneak off! I just ... *went* off."

"Well you should have talked to me about it before you *went* off. That was very high-handed of you."

"High-handed?"

He squirmed out from under her and pushed himself up on the bed, looking down at her incredulously.

"What would you have said if I *had* tried to talk to you about it first, Louisa? Sure, go ahead and walk down to Mr. Moysey's? I trust you to use reasonably good judgement? I know you can do it?"

"I *do* know you use reasonably good judgement, Martin. Very good judgement actually ... usually."

He watched her, waiting for something more, but she just returned his gaze. He tried to ignore the familiar pain in his chest and he closed his eyes, calculating the number of years, months, weeks, days.

As the tightness began to ease, he took in a deep breath and let it out slowly. "So, the other?"

She shook her head. "The other what?"

"You didn't think I could do it."

"No. I have to admit that I *didn't* think you could do it. You surprised me. But you did hurt yourself in the process, didn't you?"

He tipped his head back and waggled his nose in the air. "I wouldn't have taken the fall if you and Ruth hadn't interfered. I turned when Ruth called out to me which caused me to lose my balance."

Louisa sat up and pulled her knees to her chest. "Yes, but Ruth wouldn't have been calling out to you if I hadn't rung her up because I was worried sick after you just left without saying anything."

"I left without saying anything because you weren't listening to me anyway. What's the point in my talking if there's no one listening at the other end!"

"The point is, Martin, that you walked down Roscarrock Hill—in the dark—where you were distracted by Ruth and you fell. You could have been seriously hurt."

"I *wasn't* seriously hurt. And that would be an unlikely scenario by the way. And I need to concentrate whenever—and *wherever*—I'm up on my feet! I got distracted and lost my focus—my sense of balance, and I fell. It had nothing to do with my being incapable of going for a bloody walk down Roscarrock Hill! I *would* have been fine."

He forced out an angry hiss of air and clenched his fist. "And I *left* you a note!"

Their discussion had quickly spiralled down into a row. Louisa tried to take a step back from what seemed to her to be a sensitive area for her husband, and she approached the problem from a different angle.

"I'm scared to death that something bad will happen if you go out on your own. That something will happen and you won't be able to get help," she said softly, keeping her eyes on her lap as she inched her hand over to grasp his.

"I know it's not fair to you, but it's so much easier for me when I know that you're safe ... here at home."

Martin wrapped his arm around her, pulling her close. "Then we have a problem, don't we?"

"Hmm?"

Rubbing a hand roughly across his head he began to stammer out an awkward explanation. "*You* need me here—where you don't have to worry. And I understand that. I understand why you would worry that I'm going to do something to get myself hurt.

"But it would be helpful if—to know you have confidence in me. I would like—er, I *need* actually—I need your encouragement to do these things.

"I don't talk. I know that. So, I can't—I can't expect you to understand this—how hard this is. And—and I don't think you can be encouraging when you—when you don't understand, or when—when you don't have confidence in me."

Tipping her head back, Louisa peered up at his face. "I'm sorry," she said softly as she reached a hand up and stroked his cheek. "I *do* want you to get well and to be able to do everything you used to be able to do, but I don't want you to take chances—to get hurt in the process."

She turned his face towards hers. "I *am* sorry, Martin. I just can't bring myself to encourage you to do things that I don't think you're ready for."

He sighed and shook his head, shrugging off what he had so desperately needed her to understand. "Thank you for helping out with Evan today," he said, effectively shifting the conversation away from his needs.

"You're welcome. I'm not sure that Evan saw cleaning out your car as a punishment, though. I think he quite liked it."

Martin pulled back and looked down at her with a rapidly developing scowl. "It wasn't *intended* to be a punishment! I just wanted him to see that his actions have consequences. That what he does affects not just himself, but other people as well. *And* that he needs to take responsibility for the consequences of his actions."

Louisa rubbed her palm across his chest and reached up to plant a kiss on his cheek. "I think you got that message across very well. I'm just saying, Evan really likes you, Martin. He looks up to you. And for him, any time spent with you is a wonderful reprieve from the negativity of home. And you make him feel safe."

"Mm." He tipped his head down, gazing at her. Taking her chin in his hand, he pressed his lips to hers.

She leaned forward slightly and her pyjama top fell away from her body, allowing him a brief glimpse of her breasts.

"Do you mind?" he asked as he took hold of the bottom edge of her top.

"No." She smiled coquettishly and lifted her arms over her head.

He peeled her top away and her fragrance wafted its way into his senses, whetting the need to satisfy his desire. With a soft moan, he pushed her back on to the mattress and buried his face into her neck.

She tugged at his vest as his lips moved down to nip playfully at her collarbone. "Mar—tin!" she giggled as he slipped his left arm from the sleeve. He continued on towards the hollow in her throat.

Squirming, she grasped his head in her hands. "*Martin*, that tickles!"

He pulled back. "Mm, sorry—sorry." He shook his head. "I didn't mean to." He pressed his palm to her clavicle. "I'm sorry, Louisa."

Rolling on to his back, he slipped the right sleeve of his vest over his arm before letting it drop to the floor.

Her eyes darted over her husband's features as she tried to read his mood. "It didn't bother me, Martin. Not in the least. Quite the opposite, in fact. It was nice to share a—a playful moment with you."

"*Playful?*"

"Yes, Martin, playful. When you were tickling me."

Martin screwed up his face. "I told you I didn't mean to. And the word playful would suggest that there's some element of pleasure involved. I don't know how you can find that particular stimulus to be pleasurable."

She stroked her fingers across his cheek and rested her forehead against his.

"So—you don't find tickling to be pleasurable?" she asked mischievously as her hand sat poised at his side.

"Maybe I should examine you, Doctor, to see if your reflexes react normally to the—*stimulus*," she said as she quickly wiggled her fingertips back and forth under his arm.

"Stop that!" Grabbing hold of her wrist, he pushed away and rolled from the bed. Falling forward, he sent the lamp on the bed stand crashing to the ground before he caught himself on the bathroom door jamb.

The sudden noise woke James Henry with a start, and his cries could be heard coming from the nursery.

"Are you all right?" Louisa asked as she sat up in the bed.

He stood, staring back at her for several moments before he felt a warm wave of embarrassment. "I'm fine," he said, averting his eyes. "I'll just go see to James."

He worked his way across the room and into the hall, steadying himself with a hand against the wall. Louisa watched him, baffled by the sudden turn of events, as he disappeared around the corner.

She joined him in the baby's room a short while later, where he was sitting in the rocking chair with his son on his lap. His eyes darted up at her before quickly shifting back to the boy.

She knelt down and picked up his feet, one at a time.

"What on earth are you doing?" he whispered.

"The bulb broke on the lamp ... there was blood on the floor. You've cut yourself." She peeled an envelope open and pulled out a plaster, applying it to the bottom of his foot.

"Mm, I see."

"Here, give me James." She held her hands out for the now sleeping child, and Martin released his grip on him.

"I brought your crutch. You go back to bed. I'll look at that cut in our room where I can see what I'm doing."

He was sitting on the edge of the bed, digging his thumb into his palm when she returned to the bedroom.

"Okay, lie back and let me take a look."

"No. I can do it," he clipped, trying unsuccessfully to grab the plaster and disinfectant spray from her hand.

"Oh, Martin, stop it! Just lie back. You know as well as I do that you'll never be able to get to it on your own."

He pulled his feet up on to the bed and reclined against the headboard.

"You want to talk about it?" she asked as she shined a torch on the bottom of his foot and peeled the plaster off before looking for embedded glass.

"No."

"Martin ... did I do something to upset you? Was it the tickling thing?"

"I think I already told you I don't want to talk about it, Louisa," he grumbled, pulling his foot back reflexively from the biting sting of another shot of disinfectant.

"It might help ... to not go to sleep with this on your mind, hmm?"

He sighed heavily and glanced at her quickly. "Just how much more do you want to humiliate me tonight? I tried to talk to you earlier and nothing came of it. No, I don't want to talk about it."

"I don't think I *humiliated* you! Why would you say that?"

She pressed a fresh plaster over the cut. "There," she said, patting his foot. "You should have Jeremy take a look at that tomorrow, but it's just a small cut."

"Mm, yes. Thank you. And erm, thank you for cleaning up the mess."

"You're welcome." She crawled in on her side of the bed and slipped under the blankets before turning off the light.

Curling herself up against him, she wrapped her leg over his hip. "Too bad our ... playful time came to such an abrupt end. I was enjoying it."

"I'm sorry."

They lay in the quiet for several minutes before he said, "I don't like tickling. I'm sorry about that because you obviously enjoy it."

"So, it's not me, then? The way I approached it?"

"Nooo!"

She waited out another period of awkward silence before he spoke again.

"It has to do with boarding school."

"Oh. I see."

"It was discovered that it could have an effect on me. If that's what playful feels like, then I don't think I like playful either, I'm afraid. I'm sorry about that."

She tightened her embrace and pressed her cheek to his. "It's okay; I understand. It's in the past now, though, isn't it?"

Martin lay silent. Her hands caressed his back as she tried to comfort him.

No, it wasn't in the past. The pain he had experienced minutes earlier was every bit as acute as what he had experienced as a child. Martin went to sleep that night feeling loved, but unheard.

Chapter 23

Rain pattered against the windows as a gust of wind shook the cottage Friday morning, and Louisa moved over, spooning up against her husband's solid frame for warmth.

She pulled her feet up, slipping her cold toes under his legs, her breath catching in her throat as one of his pins scraped across her ankle. She squeezed her eyes shut and bit her lower lip before mouthing a silent, *ouch*.

Martin had been unusually quiet the previous day, hardly speaking at all at breakfast or lunch and disappearing into his consulting room immediately after dinner. His mood made her nervous, bringing back painful memories and the old sense of resentment and insecurity that she had felt in those horrible weeks leading up to the Sports Day fiasco.

She pulled her arms in, sandwiching them between her body and his. Her fidgeting roused him and he began to stir. He groaned softly as he rolled on to his back and his limbs complained, having stiffened after several hours of lying inert.

She sighed and moved over, giving him space and ceding her warm nest to the new day. "Morning," she said, her voice still thick with sleep.

"Morning." Rubbing the heel of his hand against his eye, he gave his head a shake. "What time is it?"

"A little before seven. You can go back to sleep for a while if you like. I can wake you when I'm done in the bathroom."

"Mm, no. I have Chippy Miller coming in early today."

She narrowed her eyes at him. "Martin, remember, two hours a day."

He sucked in a breath, the air whistling through his clenched teeth. Then closing his eyes, he rolled back to his side, facing away from her. "You go ahead in the shower. I'll wait."

She fought her impulse to storm off in anger and instead moved up against him, wrapping her arm over his waist. "I'm just concerned that you'll overdo it, that's all," she said as she reached up and placed a light kiss on the back of his neck.

"Martin, I've been wondering ... what did you mean the other night when you asked if I wished I'd gotten a different brand?"

His body stiffened under her arm, and there was a pause in the gentle rise and fall of his chest. "Mm, it was just something Evan said."

"Oh, so it had nothing to do with mouthwash?"

He turned on to his back again and looked over at her. "*Mouthwash?* Of course not. Why would a seven-year-old boy concern himself with what brand of mouthwash to buy?"

Propping herself up on an elbow, Louisa rested her chin in her hand and studied his face. "The source of the quote was a little ambiguous, Martin." She brushed her fingers over her husband's head before taking the small curl of hair growing out behind his ear between her thumb and forefinger.

"I need to get a haircut when we're in Truro this afternoon." He stared up at her for several seconds and then reached up to cup her cheek in his hand.

"I'm sorry that all of this is causing you anxiety, Louisa," he said as his thumb brushed along her lips.

"Let's call it worry, not anxiety. I worry because I *love* you and want to keep you safe. Anxiety sounds like something negative that you're doing to me."

Martin stretched and yawned, his arm coming down around her shoulders. "Mmmm. I believe Jeremy would say you're getting all dainty with your semantics."

She smiled and leaned over to place a kiss on his lips. "Jeremy's turned out to be a good friend, hmm?"

"He hasn't known me long enough for you to say that."

"Martin, *please* don't push him away."

"I'm not. I'm just not ready to hang that moniker around his neck until he knows me better."

"He's not going to change his mind." Louisa stared down at him, tears welling in her eyes. "I'm scared, Martin. Scared that we're both backsliding."

He turned his gaze to the grey, drizzly sky out the window. "I know, me too."

"We're talking past each other. Going 'round and 'round in circles again."

"I know."

"And you're shutting down again."

He pressed his hand to his eyes and then brushed away the moisture before turning to look at her. "I'm not shutting down. I *want* to talk to you. I just don't know *how* to talk to you—how to get you to listen. When I talk, it just seems to make things worse." He pushed himself up, swung his legs over the side of the bed, and retreated to the bathroom.

The tension was thick on the drive to Truro later that day, with Martin and Louisa dancing around their communication difficulties by discussing things as far-flung from the topic as possible.

Martin pointed out that they would need to do something about the increasing number of cracks in the ceilings upstairs, and Louisa reminded him of their rapidly aging boiler. By the time they arrived at Dr. Newell's office, they had agreed that, unless they were pressed to take more immediate action, they should postpone making any decisions about either matter until after the Christmas and New Year holidays.

Louisa now sat, watching her husband as he thumbed distractedly through the latest issue of "Hello" magazine.

"So ... do you agree? Kanye West would make a great American president?" she asked, giving him an impish smile.

He turned to look at her, his eyebrows raised. "Hmm?"

"That article you seem to be engrossed in," she said, tapping her fingernail on the glossy picture of the rap star.

Martin glanced down before pulling in his chin and tossing the rag on to the coffee table.

Rubbing her hand on his thigh, she looked at him empathetically. "We'll work through this, Martin. I've been thinking about it today. It's not like when we had our difficulties in the past. We're both admitting that there's a problem this time around, and we have someone to help us through it ... right?"

He took her hand in his and straightened himself in his chair. "Mm."

The familiar squeak of the hinges on the therapist's door could be heard as the man emerged from his office and waved his patient back. "Martin ... you ready?"

Louisa gave his fingers a small squeeze. "Love you."

"Mm, yes," he said before limping down the corridor.

"Looks like you took a tum..." Louisa heard the therapist say to her husband as the door closed behind them. *Maybe Dr. Newell will be able to knock some sense into that man.*

"So, what exactly happened?" the psychiatrist asked as he dropped into the chair behind his desk and flipped open his patient's file.

"Like you said ... I took a tumble." Martin brushed at the leg of his trousers.

"Judging by your reluctance to elaborate, I assume I'm beating the proverbial dead horse?"

"Mm."

Dr. Newell cocked his head. "How are things going between you and Louisa? Keeping the lines of communication open?"

"I guess you could say that we've found ourselves challenged in that area recently."

"Has this been a gradual regression into old habits, or is it a new issue?"

Martin stared vacantly out the window, and the psychiatrist tipped his head to make eye contact. "Martin?"

"I'm not sure I know." He sat stiffly, his hands clasping his knees as his eyes darted between the therapist and the bookcases behind him.

Coming around the desk, Dr. Newell pulled a chair up next to him. "Are we back to that dead horse again, maybe?"

"I don't understand her, or she doesn't understand me," Martin said as he shifted his attention to the man. "I'm not sure which it is, so I don't even know what needs fixing. She looks at me like she did before she wanted to leave—like she's not happy, and I don't know what to do about it. I'm just not very good at all of this. I want to learn, but I'm beginning to think I'm incapable of that."

The therapist's fingers tapped against his lips as he watched him. "Did your communication difficulties play any part in the fall you took?"

Martin pressed his fingers to his temples. "My assistant and I went to see an elderly patient the other day. We were on our way back to Portwenn when we happened upon a boy ... a student at Louisa's school. He'd had an accident with his bicycle and had an abrasion on his knee that required attention. I cleaned it up and bandaged it, then we drove the boy home.

"By the time we got back to the village it was dark. Louisa was angry about my having exceeded our previously agreed upon work hours, but I don't know what she would have had me do. Leave a seven-year-old boy crying in the middle of the road?"

Dr. Newell rolled his biro back and forth between his palms. "When you explained the situation to your wife, what was her response?"

"She doesn't listen! I could hardly get two words out of my mouth before she cut me off!"

"And when did your fall occur?"

He closed his eyes and breathed out a heavy sigh. "I went out later. I had told a patient—my aunt's neighbour—that I'd look at his clock. It had quit working.

"Louisa was upstairs with James when I remembered I was supposed to stop at the man's house. I was tired. And tired of trying to talk to her, I suppose. So, I left her a note and walked over to see the man. I was fine until my aunt called out to me from her porch. I turned, lost my balance, and fell."

"Would you handle things any differently if you were confronted with a similar situation again?"

"Of course. I'd ignore her."

The psychiatrist's brow wrinkled. "In what way do you think *ignoring* your wife would solve anything?"

Martin screwed up his face and shook his head. "Not my wife—my aunt. I wouldn't have fallen if I'd ignored her. Turning my head threw me off balance."

"What about how you handled the situation with Louisa?"

"Well, as I said before, she wasn't listening to me. I seem to have a propensity for rubbing her up the wrong way. Most of the time I'm at a loss as to what I've done. I know this time what I've done, but I have no bloody idea what I should have ... *could* have done differently."

"What about foregoing the trip out in the dark?"

Martin's head shot up. "I can't keep myself shut up in the surgery for the rest of my life. Which is what Louisa seems to need from me right now." He dug his thumb into his palm as he worked the muscles in his jaw. "I don't know how to get my independence back without causing her anxiety."

"So, you think Louisa needs you to stay at home where she doesn't have to worry about you?"

"I don't think it, I know it! She told me as much!" he said, his eyes snapping.

"Well, it sounds like she's made her needs quite clear to you. What is it that *you* need right now ... from *her*?"

"It's irrelevant because she doesn't have it to give."

The psychiatrist leaned forward, resting his arms on his thighs. "Humour me, Martin. What do *you* need?"

He blinked his eyes at the man and tipped his head. "To be independent again."

"And why do you see independence as a need?"

"Isn't that something every human being needs?"

"Yes, to some extent. Some more than others. What is it that you get from feeling independent?"

Martin pulled himself to his feet and limped over to the window. "I have a busy medical practice, or I did—should. I want to be able to do the job that I was trained to do. And I need to be independent if I'm to be able to care for my patients properly. To not need my assistant to drive me to see patients who are unable—or unwilling—to come to the surgery. And, of course, I want to be able to care for James and Louisa ... be physically able to care for them."

"In what ways?"

Martin turned from the window and gave the man a sharp nod. "You're a father. You know what I mean. I can do little more than lift James out of his cot, his high chair, hold him on my lap. He's starting to walk, and I can't even hold his hand so that he doesn't fall down ... take him up the hill to sit and watch the sun set in the evening. I could fall with him ... on him.

"And what if James and Louisa need me ... physically? Do you know how humiliating it is to have your wife think you're not even capable of going for a damn walk down the hill? I *can* do it! But I fell and now she's treating me like that seven-year-old boy who needs to be reminded to stay out of the street. God! I'm a grown man! I'm not a child!"

He turned back to the window and shoved his crutch to the floor.

The therapist sat, unflinching. "I asked how you think you benefit from being independent. You gave me several good examples of how others would benefit from your independence, but I'm not sure I'm understanding how *you* would benefit. Can you clarify that for me?"

Martin turned slowly to face him, his confident carriage belying his desperation. "As I explained to you, I'm a doctor. To be able to carry out my duties properly I need to be able to get around, and I would much rather I didn't have to rely on my assistant. Is it clearer to you now?"

"Not really, Martin. You're not seeing the real issue here at the moment. You can administer to the needs of your rural patients equally well regardless of who's behind the wheel of your car."

The psychiatrist walked to his side and picked up his crutch, handing it back to him. "Come back and take a seat, please."

He put his hand on Martin's shoulder and guided him back to his chair. Then, giving a tug on the knees of his trousers, he sat back down next to him. "Martin, you were on your own, living independently for many years. I know what came after that period, but tell me about the years before you were able to be independent."

Martin leaned his elbows on his thighs and slowly rubbed his palms together as he stared absently at a scrap of paper under the doctor's desk.

His eyes drifted shut as he took in a slow breath. "That wasn't a good time. I worked my bloody arse off trying to please my parents, but it didn't seem to change their feelings about me.

"I had no say in anything. My opinion didn't matter. Actually, not only did it not matter, I wasn't *allowed* an opinion. I never could have survived my childhood if I'd had an inkling that it should have been any better. I guess that's the upside," he said, glancing over at the therapist.

"So, the *upside* is that you took the abuse at face value?"

"That's right."

Dr. Newell squinted his eyes at him. "Can you explain what you mean by that?"

"I was the only child in my family. No siblings—no cousins. And I had no friends, so I was unaware of what life was like for other children. I just had glimpses when parents came to pick classmates up from boarding school.

"I *did* know that I was an anomaly, being the only boy to spend the holidays at the school. Aside from summer holidays ... up to a point. But you can't miss what you don't even know exists."

The therapist's penetrating gaze and rapt attention caused Martin to avert his eyes before screwing up his face. "It was all rubbish anyway."

"What was all rubbish?"

"The jolly holidays the boys talked about."

"Why do you say that? That it was all rubbish?"

"The negative experiences aren't as painful if a person doesn't have positive experiences to compare them to. I would think that would be obvious to someone in your line of work," Martin growled, his barely concealed tension bubbling to the surface.

Dr. Newell pushed himself up from his chair and returned to his seat behind his desk. "We're veering off from what we were discussing, but I think this is an important issue that's just surfaced." He picked up his biro and scribbled some notes into Martin's file and then leaned back in his chair, tapping the implement on the armrest.

"Let's talk a bit about your last statement. That the bad experiences aren't as painful if there are no positive experiences to compare them to. Can you give me an example of what you're talking about?"

Martin shifted his weight off his right hip and stretched his leg out in front of him. "Visits to Aunt Joan and Uncle Phil's. In the spring, each day at school seemed progressively more difficult to tolerate as the summer holidays approached. Then the time at the farm was—" He drew in a breath and closed his eyes, forcing back tears. "That stress ... fear was gone. When it was time to go back to school—or home—*gawd*— I had to adjust to it all over again before the cycle started again in the spring."

"Are you saying that during that month spent at your aunt and uncle's home, you got used to a more laid back way of life, and it made the rigors and formality of boarding school less tolerable?"

Martin stared back at him. "Something like that. Each year at Joan and Phil's it got worse. The first couple of summers, the anxiety about leaving Portwenn and returning to school didn't begin until my last week on the farm. But eventually there was a constant undercurrent of dread that tainted the enjoyment of being there. I couldn't relax. I couldn't sleep. I knew it was just a fleeting reprieve from my life. And if I allowed myself to—to get used to feeling good, the misery when I returned to school or home was even more intense."

Dr. Newell leaned back in his chair for a moment and closed his eyes, nodding his head gently. He rolled his chair forward and leaned his elbows on his desktop. "As a coping mechanism for dealing with that inevitable readjustment period you kept one foot in that misery of boarding school and didn't allow yourself to fully live that blissful life on the farm?"

Martin blinked his eyes slowly, his gaze fixed on the shelves of books behind the doctor. "I suppose that would be an accurate description."

"Over the course of the next week, Martin, I'd like you to keep a journal of sorts. You have a much different life now than the life you were forced to live as a child, but your brain hasn't adapted to that different life.

"Human beings are hardwired for a more efficacious response to negative experiences than positive experiences ... a self-preservation strategy that we were endowed with by mother nature.

"Because your childhood consisted of primarily negative experiences, that hardwired response has been strongly reinforced, making it difficult for you to enjoy the good things in your life.

"Your brain has been trained, so to speak, to not recognise the good things. We're going to try to retrain that brain of yours. I want you to keep a record of the things that happen each day for which you are grateful."

"How many ... *good things* do I have to record each day?" Martin asked as he watched his therapist suspiciously.

"There's no set number, Martin. Although you should always have at least one, don't you think?"

He cocked his head at the man. "I'm sorry?"

"You have a wife and son who love you."

"Ah, yes."

Dr. Newell came around to the front of his desk and perched himself on the corner. "Now, back to what we were discussing before we got side-tracked. What benefit do you get from being independent?"

Martin worked his fist around the end of the armrest and sighed heavily. "I don't have to rely on someone else."

"And in what way do you benefit from being self-reliant?"

"I'm not *dependent* on someone else!" Martin snapped. "Are you listening to me?"

"I *am* listening to you. You've defined independence for me twice now. But you haven't explained to me how you *benefit* from being independent."

Whipping his head around, Martin began to pull himself from his seat before dropping back into it. "It would make getting up out of this damn chair and walking out of this room a hell of a lot easier for one thing!" he growled.

The psychiatrist kept his gaze fixed on his agitated patient as he clicked his biro.

Martin's eyes flashed at the man. "I'm not *how* I benefit! I *need* to be independent though, I *am* sure of that! I've completely lost control of my life!"

He winced as he smacked his fist on his thigh. "Gawd! Portman chauffeurs me around—tells me when to have a lie-down! Louisa chastises me if I'm late getting home—for going out without getting permission first! I feel like a child again! When I had absolutely no say in my life! When the people who had the say despised me!" he spat out.

"Do you have any idea how terrifying that is? To be completely controlled by a man who's disgusted by you—a woman who would protect her—p-pampered poodle from the neighbourhood bullies before defending her own son?" He put his head down in his hands and swallowed back a strangled sob.

Dr. Newell returned to his chair and added to his notes before saying quietly, "Martin, how do you benefit from being independent?"

Martin slowly straightened himself and refocused his gaze on the bookshelves. "It gives me a sense of security, I suppose. I never really felt secure—safe—until I was an adult. After I refused to let my father push me into the navy. When I was at the farm with Joan ... that feeling was fleeting. I felt a sense of *permanent* security once I cut off ties with my parents."

"Once you were independent."

"Mm, yes."

"I understand. Given your experiences as a child, it makes perfect sense for you to feel the way you do."

The doctor glanced discreetly at his watch. "Well, we're out of time. You did well today, Martin," he said, pushing himself up from his desk.

The psychiatrist held the door for him and followed him out into the waiting area. "Don't forget that journal I asked you to keep."

"All done?" Louisa asked, flashing her husband a smile as he approached."

"Mm, yes."

Dr. Newell put his hands on his hips and glanced from husband to wife. "Would you both be agreeable to resuming our couple's therapy next week? Perhaps couple's therapy on Wednesdays, and I can spend time with you alone on Fridays, Martin?"

Louisa reached for her husband's hand and grasped it firmly as she gave the therapist a smile. "That would be good ... for me. If it's good for Martin," she said, glancing up at him.

"That would be fine. Good for me as well." He squeezed her hand in return before discreetly stroking his thumb across her knuckles.

"All right, then, I'll see you both next Wednesday at four o'clock." Dr. Newell turned to Martin and extended his hand. "You made good progress today, Martin. It may not feel that way, but ... good job."

Martin and Louisa crossed the parking lot in silence. Then Martin pulled the driver side door open for his wife. As she moved to get into the vehicle, he pulled her back and wrapped his arms around her tightly before placing a gentle kiss on her forehead. "We *will* be fine," he whispered.

Chapter 24

Martin didn't bring up the subject of his session with Dr. Newell, and though she was tempted, Louisa didn't ask. When she came back downstairs after putting the baby to bed that night he was sitting on the sofa with a medical journal in his hands and the leather-bound book that he used for note-taking in his lap.

The outlining of recently published papers and research studies was a practice that her husband had adopted during his years at medical school. Copying the information helped him to commit the latest information to memory.

She sat down, and Martin moved the binder to make way for the feet he knew would be plunked in his lap.

"Did James go down all right?" he asked as he wrapped a hand around her foot.

"Sound asleep."

"Your toes are cold. You should put your slippers on rather than running around in your socks, you know." He gave a tug on her pant legs, pulling them down to cover her bare ankles.

"But I like having you warm them up for me," she said, giving him an impish smile before shoving her feet under his thigh.

"Mm." He shifted his eyes back to his journal, giving a roll of his eyes.

Louisa picked up her novel from the coffee table and opened it to the dinosaur-shaped bookmark she had received from one of her students. Her gaze repeatedly flitted from the pages as her husband would raise his head and stare absently before refocusing again to scribble into the leather binder.

Returning her attention to her book, she tried to allow herself to become immersed in the tale. The descriptive narrative that had captivated her the night before, with its colourful telling of life on a Ceylon tea plantation, was failing to keep her attention from being drawn elsewhere, however.

Martin's brows pulled together as he glanced up again, before trailing more ink across the paper in his notebook. His mouth pulled up slightly as almost imperceptibly-fine creases formed at the corners of his eyes.

Louisa listened to the whispered scratches as he went to work again with his pen. "What are you doing?" she asked, curiosity getting the better of her.

His head shot up, and he glanced at her quickly before averting his eyes. "Mm, nothing. Nothing. How's your book?" He jabbed his biro at it, tipping his head back and peering down at her.

Giving him a coy smile, she shrugged her shoulders. "I can't quite get into it. I'm finding myself distracted tonight ... for some reason," she said pulling a foot out from under him and wiggling her toes against his inner thigh.

He gave a low grunt. "Maybe we should run over to Wadebridge tomorrow before the thing at the farm ... find you something that'll hold your interest." His attention was returned to his journal.

Louisa twisted up the left side of her mouth and knitted her brow before giving a small sigh, opening back up to her bookmarked page. The clock on the secretary ticked away the seconds as she tapped her fingernail, in counterpoint, on the book binding.

She peeked up furtively at her husband and shifted her foot up slightly higher on his leg before pivoting it slowly back and forth. Still nothing.

Another shift north and a few well-placed caresses finally jarred his eyes from the words on the page in front of him. His brows raised, he glanced down at his lap before giving her a sideways glance.

"Are you, erm ... still finding your book to be less than engaging?"

Louisa withdrew her feet and moved to the other end of the sofa, leaving her novel behind. "The book is quite entertaining, but *you* ... are proving to be a bit of a distraction tonight," she said as she tucked her legs under her and raised up to place a lingering kiss on his lips.

He looked back at her, his round eyes softening his typically stern facial expression into one of childlike naivete. "Mm, sorry," he said before clearing his throat and laying his pen and books aside.

Flinging her leg over him, Louisa straddled his lap. "This okay?" she asked, cupping his face in her hands. "Not hurting, is it?"

"Mm, no ... it's fine."

She tried to suppress a satisfied smile as she watched his Adam's apple rise and fall. Tipping her head, she trailed kisses down his throat before letting her lips settle in the crook of his neck while she played with the buttons on his shirt. She slipped them through the buttonholes, slowly working her way down his front before her fingers began to stroke teasingly under his vest.

He pressed his palms to the small of her back, lacing his fingers together. Then, allowing his head to fall back into the sofa cushion, he submitted himself to the pleasures of her touch and the mood of the moment.

"Mmmm," he moaned softly as the breath he had forgotten to release flowed from his lungs.

Her hands caressed, pausing as they detected the ridge of scar tissue running between his ribs. She pulled her head down and pressed her lips firmly to his chest.

Sitting back, she peered down at him, her eyes locked on his and dark with the anticipation of what was to come.

He released his grip on her and, reaching down, he groped for his belt. The sound of muted voices penetrated his ears, but barely registered. Friday night revellers down at the pub he quickly concluded before his thoughts returned to his wife's ministrations and the effect they were having on him.

His buckle jangled as the strap slid through it and he ripped the belt from the loops of his trousers and dropped it to the floor. Louisa held his head in her hands as she kissed him, the tip of her tongue brushing his lips.

He pulled his hands forward and slipped them under the front edge of her jumper, her skin warm and velvety against his fingers. He took in a sharp breath as she shifted her weight forward, pressing against him.

"Erm ... perhaps we should go upstairs?" he whispered breathlessly.

"Mmm, yes." She rolled off his lap, her eyes darting to the window.

The faint voices that Martin had tuned out moments earlier began again, this time louder and increasing in volume and intensity.

A sudden banging on the door brought about an abrupt end to the romantic interlude which had held so much promise.

"Oh, gawd! What now?" he groaned as he struggled to his feet and hastily shoved his vest back into his trousers before pulling his shirt over his shoulders.

"Doc! Doc!" PC Penhale's nasal voice resonated through the mail slot. "We have a man down here! Well, technically he's a woman ... but she's still down!"

Martin wagged his finger at his crutch which had fallen on to the floor, and Louisa stooped over to pick it up. Her head hit the corner of the coffee table with a sharp thud.

"Ow!" she yelped as she pulled up a hand, massaging the developing lump, while the other passed the crutch off to her husband.

"Oh, Louisa! Turn into the light—let me see!" Martin said, pulling his handkerchief from his back pocket and pressing it to her forehead.

"You have a small cut; hold that there. Sit down and I'll go see to the idiots at the door. Don't lie down unless you're feeling light-headed. It'll cause the wound to bleed more." he said.

He took a step towards the entryway before retreating to place a kiss on her forehead and brush his hand across her cheek. "You'll be fine." He gave her a small smile and a nod before lumbering off.

"Doc, you in there? Officer in need of assistance! We have a code three out—"

Martin jerked the door open and Joe jumped back, pulling himself to his full height before hoisting up his tool belt.

The doctor surveyed the scene in front of him, sizing up the situation. Chippy Miller, Peter Teague and several other men, clad in the waterproof yellow brace trousers worn by those in the fishing industry, stood on the terrace holding a board which supported a craggy faced woman with unruly greying hair, lying face down and in obvious distress.

"What's this about?" he asked impatiently.

"Injured female, Doc. Penetrating broken beer bottle injury to the upper, erm—" Penhale gulped and glanced down at the woman— "left buttock. I estimate the patient's age to be approximately sixty-five, give or take five ... or maybe ten years. Probably give more than take actually."

"I'm fifty-two, you stupid git!" the woman barked from her perch on the board.

The constable eyed Martin's dishevelled appearance. "Sorry, Doc, looks like you were hopin' to get off to bed early. I called for an ambulance, but there was a pile-up on the A-39, and they were all tucked up at the moment. Didn't know what else to do," Joe said, giving the doctor a shrug and a sheepish grin.

The doctor cleared his throat as his fingers fumbled at the buttons on his shirt. "That's fine. Bring her on through to the consulting room.

Martin followed after the small crowd of fishermen before squeezing past them to get to his patient.

"Okay, I can take it from here," he said as he herded them out the door. He watched, his scowl deepening, as they all settled themselves into chairs in the reception room. "What do you think you're doing?" he asked incredulously. "Go away!"

"You sure, Doc?" Chippy Miller asked, getting slowly to his feet with a hand on his back. "You might need us ta help you flip 'er over," he drawled.

"I'll manage. And you had no business lifting that woman in the first place, Mr. Miller!" he said, wagging his finger at him. "I just saw you this morning for a possible herniated disc! Good grief, do you lack the sense God gave an oyster?" Martin snatched the newspaper that Chippy clutched in his hand and hissed out a breath. "Where did you get this?"

"It was in my back pocket, Doc."

Martin threw the gossip rag into the bin and gestured towards the door. "Out! Everybody!"

The fishermen shuffled their way on to the terrace and he swung the door shut behind them before returning to the consulting room.

"All right Mrs—" He glanced up at Joe Penhale.

"Didn't get a chance to ask that particular question, Doc."

Joe leaned over and peered into the woman's face. "What—is—your—name—madam?" he enunciated loudly.

"There's nothin' wrong with my hearin'!" The woman pushed herself up on her elbows and cranked her head around to look at the doctor. "It's Tallack. Shelagh Tallack. 'E's a bit cakey, that one is," the woman said, poking her thumb at Joe. "More mouth than teeth, too. Just kept yammerin' on about the dangers of the demon drink or some such nonsense."

Martin glanced over as Joe pulled in his chin and lowered his head. "Mrs. Tallack, if it weren't for Officer Penhale, you'd still be lying on the floor in the pub right now with glass sticking out of your backside," Martin snapped back as he cut through the woman's trousers with a pair of trauma shears. "Now just lie there and be quiet."

The woman shot the doctor a black look before lowering herself back down on to the table. "It's not missus, just miss— Shelagh."

"How did this happen?"

"I fell on a busted beer bottle, what does it look like?"

Martin pulled on a pair of surgical gloves as air hissed from his nose. "*How* did you fall?"

"On my bloody arse, you idiot! Are you sure you're really a doctor?"

"That's a good one, eh, Doc? On her bloody arse." Penhale chuckled. "I bet that's just what yer gonna find under those trousers, dontcha think?" He gave Martin a crooked grin and a nudge with his elbow.

"Be quiet, Penhale," Martin said, yanking his arm away from the man. "I meant, what *caused* you to fall; did you trip?"

"'Course not. I'm rock steady." The woman gave the phlegmy cough typical of a smoker. "Gotta be when ya make yer livin' on a boat. I just got ta feelin' a bit off is all. Felt dizzy and thought I might be bein' sick, so I got up off a my stool ta go to the loo. The room set ta spinnin', and I started feelin' like a fart in a colander. Next thing's, I'm on the floor."

Martin pulled the rubberised material away from the woman's wound, stifling a gag as he turned his head away. He took a few cleansing breaths before returning his attention to the task in front of him.

"Here, hold this," he told the constable as he shoved a small basin into his hands.

"Can do, Do-*c*. You just let me know if you can't do it. I'll pull that baby out of there for you"

Martin stared at him for a moment out of the corner of his eye. He picked up a small glass vial and filled a syringe with lidocaine before injecting it into the woman's flesh around the protruding glass.

Grasping the fragment of the beer bottle with a pair of forceps, he slowly worked it out and dropped it into the basin.

"Hmm, appears to be ... Cornish Knockers. A very good choice *Ms.* Tallack," the constable said as he studied the specimen in front of him. "Flowery and fruity in the mouth with an interesting bittersweet finish.

"I actually bought you a six pack of this very fine spirit for Christmas last year, Doc. Then it occurred to me that it would be a gift that you couldn't properly appreciate ... what with yer not drinkin' and all. It's like they say, give the gift of abstinence to those who do not appreciate your presents."

"Gawd!" Martin mumbled as he jerked his head back. "It's, give the gift of your *absence* to those who do not appreciate your *presence*."

Joe pulled up his lower lip and tipped his head to the side. "That works, too, I s'pose."

The doctor gave the officer another sideways glance, curling his lip slightly as his eyes settled on the bloody chunk of glass. "Get rid of that, will you."

Pulling his hand up, the constable snapped his fingers. "Right you are, Doc. I sure wasn't thinkin' there, was I? Just standin' here...holdin' this bloody mess right in front of you, and—"

Martin pivoted and leaned over, emptying his stomach into the bin. He straightened back up and glared at the constable as he wiped his mouth on his sleeve. Then grabbing the bowl from his hand, he dumped its contents on top of the remains of his supper.

Turning his head away from his patient, Martin took in a deep breath and swallowed. "I apologise Ms. Tallack."

He inspected the wound to the woman's backside. "This will need a couple of stitches. I don't think you want me coming at you with a needle and thread right now, so I'll call my assistant to come and close the wound. I have something I need to attend to. Then I'll come back to finish up with you. If you'll excuse me for a moment."

Martin stepped into the reception room and rang Jeremy before limping off towards the kitchen. He grabbed a cold pack from the freezer and wrapped it in a clean tea towel before returning to Louisa, still sitting on the sofa with her husband's handkerchief pressed to her forehead.

"I'm going to be a little bit yet," he said as he pulled her hand away to inspect the lump that had formed above her left eyebrow.

"Is it a serious injury?" she asked, her eyes searching her husband's face.

"No, no, no, no, no. You'll be fine."

"Not *me*! Your patient. Who is it? What happened?"

His shoulders dropped, and he breathed out heavily before tipping his wife back and pulling a pillow under her head. "You'll have to get all the news from the village gossip mongers, Louisa," he said, laying the gel pack across her brow. "How are you doing?"

"Bit of a headache, but it's not bad."

"I'll check you out more thoroughly when I finish with this patient. I shouldn't be too much longer." He brushed a wisp of hair from her face and kissed her gently. "I'm sorry about the interruption to our, erm—earlier."

She smiled up at his boyish face. "It's fine, Martin. I'll just look forward to our, erm—later." she said, raising her eyebrows suggestively.

He cleared his throat and pulled himself to his full height. "Yes. I better get back to Miss—the patient."

Louisa watched as his tall frame disappeared around the corner, taking note of the shirt tail that had crept out of his waistband and was now hanging down his left side. She called out to him, "Martin! You're coming un—" She lay with his belt in her hand as the clicking of his crutch grew fainter.

"Forgive me, Miss Tallack," Martin said as he re-entered the room and took up a position next to his assistant who was now surveying the situation.

"Well, what are you thinking, Mr. Portman?" he asked.

"I'll wash it off and take a closer look, but I'm thinking a simple uninterrupted suture should do the job."

"Righto. I'll get a suture pack for you while you clean and disinfect the wound."

"You sure he knows what he's doin'?" Shelagh asked, eyeing the aide suspiciously. "Not much more than a sprog yet, is he?"

"Martin raised an eyebrow at the young man. "He's wise beyond his years, Miss Tallack. You have nothing to worry about."

The doctor watched from the side as his assistant repaired the damage caused by their patient's fall, giving him a half-smile after the final knot was made.

"You'll be a bit sore for a few days, but I'll send you home with an analgesic as well as an antibiotic," Martin said. "The wound should heal without incident as long as you keep it clean and covered. And stay off your—" he cleared his throat and pulled in his chin— "bottom."

Sitting down behind his desk, he scratched notes into Shelagh's file. "When did you last eat something, Miss Tallack?" he asked.

"'Bout noon I s'pose. I was fixin' ta get some'a them fish n' chips at the pub afore I went tits up."

"You need to be eating regularly. You probably experienced a drop in your blood sugar level. That could make you lightheaded. Come in next week, and I'll recheck your wound. My assistant can draw a blood sample—check your glucose levels."

It was almost eleven o'clock by the time Martin and Jeremy had finished with their patient and sent her out the door with PC Penhale. And it was nearing midnight by the time the aide had gone on his way and Martin crawled into bed to spoon up next to his wife.

"Louisa?" he said tentatively as he stroked his fingertips up and down her arm.

"Hmm?"

"I really had no choice tonight ... with the patient."

She wriggled under his arm, turning to face him. "I know, Martin. It's fine."

"And, erm ... I'm sorry about our interruption."

Pushing herself up, Louisa pressed her lips to his. "You *don't* need to apologise. I understand."

Martin blinked back at her and took in a hesitant breath. "No, I mean, I'm sorry—er, I'm *disappointed* that we were interrupted. I wish we'd been able to finish what we'd started."

"Oh, we'll finish, Martin. We'll finish. Just not tonight." She kissed him and then nuzzled her face against his cheek before settling in.

Martin lay, eyes closed, noticing the warmth and softness of her body, her fragrance, and her gentle breaths brushing against his neck. Then he fell asleep feeling grateful.

Chapter 25

Louisa's eyes fluttered under her lids, and her hand swiped reflexively at a tickling sensation on her forehead. Slowly, her senses began to stir.

She took in her surroundings through squinted eyes. The sun, rising in solstitial reluctance above the horizon, cast a pink glow in the room. The raucous calls of the jackdaws and gulls permeated the old stone walls of the surgery. And the pleasantly familiar scent of her husband, who was typically warm and moist as a result of her tendency to wrap herself around him as they slept, all blended together to elicit what she called her hot-chocolate-in-front-of-the-fireplace feeling. Relaxation.

She brushed again at the tickle, and Martin pulled his hand back quickly, peering down at her.

"G'morning," she said as she gave him a shy smile.

"Good morning."

"What were you doing?"

"Checking the oedema around your wound."

He made a move to peel off the plaster, and she slapped at his hand, giving him a scowl. "Martin, don't—don't do the doctor thing with me."

Martin's eyebrows twitched as his gaze drifted away from her and he dropped on to his back.

Sitting up in the bed, Louisa picked up his hand, pressing it to her lips. "Why is it so important to you? Why do you have to fuss over me when I'm sick, or when ... you know, the Sports Day thing. Why do you do that?"

His mouth opened and closed several times. "I'm a doctor. It's the thing I'm good at."

"Well, it's been my experience that you are quite good at other things as well," she said suggestively, the corner of her mouth quirking.

"Yes, but I'm concerned about—"

His breath caught in his throat as her hands slipped under his vest, and her fingernails raked lightly across his skin.

"Louisa, I'm just trying to express my—my—*Louisa!* I'm *trying* to talk to you!" He took hold of her wrist and pinned her hand firmly to his chest. "Are you interested in my answer, or is there some other reason you asked me that question?"

"I *do* want an answer, Martin. But you're going to give me the same story. I already know you're a doctor, and a brilliant doctor at that. But—I'm sorry, it can get to be a bit ... much."

"Well I apologise if you find my attentiveness annoying," he said, wagging his nose in the air. "But I can't trust that sorry excuse of a GP over in Wadebridge with my patients. I certainly don't trust him with the care of my *family!*"

"So, that's it? If we saw a qualified doctor in Newquay ... you'd be all right with that?"

Martin stared back at her. "Why are you being like this? I just want to look under your plaster—to check on your wound."

Louisa released an audible sigh. "I don't mean to make it sound like I'm unappreciative, I really don't. It's just that it feels very odd having you look at me in such a clinical way when we, erm ... you know ... you look at me in other *less* clinical ways."

"Oh, for goodness' sake, Louisa! I want to look at your forehead, not collect a PAP smear!" he said, rolling his eyes to the ceiling.

Louisa whipped her head away, her chestnut mane brushing across her face to communicate her exasperation. "Well, that image certainly threw cold water on the romantic mood! Thanks for that," she said as she withdrew her hand and reached for her dressing gown on the bedside table.

Martin blinked his eyes as he watched her drop from the bed and storm from the room. He lay, studying the cracks in the ceiling, listening to the fading angry slaps of her feet against the floor.

She was standing at the sink, staring out the window, when he entered the kitchen a few minutes later. He leaned his crutch against the table and came up behind her, slipping his left arm around her waist. "I'm sorry I spoilt the mood," he said, placing a kiss on the top of her head.

"It's all right, Martin. I was the one who asked the question in the first place." She turned, embracing him and holding him tightly. Then, tipping her head back, she offered up her injured forehead to him.

"Are you sure?" he asked before reaching hesitantly for the corner of the plaster.

"I'm sure. But hurry up, and please don't make a fuss."

Martin uncovered the wound and turned her head towards the window, scrutinising the cut for any sign of infection. "I'll redress that after you have your shower," he said as his fingers skimmed gently over the swelling that had developed.

The intensity of his gaze and the warmth and solidity of his hands as they now cupped her face caused a warm flush to spread through her. She glanced at the clock in the lounge. *Bugger.* James would be waking any moment now. Once again, their *earlier* would have to wait for *later.* "I better go ... shower before ..."

Martin dropped his hands to his sides and tried to conceal his disappointment. "Mm, yes. Yes, of course."

"*Later,*" she whispered as her cheek pressed against his and her fingertips passed across his chest.

He sighed heavily as he watched her hurry off.

The clouds had cleared and the sun was shining brightly when they got into the car to head to the farm. Louisa glanced over at her husband periodically. He was especially quiet as he stared blindly at the scenery passing by his window.

"Care to share what you're thinking about?"

His head swung around, and he tapped his fingertips against the window ledge. "We, erm ... should make a stop in Delabole—get some petrol." He wagged a finger at the fuel gauge.

"That's going to put us behind schedule. Maybe we should get it later."

"God knows what time it'll be before that circus at the farm wraps up. The station closes early on weekends. Mm, best not take the chance."

Louisa narrowed her eyes at him. "Martin, you *will* remember that this is a very big day for Al and Ruth—yes?"

He tucked in his chin. "Yes." His eyes shifted back to the passing moorland.

Delabole, a small, family-friendly community, was located northeast of Portwenn, and not far from Auntie Joan's farm. He remembered the many stops she would make there for basic supplies and to deliver her produce to the market. The egg and cress sandwiches she would buy for him, just to get him through to supper as she would say, were always the high point of the trip.

"I'm going to run inside for a minute. Can you take care of the petrol?" Louisa asked as she pulled the Lexus into Lugg & Son's a few minutes later. "I'll take James in with me."

"Yes, that's fine."

Louisa gathered up the baby and went into the station, and Martin forced himself on to his stiffened legs and limped to the pump.

He fumbled with the gas hatch, his fingers having difficulty grasping the lip on the door. Lifting the pump nozzle, he shoved it into the fuel fill hose before waging war with the handle.

His hand trembled as he struggled to squeeze it hard enough to engage the latch. He grimaced as pain shot up his forearm. "Gawd!" he muttered before giving up on his right hand and taking hold of the nozzle with his left.

He leaned back against the car and closed his eyes, listening to the whooshing and ticks generated by the pump. An open house was not the sort of activity that he would enjoy on *any* given day, but he had been dreading this event in particular.

The farm was no longer a reminder of Auntie Joan, but rather a painful reminder of her absence. And, of course, there would be the questions, comments, and awkward stares from the villagers in attendance. This would, without a doubt, be a good day to have over and done with.

The solid clunk as the machine shut off jarred his thoughts back to the present, and he pulled the nozzle from the car.

As he went to hang it up, he lost his balance, spattering drips of fuel on to his trousers. He braced himself against the metal post on the side of the machine until he had regained a sense of equilibrium. *Bugger!* he hissed.

Pulling a paper towel from the dispenser, he blotted up the wet spots the best he could.

His head now throbbing from nervous tension, he glanced towards the building. He could just make out his wife's silhouette as she stood in the queue at the checkout. Saturdays were busy days in small towns, and the little market was full of customers.

Making his way in her direction he paused when he reached the door to plan his strategy for getting inside. His crutches clattered against the glass as he fought the resistant forces to pull the door open. Louisa glanced up and flashed him a smile, taking a step to lend assistance before falling back lest she lose her place in line.

All eyes were on him as he entered the store. He kept his head down and headed for the aisle with the toiletries and over-the-counter medications.

When he returned to the checkout, the line had barely moved. An elderly gentleman was at the head of the queue, trying to unload a jar of coins to pay for his tank of diesel. The clerk stood, painstakingly counting through them as the queue grew longer.

Martin walked up and joined his wife, handing her a bottle of paracetamol.

"Hey, the queue starts back there, mate!" the grey-haired man behind them barked.

Louisa put her palm up in front of her and gave him a forced smile. "It's all right. He's my husband; we're together."

The man's eyes darted between Martin and Louisa. "I don't care if he's the bloody Queen, love. He still has to get in the back of the queue."

He reached a tattooed arm out and yanked on Martin's sleeve.

"Get your hands off me!" Martin growled as he pulled back, averting his eyes from his aggressor.

"Hey, mate, leave the bloke alone," another customer interjected. "We've waited this long, we can wait a while longer."

"Stay outta it, Nigel," the grizzled man warned.

James Henry watched, his eyes widening as he sensed the tension building.

"Yer a pretty thing. What are ya doin' with the crip?" the man said as he poked a finger into Louisa's shoulder.

Martin flicked the man's arm away, his eyes flashing. "Get your hand off my wife," he warned, his voice low and threatening.

Louisa put her palm against her husband's chest and looked up at him, her eyes pleading. "Just leave it, Martin," she whispered.

He took in a deep breath before it hissed from his nose. "Yes."

James reached his arms out and grabbed on to his father's shirt.

"No, James. You're too heavy for your daddy right now," she said as she pried the fabric from his pudgy fingers.

Martin's eyes flitted behind him, then he leaned over and said in an undertone, "Why don't you let me pay. Take James out to the car; I'll be out in a minute."

"You sure?" she asked, casting a furtive glance in the rude man's direction.

"Yes, just go."

Louisa passed the bottle of tablets back to her husband along with a box of tampons. Martin looked down at his hands and quickly tucked the item under his arm as his wife and son moved towards the door.

The clerk had finally finished counting out the elderly gentleman's coinage, and the line had begun to move. Martin tried to keep his mind off the earlier unpleasantries by making a mental list of the patients he had seen over the course of the last week. Once he finally reached the counter he settled his bill before limping to the door and pushing into the cool fresh air.

Louisa had moved the car to a parking place near the building where she waited anxiously for him. She breathed a sigh of relief when he dropped into the passenger's seat.

"Everything go okay? Did that man give you any more trouble?" she asked as she shifted the car into reverse.

"*No.* Let's just go."

When they arrived at the farm a short time later, Morwenna was outside. A group of youngsters gathered around her as she pushed wire hoops into the ground for a game of croquet.

"I'll get James settled inside with Poppy, then come out and give you a hand," Louisa said as she shifted her son on her hip.

"Good, I think this lot is gettin' tired of me. Don't really have the maternal instinct thing I'm afraid." She picked up a bag and dumped the coloured wooden balls out on to the ground. "I'll get 'em goin' on a game—keep 'em busy till you get back."

Louisa put her hand on the girl's shoulder. "You're doing *fine*, Morwenna. The children all seem to be having a good time!"

"You doin' okay, Doc? You look a little peaky." Morwenna said, studying him with the eyes of an experienced medical receptionist.

"I'm fine." Martin clenched his jaw in preparation for the inevitable ensuing questions.

"You sure? 'Cause you look kinda pale. And you got dark circles under your eyes. Could be you're comin' down with somethin'. They got some food inside. Maybe that's what you need. Get some—"

"Morwenna! I said I'm fine! Now leave it!"

Martin turned and moved off towards the house with Louisa and James following close behind.

"Gawd, I bet half the village will be at this thing," he grumbled as his footsteps slowed and he began to breathe heavily.

"Try to look on the bright side, Martin. Joe Penhale's not here. That's a positive, hmm?"

"How do you know that?"

"I don't see his Land Rover, do you?"

"The absence of evidence is not evidence of absence, Louisa."

"Well, maybe you could just hide in a corner somewhere until it's over."

Martin stopped in his tracks and turned to look at her. "You'd be okay with that?"

Louisa struggled to suppress a smile. "Maybe you could mingle just a bit before you go looking for your corner, hmm?"

She slipped her hand between his arm and his crutch, wrapping her fingers around his wrist. "It'll be over before you know it."

"Hullo, Doc ... Louiser." Al greeted them with a tray of canapes in his hand. "Glad you could make it. May I offer you an hors d'oeuvre?" he asked, gesturing with a flourish.

"None for me, thank you," Martin mumbled as he kept his head down and looked furtively around the room.

"Got some nice quinoa-stuffed peppers that you might enjoy, Doc." The younger man rotated his finger over the bright red vegetables.

"I'm not hungry, Al!" he snapped back before wending his way through the guests clustered together in animated conversation. He made his way towards the rank of windows on the far side of the room.

The wall between the dining room and living room had been taken out during the renovations, opening the area up into one expansive space with a view overlooking the sea. Martin's eyes fixed on the gazebo in the distance.

Well, that's one bit of Auntie Joan that was spared the skip.

A vague ache settled in his chest as he remembered the last time he had shared tea and conversation with her there. That visit with Joan and his parents had changed him. His parents had stripped him of the tenuous grasp he had held to any sense of family.

They had placed an excruciating, albeit temporary, wedge between him and Joan, extorted money from him, and made clear that he had never been wanted.

When his parents had said their goodbyes the following day, Martin knew that the final remnants of his existence in his parents' lives had been erased with his father's betrayal and his mother's brutally honest confession. And that was the day he had alienated the woman he had dreamt of marrying when he rudely rebuffed her kindly advances.

"Nice to see the other half of the dynamic duo was able to make it to this *auspicious* even-t."

Martin groaned softly as he turned to face Portwenn's constable. "Penhale."

"It was nice last night, eh? Workin' as a team again to protect our village from all manner of potential disasters ... big and small."

Martin gave him a grunt as he looked about the room for an escape plan.

"Returning law and order in the midst of—lawlessness. Preventing our community's descent into total anarchy. Saving it from the likes of ruffians such as *Ms. Tallack*."

"You mean the fifty-two-year-old woman who fell off her bar stool?"

Joe tipped his head down and peered up at the doctor, the corners of his mouth lifting into a clownish grin. "Now, you and me both know that was just an alibi, don't we, Do-c?"

"Don't be stupid," Martin grumbled. "Where's your police vehicle? I didn't see it outside."

"It could have put people off, so I parked it behind the barn. Didn't want the guests to be aware that there would be a police presence."

Martin gave a derisive snort. "What is it you want, Penhale?"

The constable gave his shoulders a shrug as his gaze drifted to the floor. "Just tryin' ta be friendly, Doc."

Martin felt a pang of guilt as the man turned to walk away. "Erm, Penhale," he said. "Thank you for your assistance last night. I, er ... I appreciate it."

Joe flashed him a smile and stuck his thumb up in the air. "You can always count on me, Do-*c*."

Martin startled and whirled around as a hand settled on his arm. "Mm, hello," he said, his wife's happy face teasing a small smile from his own.

"Just thought I'd see how you're making out before I go outside to help Morwenna with the children. Can I get you anything before I go?"

"No, I'm fine." Air whistled through his teeth as he contemplated the wisdom of his next words. "How long do we have to stay?"

Louisa pulled her lips into a taut line as she glanced at her watch. "We have been here for less than ten minutes, Mar-tin. This means a lot to Al and Ruth. I need to go out and help Morwenna with the children. And you can go mingle a bit more before you go to find your corner. Does that answer your question?"

He blinked back at her, clenching his tongue in his teeth lest he say what he was thinking. "Yes." he forced out through pursed lips.

Her face softened, and she stretched up to place a discreet kiss on his cheek.

"Oh, ho, there, Doc. Gettin' a bit frisky."

Martin's head shot up at the sound of Bert Large's sialorrheic voice. He looked pleadingly at his wife.

She gave his hand a squeeze and turned to face the portly man. "Hello, Bert! How are you?"

"Funny you should ask. I was just comin' over to have a chat with the doc here about that. You see, I been havin' this pain in my chest. I think it could be that drastic reflex thing."

Martin screwed up his face at him. "Do you mean gastric reflux?"

Louisa looked from Bert back to her husband. "I think I'll just go. Leave you two to do whatever it is you're going to do."

"Mm, yes. Goodbye," Martin said as her hand slipped from his.

"So, Doc—is that what you think I've got then?"

"I haven't the foggiest idea *what* you have, Bert—*if* you have anything. Why do you think you have gastric reflux?"

"I get heartburn all the time. Maybe it's somethin' I ate. Do you think that could be it—somethin' I ate?"

"Quite possibly, given your dietary habits. Does there seem to be a correlation between what you eat and how your heartburn manifests itself?"

Bert gave him a blank stare. "Not sure what you mean by that."

Martin grimaced. "Does your heartburn seem to be worse when you eat certain foods? Greasy foods, spicy foods, alcoholic beverages?"

"Oh. Yeah, yeah. All of them, Doc. So, you think that's what I got then?"

"It's a possibility, yes."

"You can write me a prescription for it then, right?"

"No, of course I can't! I'll need to perform a thorough examination before I can make a proper diagnosis. Make an appointment with Morwenna on Monday."

"Oh, sure, sure, Doc. But you could give me somethin', just to get me by until then, right?"

Martin glanced around at the people who had gravitated towards them. "Bert, I'm not going to write you a prescription until I've made a proper diagnosis. And I can't make a proper diagnosis until I've conducted a thorough examination. *Which* I'm not going to do standing here in a room full of people."

"Right you are. That conversationality thing."

"Confidentiality?"

"That's it. Gotcha there, Doc." The man looked the doctor up and down. "And how 'bout you? You feelin' any better?"

"I'm improving." Martin began to scan the room again for an excuse to avoid further discussion with the man. "I need a glass of water," he said before moving off quickly.

He snaked his way across the room and out to the kitchen. Searching through the cabinets, he pulled down a glass and filled it at the tap, sipping on it while watching his wife through the window as she played with the children. *Thank God James has one parent who can teach him how to enjoy life.*

Joan knew how to enjoy life; she knew how to enjoy people. He was sure that she was disappointed with the man he had become. Had too much time, too much history passed for him to be able to change?

He squeezed his eyes shut and took in a deep breath. It hurt terribly to think about how he had failed his aunt. She died not having seen that he could actually be a husband and accept the love of his wife. She died before she could learn to know James Henry, to see that he could be a loving father. But what pained him the most was that she died not knowing she had been his saving grace. That he loved her.

He felt a warm hand on his arm and he turned. His crutches clattered to the floor as he recoiled from the village chemist's touch. "What on earth are you doing!"

"I'm sorry, Dr. Ellingham. I didn't mean to startle you. I just thought you looked like you might be in need of some companionship ... a willing ear, so to speak."

"Mrs. Tishell," Martin said in awkward acknowledgement of the woman. "I'm fine." He brushed himself off where her hand had settled on his wrist. "What do you want?"

She looked up at him, her head listing slightly. "Mrs. Norton was a *lovely* woman, wasn't she?"

"Mm. Yes. Yes, she was."

"*Always* a kind word for me whenever she came into my shop."

"Is there something I can help you with?" Martin asked as he squirmed under the woman's intense gaze.

Sally pressed her hand to her chest and looked longingly at him. "No doctor, but there is *so* much that I could do for—"

The latch on the kitchen door rattled before Chris and Carole Parsons stepped into the house, sparing Martin the chemist's forthcoming expression of sentiment.

"Chris ... Carole! Hello!" Martin said. "I'm glad to see you!"

The couple exchanged bewildered glances.

"We can take this up again later. Hmm, Dr. Ellingham?" Mrs. Tishell said, her hand again alighting on his arm as the tip of her tongue quivered against her upper lip.

He took hold of the woman's wrist and pushed her away. "Goodbye, Mrs. Tishell."

Chris stood watching, slack-jawed, as Sally swayed from the room.

"Gawd!" Martin shuddered.

"Do you have something you'd like to share, Mart?" Chris asked.

A deep line developed between Martin's eyebrows as he shot his friend a warning look. "*That* was the chemist who kidnapped James."

"Ah!" Chris let out a low whistle as his eyes drifted to the doorway. "I'd watch that one, mate."

"Yes, obviously!"

Carole walked over and embraced him. "How are you, Martin?"

"Improving."

She stepped back and put her hands on her hips. "Martin."

"Erm, yes. I'm back to work. Just a couple of hours each day right now."

He glanced over as Chris folded his arms across his chest and leaned back against the counter.

"Maybe a bit more, now and then."

Chris shook his head. "Just so you know, Mart, Ed has Portman keeping track of your hours. You're walking on thin ice, my friend."

"Did you come for tea and biscuits or did you come to lecture me?" he snapped back.

"Maybe you two could discuss this at a more appropriate time?" Carole suggested, raising her eyebrows at her husband.

"All right. Where *are* the promised refreshments?" Chris asked as he straightened himself and rubbed his palms together.

"Mm. The dining room."

"Oh, how lovely!" Carole gushed as she stepped through the doorway and surveyed the changes. "It hardly looks like Joan's house anymore!"

"Yes." Martin replied, lowering his head.

"Dr. Parsons, hello. I didn't realise you were coming," Jeremy said as he looked up from the opposite side of the refreshment table.

Chris reached for a canape. "Martin and Louisa invited us, and we couldn't pass up the chance to do some reminiscing about our medical school days."

"We kind of fell in love in this house, I guess you could say," Carole said giving her husband a knowing smile. She reached for a salad tomato and popped it into his mouth.

"Oh, gawd," Martin muttered under his breath.

Carole gave his arm a back-handed slap. "Hush up."

"The doc here looks about as dour as a teetotaling Scotsman now, don't he?" Bert Large chuckled as he approached the table. "Nothin' ta be so glum about, Doc. I mean, is this or is this not the nicest assortment of fine cuisine you've ever feasted your eyes on?" he said as he pushed in between Martin and Carole to reach for another bacon-wrapped sausage.

"Full of fats, sugars, salts—God knows what else," Martin said, sizing up the array of cheeses, cured meats, pate, cakes and biscuits.

"Oh, come on, Doc. You gotta admit, there's some mighty tasty titbits to be had here." The ex-plumber rubbed at his cheek as he studied the spread in front of him.

"Why are you doing that?" Martin asked, eyeing the portly man suspiciously.

"I'm tryin' ta decide, Doc. I don't take these things lightly."

"Mm." He tipped his head back and peered down at him for a moment before his attention was diverted by his wife.

"Chris ... Carole! It's so good to see you! How was the drive over?" Louisa said as she wrapped one arm around her friend while she balanced James Henry on her hip.

"Fine, just fine. The house looks wonderful, doesn't it?"

"It does. You'd hardly know it was the same place," Louisa said, glancing up and flashing her husband a smile.

With his wife immersed in conversation with their friends, Martin slipped away quietly and sought solitude upstairs, turning into Joan's old room.

He stroked his fingers along the chair rail, pausing when they touched a gouge in the wood, still there more than forty years after he knocked over a wrought iron floor lamp, marring the rail and breaking the lamp. It was an accident that occurred during a boisterous game of hide and seek with Uncle Phil.

He felt the air being sucked from his chest, just as it had been that day. His fear of the punishment that he was sure would follow sent him fleeing down the stairs and outside, where he had hidden in the tall grass that grew up behind the house.

He walked over to the window and peered down. The progeny of the very grass he had cowered in now stood lifeless and winter-brown. Looking from this second-story perspective, it was obvious how Auntie Joan had found him so quickly. The corner of his mouth pulled up slightly as he now realised how easily he would have been spotted from this vantage point.

He had experienced a blinding fear that day as he watched his aunt wading through the grass towards him. He had expected some sort of painful retribution, but what he received was love and understanding.

Joan had seated herself in the grass and pulled him into her lap, rocking him back and forth. The soothing motion and the comforting *lub-dub* of her heart had calmed him quickly.

She had assured him that accidents happen to everyone and that she wasn't angry. They made a pact that he would never run off again, and neither she nor Phil would ever lay a hurtful hand on him. Then they sealed the deal by sharing treacle cookies and milk.

Martin was shaken from his reverie by the sound of Al Large's panic-stricken voice.

"Doc! We need you!"

Martin turned from the window to see the ashen-faced young man standing in the doorway. "It's Dad, Doc. I think he's havin' a heart attack!"

Chapter 26

Martin's thoughts raced as he limped towards the stairs. He hoped that Bert had been correct earlier with his self-diagnosis of *drastic reflex*, but he had been suspicious when he noticed the man rubbing at his jowl.

He began to mentally prepare for a worst-case scenario. *My medical bag and the defibrillator are back at the surgery. Morwenna can go for it. Chris and Jeremy will have to do compressions until she gets back.* He flexed the fingers of his right hand subconsciously.

Al's strident voice echoed in the large dining room. "Dad! Dad! Come on, Dad, you're gonna be okay! The doc's comin'!"

Martin reached the bottom of the staircase and scanned the room. "Louisa, where are Chris and Jeremy?"

She knelt on the floor next to Bert, slapping a hand against his cheek. "They were going outside—down to see the lake! Martin, *do* something!"

"Al, run down and get them. And tell Morwenna to get the defibrillator and my medical bag from the surgery. *Quickly,* please!"

"I called for an ambulance, Doc," Joe Penhale said as he began to move the crowd to the other end of the room. "All right, everybody. Let's give the doc some room to work."

He put his hands on his hips and narrowed his eyes at the reporter from the Telegraph who had been sent to cover the event. The man stood with his camera poised in the air. "You too, sir."

"But this would be a brilliant human interest story ... draw a lot of attention to this B&—

"Lower the camera and step back—now." Joe set his jaw and glared at the man until he turned in a huff and joined the rest of the crowd.

Martin shoved the onlookers aside as he made his way to his patient. "Out of the way!"

He threw one of his crutches to the side and used the other to lower himself to the floor. Dropping heavily, he grimaced when his stiffened knees hit the hardwood.

Bert groaned softly as Martin took hold of his wrist, noting his clammy skin and racing pulse. He pulled the man's tie from around his neck and ripped his shirt open, pressing an ear to his chest. The furrows in his brow deepened as his heart beat increasingly erratically before slowing and then arresting completely. "*Bugger!*" he hissed.

"Louisa, take your jumper off and put it under his neck."

He turned and scanned the room, his eyes settling on the police constable. "Penhale! Call and tell them we need a helicopter! Then get over here; I need you!"

Joe put in the call before hurrying to Bert's side, dropping down beside him. "What d'you want me to do, Doc?"

"I need you to do chest compressions when I tell you to," Martin said, tipping his patient's head back and pulling his chin down to force his mouth open. Using his index finger, he swiped down his throat and removed a chunk of sausage, tossing it on to the floor. He leaned over and blew two breaths into his mouth before glancing up at the constable. "*Now,* Penhale."

Joe positioned his hands over the centre of Bert's chest and began the hard compressions used to keep oxygenated blood pumping through a patient's body.

Martin counted silently, *One and two and three and ... thirteen and fourteen and fifteen.* "Okay, stop."

Leaning over, he pinched Bert's nose shut and forced two more breaths into his mouth. "Again, Joe," he said giving a forceful nod to the policeman.

The doctor's fingers probed the jowly neck, searching for a pulse, before moving to the man's wrist. Nothing. "*Harder*, Penhale! You're compressing through a lot of fat layers. You've got to be more forceful!"

Martin shifted as he could no longer tolerate the pain shooting through his legs. He palpated again for a pulse. "You've got to give it everything you have, Joe! Your compressions aren't doing anything!"

"I *am* givin' it everything I've got, Doc!"

Martin looked on in frustration, cursing the man lying on the floor for having allowed himself to become so obese as to curtail their efforts to revive him.

He searched again for any sign that the compressions were doing any good. Then, hissing a breath of air from his nose, he pushed Joe's hands away. "You take the ventilations."

Louisa looked frantically from her friend who lay dying on the floor, to her husband. "Martin, I don't think you should!" she breathed out.

"Louisa, be quiet!" he snapped back.

Ruth came up from behind and bent down, resting her hands on the younger woman's shoulders. "He doesn't have a choice, dear."

Joe Penhale was physically fit, but he lacked the height, weight, and upper body strength needed to do the compressions effectively on a patient as heavy as Bert Large.

The doctor placed his hands over the patient's sternum before throwing his full weight into his thrusts. *One and two and three and ... thirteen and fourteen and fifteen.*

His contorted face and set jaw betrayed his pain as the intense applied force necessary to reach Bert's heart was repeated again and again.

"Oh, Martin!" Louisa breathed out softly.

He lifted his hands and Joe blew into Bert's mouth.

"See if you can find a pulse while I'm doing the compressions," Martin said as he resumed the pumps to the patient's chest.

Joe pressed his fingers to Bert's neck.

"Not—there—his wrist!" Martin panted.

"Yeah, Doc. I can feel it ... a bit," the constable said, his face drawn up in concentration.

A commotion could be heard in the kitchen as Al hurried in with Chris and Jeremy close behind.

"Move!" Chris barked as he pushed his way through the guests who had crept back in to watch the drama unfold.

"Where do you want us?" Chris asked as he knelt down beside his friend. Martin kept up his thrusts, jerking his head in Joe Penhale's direction.

"I can take over here," Chris said as he slipped in to replace the policeman.

Jeremy joined the others on the floor, taking note of the physical fatigue apparent on Martin's face. "Let me take over for a while, Dr. Ellingham."

Martin kept his head down, shaking it vigorously. "You don't—have—enough weight!" His sweat-saturated shirt clung to him, pulling annoyingly on his skin, and his nostrils flared as air rushed in and out of his lungs. When he paused for Chris to breathe the two ventilations into the patient, he held his left arm out to Jeremy. "Pull up my sleeve!"

The aide slipped the button through the buttonhole and hurriedly rolled the doctor's cuff back.

"Doc, Dad's gonna be okay, right?" Al asked as he hunched over his father.

Martin tuned the young man out along with the increasing pain in his limbs and waning strength in his arms. He resumed the compressions to the portly man's chest.

The back door slammed again and Morwenna raced into the room, dropping the medical bag next to Martin and setting the defibrillator on the floor. She flipped the lid of the machine open and turned it on.

Martin reached his hand back, and Morwenna slapped a plastic package into it. He fumbled, his fatigued right hand unable to grasp hold of it. "Open that!" he said shoving it back towards her.

Their eyes met as she passed the adhesive pads to him, and they exchanged worried glances.

He affixed the electrodes and then pressed the paddles to Bert's chest. "Everyone, clear!"

The patient's body jerked violently as the high-pitched charging whine of the machine began again.

Martin handed the paddles to Chris and grabbed for his medical bag. Chris administered another jolt of electricity. Still nothing.

"Get this—started for me, Jeremy." Martin said as he handed an IV kit across Bert's lifeless body, to his assistant.

Removing a small vial from his bag he drew up the clear liquid into a syringe and gave it to the aide.

"What's that?" Louisa asked, brushing tears from her cheeks.

"Vasopressin. It raises the blood pressure," Martin answered quickly as he pulled his stethoscope from his bag and inserted the tips into his ears.

He shook his head at Jeremy and Chris as he listened for the hoped for *lub-dub*. He began chest compressions once again.

Chris readied the paddles and Martin pulled his hands back. Another jolt. "*Come on, Bert!*" Martin hissed. Still no response. "*Damn!*"

"Doc, you can't let 'im die!" Al pleaded as he watched helplessly.

Pulling a second vial from his bag, Martin filled another syringe and passed it to Jeremy before starting back in with the compressions.

"Ready," Chris said as Martin lifted his hands into the air.

Again, the patient's body convulsed, but the shrill, flat-line alarm still intoned.

Martin lunged forward again, willing the inert muscle to respond.

"Mart," his friend said softly.

"Shock him again, Chris." Martin pinched Bert's cheek and leaned over, putting his mouth to the man's ear. "Don't you *dare* die on me, you shiftless laggard! *Come on, Bert!*"

"Martin." Chris looked sympathetically at his friend.

"Just do it, Chris!" Martin sputtered, his face red and glistening from exertion and stress.

Chris placed the paddles on the man's chest one last time, and Bert's body lurched up off the floor. The shrill tone was interrupted suddenly by erratic beeps that gradually fell into a steady rhythm.

Martin slapped his stethoscope to his patient's chest and breathed out a shaky sigh. "That's better."

"He okay, Doc? He's gonna be okay, right?" Al asked, his eyes glued on Martin as he waited for a response.

"He's alive, Al."

Bert's eyes cracked open and he moaned softly. Al dropped down next to him and wrapped his arms around him. "Yer gonna be okay, Dad. Yer gonna be okay."

The *whup-whup-whup-whup* of the approaching helicopter grew louder as it neared the farm and landed in the tall grass behind the house.

Martin reached into his bag and retrieved his blood pressure cuff, wrapping it around his patient's arm.

His head nodded approvingly. "That'll do for now," he said as he folded the stethoscope in his hand.

Bert's head turned slowly towards Martin, and he looked up at him. "Doc. I'm not—shift—less," he said, his voice soft and brittle.

The doctor's mouth twitched as he leaned down. "I apologise, Bert. Now be quiet."

Chris and Jeremy helped Martin to his feet as the ambulance crew prepared the patient for transport.

"Al ... I would imagine you'll want to go with your father in the helicopter." Martin said, jerking his head towards the door.

"Erm, yeah, yeah. That okay, Ruth?"

"Oh, for goodness' sake, Al! Do you really think you need to ask permission?" Ruth put her hand on his back and pushed him forward. "Of course! Go! Go!"

Bert was wheeled out to the air ambulance, an entourage of well-wishers accompanying him as far as they were allowed. Martin watched as they loaded the man on to the helicopter and then turned, quietly slipping away.

Inside, Carole sat with Louisa at the old table in the kitchen. "Do you think he'll be all right?" Louisa asked, peering at her friend over the rim of her teacup.

"I'm the wrong one to ask, I'm afraid. Martin probably has a pretty good idea, though. Ask him."

"Mmm, no," Louisa said, taking in a breath to speak again and aspirating a bit of tea. She coughed and then cleared her throat. "I *meant* Martin."

She dabbed at her mouth with a napkin before replacing it on her lap. "He would have been up front with Al if he wasn't confident that Bert would be okay. I trust Martin to take care of Bert, but I could tell doing the CPR was hurting him. And he acts as if he doesn't like Bert, but—" She gave her friend a weary smile.

James began to fuss and squirm to be free of his constraints, and Carole set him down on the old slate floor. "There again, you're going to have to ask Martin, Louisa."

She went to the cupboard and pulled out a metal pot and a wooden spoon before crouching down to offer them to the boy. He gave her a gap-toothed grin.

"You sure look like your daddy, James Henry." Glancing up at Louisa, she added a hesitant, "Aside from the smile that is."

A slight breeze moved past them as Ruth and Chris stepped in from the crisp fall air.

"What's become of my nephew?" the old woman asked as she peered into the dining room.

"I thought he was with you," Louisa said. Her chair legs screeched against the stone floor. "I better go find him."

"Let me go, Louisa. You stay here with James." Chris gave her a reassuring nod and stepped towards the door.

"Try the barn, Chris. I suspect that's where you'll find him," Ruth said as she pulled up a chair and took a seat next to Carole.

Louisa looked across at her, worriedly, and Ruth placed her hand on her arm. "Chris understands what Martin's feeling right now. It's better that he goes ... really."

Martin sat down on the old camel-back trunk in the dimly lit back corner of the barn. He tried to wedge his hands into his armpits to stop them from shaking, but the swelling in his right elbow wouldn't allow his arm to bend. So, he laced his fingers together in his lap. His diaphragm spasmed as he tried to take in a breath, and his stomach churned violently.

The events of the day replayed in his head, and the stew of emotions that had been brewing in him began to boil. Anger at himself for his awkwardness with marital communication. The fear triggered by the aggressiveness of the man at the petrol station, and the humiliation for what he perceived to be his cowardice and impotence in handling the incident. The grief he felt over the loss of his aunt. And finally, his desperation as Bert Large lay dying in front of him. He began to list the one hundred and eighteen elements in the periodic table in an attempt to ease the panic attack that he sensed coming.

The tactic, which he normally found quite effective in situations such as this, proved inadequate to override the stresses that had piled up on him over the course of the day. A tidal wave of emotions washed over him, and he erupted in a rage. He tried to hurl his crutch across the barn, but his right arm fell limply to his side and the crutch dropped a few feet in front of him.

"Arghh!" He gave a stack of boxes a forcible shove with his left hand, knocking them to the floor. Their contents spilled out, and he kicked repeatedly at the anachronistic assortment of worthless objects, the pain that shot through his leg with each impact feeding into his fury.

Chris heard the commotion as he neared the barn, and he raced ahead, pushing through the door.

"Martin! Stop it, you're going to hurt yourself!" he said as he watched, uncertain as to how to subdue the much larger man. "Dammit, Martin! Stop that!"

Martin could hear his voice, but he was immersed in anger and his words were an annoyance and a distraction from his venting. It further enraged him and he whirled around. "Shut up! Just *shut—up* and leave me alone!"

Chris held his hands up in front of him and levelled his voice. "Mart, you need to calm down before you injure yourself. Let's go back in the hou—"

"*I—said—shut—UP!*" Martin took several steps towards a tower of old milk cans and swung his arm at them, sending them rolling towards his friend. "Get out! Just leave me be, for Chrissake!"

Chris took a hesitant step towards him. "Let's find someplace to sit down and talk abou—"

"Get—out, Chris!"

Martin's nostrils flared, and his eyes darted rapidly from his friend to the barn door. He wanted to get away. To be on his own until he could get the turmoil that he was feeling under control. He sucked in ragged breaths. "Please—just leave me—be," he pleaded.

"Mart, I understan—"

"No! No! Don't you dare say you understand, Chris! You don't understand—at all! God! That *idiot!!*" Martin staggered forward and batted a clay pot from its perch on a crate, sending it shattering into pieces against the barn wall.

"All for a few extra pounds in his bloody pay cheque! Probably so he could—could go swill it down at the damn pub on Friday night! My life has been completely bollocksed up, Chris, all for a few extra bloody pounds in the idiot's pay cheque! You don't understand a goddamn thing! You can't *begin* to understand the pain—the humiliation through this whole thing. All that I've lost because of this!"

Chris nodded his head. "You're right, Mart. This has been hell for you. I know that. And I can't possibly understand because I've never experienced anything like it. And I hope I never will. But I *do* know that you'll continue to improve. Life will get back to normal in time."

"Oh, will it!" Martin scoffed. "You can stand there and tell me that I'm not going to walk with a limp? *Can you?* That I won't be gulping down morphine every time the weather changes?"

"It's been a really stressful afternoon, mate. Things look—"

"Can you tell me that Louisa's not going to spend the rest of our married life worrying about me every time I go for a goddamn walk, Chris? That she's not going to be trying to defend me every time some moron insults me? That I'll be able to do more to protect her and James than to put distance between us? That's what happened today you know!"

Chris took a step towards his friend. "Let's sit down, Mart ... talk about it."

"I don't *want* to sit down! I want you to get out! Leave me be!" Martin stood, his brow drawn down and his head tipped to the side. *"Please."*

"Mart, you're reeling from what's happened. Performing CPR is physically and emotionally exhausting for anyone, but you have your injuries as well as your friendship with this guy that's compounding the expected blow-back."

Martin's head shot up, and he scowled back at him. "Bert Large isn't my *friend*. He's a patient—a-a-a bloody villager!"

"Ah, I see," Chris said with a nod of his head. "Mart, let's get you back to the surgery. Jeremy and I can check you over, make sure you're all right. That was an awful lot of force on that arm and shoulder, you know. How's it feeling?"

Martin shifted his gaze back to the floor. "I'm fine."

Take another wary step forward, Chris reached a hand out slowly. "I'll take a look at you back at the surgery. Then Carole and I'll take you and Louisa to get some dinner, how does that sound?"

"I'm fine. I just want to be left alone."

Chris felt his friend stiffen and recoil as his hand made contact with his arm.

"I can manage on my own!" he snarled. He glared at him before his expression eased, and he breathed out a heavy sigh, squeezing his eyes shut. "Just give me a few minutes on my own—please," he said softly.

Chris hesitated and then dropped his hand to his side. "All right, I'll be right outside if you need me."

Martin watched as the barn door swung shut then he reclaimed his position on the old trunk. He looked around at the mess that now lay at his feet, his eyes focusing in on a pile of papers.

Leaning over, he picked up the bundle and pulled at the yellowed piece of string holding the stack together. On top was a folded piece of paper with a child's rendering of two people in stick figure form.

They stood, hand in hand, in a carpet of grass. Boats rested atop a wavy blue line in the background. On the inside, in the constrained penmanship of early childhood, were written the words, *You are my most favourite person. I will miss you a lot. From Marty.*

He flipped through the other pieces of paper—letters all beginning with, *Dear Auntie Joan.*

The hinges on the old barn door creaked wearily, and his gaze shifted towards the sound.

"Mind the company of an old woman?" Aunt Ruth asked as she stepped carefully through the debris field.

"Mm. Sorry about all of this. I'll clean it up before I leave."

She put her hand on her nephew's shoulder to steady herself before joining him on the trunk.

"I'll have Al get it. You've done enough for today." The elderly woman scrutinised him, noting his still flushed face, the wet shirt adhering to his back, and his artificially phlegmatic affect.

"Well, your exceptional medical skills were certainly on display today. The man's very fortunate you were there."

Martin jerked his head to the side and jutted out his lower lip. "A simple matter of a size advantage."

Ruth breathed out a heavy sigh before she peered up at her nephew as he continued with his explanation.

"I'm taller than both Chris and Jeremy, so I had a greater distance with which to build momentum with my thrusts. Not to mention that I have more weight to put into each thrust. And my upper body strength has increased due to the use of the cru—"

"Oh, Martin! Must you minimize the significance of every one of your accomplishments?" she said. "It's a terribly unfair impulse bequeathed you by your lovely parents. And one you would do well to break yourself of, I might add!"

Martin gave her a scowl. "Would you rather I strut around like a peacock with a swelled head?"

"That might not be *ideal*, but it would be an improvement over your tendency towards self-deprecation." Ruth placed a frail hand over her nephew's solid paw. "I'm attempting to extend a compliment, but I don't seem to be having much success."

He dropped his gaze to the floor. "I did what any competent doctor would do, Ruth."

"I disagree! Your friend, the *very* competent Dr. Parsons, was ready to give up ... declare the man dead. You are a determined man, Martin. You don't give up easily. And thank goodness for that! I suspect your pertinacious temperament has had much to do with your great success in life."

Ruth surveyed the littering of objects at her feet and then turned to face her nephew. "Joan was *very* proud of you. You do know that, don't you?"

Martin brought his head up slowly and turned to look at her. "I never told her..." He sucked in a ragged breath and swallowed. "I never told her that I loved her. She died not knowing that, Aunt Ruth."

"Oh, Martin, she knew. You take those letters with you and read them," she said, tapping a bony finger on the papers in his lap. "She knew."

The elderly woman placed a warm hand on her nephew's back. "Oh, good lord, Martin! You're shivering! You must be freezing out here in those wet clothes!"

"I'm *fine!*" he said, shaking his head and pulling away from her.

"Don't be perverse. You're cold and wet." Ruth pushed herself to her feet and peered down at him imperiously. "Well, come on. You're not going to get any *finer* sitting there staring at your shoes."

Martin gave a derisive snort and pulled himself to his feet before his fatigued muscles resisted, landing him back on the trunk. He took in a trembling breath as a shiver went through him. Then he forced himself upright again, and the two made their way together towards the door.

"Martin, Joan *was* very proud of you, and—and I am as well," she said taking hold of his sleeve and bringing him to a stop.

"And, as I'm not getting any younger, I want you to know..." Ruth looked up at him as he towered over her. "I want you to know that I love you, Martin. Joan's death was a blessing in disguise for me, I suppose, because it gave me a chance to have my own family. So, I hope you'll forgive my occasional dalliances in maternalism. I can't quite help myself."

Martin stared at her, taken aback by her words. He clenched his lip in his teeth and gave her a slow nod of his head, blinking back tears.

The elderly woman pressed a hand to his back, impelling him forward. "Let's go find your wife. I think she may be wondering where you got off to."

Chapter 27

Louisa peered out the kitchen window, raising up on her toes to see over the shrubs. "I wonder what's keeping them?"

"Try to relax, Louisa. It won't be of any help to Martin if you have yourself all worked up when he gets back here, will it?" Carole said.

"No, s'pose not. But, they *have* been gone a while." She stood, patting her palms together, and then hurried to the coat rack. "I think I'll just walk down—"

"Louisa! Sit down and relax. Chris is there to help him, and if he proves useless, Ruth will certainly know what to say to him. And for goodness' sake, maybe the poor man just needed a bit of air, hmm?"

Louisa hesitantly slipped her coat back over the peg and returned to her chair. "I'm just worried."

Her fingertips tapped out a frenetic rhythm on the table top before she got to her feet and again took up watch at the window. "Oh, thank goodness! Here they come now."

"Is everybody in one piece?" Carole asked.

"Ha, very funny." Louisa scrutinised the trio. "Chris looks a bit peevish, Ruth looks ... well, like Ruth always looks, I guess."

"And, Martin?"

"Well, he's moving pretty slowly. He seems to be dragging his right leg a bit. But mostly, he just looks exhausted."

"Oh, dear," Carole said. She got up from her place on the floor next to James Henry and bent down to hoist the boy into her arms.

The door from the little porch off the kitchen opened, and Ruth hurried in, her arms wrapped around her.

"Oh, it's getting cold out there!" she said, giving a theatrical shudder. "I think there's weather brewing."

"Is Martin all right, Ruth?" Louisa asked, keeping one eye on the window as her husband neared the house.

"Yes, he appears to be fine ... on the surface anyway. It's been a very rough day for him though and it shows. He won't admit it, but he's cold and he hurts," Ruth said as she plopped into a chair with a sigh.

Louisa patted the woman's shoulders. "I'll make a pot of tea."

Taking a container of Melba toast from the nappy bag, Carole slid in next to the elderly woman, settling James Henry on her lap. "Well, I must say, Ruth, you and Al certainly know how to create an atmosphere at your parties. Is this indicative of what you have in store for future guests?"

"A *bit* of a damp-squib, possibly. I think the locals showed up out of sheer nosiness. But the down from towners, who hold the *real* business potential, were quite impressed with the place *and* impressed with your husband's heroics," the elderly woman replied, raising an eyebrow at Louisa.

Her index fingers tapped together slowly. "I should send Bert Large some flowers," she said, making a mental note. "He certainly made the occasion a memorable one for all."

Louisa set a teacup down in front of her husband's aunt and filled it with hot water before taking a seat at the table.

All heads turned when footsteps were heard on the back porch.

"...be a good idea to keep that arm in a sling for a few days," Chris said as he pushed through the door, holding it open for his friend. "I'll check you over thoroughly when—"

"Will you *stop!* How many times do I have to say it? I'm fine!" Martin's face bore a deep scowl as he made his way across the room.

Louisa rose quickly to follow him, but grudgingly returned to her seat when Chris gave her a vigorous shake of his head as he followed after him.

"*Now* where do you think you're going, Mart?"

"I'm *going* to pee! I suppose you want to come with me?"

"Yes, as a matter of fact I do. You're exhausted, mate. I don't want you keeling over into the..."

The two wives exchanged glances, listening to the decrescendo of voices as their husbands moved away from the kitchen.

Carole bounced James on her knee and rolled her eyes. She leaned forward and said conspiratorially, "I swear, sometimes those two sound like an old married couple that never quite got the hang of things."

Louisa's taut features relaxed slightly into a vaguely amused smile. "I sure hope Martin and I never end up like that."

"Well, that's water over the dam *now*." Ruth quipped.

Her ponytail flicking, she narrowed her eyes at her husband's aunt. "What do you mean by that?" she asked, her voice suddenly crisp.

"Oh, I didn't really mean *anything* by it, dear ... just reminiscing. As soon as Martin moved to Portwenn, Joan started calling with weekly reports about you two."

"The on-again off-again nature of your relationship. How neither of you could own up to the fact that you each had designs on the other. How Martin would offend you in his uniquely clumsy manner every time he made an attempt at conversation with you. And *you*, quite naturally I'm sure, would take offense."

Ruth peered over her teacup and circled a hand in the air. "Like I said, you've both moved beyond all that."

"Right." She threw a spoonful of sugar into her cup and stirred it in before tapping the utensil impetuously against the rim.

Glancing towards the doorway, Ruth put her hand on her arm. "By the way, I suspect your husband could probably benefit greatly from some bodily contact tonight ... if you catch my drift," she said, her words hushed.

Louisa's face burned as she saw a smile spread across Carole's face.

"Oh, I didn't intend to embarrass you, dear. Just a bit of clinical advice," she continued, quasi-confidentially. "It's been my experience that males show a definite proclivity for a physical release of emotions as opposed to the female need to verbalise them."

The younger woman pulled in her chin and glanced self-consciously at her friend. "I'll take that into consideration, Ruth. Thank you."

Ruth fixed her gaze on her. "And be ready with tight lips and open ears as well. Although Martin *did* get some of it out in the barn," she said, eliciting an inquisitive glance from her nephew's wife.

She set her now-empty teacup down on the table and got to her feet. "Well, if you ladies will excuse me, I believe I'll head on home."

She dangled a set of keys in front of Louisa's face. "I trust you can lock up when you leave?"

"Yes, we'll take care of it, Ruth," she replied, donning a plastic smile.

"I'll stop by in the morning to collect my keys," the old woman said before pulling the door shut behind her.

Louisa watched her walk past the window and then whirled around towards her friend. "*Oh*, that Ruth! She can be all too forward at times ... suggesting that Martin and I can't communicate!" she hissed.

Carole cocked her head at her. "I thought she was just saying that you and Martin had difficulties at one time in your relationship, but that's in the past now. You think she was insinuating something else?"

"Ruth's comments are never so benign, Carole. I know the woman well enough by now to see when she's trying to get in my head. She was up to something with that remark."

Her fingers drummed against the table as she stared into her teacup. Then she straightened herself and brushed her hair back from her face. "Oh, never mind. You're right, she probably meant nothing by it. The other, however..."

Carole put a hand over her mouth as she began to giggle over the old woman's words. "So, about that bodily contact ... are you planning to heed her advice?"

"Carole." Louisa narrowed her eyes at her. "*That* is none of your business."

James wriggled in Carole's lap, trying to worm his way out of her arms and get to the floor. Setting him down to resume his play with the pot and spoon, she looked up at her friend. "Sorry, you're right. But ... *are* you and Martin doing okay?"

Louisa tipped her head to the side as she ran a finger along her cup handle. "Yeah ... yeah, of course. Just maybe a *bit* of a backslide lately."

"Nothing serious, I hope." Carole sat back down and stared across the table. "Martin did seem a bit off today. It's not the depression again, is it?"

"No. We just had a difference of opinion about how much freedom he should have."

"Freedom? What in the world does that mean?"

Louisa tugged at the sleeve of her blouse, smoothing out a wrinkle. "Well, *freedom* may not have been the best choice of word. I guess it might be more accurate to say independence. Martin wants to do things that I just don't think he's ready for. He took a terrible spill a few days ago because he walked over to see a patient after it had gotten dark."

"Oh, dear! I don't think Ed filled Chris in on that. He's going to want to know."

"Martin didn't see Ed about it. I helped him get the scrape on his arm bandaged and Jeremy checked it the next day. It's healing now, thank goodness."

"So ... maybe you were exaggerating just a little about the *terrible* spill?" Carole said warily.

"He could have really hurt himself, Carole!" Louisa snapped her head to the side. "I just don't want anything to happen to him ... to set him back. I thought for sure you'd be able see things from my perspective."

"Well, I can understand your concerns, but Martin certainly doesn't have a devil-may-care attitude when it comes to his health. Don't you think he's trying to balance the benefits with the risks? He does need to be increasing his activity level, right?"

"Yes, I realise that, but..." Louisa patted her hand against the table and then craned her neck to see through the doorway. "What's keeping those two?" she said, shifting the subject away from the argument she knew she was losing.

She sat quietly for a moment before her brow furrowed. "What do you mean, Martin seemed a bit off? A bit off, how?"

Carole got up from the table and went to the sink, filling her cup with water. She turned, pulling a hand under her arm. "I Imm ... sullen I would say. I would have thought he'd be pleased with all the improvements to Joan's old house ... to know it's being well cared for."

Louisa took a sip of tea and waved a dismissive hand in the air. "I think he's just tired. Those bloody fixators make it very hard for him to sleep. And he's healing."

"You're probably right." Carole's gaze shifted as she noticed their husbands coming towards the kitchen. "There you are. What have you two been up to?"

Chris glanced over at Martin, then gave a small shake of his head. "Just talking."

Martin eyed his wife, giving a nod towards the door. "Can we leave?" he asked, an edginess in his voice. "*Now.*"

"Erm, yeah, Ruth left already. We're supposed to lock up."

Louisa reached over and took her husband's hand as they wound their way back towards the village a short time later.

"I was so afraid for you today," she said, caressing the backs of his fingers with her thumb.

He glanced over. "There was nothing else I could do, Louisa."

"I know. I was afraid, but I was also very proud of—"

"Can we please not talk about it right now?" He pulled his hand away and swallowed hard before taking in a deep breath.

"Erm, sure." She focused her eyes on the road ahead as feelings of insecurity crept in. "So, Chris and Carole will pick up takeaway and come over for dinner. That's nice, hmm?"

"I would've preferred to go home and have the house to ourselves tonight."

"They won't be staying long, I'm sure. It'll be okay." Louisa felt his muscles tense as she placed her hand on his thigh.

James Henry, having missed his usual afternoon nap, had dropped off to sleep quickly once the car was moving, and his mother adjusted the rear-view mirror to quickly check on him. He stretched in his sleep and his brow furrowed as he pursed his lips.

Louisa turned to Martin, a smile spreading across her face when he glanced over at her.

"What?" he asked defensively.

"Oh, just seeing my two handsome men. It makes me happy."

"Mm. I see."

She wiped her fingers across the condensation that had begun to accumulate on the inside of the windscreen, eliciting an indignant hiss from her husband.

He reached out and flicked the defrost knob. "You leave streaks on the glass when you do that, you know."

She gave a shrug of her shoulders. "Sorry, force of habit." Eyeing him, she asked hesitantly, "Do you think Bert will be okay? I mean, I know you can't say much, but—"

"They'll run tests in Truro to see what further medical intervention is necessary, but yes, I think he'll be fine. Although, if he doesn't drastically change his lifestyle, get more exercise and modify his eating habits, he will almost certainly experience further problems, and quite likely an early death."

She reached over and ran her hand across his cheek, giving him a soft smile. "I've watched you save lives before, but today—" Her voice caught in her throat at the pride she felt in him.

"Mm, yes." His gaze flitted towards her briefly before he pulled in his chin and wagged a finger in front of him. "You should keep your eyes on the road when you're driving."

By the time the Lexus descended the long hill into the village, James had begun to stir and fuss hungrily for his supper. Louisa manoeuvred the car into the parking place by the surgery and shifted the gearbox into park.

She pulled her son from his car seat, keeping one eye on her husband as he pulled himself slowly from the vehicle. His stiffened joints and swollen limbs complained with each step, and his movements were halting as they made their way around to the back of the cottage.

Pushing the kitchen door open, Louisa stepped aside to let him pass by.

"Why don't you go lie down on the sofa for a few minutes, Martin, while I get James a snack to tide him over until dinner.

Have a short rest before Chris and Carole get here with the food, hmm?"

"I'm fine," he said before gesturing towards his son. "If you give him something now we won't get a proper meal in him later."

Louisa sighed and brushed her hand over the boy's head. "Yeah, I s'pose you're right." Her eyes softened as she took note of her husband's antalgic stance. "Martin ... you're exhausted. *Please*, go sit down and at least put your feet up for a while."

"If I sit down on that sofa, Louisa, I don't think I'll be able to get back up. So, if you had in mind that we'd sleep in the same bed tonight, stop arguing with me."

James Henry let out a screech to protest his imposed delayed gratification, and Louisa hurriedly removed his jacket and slipped him into his high chair. "We'll eat in just a minute, James," she said, placing a Sippy cup of water and the child's toy fire engine on the tray.

The bell on the front door rang, and she hurried off to greet their guests.

Martin eyed Chris as they sat at the kitchen table a short time later, scowling as his friend devoured the bacon butty he had picked up at the Bridge On Wool, a little pub in Wadebridge.

"You're going to end up like Bert Large if you're not careful, you know."

"Mind your own business and finish your egg and cress, Martin. Then we'll go to your consulting room, and I'll look you over before we leave." Chris popped the last of his crisps into his mouth and wiped his face with his napkin.

"You already did that at the farm," Martin replied. He picked up his glass and swallowed down his milk.

Chris leaned back in his chair and folded his arms across his chest. "All I did was rebandage that scrape of yours. I'm not leaving here until I've checked you over carefully and I'm satisfied that you didn't do any damage when you were doing the chest compressions this afternoon. Or in the barn for that matter."

Martin glanced uncomfortably at his wife and then hissed out a breath before shoving himself away from the table. "Fine!" he barked irritably as he made his way towards the hall.

Chris exchanged glances with Louisa and then followed after him.

The two women were visiting in the lounge when their husbands returned. Louisa looked over at Chris, anxiously.

"Nothing too alarming to report," he began. "The stress on those fractures has caused a fair amount of oedema. And despite the fact that I couldn't get an admission out of him, I know he's having pain, so I gave him an injection of Toradol. That should help relieve his discomfort tonight.

"Otherwise, you know the drill—rest, elevation, ice. Jeremy will stop by in the morning to check up on him, but if you have any concerns before then don't hesitate to call me, okay?"

"Yes, thank you, Chris. And thank you, both of you, for coming over today. I'm just sorry that you didn't get much of a chance to stroll down memory lane."

Martin cleared his throat and averted his eyes as his wife proffered her customary hugs before seeing their guests to the door.

When she returned to the lounge, Louisa came up behind him and wrapped her arms around his waist, joining him as he gazed down at the young life they had created together. "Well, Dr. Ellingham, it's finally just you and me. And James, of course."

"We very nearly lost all of this you know, several times," Martin said, his breaths uneven. "Only one of those times was beyond our control."

Louisa pressed her cheek to his back and tightened her grip on him. "I'm not sure what you're saying."

"Mm. I suppose I'm saying we need to be more advertent ... more proactive than we've been in the past. But I think we've been doing better ... don't you?"

"Yes, Martin, we have. I think that after our wedding I expected everything would take care of itself. That we were kind of on autopilot now that we were married.

"But that's not the way it is. We need to be making constant adjustments here and there and paying more attention to each other."

He turned in her grasp and buried his face in her hair. "It's past James's bedtime. Maybe I could read to him tonight?"

Louisa tipped her head back before reaching up to kiss him. "James would like that. And it would give me time to have a relaxing bath before bed. If you don't mind."

"No. That would be good!"

After getting Martin situated with James in a chair in the baby's room, his legs elevated and enclosed in cold packs, Louisa went to run her bath.

When she returned a half hour later, wrapped in her dressing gown, James was asleep and Martin was staring, pensively, at his son. She hated to disturb them, but it was quite obvious that the child was in need of a nappy change.

Martin raised his head and shifted when she leaned over to lift the blue packs from his legs. "Erm, he needs tending to," he said softly.

"I noticed," she whispered back.

She pulled the boy from Martin's lap, leaving him feeling exposed and vulnerable without James Henry's comforting warmth and weight.

"I left my candles burning in the bathroom. I thought you might find it relaxing while you take your shower—help you to leave the stresses of the day behind, maybe?"

He pulled his legs from the footstool, the movement causing a deep bone pain to shoot through his limbs. A soft groan slipped out before he could stop it.

"You okay?" Louisa asked, squinting her eyes at him.

He quickly dismissed her concerns with a wave of his hand. "Goodnight, James," he said softly before touching his fingers to the boy's forehead and leaving the room.

Louisa readied her son for bed and tucked him in before making her way back across the landing.

She could hear water trickling as she entered the bedroom, and she tapped lightly on the bathroom door. "Martin, may I come in and brush my hair?" she said softly.

Her brows drew together as she placed her ear to the door. "Martin, is everything all right?" She waited a moment and then pushed the door open.

The candlelight cast a warm glow in the room as it played off the glass shower door. Martin stood, leaning up against the tiled wall, his inhalations catching convulsively.

She let her dressing gown slip from her shoulders and stepped in under the water with him. "Oh, Martin," she breathed out as she reached for him.

Grabbing hold of the assist bar, he turned away from her as the grief that he had quelled, through sheer denial, for more than a year washed over him.

"Martin," she said quietly, "It's all right."

Louisa moved closer and pressed herself against him. The warmth of her body against his and the sense of security it gave him was all it took to break down the last bit of resistance that he had been holding on to, and his emotions poured out of him in heavy sobs.

"God, I was so afraid! I thought Al was going to lose his father today, Louisa! I came so close to leaving him on his own. To leaving him with no one who cares about him!

"You have no idea what that feels like ... to be left on your own with no one who cares about you! He has *one* person who cares about him, and I came so close to being responsible for—" Martin squeezed his eyes shut as he tried in vain to swallow back a sob.

Ruth's words replayed in her head, and Louisa said nothing as she moved around to face him. She laid her ear against his chest and focused on the scar that disappeared under his arm. Her heart ached for him as he poured out his soul to her.

"I miss Joan. I miss Auntie Joan. I didn't want to go to the farm today because nothing's the same anymore. It doesn't look like Joan's. Or feel like Joan's. No clutter. No collections of books. The stacks of empty biscuit tins and recipe books in the kitchen. The ridiculous assortment of old ledgers and piles of outdated magazines—those Old Farmer's Almanacs in the living room. It's all gone. The house doesn't even *have* a bloody living room anymore!"

She felt her husband's chest expand as a stammered breath filled his lungs. His body relaxed and he brought his arm up around her. "There's so little evidence that she ever existed, and yet she was the most influential person in my life. How can that be, Louisa? How can a person be so vitally important to another only to have any trace of their existence erased once they've died?"

Reaching for the tap, she shut the water off and pulled a towel from the rack on the door.

"I think you're forgetting one very important piece of evidence," she said, rubbing the towel over his head. "You finish up here, then I want to show you something." Pulling his hand up, she dropped the towel into it.

She stepped out and dried herself and then pulled her dressing gown back on before wrapping her towel around her husband's waist.

"Come on," she said as she took his hand and led him across the landing.

"Look at that little boy, Martin. If it weren't for Joan, he wouldn't be here," she whispered. She gave a gentle tug on his arm, and they slipped back across to their bedroom.

"You wouldn't have been able to overcome your horrid upbringing to become a surgeon if it hadn't been for the six weeks of love and encouragement that you got from Joan every summer. And you wouldn't have been inspired to come here to be a GP in this sleepy little village either. Think about all the lives that have been positively affected by your presence here. If it weren't for Joan, none of that would have been possible. And most of all, you wouldn't have been here to woo the local school teacher, propose to her, *and* to follow up that proposal by immediately conceiving a child with her, by the way!"

Louisa was now standing so close that Martin could feel her breath brush against his bare chest as she spoke, and he felt the accumulated stresses that remained of the day evaporating as quickly as the distance between them.

"*You* are the most important bit of evidence of Joan's existence, my extraordinary man. You and James Henry." She raised up on her toes and kissed him.

Her lips were slightly sweet with a hint of mint as her tongue grazed over his. She cupped his face in her hands, her gaze penetrating, and she raised up once again, this time her affections more passionate.

Martin sat back against the dresser and slid his left arm under her backside, pulling her tightly to him as he nuzzled into her neck. The scent, that was intrinsically his wife, was intensified by the warmth and dampness of her skin, and it sent his senses reeling as his inhibitions fell away.

"Oh, Louisa," he sighed before pulling his head back to look at her. "You are *so* very beautiful."

She drew away slightly, and Martin let her slide to the floor. Then taking his hand she led him to the bed.

She untied her dressing gown and, after being given a small nod of encouragement, he slipped the satin garment from her shoulders and the towel from around his waist.

"Martin, please ... make love to me." Her words spilled languorously from her mouth.

Dropping to the bed, he pulled her into his lap, his hands constantly caressing. "I suspect I'm going to need a bit of help," he said apologetically.

"I think I can accommodate you." She kissed him once more before rolling from his lap and under the covers.

He flipped the switch on the bedside lamp and joined her.

Their lovemaking was extraordinarily sensual. The deepening of the bond of trust between them laid bare a connection that they had never before experienced. It exposed raw emotions that leant a complexity to the intimacy and heightened their sexual responses.

Martin held tightly to her as he rolled to the side, unwilling yet to part from her. He lay, taking in the nuances of her features and marvelling at her beauty.

Louisa smiled at him and shook her head slowly. "That was..." She breathed out a ragged breath. "I don't know that I have the words, Martin," she said as she gazed into his eyes, still dark with lust. "I do know that I have never felt so fully satisfied or thoroughly cherished before. Or loved you as completely as I do at this moment," she said, brushing her hand over the sheen of moisture that glistened on his forehead.

Martin swallowed hard as he blinked back tears. "Mm, yes. I know. I mean ... me, too."

Turning her head to the side, Louisa pressed her cheek to his chest, listening to his heart as it still pounded from arousal and exertion. "Martin, I'm sorry that the farm isn't that special place for you anymore ... that you've lost that connection to Joan."

He breathed out a heavy sigh and pulled her closer. "It's all right. She's not my only person anymore."

Chapter 28

"Louisa," Martin whispered through clenched teeth. "Louisa, I need your help!" The vehemence in his hushed voice finally roused his wife from her slumber.

"What is it?" She sat bolt upright in bed, trying to shake the torpidity from her head.

"I need you to get—some more Toradol for—me." His voice was halting as stabbing pain radiated through his hand and arm and into his shoulder.

Reaching for the bedside lamp, she flipped the switch, slapping a hand to her eyes as the bright light hit her dilated pupils.

She dropped her arm as she adjusted to the glare of the incandescent bulb. "What's wrong, Martin?"

"The Toradol—get it! In my medicine cabinet—right side on—the bottom. And get an alcohol swab and a syr—syringe from my medical cart."

"Yes. Yes, I'll be right back," she said as she ran towards the stairs.

"Louisa!"

She whirled around. "Yeah?"

"Don't—rush. I don't want—you to fall," he said as he gave her a weary nod of his head.

She took in a deep breath and slowed her pace. When she returned a few minutes later her husband was sitting up in the bed, his arm cradled in his lap.

"Let me see," Martin said, scrutinising the label on the small vial.

She eyed him anxiously. The strain on his face was obvious. "I didn't know what size syringe thingy you needed so I got an assortment."

"The three-cc syringe. Take the cap off and draw up—*arrgh!*" He clutched his arm to his stomach as his face contorted in agony.

Louisa put her hand on his shoulder. "I'm going to call Jeremy."

"No, no, no! It'll be—fine." He blinked the tears from his eyes and gave a nod towards the vial of Toradol. "Draw up a millilitre from the bottle." he said.

"Like this?"

"Nope, the other—end up."

She held the syringe out to him. "Is that right?"

"Hold it needle end—up. Push the air out."

Louisa pressed on the plunger, and a small amount of the yellow-tinged liquid squirted out, landing on her leg.

Martin pushed the blankets away and reached for the packet containing the alcohol swab, grasping it in his teeth and tearing it open. He scrubbed his thigh with the enclosed pad and then reached out to his wife.

"Give it to me."

He took hold of the syringe and took a deep breath, trying to quiet the tremors in his hand. "Bugger! Here, you'll have to—to do it. My hands are shaking too much."

"Oh no, Martin! I'm not sticking that thing into you!" she said, shaking her head as she looked at him, wide-eyed.

"Louisa, it's either you—do it or you—call Jeremy and I have to wait until—he gets here." He watched her, his eyes pleading. "You can do it," he said, giving her a feeble smile and an encouraging nod.

Louisa looked at her husband's face—his brow furrowed, jaw set, and beads of perspiration on his forehead.

"Oh, gawwd; I *hate* needles!" She reached out and took the syringe from his hand. "Tell me what to do."

"Hold it like—a pencil—a pub dart."

"Oh, Martin," she fretted as she screwed up her face and positioned the implement between her fingers.

"Now take hold of the muscle—on the front of my thigh. Pull up, then in—insert the needle at a ninety-degree angle."

"How deep do I have to stick it in?"

"All the way. Just do it quickly," Martin said as he grimaced in response to another jolt shooting through his arm.

"Oh, gawwd!" Louisa leaned over and kissed his head before taking in a deep breath, jabbing the needle into his leg.

"I'm sorry! I'm sorry!" she said as she felt his body tense in response to her grudging assault.

"Mm, it's okay. Now, pull the p-plunger back. If—if there's blood you need to try a different spot."

Louisa's stomach churned as she followed his instructions. "No blood—now what?"

"Go ahead and in—inject the Toradol. Then pull the needle back out at a-a ninety-degree angle."

She did as he instructed and then breathed a sigh of relief, laying the syringe on the bedside table.

"Erm, would you mind—mind getting me a hot flannel?" he asked, rubbing at his thigh.

"Bet you won't ask me to do *that* again, hmm?" she said, brushing her fingers through his hair.

"You did fine ... good. It's just that—the Toradol burns, you know. Heat helps."

She touched his leg gingerly and then went to the bathroom, returning with the hot cloth. Tipping her head down, she furrowed her brow at him. "I should call Jeremy and let him know what's going on."

"Oh, for goodness' sake, Louisa! It's half three in the—the morning!"

"I'm *aware* of the time, Mar-tin."

His wife's taut lips and crossed arms were mannerisms which Martin was all too familiar with, and he wisely changed his tack.

"Yes. Come here, you must be getting cold," he said as he worked his way over on the bed, leaving her room to slide in next to him. He pulled the blankets up around her before brushing his fingers along her jaw.

"Thank you, you're nice and warm," Louisa said softly, nestling herself under his good arm. "It scares me you know."

"It's a com—mon fear. It's thought to be linked to an evolu—evolutionary survival response." Martin looked down at the top of his wife's dark head, noting a few small flakes of dandruff. He thought better of pointing it out. "I could research some possible co—coping strategies if you—"

"Martin, stop talking. This isn't about needles anymore. I just want it all to be over with. To know that nothing's going to happen to you."

"I'm fine, Louisa. The stress to the fractures caused some oedema and aggravated some existing neuropathy, but these symptoms should abate with—"

She pressed her palm to his mouth. "You're waffling, Martin. Your medical reassurances aren't going to help, you know."

He knitted his brow and gave his head a small shake. "Well, what *will* help then?"

Louisa looked up at him apologetically before her face crumpled, and she collapsed against him in tears. "I don't know! Why can't you just stay at home until you're well? I know that doesn't *sound* reasonable, but when I worry that you'll fall and get hurt again it puts me right back to those days after the accident. When I didn't know if—if you were going to—"

Martin grimaced at both another jolt in his wounded appendage and his wife's affectability. Her quick temper and unpredictable mood swings were unsettling, but he was at a complete loss during times such as this. "Well, statistically speaking, a fall is much more likely to occur here at home than when I'm out and about. And the odds of—"

"Martin! Will you stop, *please?*" Louisa pushed herself up and brushed the tears from her cheeks. "A logical explanation isn't going to make me feel any better when this is an illogical reaction, is it?" she asked him softly.

He fought the temptation to point out the futility of illogical reactions and grasped for any words befitting the situation.

A smile began to spread over his wife's face as she realised how utterly bewildered he was.

"I'm sorry, Martin," she giggled. "It's just ... your face when you don't know what to do with me," she said as she reached up and caressed his cheek. "It's really quite adorable."

He gave her a roll of his eyes before a sudden pain caught him off guard. Pulling his good arm protectively over the source of his distress, an involuntary groan reverberated in his chest.

Louisa reached for his left arm, pulling it away to examine the fractured limb.

"Oh, Martin! This is *really* swollen!" She jumped from the bed and picked up her mobile. "I'm calling Jeremy."

"No, no, no, no, no! It looks worse than it is Louisa. If you call him, he's going to come over here and tell you exactly that."

She slid off on to the floor and flapped her arms in the air. "Well, then, what am I supposed to do?"

"Go get the cold packs. That would be helpful." Martin said, nodding towards the doorway.

Giving an exasperated huff, she hurried off, returning a short time later with the requested items in hand.

"I'm sorry," he said as he shifted back to his side of the bed before lying down. "I didn't want to disrupt your sleep."

"Is that why you waited to wake me—until you couldn't stand the pain any longer?"

He looked at her sheepishly, "I thought it might ease ... a bit."

"Oh, *Martin!* Sometimes ... grrr!" She crawled in on her side of the bed and turned out the light. "Do you honestly think that I'll be able to get any sleep at all if I'm worrying about something like this happening—that you won't wake me, and I'll sleep through it?"

She pulled one of the extra pillows from the stash by the bed and tucked it under her husband's arm before placing the cold packs on top.

"I guess I should have taken care of the Toradol sooner," he admitted. "I'm sorry that you had to do that."

"Yeah, I *bet* you are. I suspect my technique left something to be desired."

"I suspect your technique left a healthy bruise on my leg."

Louisa gave him a playful slap before laying her head on his shoulder. Pulling his arm around her she worked his hand under her pyjama top and pressed it to her breast.

"You actually did very well, Louisa."

His hand caressed her curves, his thumb flicking lazily over a nipple. "Martin, what did Chris mean about the barn? What *happened* in the barn?"

His hand froze. "When?" He stalled, unwilling to open up that Pandora's box of emotions again.

"You know, Martin ... after the helicopter left. I'm assuming that's what Chris and Ruth were referring to."

"Mm. I see. It was nothing."

She tapped her fingertips against the back of his hand.

"I don't think the pain's as bad now. We should get some sleep." Martin's internal voice was warning him against his duplicity, causing a heaviness to settle in his chest and belly.

"Hmm. You have to promise to wake me up if you're too uncomfortable to drift off ... *all right?*"

He gave her an ambiguous grunt before lifting his head to kiss her.

She tipped back, returning the gesture of affection. "Goodnight, Martin."

"Mm. Goodnight."

Chapter 29

"Ruth! You're out and about bright and early," Louisa said as the elderly woman stepped into the kitchen the following morning. "Would you like some breakfast?"

"No, thank you. I've already eaten." She slipped her coat over a hook on the rack by the door and walked unsteadily towards the table.

James released a string of nonsensical utterances in greeting to his great-aunt, eliciting a crooked smile in return.

Louisa's brow furrowed as she watched the woman. "Are you limping, Ruth?"

"Oh, it's nothing," she replied, quickly diverting the conversation. "I just thought I'd stop by and pick up my keys ... see how my nephew's doing. Any ill effects from yesterday?"

"He had a very bad night. He's just now getting up in fact." Louisa removed the bowl from her son's high chair tray and reached for the kitchen roll.

"Chris gave him some Toradol before he and Carole left last night, but it wore off around three o'clock in the morning. I gave him another injection then and some more just a bit ago," she said, shuddering demonstratively.

Ruth raised an eyebrow at her. "Don't have the nursing gene in your DNA, dear?"

"I do just fine with the *nursing* part," she replied, looking at the woman through narrowed eyes. "I just don't happen to like stabbing sharp metal objects into my husband."

"It was in no way meant as a criticism, Louisa. I can't stand needles myself. But as a physician, I've learned to bypass the usual thoughts that trigger a negative reaction. I'd be happy to lend you some reading material that might prove useful."

Louisa turned back to the sink before rolling her gaze towards the ceiling. "I think I can muddle through this rough patch without too much difficulty. Thanks all the same, Ruth."

"Suit yourself." She tapped her fingertips on the table, giving her great-nephew a wry smile as he squeezed banana through his fingers before licking it from the back of his hand. "What does your father have to say about your table manners, James Henry? I can hardly imagine he approves."

The child gave her a wonky grin before spitting a mouthful of macerated fruit back into his fist and thoroughly inspecting it.

"What are you doing here?" Martin asked as he came through under the stairs.

Ruth whirled around at the sound of his voice. "Well, hello to you, too. Should I come up with a plausible excuse or just come clean and admit that I'm here to check up on you?"

"Well, if that's the case then you made an unnecessary trip up Roscarrock Hill," Martin informed her as his gaze fixed on Louisa. "I'm fine."

"Oh? Louisa said you had a less than restful night?"

"Mm, yes. Just some oedema and neuropathic pain. The problem should resolve given a bit of time."

Martin took several more steps forward before sidling up next to his wife as she stood at the counter. "Morning," he whispered in her ear, slipping an arm around her waist.

Louisa looked up at him wide-eyed. "Good morning," she whispered back. "All okay?" She cocked her head and peered up at him.

"Mm, yes." He squirmed self-consciously under her intense gaze, dropping his arm and averting his eyes.

She flashed him a smile before turning and placing a cup of coffee on the table for him.

"I'll just go and ... sit," he said, pulling in his chin and clearing his throat before limping over to take a seat next to his aunt.

"Maybe you should have Jeremy take a look at you," Ruth suggested as she tried to take hold of her nephew's wrist.

"What are you doing?" he bristled, pulling his hand away and giving her a stern scowl.

"I just wanted to have a look, Martin. You *are* monitoring for compartment syndrome, I hope."

"Oh, for goodness' sake, Ruth!" He reached for his cup, knocking it over as the fingers of his right hand closed convulsively.

"Bugger!" he said, shaking his arm, trying to rid himself of the drips of hot brew.

Getting to her feet, Ruth limped to the counter to get a kitchen roll before returning to the table to wipe up the spilt coffee.

Martin eyed her suspiciously, his brows drawing together. "Why are you walking like that?"

"Like what?"

"You're limping," he said, wagging a finger at her skirt-clad legs.

"Don't change the subject. Let me see your hand." She reached again for his wrist, catching him off guard and grasping on to it.

"I said it's fine, Ruth. Just leave me be."

Ruth ignored his plea and turned towards Louisa. "Get me a cold wet flannel please, dear."

She wedged her fist against her hip, staring her nephew down. "You know, I quickly lose patience with you when you persist in denials."

"I persist in denials because I *am* fine. I suppose you're going to ban me from hot liquids now, too?" he said, screwing up his face.

"*I* won't. Although what your wife does is her business."

Louisa returned to the table with a cold cloth, and Ruth laid it over her nephew's hand.

"Did he get a burn, Ruth?" the younger woman asked, worrying her lip.

Ruth peeked under the cloth. "There *is* some inflammation."

"What about blistering?"

"Oh, good grief!" Martin snapped, yanking his hand back and slapping the flannel down on to the table top. "If anyone had bothered to ask, I'd tell you it doesn't hurt. As I said already—it's fine. There *is* no problem here, so get off."

Ruth took a step back and shook her head. "I'm beginning to see your point about him, Louisa. He *can* be quite difficult, can't he?"

Martin's head snapped towards his wife.

She watched him warily. "Well, I don't know that I'd say Martin is *difficult,* Ruth. Maybe a bit trying at—"

"Excuse me, you do see that I'm sitting right in front of you, don't you?" Martin blustered.

"You're rather hard to miss, Martin," Ruth said. Pulling out her chair, she again took a seat next to him. "Now stop your mithering and let me see."

Martin waggled his nose in the air but reluctantly held out his hand. "I *am* a doctor, you know."

"Yes, I'm aware of that. I'm also aware that doctors make abominable patients, so hush up," she said as she inspected the burned area. "No. You're fine, just a bit pink is all. Nothing to make a fuss over."

"Pfft! I *wasn't* making a fuss."

He leaned towards his aunt, his eyes boring in at her. "Now … are you going to tell me why you're limping?"

"Oh, mind your own business, Martin."

"How in the hell is *that* fair?" he sputtered.

Ruth tipped her head down and peered up at him. "Life isn't fair, Martin."

Turning back to the table, she picked up her cup of tea, taking a sip as she glanced surreptitiously at her nephew. "And you should watch your language. Do you want your son's first words to be profanities?"

Louisa raised an eyebrow at him while trying to keep a straight face. She recognised the deepening creases in her husband's forehead as the calm before the storm, however, and decided it would be best to head off a full-blown conflagration between the pair. "Ruth, Martin's concerned, as am I. We would really appreciate it if you would tell us why you're limping."

The old woman brushed the hair back from her face and grimaced. "Oh, very well. But I don't want you throwing this in my face every time the subject of my age comes up in a conversation, Martin," she said, wagging a bony finger in warning.

She turned and stared at her teacup, running her fingertip along the handle. "I had a bit of a spill coming over here," she mumbled.

"What! Why didn't you *tell* me?" Martin got to his feet, and the table legs screeched along the slate floor as he pushed it forcefully out of the way. "Where did you fall? How did you land?" he asked, tugging at the hem of his aunt's skirt.

Ruth brushed his hand away. "Oh, do stop that Martin! I knew you'd overreact. *This* is why I didn't mention it. Well, that and the surety that you'll remind me of this every time you feel my senescence is an issue."

He leaned down, studying her face. And where *did* you fall?"

"On the cobblestone path by my house. But I'm fine. I walked all the way up here, didn't I?"

"And how did you land? On your knees or your backside?"

"My backside," Ruth grumbled, fidgeting under her nephew's fixed gaze.

"All right, up you get. Here, take my arm," Martin said as he reached down and pulled his aunt to her feet. "I need to scan you."

"Oh, please don't make a fuss! I'm fine!"

Louisa tossed the tea towel down on to the table. "Oh, for goodness' sake! *You two!* I have lost track of how many times I've heard the words *I'm fine* uttered in the past ten minutes! Ruth, go with Martin right now ... let him examine you. And Martin, when you're finished with Ruth, call Jeremy and tell him that you need him to stop by and take a look at you."

Martin stood watching her, slack-jawed. "But Louisa, it's not really—"

"Martin, I've had all the Ellingham bravado and bullheadedness that I can take for one morning!" She snapped her fingers towards the hallway and pinched her lips together. "Go! Now!" she hissed.

"Yes." Martin ducked his head and then led his aunt slowly under the stairs before turning into the consulting room.

When they returned to the kitchen a short time later, Louisa had a bowl of hot scrambled eggs on the table and had refilled their cups with tea and coffee.

"Well, did everything check out okay?" she asked as she set a plate of toast down before taking a seat.

"I can't say. You'll have to ask Ruth," Martin said.

The old woman rolled her eyes at him and dropped into her chair. Then she turned to Louisa. "I'm fine. A nice contusion to the left gluteus maximus is all. Nothing broken."

Martin went to the freezer and returned to the table with a cold pack, tipping his aunt to one side and slipping it under her hip. Pulling out his chair, he sat down before eagerly piling eggs on to his plate. "I'm going to get someone to build a set of steps at the other end of your porch, Ruth. I don't want you on those cobblestones anymore."

The elderly woman curbed her reflex to object and instead gave him a small smile. "Thank you, Martin. I'd appreciate that."

"That's an excellent idea," Louisa said as she stretched a foot out under the table and stroked her husband's calf, eliciting a look of incredulity from him.

He peered under the table at her wiggling toes. "Mm."

Turning his attention back to the more serious matter at hand he said, "I'll have that Granger fellow who did the shower—"

"*Grady*, Martin," Louisa prompted.

He gave her a quick glance. "Yes. Grady Granger. He's going to be taking care of the locks around the house. I'll ask him if he can do the steps at Ruth's."

"That would be wonderful. But Martin, when you talk to the man, try to remember ... his name is Grady. *Lawrence— Grady.*" She scooped up a forkful of egg as she gave a small shake of her head.

The remainder of the day was mercifully quiet at the Ellingham home. Martin sought solitude in his consulting room, working on Ruth's clock, and Louisa took James out for a short walk to the Platt before making dinner.

Engrossed in what he was doing, Martin didn't notice his wife enter the room that evening. He startled when she slipped in behind him and nuzzled her face into the crook of his neck.

"For heaven's sake, Louisa! Give me some warning before you do that!" he said as he placed a palm against his pounding chest.

Her arms snaked around him and she held him tightly. "Sorry 'bout that. James is down for the night."

"Ah ... good."

"What are you doing?"

"Looking over these gears—checking for any burrs." He picked up a small metal disk, holding it up to the light streaming in the window. "See here ... how this little tooth isn't smooth."

Louisa undid the top button of his shirt and slid her palms inside before placing a quick kiss on the side of his head. Leaning over his shoulder, she peered at the object pinched between his thumb and index finger. "That *little* tiny thing sticking out?" she said, tapping it with the tip of her fingernail.

"It may look insignificant, but the drag caused by that little burr will be magnified exponentially as it's transferred to each consecutive component in the works of the clock."

"So, then you have to get a new part?"

He pulled a small metal file from the fabric pouch unrolled in front of him and brushed it gently over the imperfection. "That should do it," he said as he inspected his work carefully.

"Quite impressive, Mr. Ellingham." Louisa nipped gently at his ear.

"It's a simple procedure."

She watched as his large fingers painstakingly manipulated the tiny cogs. "Do you miss it, Martin?" she asked, pulling a hand up protectively against his neck as she pressed her cheek to his.

"Miss what?" He fitted his loupe to his eye before scanning over his work, assuring himself that the little tooth was completely smooth.

"Surgery. How much of a loss was it for you when your blood sensitivity hit?"

His throat rose and fell against her palm as he swallowed slowly. "It's what I trained all my life to do, really."

A tear worked its way between their cheeks, and she felt his chest vibrate under her hand as he took in a ragged breath.

"I'm so sorry, Martin," she said, pressing her lips to his head.

Their tender moment was brought to an abrupt end by a raucous pounding on the front door.

"Oh, gawd. What now?" Martin said, letting the clock part drop to his desk.

"Doc! Doc! You home!"

"I'll get it," Louisa said before rushing out through the reception room as her husband struggled to his feet.

Chippy Miller stood facing her as she pulled the door open, his face red as he gasped for air. "Louiser, it's Irene. The baby's comin' early. It's not s'posed to be 'ere till the middle of January."

Martin moved in behind her. "Well, call an ambulance!"

"I did, Doc. But I don't think they're gonna make it in time, an' Irene seems to be havin' trouble. I think somethin's wrong. I need yer help ... please."

Martin turned to Louisa. "Can you get my medical bag? Then call Jeremy ... tell him what's going on and have him meet me at the Miller's."

"Ah, yeah—yeah!" She gave him a nod before hurrying back to the consulting room, returning moments later with his bag.

"Thank you," he said before placing a kiss on her cheek and limping out the door.

Chapter 30

Martin's anxiety over what he might face at the Miller home increased as Chippy related additional details on the drive up Church Hill and down the winding Cornish lanes. Both the fisherman and his wife were past prime childbearing age, and the clinical signs the man described raised red flags for the doctor.

He pulled his mobile from his belt and called Jeremy. "I need you to stop at the surgery before you come to the Miller's. Pick up a tank of oxygen. Then stop at Mrs. Tishell's and get a bottle of magnesium sulphate. Be quick about it, too."

He rang off and turned to Chippy. "What did Dr. Lippolis say about the glucose screening test? Was that normal?"

Chippy gave him a vacant glance before turning his attention back to the road. "Don't know what yer talkin' about, Doc."

"The test for gestational diabetes! What did it show?" he asked impatiently.

"Sorry, Doc. That kinda stuff just flies by me. I figured if there was somethin' wrong the guy over there in Wadebridge would've told us, wouldn't 'e?"

Martin gave a grunt as his fist closed tightly around the handle of his medical bag.

Irene Miller was a superstitious soul and had put off seeing a physician until well into her second trimester. She had experienced two miscarriages already and had convinced herself that the Fates would surely curse this one as well if she revealed it to anyone.

She kept her condition to herself for almost five months until she could no longer hide the pregnancy from her husband.

"That was idiotic!" Martin blurted out.

"I know it was, but don't get into a bate with her, Doc. She was just scared."

Chippy rubbed his palm across his forehead and looked over at him. "She's gonna be okay now, though. I know *you* won't let anything happen to her."

Martin breathed out a heavy sigh. He decided it best to not mention that he could count on one hand the number of babies he had delivered since becoming a GP.

"Irene was havin' a headache tonight, so she went to bed early," Chippy explained as he led the doctor through the house. Martin cautiously scaled the stairs. There was no handrail on either side, so he placed his palm on the wall and inched his way up to the second story.

The very heavily pregnant woman was lying on the bed, her brow furrowed as she pressed her hand to her head.

"Hi, Doc. Sorry ta be disturbin' yer weekend," she said, giving him a weak smile.

"It's all right, Mrs. Miller." He sat down on the bed next to her and pulled the blankets back from her legs. "Good, God! How long has your oedema been this bad?" he asked, noting the pits left in her ankles when he pressed his fingertips against her skin.

"Just for the last few days. I weren't worried about it. The doc over in Wadebridge said it were normal this close to the baby bein' born an' all."

Martin's jaw tensed as he planned an immediate course of treatment. Pulling his blood pressure cuff from his bag, he wrapped it around the woman's arm, his brow knitting as he watched the needle on the gauge drop.

Irene reached out suddenly, her hand grasping on to his shirt sleeve as a contraction began. He reflexively yanked his arm away before quickly composing himself and turning his wrist to eye his watch as the seconds ticked by.

"What are ya doin' now?" Chippy asked as he watched the doctor press an instrument to his wife's belly.

"It's a foetal heart monitor. I'm just checking to see how your baby's doing." A faint smile slipped across his face as the anticipated rhythmic whooshing sound emanated from the device.

He gave a satisfied nod before cocking his head, his breath catching in his chest. He had detected a faint sound as he moved the device around. Sliding the transducer higher on his patient's belly confirmed his suspicions.

"Erm, when you had your scan done, what were you told?" Martin asked, looking from Chippy to Irene.

"Irene didn't want one, Doc. She'd 'eard them things can hurt the baby, and the doc at the clinic over there said it wasn't real necessary."

"That's ridiculous! Studies have repeatedly shown them to be harmless. If your doctor had an ounce of sense about him, or at the very *least* been compliant with NHS recommendations and done the scan, he would have determined that you're pregnant with twins, Mrs. Miller. We're now dealing with a preeclamptic mother and two babies who will be born both prematurely and away from hospital where they could have been cared for properly!" Martin grumbled unintelligibly as he began to dig through his bag, laying supplies out on the bed.

Glancing up, he saw his patient shudder and wipe tears from her cheeks. "Mrs Miller ... I'm—I'm sorry. I didn't mean to upset you. Your doctor should have provided you with accurate information, and stressed to you and your husband the importance of these prenatal scans. Let's just focus now on delivering these babies safely and getting you and your new family sent on to hospital."

"Oh, bless yer heart, Doc! I'm not upset about all this. I know you'll take good care of me ... us. I just wasn't expectin' to have two babies is all. It's wonderful news! All the years of tryin' and now two little bairns! It's tears of—"

Irene's words were choked off by another contraction, and she let out a long groan as her muscles clamped down in an effort to force the new lives into the world.

Footsteps could be heard thundering up the stairs before Jeremy appeared in the doorway, red-faced and out of breath. "What do you want me to do?" he asked as Martin pulled the blanket up and helped his patient to bend her legs.

"Help Mr. Miller get a pile of clean towels together. Then see if you can find a sturdy box. Or better yet, empty out a dresser drawer. Then chase up some cling film."

"Cling film?" Chippy looked at Martin, his bushy brows drawn together.

Jeremy put his hand on the man's back and led him towards the door. "I suspect Dr. Ellingham is wanting us to..."

Martin glanced over his shoulder as his assistant's voice faded away and then pulled the blanket back so that he could examine his patient.

"This will be uncomfortable, Mrs. Miller, but I need to assess your progress." Martin completed his brief examination, peeling off his gloves and dropping them into the bin. "Are you having any urge to push?"

"Not real sure I know, Doc. I feel like a right moron—at my age and not knowin' nothin' about this and all."

"That's what I'm here for. You just do as I tell you. I'm going to give you a bit of Pitocin, just to speed things up a bit," Martin said as he started an IV in the back of the woman's hand. A bit of blood oozed out around the injection site, and the doctor turned his head away, taking in several deep breaths as the nausea abated.

"You okay, Doc?" Irene asked as she rested her hand on his arm.

"Mm. I'm fine. You should be prepared for a noticeable increase in the intensity of your contractions once I've administered the medication," Martin said as he injected it into the catheter. "Things will probably progress quickly from this point on."

"Where's my husband?" Irene asked, looking nervously towards the hallway. "I want 'im 'ere!"

"Jeremy!" the doctor barked over his shoulder.

Footsteps could be heard approaching and Chippy hurried into the room, kneeling down beside the bed. "How're ya doin, darlin'?"

"Doc says—" the woman reached for him, moaning as nature took control of her body. "Chippy, don't leave again ... promise me," she said tearfully, pulling him to her.

"I'm not gonna go nowhere, Irene," he said, wiping his hand across her cheek.

"Need me to do anything?" Jeremy asked.

Martin glanced up at the young man before turning to the fisherman. "Erm, Chippy, do you have any hot water bottles?"

"In the bathroom cabinet—under the sink."

"Can you get whatever they have in there ... fill 'em up with hot water." Martin said as he squeezed the bulb on the blood pressure cuff again.

Jeremy hurried off down the hall, retrieving the items and returning quickly.

"Put them in the bottom of the drawer, then cover them with towels," the doctor instructed. "Okay Mrs. Miller, on the next contraction, I want you to push as hard as you can." He laid two towels out on the bed next to him.

"Oh, dear God, please let them be all right," Irene pleaded as she felt the band of muscles across her abdomen tighten.

"Now, Mrs. Miller. Push, push, push, push, push!" Martin glanced up at her and gave her a small smile and an encouraging nod of his head. "You're doing great; keep pushing. I can see your baby's head ... lots of dark hair."

The fisherman's gaze darted between his wife and Martin, a broad smile spreading across his face as he became a father for the first time.

The doctor supported the head as the tiny body made its way into the world. He manoeuvred the shoulders through the birth canal, one at a time, before the child slipped out completely.

"It's a girl!" Martin said as he lay the tiny form in his lap. He wiped the mucous from it's nose and mouth before clamping and cutting the umbilical cord.

The fresh little being lay in his hands motionless, and the doctor's own breathing was suspended as he rubbed up and down the baby's back. The child finally startled, it's arms flailing and fingers spread as it let out a soft mewl. "There, that's better," Martin said as air rushed back into his own lungs.

He counted the fingers and toes and then bundled the baby girl securely in a towel and handed her to his assistant.

Quickly examining his patient, he breathed a sigh of relief that the second baby was also in a head-down position.

"A good hard push now, Mrs. Miller."

Irene's face tensed again as she pushed one last time. The birth of the second child was rapid, hardly giving the doctor time to prepare.

"Well, Chippy, you have a son," Martin said as tears welled in his eyes. He discreetly wiped the moisture from his cheeks on to his sleeve as the baby boy let out a loud wail, protesting the abrupt change to his environment.

After cutting the second umbilical cord and swaddling the youngest infant, the doctor caught his assistant's eye and gave a nod towards the Miller's. "Shall we give the new family a bit of time, Mr. Portman?"

The aide handed his tiny parcel to Irene, and Martin held the couple's new baby boy out to Chippy.

"Naw, I don't think I better, Doc. I might hurt 'im. He's awful tiny," the burly fisherman said as he pulled at the towel to peer in at his son's face.

"You'll learn, Chippy." Martin pushed the infant towards his father.

He reached out hesitantly and took the child, and Martin returned his attention to Irene, rechecking her blood pressure while waiting for the placentas to be delivered.

Once the final stage of the birthing process had been completed, Martin excused himself and limped down the hall to the bathroom, where the nausea that he had been able to quell during the intensity of the emergency finally got the better of him.

He flushed the toilet and then splashed cold water on his face before taking in a deep breath and returning to the bedroom.

"We need to get the babies situated for the trip to Truro," he said as he sat back down on the bed. "Mr. Portman, could you take the little girl. And Chippy, can you lay your son in our rather crude incubator?"

The two men nested the infants into the drawer, head-to-head, before the doctor and his aide sealed the top with a cover of cling film.

Martin pulled his biro from his pocket and poked a small hole in the plastic, inserting the tubing leading from the oxygen tank. Then, he took a roll of bandage tape from his bag and affixed the tube to the side of the incubator before securing the cling film. "That should hold them until the ambulance arrives," he said as he adjusted the valve on the tank.

"Your son and daughter are small. I would estimate around four and a half to five pounds. But Mr. Portman gave them Apgar scores of six for your daughter and eight for your son at one minute and eight and ten at five minutes."

"Sorry, Doc. Don't understand any of that," Chippy said, giving him a shrug of his shoulders. "Are they gonna be okay is all I need ta know."

"They appear to be perfectly healthy, Chippy. And your wife's blood pressure is under control at the moment. The doctors in Truro will want to keep her a day or two ... monitor her condition. But I don't anticipate any further problems." Martin glanced at his watch and then at his aide. "Could you check to see what's keeping that ambulance?"

"Yeah...yeah." Jeremy stepped into the hallway to make his call.

Chippy leaned over and kissed his wife. "I was worried."

"Oh, you shouldn't 'ave been, love. I knew Doc Martin wouldn't let nothin' bad happen." Irene reached up and squeezed her husband's fingers.

Martin cleared his throat and busied himself with gathering together the medical waste and putting it into a plastic bag.

"They just passed St. Endellion, Dr. Ellingham. Should be here in just a few minutes," Jeremy said when he returned from the hallway.

Martin got to his feet and walked over, extending his hand to his patient's husband. "Congratulations, Chippy. You have a fine family."

The fisherman looked down at Martin's injured arm before gently taking his hand and shaking it. "Thank you, Doc. For all of it ... watchin' out for Irene and keepin' the young ones safe 'n all."

"You're welcome." Martin tucked his chin and put his stethoscope back in his ears before checking Mrs. Miller's blood pressure one last time.

Louisa was wrapped up in a blanket on the sofa when Jeremy dropped Martin at the surgery. She looked expectantly at him as he ducked through the doorway and entered the lounge. "Well?"

"Louisa—"

"Oh, Martin. Do I have to wait and call Bert in the morn— Oh, no! I *can't* call Bert! Martin, how am I going to find out if you don't tell me?" she asked, looking at her husband with pleading eyes.

"I'm sorry, I can't discuss—"

She slapped her book to her lap. "Sometimes I really hate that you're a doctor, you know."

Martin stood in front of her, his fingers twitching at his sides. "I'm sorry."

Louisa got to her feet and took his hand. "It's okay. Most of the time I'm very happy that you're a doctor ... and very, very proud of you." She reached up and kissed him. "You ready for bed?"

"Mm, very."

The warmth and softness of his wife was comforting as they lay side by side a few minutes later. Though it was a happy outcome, it had been a stressful evening.

And Martin knew that he would again have to address the issue of the incompetency of the Wadebridge GP when he spoke with Chris in the morning.

Louisa wrapped her arms around him and nuzzled her nose into his neck, inhaling his scent. "Goodnight, Martin. I love you," she said softly.

He turned his head and placed a kiss on her cheek before breathing out a whispered, "Goodnight."

He lay for several minutes, recalling the events at the Miller's and thinking back on the memorable day a year and a half before when James Henry Ellingham came into the world.

"Louisa."

"Hmm?" She nestled in closer, tightening her hold on him.

"Boy *and* girl."

Chapter 31

"Thank you for telling me, Martin," Louisa said, patting her husband's cheek as she passed him on the way to the sink with her breakfast dishes. "I'm glad I wasn't the last one in the village to hear the big news."

She ran her bowl under the tap before gazing out the window for a moment. She whirled around. "Oh, gawd! I just had a horrible thought! What if Mrs. Tishell had been the one to tell me! I can just hear her. *Oh? Dr. Ellingham didn't rush right home to share the good news with his wife?*" Louisa said in mock singsong before adding, "*I just assumed the two of you talk. But I would imagine you don't share the same level of interest in the latest medical information that the good doctor and I do. I'm sorry, I shouldn't assume. I'm sooo sorry!*" Louisa grumbled unintelligibly before slapping the tea towel down next to the sink.

Martin stared up at her for a moment before pulling in his chin and grunting. He returned his attention to the newspaper.

Louisa leaned back against the counter, staring across the room. "I still can't believe it! Chippy Miller—a dad. And to twins, no less! What did they look like?"

Martin lowered the newspaper and looked at her uncertainly, hesitating as he tried to mentally fill in the blanks between the snippets of conversation he had picked up on. *Something about Chippy Miller, assumptions, news ... or maybe it was information—and twins. What did they look like?*

"Mm. Surprised. I'd say they looked—erm, yes—surprised. Yes, they looked surprised." He gave his wife a small smile and a confident nod of his head before returning to the morning's news.

She walked behind him, pulling the distracting object from his hands and giving it a toss on to the floor. "You weren't listening, were you?" she said tipping his head back so she could make eye contact with him.

"Mm, sorry. I was ... reading." He reached down to retrieve his paper from the slate below, but pulled back quickly as his wife's foot came down hard next to his fingers. "Louisa! That's my one good hand!"

Plunking down on the chair next to him, she huffed out a breath. "Martin, I'd just like your attention for a few minutes! I won't be able to make it home for lunch, and I want a little time with you before I leave."

"I see." He surreptitiously eyed the article that he'd been reading, warning of a series of winter storms predicted to move across Cornwall over the course of the next several weeks.

*"Mar-*tin!"

Forcing himself to forget about the expected rain, wind and cold temperatures, he turned to his wife. "Yes, I'm listening. What is it that you're wanting to talk about?"

She stared at him for several seconds before clarifying her earlier question. "I was referring to the babies, Martin. What do the *babies* look like?"

Straightening in his chair, his head bobbed vigorously. "Yes, I see! Ah, typical preterm neonates. Small—four-and-a-half to five pounds, as best as I could tell.

"They seemed healthy overall, however. Both exhibited good breath sounds, strong and regular heartbeats, normal reflexes.

"Of course, both infants presented with the liberal coating of vernix that one would expect with an early birth, and their heads were less misshapen than one would see with a term pregnancy.

"Naturally, their craniums are small, so there was, of course, less deforma—"

Louisa pressed her fingers to his lips and tipped her head down at him. "I was wondering, Martin, what they *look* like."

"I was *trying* to explain, Louisa." His eyebrows pulled down—his face thoughtful. "Perhaps you weren't listening?"

"Martin, who do the babies look like—Irene or Chippy?" she asked sharply.

He took note of her pursed lips and crossed arms and tried to tamp down his own growing frustration.

"Louisa, they're babies," he explained slowly. "At this point, they hardly look human, let alone like one or the other of their parents. But I *can* tell you that one of them has a lot of dark hair, and one is bald. Is that the sort of information you've been fishing for?"

She squeezed her eyes shut and shook her head. "Why couldn't you have said that when I first asked?"

"Because that's *not* what you asked! If you wanted to know if they have hair, why didn't you just ask if they have hair? I find you very confusing at times."

"Oh, *Martin!*" She picked her son up from his high chair before heading off towards the stairs, her ponytail flicking.

Martin sighed, pushing himself away from the table before refilling his coffee cup and heading off to his consulting room.

His first patient of the morning was Shelagh Tallack. He sat behind his desk reviewing her blood glucose results.

"Doc," the woman said as she entered the room.

"Miss Tallack. Take a seat on the exam couch and I'll check your wound. Any problems with it?" he asked.

"Not so much problems. Just inconvenience. It's costin' me a fortune sittin' at home. I should be out on my boat, you know."

He scrutinized her as she walked unsteadily before climbing on to the table.

"Have you been drinking?"

"Of course not, you stupid git! It's not half ten in the mornin' yet!"

"Mm." He picked up his ophthalmoscope and leaned forward to look at her eyes.

Shelagh pulled back and batted his hand away. "What do you think yer doin?"

"I'm trying to examine your eyes. I can't very well do that if you don't sit still, though, Miss Tallack," he said, waiting for her to stop squirming.

"You got hold'a the wrong end'a the stick, then. It's my arse yer s'posed ta be lookin' at," she snapped.

He pulled in his chin and looked at her askance before resuming his examination. "Have you had any more falls?"

"No, but I weren't quite right all weekend—a bit squiffy feelin."

Martin grimaced at the colloquialism. "Squiffy? What do you mean, *squiffy?*"

"You know, Doc. Kinda that feelin' you 'ave when yer out in the mizzle and can't quite git yer bearins'."

"Oh, yes. It's crystal clear now," he grumbled as he moved his scope to examine his patient's other eye.

She pulled her head back, shaking it from side to side. "What's takin' you so long there? Can't 'ardly see straight now; thank you very much!"

"What do you mean? You're experiencing double vision?"

"Maybe."

Martin hissed out a breath and laid his scope down on the table. "I need you to slip your coat off so I can check your blood pressure," he said, wagging a finger at her.

Shelagh struggled, trying to keep her weight off her injured hip while pulling her arm from her sleeve. He took hold of the cuff and began to tug.

"Get yer 'ands off me!" she said, yanking her arm away. "I oughta report you to—to—" She stared vacantly across the room before her eyes snapped back at the doctor. "Just keep yer 'ands to yerself, ya tosser!"

Martin pulled back and watched her for a moment. "Morwenna!" he called out.

The clattering of plastic jewellery grew louder as the receptionist approached. "What d'ya need, Doc?"

"Could you help Miss Tallack off with her coat, please?"

Morwenna cast a puzzled look at him.

"Don't want 'im tryin' ta take advantage of the situation," Shelagh said, holding her arm out to the young woman.

The receptionist reached for the woman's sleeve, looking at her boss wide-eyed. "What have you been up to in here, Doc?"

"I haven't been *up to* anything! Just get her coat off so I can proceed with my examination."

The woman's outer garment was removed and he gave a grunt. "Can you roll up her sleeve?"

Morwenna gave a shrug of her shoulders before doing as he asked.

"What about the dizziness and confusion. Anymore episodes?" Martin said, wrapping his blood pressure cuff around the woman's arm.

"I told you ... I been feelin' squiffy. Clean out yer ears, boy!"

Martin's jaws clenched as he ripped the Velcro from around the woman's elbow. He placed his stethoscope against her chest. "You're palpitating."

Turning to his receptionist, he said, "Get the bottle of honey from the kitchen, Morwenna. Up and to the right of the cooker. And bring me a teaspoon, too."

The young woman gave him a quizzical look as she moved towards the door.

"And tell Mr. Portman I need him in here!" he barked after her.

"I want my assistant to draw some blood, Miss Tallack. I'll send it off to the lab in Truro." he said as he placed a tourniquet around her arm and tightened it.

Jeremy entered the room. "Morwenna said you needed my help with something?"

"Mm. I want you to draw a sample on this patient."

The crusty woman stared threateningly at the aide but slowly relinquished her arm.

Morwenna came back through the door. "Here you go, Doc."

Martin filled the spoon with honey and pushed it towards his patient's face. "Swallow that. The sugar should raise your glucose level, thereby slowing your heart rate and ameliorating your—strange behaviour."

Shelagh looked uncertainly at Morwenna, and the receptionist gave her a smile and a nod of her head.

"He's not tryin' to dope you or anything ... I promise."

The woman opened her mouth and downed the sugary substance.

Martin handed the bottle and spoon back to his receptionist and then retrieved several gauze pads, disinfectant, and bandage tape. "Lie face down on the table and I'll check that wound."

Shelagh's eyes twitched and narrowed at him. "Don't you try nothin' funny ... you 'ear?"

Morwenna let out a small snort. "Ha, not a chance! The doc doesn't *do* funny."

Martin's head whipped around and he furrowed his brow at her. "Hold this," he said, clearing his throat and shoving the small tray of supplies into the girl's hands.

He cleaned and dressed the woman's wound and then helped her to sit back up before his hands were slapped away.

"Why do I bother?" he muttered, returning to his desk.

"I suspect you have an insulinoma ... er, a tumour on your pancreas. If your test results support my diagnosis, Miss Tallack, you'll need to have an MRI scan and probably surgery to remove the tumour."

The woman walked slowly back to take a seat in the chair, working the buttons of her coat through the buttonholes. "Pancreas cancer ... that's a bad one, innit, doc? Gonna be the end of me, right?"

Martin glanced up from his desk at the blanched face in front of him. "No, no, no, no, no. Not pancreatic *cancer*. A tumour on your pancreas. Insulinomas are rare and nearly always benign ... er, relatively harmless. In fact, if your disease is limited to one tumour, your doctor in Truro will probably be able to remove it through a simple laparoscopic procedure and just a small incision. Most people experience a complete recovery and no further problems."

He jotted a few notes into the woman's file before going around to perch on the front of his desk. "I'd like to listen to your heart again before you leave. Can you stand up for me?"

"What fer?" she replied, eyeing him suspiciously.

"I'd like to see if the honey that I gave you had any effect on your heart rate."

The woman gave a grunt and stood up, pulling the collar on her shirt open.

"That's better," Martin said as a steady *lub-dub* pulsed through his stethoscope.

He pulled several tissues from the box next to him and handed them to her before getting up and walking to the door. "The people in Truro will be in contact with you to set up an appointment, but until the issue is resolved, you shouldn't be driving. Morwenna will call for a taxi to get you home today, and you can make arrangements for transportation to and from the hospital when the people in Truro call."

Shelagh got up from her chair, and as she neared the doorway, she turned suddenly, throwing her arms around Martin's neck and planting a kiss firmly on his cheek. He pulled his hands up to push her away, but fearing further insinuations of impropriety, he held them out from his sides as his assistant and receptionist looked on in amusement.

"Thank you, Doc. I knowed somethin' were wrong. It's a relief to find out what it is."

"Mm ... well, yes."

The morning seemed to drag more and more slowly as Martin carried out the most mundane of duties. His head had begun to pound and his back ached, making the completion of patient notes particularly laborious. By the time he finished with his final case of the day, his stomach had begun to churn as well.

He lifted his head from his desk when he heard a knock on his door. "Come!"

Jeremy entered the room and swung the door shut behind him. The latch clattered loudly, the sudden noise bringing Martin's hands to his head. "*Must* you slam that door every time you come through?"

"Oh, sorry." The aide cocked his head at him. "You having those ice pick headaches again?"

"*No*. In fact, I want you to call Ed. Let him know that I've been headache free for the last week, and I'm fine to drive again."

"Yeah? You sure about that?"

Martin rolled his eyes at the young man as he tapped a stack of notes into a neat pile. "Oh, for goodness' sake, Jeremy. I'm not going to take unnecessary chances. Do you think I want to land myself back in hospital again—repeat this nightmare?"

"I suppose not. I'll call him before lunch." The aide squinted his eyes at his patient. "You look a bit peaky. Everything okay?"

"I'm fine," Martin said, waving a hand through the air. "I'm just tired."

"Okay, I'll let you know what Mr. Christianson has to say. But you better go and eat some lunch and then have a lie down."

"Yes, I will!" Martin bristled before pushing himself from his chair and snatching the notes from his desk. He limped through the reception room, stopping long enough to drop the pile in front of Morwenna. "Get those filed," he grumbled before heading for the stairs.

"Please?"

Martin turned and glared at her, "Just—do it!"

The young woman shook her head at him as he scaled the steps.

When Jeremy stuck his head into the bedroom a short time later, Martin was already asleep. The aide reached down and placed the backs of his fingers against his forehead before leaving the room, returning with a thermometer. He gave a soft sigh before heading back downstairs.

Jeremy stayed through the afternoon, not leaving until Louisa had arrived home.

"It appears to be a virus," he told her. "But he's still on the IV antibiotic. Hopefully, it'll prevent any bacterial infections from setting in," he explained. Morwenna's already cancelled his appointments for tomorrow."

"Thanks, Jeremy. So, you don't think it's anything to be concerned about then?" Louisa asked, her teeth worrying her lip.

"Any illness will be cause for concern for the next year or two, Louisa. But it *is* to be expected, and we'll stay on top of it."

"What should I do? How do I know when to call you?" she asked as she hoisted her son higher on her hip.

"Keep track of his temperature. It's been holding steady at a hundred and one point three. Call me if it goes *any* higher.

"Do what you can to keep him in bed. I know it's a tall order, but what he needs most is rest. Hopefully, this is one of those twenty-four-hour viruses and he'll be right as rain by the end of the day tomorrow."

Jeremy's heels clicked against the slate kitchen floor as he moved towards the door. Grasping on to the doorknob, he turned his head. "Oh ... tell Martin he has Ed's blessing to start driving. That should make him feel a bit better."

Louisa gave the young man a tepid smile before he pulled the door shut behind him. Then she scaled the steps to check on her husband.

Martin's eyes began to flutter open as the scent of his wife's perfume roused his senses. He rolled on to his back and looked up at her from under heavy lids. "Mm, hello. How was your day?"

"My day was ... routine. Aside from the meeting over lunch about the Christmas market, that is. That was interesting."

James Henry wriggled from his mother's arms and crawled up and over his father's midriff. Martin moaned, pushing the boy off and on to the bed. The child giggled, scrambling across the mattress before dropping on to the floor.

"Sorry 'bout that," Louisa said, brushing her fingers through his hair.

"It's okay. I just have a bit of a stomach ache."

She furrowed her brow and quirked the left side of her mouth. "Hmm. Jeremy left a message for you." She tipped her head down, peering at him with a taut face. "He said you have Ed's blessing to start driving again."

Martin's cheeks nudged up as the words brought him another step closer to the life he'd had before his accident. "Good ... that's good news."

"Yeah, I hope so." Louisa's doubts were audible in her voice, and some of the happiness Martin had felt at the news slipped away.

He put his hand on hers. "I'll be careful."

Leaning over, she pressed her lips to his hot forehead. "How are you feeling?"

"Tired and a bit achy ... nauseous. You really shouldn't have James in here. I'm probably contagious."

"I'll take him out in a minute. Cupping his cheek in her palm, she asked, "Do you think you picked up a bug at the open house this weekend?"

"Quite likely. No doubt giving Bert Large mouth-to-mouth," he grumbled, turning up his lip. "The man's disgusting—a walking petri dish of bacteria, viruses and God knows what else. That's what having your arm down toilets for four decades will do."

"Oh, Martin," Louisa hissed disapprovingly. She sat quietly for a few moments and then gazed down at him. "You complain about them, but you do care about them ... don't you."

Martin took in a breath and held it, unwilling to admit to the truth of his wife's words.

James saved him the indignity when he pulled himself up beside his mother, grabbed for the thermometer on the bedside table, and shoved it into his father's ear.

"Hmm, a budding doctor, maybe?" Louisa said while holding on to their son's hand, helping him to conduct his examination. The instrument beeped softly, and she showed it to the boy. "It says one hundred point four, James. Daddy's doing a bit better!"

"Da-ee!" he squealed as he slapped his hand against Martin's arm.

"Jeremy thinks this is just a twenty-four-hour virus, and you'll be better by tomorrow afternoon. Your temperature's down, so maybe he's right," Louisa said.

"Jeremy said that? That he thinks it's a twenty-four-hour virus? He has no way of knowing that." Martin took the thermometer from his wife's hand and slapped it back down on to the table. "Frankly, I'm disappointed in him."

She shifted on the bed. "Well, could be he didn't say that *exactly*. But I believe he did mention the possibility."

Her brow drew down as she cupped his cheek in her hand. "Could be wishful thinking on my part, too. I just want you well. It makes me very nervous to have you sick."

"Mm, sorry." Martin's eyes drifted shut again. Louisa tucked the blankets under his chin before gathering James into her arms and heading for the landing, pulling the door shut behind her.

Chapter 32

Slipping quietly from the bed on Wednesday morning, Louisa showered and prepared for the school day while allowing her husband a lie-in.

He had slept through most of Tuesday, but his fever had broken by late afternoon and his appetite had returned with a vengeance by dinnertime.

Sitting down on the edge of the bed, she leaned over and nuzzled her nose into his neck. He groaned softly before rolling stiffly on to his back, squinting up at her. "Morning," he said hoarsely.

"Good morning. How did you sleep?"

"Mm, fine." Pushing himself to a sitting position, he cocked his head to the side. "Are you experiencing any symptoms of illness? Body aches, nausea, sore throat. Any sign you could be coming down with this?"

"Nope, just me and my regular pulse," she said, giving him a grin and another kiss.

"Mm, good. What about James? Is he asymptomatic? Have you been monitoring his temperature?"

Louisa picked the thermometer up from the bedside table, and then grasping on to her husband's head, she inserted it into his ear.

"We're fine, Martin. Stop your fussing." She pulled her hand up and tipped the instrument so she could read the numbers on the small display. "Hmm, ninety-eight point nine. You're still a bit warm. How are you feeling?"

"Much better." He glanced at the clock. "Oh, gawd," he groaned, quickly swinging his legs over the side of the bed. "I have patients this morning. I'm going to be late. Why didn't you wake me?"

"Martin! You can't see patients today! You're losing your voice for one thing. *And* you're still feverish!" she said as she followed after him.

He turned and shook his head. "No, I'm not. A temperature of ninety-eight point nine is within the normal range. And I'm not losing my voice. It's been like this since yesterday."

"Let's talk to Jeremy about it ... please?" She put her hand on his arm and gave him a hesitant nod. "Please, Martin. I'd feel a lot better about going off to work today if you'd call him."

His chin dropped to his chest as his eyes shifted again to the clock by the bed, the steady ticking warning of the rapidly dwindling amount of time before the surgery was to open. "Yes," he huffed, reaching down and snatching his mobile from the bedside table. He sequestered himself in the bathroom and then rang his aide.

Louisa listened, her ear to the door, feeling a brief pang of guilt for not trusting her husband to follow through with the phone call.

"Normal," she heard him say crisply.

Tell him to be specific, Jeremy! she willed the aide to say.

"Normal—ninety-eight point nine."

The door to the cabinet over the sink squeaked open. As per his usual routine, Martin would be pulling his razor from its designated place, slightly right of centre on the bottom shelf.

"Oh, for heaven's sake, Jeremy. It's just a bit of residual laryngitis."

Louisa worried her lip as she brushed the hair away from her face, pushing her ear more tightly to the old plank door.

The sound of water running into the sink momentarily obliterated her husband's end of the conversation.

The tap squeaked shut, and she heard his voice once again. "... a bit anxious. Maybe if you could talk to her, tell her that you approve?"

The latch rattled as the door was pulled open unexpectedly, and Louisa tumbled forward, her momentum stopped as she came to rest against her husband's chest.

"Mm. Yes, she's right here," Martin said, looking down, perplexed, before handing the mobile to his wife.

She peered up at him sheepishly, taking the phone from his hand. "Good morning, Jeremy."

Martin watched as her features tightened, and she blew a hiss of air from her nose.

"Yes, I *do* understand from a clinical point of view. I just think that he should give it one more day. Would that hurt anything?"

Louisa stepped back into the bedroom, and Martin returned to his preparations for the work day. His head began to throb as he filled the sink with water and listened to his wife's arguments in favour of another day of forced bed rest.

Looking into the mirror, he pulled his upper lip down and ran his razor across the stubble that had grown out since Monday.

Louisa's reflection appeared behind his own, and he watched warily as she folded her arms across her chest.

"Okay, I give up. Jeremy seems convinced that you're okay to go back to work. But Martin, you have to promise me that you'll go right to bed if you start to feel any worse. Agreed?"

He laid his razor down on the edge of the sink and turned slowly. "Louisa ... I'm sorry. I'm doing my best to hurry the process along—get this over with. But ... well, maybe that's just making things worse for you."

Her head whipped back and forth, her ponytail brushing her cheeks. "Why are you in such a hurry? For the first time in your life you could enjoy being truly cared for, and yet you seem to not want it."

"Louisa." Martin struggled to put his thoughts in order, but her fingers tapping impatiently against her elbow were having an amnesic effect on him. What Dr. Newell had managed to make so clear to him on Friday now seemed muddled and nonsensical.

He closed his eyes tightly and breathed out a heavy sigh before pushing past her and into the bedroom. "I'm going to be late."

The soft contented sounds of baby chatter emanating from across the landing escalated suddenly into demands for breakfast, and Louisa gave her husband a final flick of her locks before moving off to rescue her son from his confines. Martin watched her disappear and then pulled a clean shirt from the wardrobe.

Louisa stayed at the school over the lunch hour so that she could leave early for their appointment with Dr. Newell in the afternoon.

It had been decided that Martin would drive from Portwenn to Wadebridge, and Louisa would drive the busier stretch from Wadebridge to Truro.

Although he'd been eager to get back in the driver's seat, Martin felt an unexpected wave of apprehension when he picked the car keys up from the basket on the kitchen counter.

He stopped at James's high chair, where his son sat gnawing on a rice cake, and let his hand rest on the boy's head. "Be good for Poppy, James," he said, glancing over at the childminder.

"You're always a good boy, aren't you?" Poppy dropped several cubes of cheese on to the child's high chair tray before turning to her employer. "You might wanna keep an eye on the weather, Dr. Ellingham. Sounds like a nasty storm moving in overnight.

"Yes. We'll try not to make it too late." His thumb brushed against his son's cheek before he moved off towards the door.

The ambient temperature increased suddenly as he stepped out from behind the long shadow of the cottage and into the bright sunlight. As he pulled the door to the Lexus open and dropped into the driver's seat, his head hit with a thunk against the door frame above him. He grimaced, rubbing his hand above his ear.

His leg bent reluctantly as he tried to swing it into the vehicle, his foot hanging up on the bottom of the door opening. "Bugger!" he snapped as his knee collided sharply with the steering wheel. "Good gawd! How does she fit in here?" he muttered.

The motor hummed as the seat dropped slowly and moved backwards, finally clicking into its lowest and rearmost position. Stifling a groan, he worked his legs in front of him and raised the steering wheel before hitting the pre-set button.

He leaned his head back against the headrest, inhaled deeply, and closed his eyes for a moment before shifting the gearbox into reverse.

Easing the Lexus down Roscarrock Hill, he pressed his foot to the brake pedal, tuning out the hot ache that had begun to pulsate through his lower leg. He focused his attention on the van turning on to Fore Street from Church Hill. Rolling across the level area of the Platt he rounded the turn by the pub to continue on up the hill towards Portwenn Primary.

Louisa came out of the school just as he pulled into the parking lot. The smile he had become accustomed to seeing wasn't there today, however. And her tightly drawn features gave him an immediate sense of unease.

"Martin, what in the world are you doing?" she asked as soon as the passenger side door opened.

He stared at her blankly. "I'm picking you up. Wasn't that the plan?"

She slid into her seat and pulled the door shut with a loud thud. "*You* were going to drive from Portwenn to Wadebridge, and *I* was going to drive the stretch from Wadebridge to Truro."

"Problem?" he asked, his eyebrows raised.

"Well, I thought ... I *thought* we would go together."

"We *are* going together!"

"Well, I don't think you driving over here by yourself was a good idea, do you ... Martin?"

"I'm sorry, I don't know what you expected me to do!"

Louisa took in a deep breath, twisting her purse strap in her hand. "I thought I'd walk home, and we'd leave from the surgery together. You don't really think it's a good idea for you to be driving alone ... do you?"

His eyes blinked slowly before he huffed out a breath. "Are you saying I'm still required to have a bloody chaperone?"

"Well, not a chaperone, as such. Just ... maybe an extra set of eyes. Just to start out." She leaned forward and straightened her skirt, giving him a sideways glance.

"My eyes weren't damaged in the accident, Louisa. And I'm not a teenager," he said as he shifted the car into drive and pulled back out on to the street.

They rode in silence, Louisa trying to discreetly monitor her husband's movements and to watch for oncoming traffic at intersections. And Martin tried not to let on to his wife that the position of his limbs and the movements required to operate the vehicle were causing him pain.

"Maybe you could pull into the showground after we get through town. We can switch off there, hmm?" Louisa suggested as they passed through the first roundabout. She gave him a nervous smile.

"Mm," he grunted back, avoiding eye contact with her and showing feigned interest in the buildings passing them by.

They neared the River Camel bridge and Martin wiped his palms, one at a time, on his trousers, attempting to rid them of perspiration. He pleaded silently that traffic would be light and was relieved when they made it across the span with only a few cars passing from the opposite direction.

Pulling the Lexus into the showground lot, he slipped it into park. Louisa watched as he worked to extricate himself from the vehicle, his face refusing to disclose the pain he was experiencing.

She hurried around to help him from the car, but he brushed her away, once again avoiding eye contact.

"You okay?" she asked as he limped around past the front bumper to get in on the passenger side.

"Fine. But we don't have time for idle chatter. We're going to be late for our appointment if we don't keep moving."

They sat, side by side, in front of Dr. Newell's desk thirty minutes later, the therapist rocking back and forth in his chair while taking note of Martin's wooden aspect.

"How have things been going since our last couple's session?" he asked, fixing his gaze on Louisa.

She smiled back at him. "Well, I don't have to tell you that we've had a few challenges since then. Overall though, I think we've been doing quite well. We're communicating more effectively ... for the most part."

The psychiatrist leaned forward, studying her face as he tapped his biro on his notepad. "For the most part? Are you saying there have been a few bumps in the road?"

Martin worked his hands around the armrests of his chair and focused on the large flock of geese moving across the sky outside the office windows.

"It's been a bit ... tense today. Martin's been sick, and I didn't think he was ready to go back to work. He's still running a bit of a fev—"

"Ninety-eight point nine does *not* qualify as a fever, Louisa! I was warm because you seem compelled to attach yourself to me in the morning, and it makes me—hot!" Martin blurted out.

She looked back at him, tears stinging her eyes, and then shifted her gaze to her lap.

Pressing his fingertips to his temples, Martin huffed out a breath. "I'm sorry."

"How do you feel about Louisa's reluctance to see you back at work today, Martin? About her concern for your health?" the therapist asked.

"It's unwarranted."

Dr. Newell rocked back in his chair. "And that frustrates you? That her concerns are unwarranted?"

"Medically speaking, there was no reason I couldn't see patients today. So yes, it frustrates me." He brushed at his trousers, keeping his eyes fixed on the floor.

"And you feel your concerns *were* warranted, Louisa?" the psychiatrist asked.

She twisted her purse strap in her hand and glanced over at her husband. "I guess, as Martin said, *medically speaking* there was no reason he shouldn't see patients. But he's so vulnerable right now."

Dismay spread across Martin's face before hardening into anger. "I'm not vulnerable! I'm perfectly capable of taking care of myself."

"Maybe, vulnerable was a poor choice of word. But I don't get this—this—*desperation* to be in control."

Martin looked up at Louisa, furrowing his brow and giving his head a shake. "I wanted to talk to you earlier, but—" Sitting silently for several moments, he rubbed his palms together as he tried to collect his thoughts. "I couldn't."

His gaze drifted towards the therapist. "Well, what sounded perfectly logical when we discussed it on Friday wouldn't come together in any cohesive manner in my mind this morning. I didn't know how to explain it."

Dr. Newell stood up and walked around to take a seat on the corner of his desk. "I think it's important that Louisa understands where you're coming from here. Why don't you take a moment and try to put your thoughts into words?"

Louisa looked questioningly from the psychiatrist to her husband.

Martin's fingers tapped against his knees as he sat pensively for several moments before hissing a breath from his nose. "I don't know."

"Would you like me to help you out here?" the therapist asked.

"I don't seem to be managing very well on my own."

Dr. Newell spun his wedding band back and forth on his finger. "For you as a child, what was it like to be dependent on others, particularly your parents?"

"It was a lose-lose situation," Martin said hoarsely, turning his head back towards the view out the window.

"Can you explain what you mean by that?"

"There were things that I wanted or needed ... things I was required to have for school. If I asked for something there were negative consequences."

"Negative consequences. I assume that means punishment?"

"Quite often punishment. Yes. But certainly, a negative reaction."

His eyes flitted towards his wife before focusing intently on the fixator attached to his arm. "I tried to make do on my own. All the boys were given a stipend to be used for activities unrelated to school. Movies, trips to the museum, concerts, that sort of thing. I found if I skipped those activities and saved that money, I could cover many of the incidentals myself.

"My father would sometimes give me pocket change if he took me with him to the shops. I wouldn't spend it. I'd tell him

I'd lost it … save it for what I might need at school. My father took it as further evidence of my lack of financial nous."

The psychiatrist leaned forward, his elbows resting on his knees, watching his patient intently. "Did being able to take care of some of those expenses yourself give you some sense of control … security?"

"Mm. I found my life was much less stressful when I didn't have to go to my parents for these things."

The doctor's voice softened. "And the non-material needs that every child has … the need for affection, a listening ear, encouragement. How did you manage that?"

Martin sat, unresponsive for several moments before looking up at him. "I think I outgrew that fairly quickly."

"In what way do you think that early emotional independence worked in your favour?" Dr. Newell asked as he pushed himself from the desktop and returned to his chair.

"I didn't have to risk upsetting my parents, obviously."

"So, before your emotional independence, hoping to receive praise for an achievement or asking for affection … maybe even *showing* affection … that was a risky proposition?"

Martin gave his wife a sideways glance and then looked at his doctor, shrugging his shoulders.

"All right, think on that a bit, Martin, and maybe we can come back to it another time.

"Let's discuss your discovery of the benefits of semi-autonomy. You found being less dependent on your parents brought some relief from stress— the stress coming from the punishments or negative consequences that you would receive. Am I understanding you correctly?"

"Yes, I would say that's accurate."

Dr. Newell picked up a small rubber ball that lay in a green bowl full of paper clips, squeezing it several times in his fist. "You've told me enough about your parents that I would be surprised if they were proud of you or rewarded your steps towards independence in some way."

"I didn't need anything from them. The absence of punishment was a reward in itself."

"I think it would be helpful to your wife if she could understand your ... *need to be in control,* as she puts it ... if you could tell her how being dependent made you feel as a child. Don't overthink this, just give her one word."

Louisa watched Martin as he dug his thumb roughly into his palm.

"Unsafe," he said hesitantly before directing his gaze at the bookshelves behind the therapist.

Dr. Newell reached across his desk and handed Louisa a tissue before again addressing Martin. "And when would you say you finally felt a stable sense of security?"

Reaching out, Louisa took her husband's hand and caressed it with her thumb.

Martin grasped on to her fingers reflexively. "When I was completely independent."

"I think it will be helpful for you, Louisa, to remember that autonomy is important to your husband's sense of well-being."

She looked uncertainly at her husband. "I'm not sure I understand. Does it make you feel insecure when I worry about you?"

"Nooo. *That* makes me feel guilty. Not being independent makes me feel insecure."

"Oh. When I take care of you ... that makes you feel insecure?" she said, her shoulders drooping.

"No, no, no, no, no!" Martin rested his hand on hers and cocked his head as he attempted to choose his words more carefully. "I *like* that you take care of me ... usually. Louisa, your caring feels good to me, but when you care for me by taking away my independence—"

"That *doesn't* feel good," she said, finishing his thought.

"Mm, yes."

She tipped her head down and peered up at him. "Is that why you won't talk about what happened in the barn? Because you think I'm going to start in with a lecture about how you shouldn't have been doing whatever you were doing out there?"

Martin groaned. "I was hoping you'd forgotten about that." He fidgeted in his chair and then got up and walked to the window, leaving his crutch behind.

"Is this something you'd like to discuss now?" Dr. Newell asked as he observed the nervous tapping of his patient's fingers against his thighs.

Martin watched the queue of cars lining up at the stoplight on the corner for a few moments and then turned to the psychiatrist. "We had an event at my aunt's farm on Saturday. Things happened. I'd had all I could take, and I tried to get away ... to find a place where I could be alone to—to get it out of my system.

"Unfortunately, such a place doesn't exist around Portwenn," he said with a sneer. "And Chris Parsons walked in on my meltdown. My aunt came into the barn a short time later and added a few more unsolicited words of advice before we returned to the house. I embarrassed myself. That's all there is to it."

"Martin, you saved a man's life! You prevented Al from losing the one person who loves him!"

Dr. Newell cleared his throat and turned his attention to Louisa. "I think a bit more information might be needed if I'm to get the complete picture here."

"One of the guests at Ruth's open house, Bert Large—well let's just say that he's a man of sizeable girth," Louisa explained, her hands gesturing around her midsection.

"Anyway, Bert had a heart attack. Martin performed CPR and saved his life. And Martin, don't deny that it wasn't painful for you to do those chest compressions. Or that it wasn't even *more* painful later," Louisa said, wagging a finger at him. "You most certainly did *not* embarrass yourself!"

"Mm," Martin grunted, casting a glance over his shoulder.

The psychiatrist swivelled his chair from side to side, watching the interaction between the couple. "When you say meltdown, Martin, what do you mean?"

"Well, what do you think? I'd had it! I never would have been able to defend you and James against that arse at the petrol station, Louisa," he said as he turned, rubbing a hand over his head.

"I'd had it with Bert for eating himself into such a morbidly obese state that chest compressions were nearly impossible. I'd had it with these—these damn—*fixators!*" he said, shaking his injured arm. "I can't—I'm not—none of it would be a bloody issue if that—*moron*—hadn't—!"

He smacked his fist against his thigh, grimacing as his knuckles hit sharply against the metal hardware.

"The *moron*, out of pure selfish avarice, deprived himself of sleep, which resulted in an accident that nearly cost me my life!"

He gesticulated wildly towards his wife. "Gawd! All that Louisa's had to endure! That my aunt's endured! Good God— all of Portwenn's been affected in some manner!"

He paced, unsteadily, back and forth. "But my wife! What that—*idiot*—!"

Burying his fist in his hair he spat out, "What goddamn—*idiot* put my—!" The last word caught in his throat as he batted back tears.

Louisa could see her husband's fingers trembling at his sides as he turned to face the window. She walked over, standing behind him, taking his hands in hers as she tried to calm his shaking.

"Martin ... it's all right," she said softly.

He pulled away and whirled around, staggering to regain his balance. "It absolutely is *not* all right! How can you say that?"

"Louisa, why don't you come and sit back down while we discuss this," Dr. Newell said, giving her a firm nod of his head as he got up from behind his desk.

She hesitated before returning to her seat.

The psychiatrist pulled two chairs over by his patient, gesturing towards them. "You're making me just a little nervous, Martin. Would you mind?" he asked quietly.

Martin glared at the man for several seconds before complying, and the therapist took a seat next to him.

"I'm sorry. I was out of line," he said. He sat, slumped, his hands folded in his lap.

"No apologies are necessary for things said in this room," Dr. Newell reassured him. "Your accident, and the fallout that resulted from it, has hit you hard from many different angles."

Martin leaned forward, resting his elbows on his knees and his head in his hands, trying to tune out the psychiatrist's voice, as he attempted to regain a sense of control over his emotions.

"As I listened to you so clearly describe what you were going through on Saturday," the man continued, "I could imagine how I may have been reacting to it all. I think for me, I would have been feeling a frightening weakness. I might even say feeling impotent. Does that strike a chord with you?"

Martin straightened himself and drew in a ragged breath. "Yes."

"This is a process, Martin. You have a lot to get your head around. Today you felt real anger, but your emotions will change from day to day. You're going through a grieving process on several levels, so expect your emotions to be all over the place for a while."

The doctor tipped his head to make eye contact with Louisa. "What are your thoughts about what Martin had to say?"

"Well, I don't see him as weak at all," she replied as she uncrossed her legs and shifted in her seat. "You're the strongest, most courageous person I know, Martin. I can't imagine, after all you've endured in your life, how you can see yourself as weak."

Dr. Newell rested his elbows on the armrests of his chair and steepled his fingers in front of him. "It's important to remember that, although you may not agree with him, both your perspective and Martin's are valid. However, Martin's perspective will change as he goes through this process."

He lowered his hand and looked at his watch and then got up and walked towards the door.

"Our time appears to be up. I would suggest you wait a day or two before discussing our session today. The emotions are raw right now, so just let it sit for a while."

There were a few stars peeking out from behind the clouds peppering the sky when Martin and Louisa left Truro, but by the time they pulled into the parking space outside the surgery, a heavy mist had begun to fall.

Fickle winds whipped around the little stone cottage, dampening their faces quickly as they walked around the building to the kitchen door.

By the time Martin made his nightly rounds before going up to bed—checking that the doors were locked, toys had been gathered together and piled into the playpen, and collecting his glass of water from the kitchen—the winds were howling and streaks of lightning illuminated the roiling sea. The first big storm of the winter season was upon them.

Louisa had piled a heavy down comforter on top of the usual layers of blankets and had burrowed underneath them, her head barely visible to Martin as he entered the room.

He hurried through his bathroom routine before dropping his trousers, sitting down on the edge of the bed to don his vest and boxers.

The mattress undulated, and his wife's warm hand settled on his back. "I heard you coughing a minute ago. Are you okay?"

"Mm, it's nothing. Just dry air," he said as he pulled the blankets back and crawled in under them.

Louisa sat up, reaching across his chest and picking up the thermometer before inserting it into his ear. He slapped a hand to his eyes a few moments later as the lamp on her side of the bed switched on.

"Oh, Martin, it's one hundred point one! *See* ... I told you!" she said as she dropped her hands into her lap and screwed up her face at him.

"Louisa, I'm tired. I would expect that my temperature would go up a bit with fatigue. Just lie down and go to sleep."

Giving him one final scrutinizing look, she flicked the switch and settled in next to him. She lay thinking about what had been discussed in their therapist's office that afternoon and began to giggle softly.

"Now what?" Martin moaned.

Brushing her hand across his cheek, she leaned over, kissing his forehead. "I was just thinking about what Dr. Newell said. About you being—" A snort escaped through her nose before she began to giggle again. "About you being—*impotent!* He doesn't know how far off the mark he was with that one, hmm?"

"*Feeling*, not being, Louisa. Good grief, can we please go to sleep?"

"Yes, Martin." Nestling her head on his shoulder, she sighed contentedly before drifting off.

They slept, warm and undisturbed by the rumbles of thunder, until shortly after midnight when they were awakened abruptly by the shrill tone of Martin's mobile.

He groped around on the little table next to him until his hand landed on the phone. "Ellingham!" he answered gruffly, annoyed by the nocturnal intrusion.

"I need your help, Dr. Ellig-am!" the small voice on the other end said.

Don't miss out!

Click the button below and you can sign up to receive emails whenever Kris Morris publishes a new book. There's no charge and no obligation.

Sign Me Up!

https://books2read.com/r/B-A-PAJD-BLQL

Connecting independent readers to independent writers.

About the Author

Kris Morris was born and raised in a small Iowa town. She spent her childhood barely tolerating school, hand rearing orphaned animals, and squirrel taming. At Iowa State University she studied elementary education. But after discovering a loathing for traditional pedagogy and a love for a certain tall, handsome, Upstate New Yorker, she abandoned the academic life to marry, raise two sons, and become an unconventional piano teacher. When she's not writing, Kris builds boats and marimbas with her husband, who she has captivated for thirty years with her delightful personality, quick wit, and culinary masterpieces. They now reside in Iowa and have replaced their sons with ducks.

Read more at www.ktmorris.com.

Made in United States
North Haven, CT
24 January 2022

15229812R00226